one good thing

Alexandra Potter is the bestselling author of numerous romantic comedy fiction novels in the UK, including *Confessions of a Forty-Something F##k Up* and *One Good Thing*. These titles have sold in twenty-two territories and achieved worldwide sales of more than one million copies (making the bestseller charts in the UK, Germany, Czech Republic, Slovenia and Serbia).

Yorkshire born and raised, Alexandra lived for several years in LA before settling in London with her Californian husband and their Bosnian rescue dog. When she's not writing or travelling, she's getting out into nature, trying not to look at her phone and navigating this thing called mid-life.

Also by Alexandra Potter

ALEXANDRA POTTER

one good thing

MACMILLAN

First published 2022 by Macmillan
an imprint of Pan Macmillan
The Smithson, 6 Briset Street, London EC1M 5NR
EU representative: Macmillan Publishers Ireland Limited,
1st Floor, The Liffey Trust Centre,
117-126 Sheriff Street Upper, Dublin 1, D01 YC43
Associated companies throughout the world
www.panmacmillan.com

ISBN 978-1-5290-2286-5

1 3 5 7 9 8 6 4 2

A CIP catalogue record for this book is available from the British Library.

Typeset in Sabon by Palimpsest Book Production Limited, Falkirk, Stirlingshire
Printed and bound by CPI Group (UK) Ltd, Croydon, CR0 4YY

Visit **www.panmacmillan.com** to read more about all our books
and to buy them. You will also find features, author interviews and
news of any author events, and you can sign up for e-newsletters
so that you're always first to hear about our new releases.

Dedicated to Elton.
And all the wonderful animals
who change our lives for the better.

Prologue

Hey you,

Remember when we were kids and used to write thank-you letters? It was usually for Christmas or birthdays and we'd do our best handwriting. Well, this email is my thank-you letter to you.

When everything fell apart, I couldn't see a future. Leaving my old life to try to start a new one was terrifying. You know how scared I always was of taking risks. I was never as brave as you. What did you always say? That life happens at the edge of your comfort zone.

Well, in the end I took your advice. Because you know what's more terrifying? The thought of never feeling happy again. There are people with broken hearts all around us, yet I still felt so alone.

But by coming here I've learned that it's only by losing what you love that you find what matters most. And I've discovered a secret. All you need is one good thing to turn your life around and make it worth living again. Like a smile from a stranger, a hug from a friend or some small, random act of kindness. Or an old, scruffy dog with no name.

Just one good thing can change the course of everything. It has the power to heal your heart, inspire courage and joy and create true friendships that can bring a whole community together. It can even save someone's life.

So anyway, thanks for the advice. I know it's not Christmas or my birthday, but when I needed it most, your words gave me the greatest gift of all: hope.

x

The Seven Stages

The seven stages of grief are widely used to explain the complicated process we go through when we experience any major loss. They are based on the famous theory by psychiatrist Elizabeth Kübler-Ross. Loss can be caused by many different situations: the death of a loved one, the end of a relationship or any big life change. Divorce, especially, represents the death of a marriage and all the hopes and dreams that went into it, and this needs a grieving process for healing.

After the initial shock and disbelief, you will begin a journey that will take you through a series of complex emotions, until finally you will begin the upward turn towards acceptance, hope and even joy. In reality, however, grief is not linear; feelings are messy and difficult, so only use the seven stages as a general guide. Loss is universal, but it is also very personal and everyone's journey is their own.

STAGE 1
WTF

Yorkshire

'So what do you think?

Having finished looking around downstairs, the estate agent pushes open a stripped-pine door and shows me into the master bedroom.

It's an innocent enough question, but probably *not* the wisest one to ask a recently divorced woman. One who has made the impulsive decision to leave London and all her friends, resign from the teaching job she's held for the last ten years and move several hundred miles away to the Yorkshire Dales, where she knows no one.

I think lots of things. Mostly that I'm still in shock. That I can't believe my marriage is over. That I haven't slept properly in months. That I'm clearly having a midlife crisis. That yesterday I looked for my keys everywhere and found them in the fridge. That I've gained five pounds – oh, who am I kidding? More like fifteen. That I feel lost and bewildered. That I lie awake in the darkness thinking this is all a bad dream. That it's all my fault.

That I love him.

That I hate him.

That secretly I wish I was the kind of woman who did crazy, angry, revengeful things to her cheating ex with frozen prawns and spray paint, instead of being the kind of woman who ran the iron over his shirts, folded them neatly into bin bags and left them in the garage, for when he came to pick up the rest of his things.

'It's very nice,' I say politely, looking around the dimly lit room, with its old-fashioned flowery wallpaper and faded brown carpet, darker in parts where the furniture used to be.

I think I've gone completely bonkers and this is all a terrible mistake.

A strong fusty smell reaches my nostrils and I feel painfully homesick.

Only I no longer have a home to feel sick for. It's been sold, subject to contract, as part of the divorce. The new owners, a couple with two young children, are due to move in in the New Year. My ex-husband has moved out of our home and in with his new girlfriend. His son, Will, my beloved stepson, who would spend weekends and holidays with us, has finished university and gone travelling. It's just me and an empty house full of memories.

Which is why, a few weeks before Christmas, while the rest of the world is shopping for gifts and decorations, I'm shopping for a new place to call home.

'I know on your search criteria you said you're looking for a flat, preferably something that doesn't need any work doing, but I thought I'd throw in a bit of a wild card for the final property.'

It's late afternoon and this is my last viewing before I travel back to London. It's been a long day. I caught the express train from King's Cross station at first light, changing at Leeds onto the local railway line, which took me on a slow but breathtaking journey through a dramatic landscape, before finally pulling into the small windswept station on the edge of the Yorkshire Dales.

There I was met by Mr Hardcastle, an estate agent who, until today, I've only corresponded with by email, after he replied to my enquiry about properties for sale in the area. Ruddy-faced and larger than life in his waxed jacket with corduroy collar, he's nothing like his slick-suited counterparts in London. Cheerfully squeezing the life out of my fingers as he shook my hand, he ushered me into the passenger seat of his old Rav4 and drove me deep into the Dales, past fields full of cows and sheep, showing me everything on the market while providing a chirpy commentary on the weather, in an accent that is pure Pennines.

'They've given rain . . . By, it's a bit nippy . . . You're lucky, yesterday it was fair tipping it down . . . There's talk of snow on the tops . . . Looks like it's clearing, I can see a patch of blue . . . With any luck, weekend should be grand after all . . .'

Considering it's the beginning of December, his optimism in the weather is remarkable. As is his ability to see anything positive in this three-hundred-year-old stone cottage, originally built for farmworkers in the small but beautifully picturesque village of Nettlewick. With its dark, poky rooms, rotten windows and nicotine-stained walls, it's old and tired and in desperate need of a makeover.

I know the feeling.

'It's got a certain charm, don't you think?'

'I'm not sure I'd call damp charming.' I point to some scary-looking mushroom growing out of the wall. 'Or wood-worm.' I peer more closely at the suspicious-looking pin-prick holes in one of the large beams running across the ceiling.

'The vendor's very open to offers,' he continues brightly, rocking on his heels. 'And there's a lovely westerly view from the back garden. There are a few houses, but mostly you can see straight across the Dales.'

'What's the view from the front?' Walking across to the sash window, I pull back the greying, stained net curtain. 'Oh – a graveyard.'

'At least it'll be dead quiet.' He chuckles at his own joke.

9

And now I'm thinking dead people. I'm thinking Michael Jackson's 'Thriller' video.

'Apparently he inherited it from his great-aunt, but he lives abroad and has no use for it.'

It's dark outside, and my reflection stares back at me in the windowpane. I look tired. Old. Pale as a ghost.

No use for it.

That's how my husband must have felt about our marriage when he walked out. The thought drops like a weight on my chest. With my back still turned, I squeeze my eyes shut, pinching the tear ducts with my thumb and forefinger. I mustn't cry. Not here.

'Well, like I said, it was a bit of a wild card.'

As he flicks off the bare bulb overhead, I open my eyes and linger for a moment by the window. My reflection has disappeared and my gaze extends over the high stone wall and through the skeleton branches of the trees, into the graveyard's dark recesses. It's only four o'clock, but it's already pitch-black.

'So, going back to the new mill conversion we first looked at in town.'

I can hear the clicking of switches behind, in an attempt to find the one to illuminate the staircase. Maybe I should call this whole move off. Admit I've made a mistake and acted too rashly. Rent something in London and beg for my job back. After all, this is so unlike me. I don't *do* impulsive. I'm sensible. Cautious. 'Risk-averse', according to my pension-fund provider.

Plus all the self-help books advise against making any major decisions for at least a year after a divorce, and I have a whole stack of them on my bedside table.

'The one with the roof terrace that you liked, ten miles from here. There's been a lot of interest in that one, what with it being in a bustling market town near the big shops, station and amenities . . .'

In the background, the estate agent is giving me his sales pitch.

'So if you're serious I'd advise acting quickly.'

Still staring out of the window, I catch sight of something. A flash of pink. White spots. I peer more closely. It's started to rain and drops are hitting the window, forming rivulets down the glass. It's an umbrella. A bright-pink polka-dot umbrella. I follow it as it moves across the graveyard, its owner hidden underneath. Something about it makes me smile. It looks so incongruous, this spotty flash of colour bobbing cheerfully along in the wintry bleakness, weaving in and out of the graves. Like a beacon of light in the darkness.

'I'd like to make an offer.'

Turning away from the window, I look across at the estate agent, who is waiting for me at the top of the stairs, studying the screen of his smartphone. He looks up, his expression like one of my pupils caught misbehaving.

'Christmas shopping,' he explains sheepishly. 'Perfume. For the wife. I get her the same thing every year.' He puts his phone away quickly. 'Sorry, what did you say?'

'I want to make an offer.'

'Oh! Excellent! A very wise decision. Our warehouse conversions are always very popular with professionals such as yourself—'

'No, I want to buy this house.'

'*This house?*' he repeats, as if he can't quite believe that his sales pitch actually worked.

His incredulity only makes me more determined. There's something about this house – the way it's been neglected and unloved – that's stirred something inside me. It needs someone to love it back to life. I begin descending the steep, narrow staircase.

'I'll offer close to the asking price, as long it's taken off the market and we can exchange by the New Year.'

'Right. Yes. Absolutely . . . I'll get straight on to the vendor in Singapore.' His footsteps follow hurriedly behind me. 'Rest assured, Ms Brooks, at Hardcastle and Son your problems are our solutions,'

'Oh, and Mr Hardcastle.'

Reaching the bottom of the stairs, I turn to see him banging his head on the low beam and wincing.

'Buy your wife something different this Christmas. Take it from me, she's sick of that bloody perfume.'

London

Six weeks later

'Is that everything?'

The removal men take the last of the packing boxes from the hallway.

'Yeah, I think so.'

Moving Day has finally arrived. After weeks of being surrounded by masking tape and bubble wrap, the house is finally emptied of its contents.

Standing on the doorstep, about to lock up, doubt flickers within me.

'Actually, hang on,' I call out as the removal men disappear down the front path, 'let me do a final check.'

I do a quick walk-through of the empty rooms. I've left behind all the curtains, but my footsteps still echo on the wooden floors and my mind flicks back to when we first moved in a decade ago, as newly-weds. Only then the rooms were unfamiliar and exciting, and I dashed around them bursting with energy and enthusiasm, my head full of colour schemes and a million ideas—

I stop myself.

I might have packed away all my belongings, but my memories are still imprinted into these walls. Still, now is not the time to be taking an emotional trip down memory lane. Spotting a small-framed photograph on the empty bookshelves in the living room, I snatch it up, feeling vindicated.

The photograph is one of those square ones with the white border that was taken in the seventies. It's of me and my big sister Josie, though she wasn't so big then. Neither of us was. We're wearing matching denim dungarees and sitting on the wall in front of my grandparents' house in Yorkshire, grinning into the camera and eating ice-lollies shaped like rockets. We lost our mum when we were still very young and would spend all our school holidays there. Brought up by a single dad, who threw himself into his work in an attempt to cope, our house always felt sad and empty, but their home in Nettlewick was a warm and welcoming escape. Which is why I've chosen the village to start over again. I want to be surrounded by happy memories. To wake up in a place where, whatever happened, it has always felt like my one true safe harbour.

Slipping the photo in my handbag, I quickly finish checking over the rest of the house, then lock the front door behind me and post the keys through the letter box. The estate agent has a set, so I'll leave these ones for the new owners. As I hear them land on the doormat, I remember I haven't taken off the key ring – a silly souvenir from a weekend spent in Italy a few years ago for my birthday.

My mind goes somewhere, but I force it back again. Who wants some stupid Leaning Tower of Pisa key ring anyway? It didn't even lean the right way.

The removal van is parked up outside with its hazard lights on. The house is on a busy main road and, like the homes of most people living in London, it doesn't have a driveway, so the van has wedged itself on the street corner, next to the pile of discarded Christmas trees. It's the third week of January, but the council is slow to recycle them and they lie there in a sorry-looking pile, devoid of their needles and decorations. Life can be brutal, even for Christmas trees.

'Olivia.'

14

As I watch the removal men loading the last of my possessions into the back, I hear a voice over my shoulder.

'Oh, hi, Madeleine.'

Forcing a bright smile, I turn to see my neighbour on the corner appearing from her garden gate. Madeleine likes to know everyone's business – she *is* the Neighbourhood Watch – and ever since my ex-husband moved out, she's been stationed behind her plantation shutters, like a sentry on lookout. Luckily, through a mixture of stealth and having to rush off early to work, I've managed to avoid being trapped in conversation with her.

Until now.

'I've been hoping to catch you for ages. Roger and I wanted to tell you how sad we were to hear about you and David . . .' She wraps her waterfall cardigan around her and folds her arms against the cold. She's obviously just shot out from behind her shutters, as she's still wearing her Peruvian sock-slippers. 'How are you?'

'Oh, you know . . .' I trail off lamely.

But of course, no, Madeleine doesn't know. She has no idea. Married for forty years to Roger, a retired accountant, Madeleine has a life of strict routine. Of local church meetings and Ocado deliveries, and weekends washing Roger's shirts, which she pegs out on the line with such regularity, I'm certain she must use a tape measure.

Hers is not a life of divorce lawyers and chaos, and a husband running off to live with the pretty young American he'd met at Bikram yoga.

To be honest, I can't believe mine is, either. David, of all people! David who likes playing golf, and New Zealand wine, and his Rotary Club dinners. A man who wears boating shoes and button-down collars and was forever teasing me about my love of vintage clothes.

15

'You old hippy,' he would laugh, when I would proudly show him my charity-shop finds. But at the same time he always looked perplexed. 'You know, if your teacher's salary won't stretch, take my credit card. I don't want our friends thinking my wife can't afford new clothes.'

Now the boating shoes and button-downs are nowhere to be seen. Instead, when he came to pick up the rest of his things, he'd gone all *Peaky Blinders* and was sporting a tweed cap, a waistcoat and skinny ankle-jeans. Only he was less Tommy Shelby and more fifty-year-old dentist with high blood pressure. Which was the reason why I'd encouraged him to take up Bikram yoga in the first place. Oh, the irony. It would have been funny, if it wasn't my husband of ten years standing on the doorstep.

At least I think it was my husband. I barely recognized him. And I'm not talking just about his appearance.

'You look tired.'

I zone back to see Madeleine peering at me.

'Moving is tiring,' I reply.

Why do people say that, when what they really mean is: you look awful?

'Roger and I have been so worried about you,' she continues, her head tilting sideways.

I shift uncomfortably. It's the dreaded pity-tilt. Since news of our divorce broke, it's how everyone looks at me these days.

'Liv! You old tart!'

Well, not everyone. We're suddenly interrupted by a figure scootering towards us on the pavement, waving.

'Naomi!' It's totally unexpected. 'What on earth are you doing here?'

'Well, I couldn't let you leave without saying goodbye.' She grins, her dark eyes flashing as she hops off the scooter and hugs me, enveloping me in her big furry teddy coat. 'It's lunch break – no one's going to miss me if I play hooky.'

I feel a burst of gratitude. 'It's so nice to see you.'

Naomi is one of the teachers from my old school and one of my closest friends. We met on my first day at Carlton Comprehensive. I'd been brought in as a support teacher to cover maternity for Year Nine English and was feeling nervous, but she immediately put me at ease, cracking raucous jokes in her strong Glaswegian accent. We share the same sense of humour and we've had a lot of fun together over the years.

'I can't believe you're leaving me to deal with all the unruliness and disobedience by myself!' she reprimands, letting me go. 'And that's only the teachers,' she adds with a throaty laugh.

Handing in my notice had been tough, but in true Naomi style, she's cheered me on, telling me I'm doing the right thing and making jokes about it being the Great Escape. 'Just think, Liv, you're finally getting out of here! No more having to sit through one of Godfrey's godawful assemblies.' Mr Godfrey was our headmaster and his famously dull assemblies had been known to literally put both teachers and pupils to sleep.

Still, underneath all the encouragement and joking, I know I wasn't the only one finding it hard to say goodbye.

'Whose is the scooter?' I ask.

'I dunno – I stole it.'

'From a pupil?'

She grins sheepishly and adjusts her woollen bobble hat, underneath which she's tucked her hair. 'Stealing scooters and playing hooky: what am I like?'

'Naomi, are you insane? You're going to get yourself into major trouble if Mr Godfrey finds out.'

'See what happens, now you've left! I've got no one to keep me on the straight and narrow.'

'Seriously, you should go, before you get caught.'

'Sorry, Miss.' Suitably told off, Naomi hangs her head dutifully.

Despite myself, I find myself smiling. Naomi has a knack for making me laugh, whatever the circumstances. I've lost count of the number of staff meetings I've held where I've had to stifle my guffaws behind an A4 folder.

'So how are you feeling about the move?'

'Excited. Fresh start and all that.'

'That's good.'

'Bit nervous, though . . .'

'That's normal.'

'Terrified actually.'

'Well, you know that's because fear and excitement are essentially the same thing, right?'

'They are?'

'Yeah, it's all to do with the hypothalamus part of your brain. Both emotions trigger the same physiological response, which releases cortisol and causes your heart rate and breathing to increase, preparing yourself for the fight-or-flight response.'

'This is why you teach biology and I teach English. *Hippo-what?*'

She laughs. 'So have you started applying for any jobs yet?'

'No, not yet. I'll have some money left over from the sale of the house. Not a huge amount, but enough to do up the cottage and keep me going for a while. I'm hoping to find some freelance work as a tutor.'

'Lucky you – what I wouldn't do for a bit of freedom from the classroom.'

'OK, so we've finished loading everything.'

I turn. It's one of the burly removal men.

'Great, thanks.' I glance over at the truck. So that's it. My whole life. Packed into cardboard boxes and wrapped in packing blankets. I'm struck by how little I've got to show for it.

'I'm going to follow you up in my rental car,' I tell him. 'You've got the address. The estate agent is going to meet us there with a set of keys.'

'Right, we'll get on the road then.' He whistles to his colleague, who gives a thumbs-up and pulls down the back of the truck. It makes a loud rattle. 'We've got a long drive ahead of us.'

'*A long drive?*'

I'd forgotten all about Madeleine, but now I turn to see she's still standing a few feet behind me on the pavement, listening.

'Are you moving far, then? Roger and I were curious as to where you were going, but obviously we didn't like to pry.'

Obviously.

'The Yorkshire Dales.'

Her eyes go wide. 'You're leaving London?'

You'd think I'd just told her I was moving to Mars.

'And what about David? Is he leaving too?'

'No, he's living in Hackney with his new girlfriend.'

For a split second I couldn't tell which she finds the most shocking. That he's got a new girlfriend or that he's moved to Hackney.

'Goodness, I had no idea.'

'That makes two of us.'

I suddenly realize I've got more in common with Madeleine than I thought. She's not the only one looking for answers. I'm still struggling to make sense of it all.

19

'Olivia, you poor, *poor* thing, you must be *devastated.*'

'Thanks, but I'm OK.'

'But are you *really?*'

Madeleine's head-tilting is so out of control, it's practically horizontal.

'Didn't you hear her? She's just fine,' snaps Naomi, glaring at my neighbour as if she's one of her disruptive pupils. 'Spare your concern for the new girlfriend.' Stepping closer, she leans towards Madeleine's ear as if letting her in on a secret. 'David has a tiny penis.'

Madeleine blinks rapidly.

'Seriously. *Tiny!*' Naomi pinches her thumb and finger together to make her point even clearer. 'Liv is going on to much bigger and better things.'

'Goodness, is that the time already?' Clutching at her wristwatch, Madeleine steps backwards and misses her footing. She stumbles over the kerb in her sock-slippers. 'Well, I must be getting on . . . I've got the grandchildren coming over. Safe journey, Olivia.' And, beating a hasty retreat up her path, she disappears behind her front door.

'Well, that got rid of her.'

'Why on earth did you say that?' Finding my voice, I round on Naomi.

'I don't know,' she confesses and, admittedly, she does look sheepish. 'Still, it's not like she's going to see David again, is it?'

'He's their dentist.'

She claps her hand over her mouth, looking stricken. '*Shi-it!*'

For a moment we stare at each other, then she bursts out laughing and I can't help but do so too. It's infectious.

'I'm such a juvenile. I get it from teaching thirteen-year-olds.' Naomi stops laughing and pulls an anguished expression. 'Sorry, Liv, she was just so annoying; the way she was going on at you, trying to get gossip under the guise of being concerned.'

'Don't be. I can't remember the last time I actually laughed.' I shake my head, remembering poor Madeleine's face, then check my watch. 'It's getting late – I should go. I've got a long drive ahead of me.'

'If I get up to Scotland at Easter to see the folks, I'll try to come and visit you. Ellie hasn't seen her grandparents forever.'

'That would be great.'

But I know it's unlikely. Naomi's relationship with her churchgoing parents has been strained ever since she announced her decision to have a child on her own with the help of a sperm donor. Now they couldn't love their granddaughter more, but in the beginning it caused a deep rift. More recently their disapproval of Naomi's boyfriend Danny, a musician, has been the cause of more discord.

'Promise to keep in touch.'

'Promise.'

We give each other a hug, and then I climb into the car. I'm putting on my seatbelt when she raps on the window. I buzz it down.

'I did mean what I said, you know. About the other thing. I do think you're going on to much bigger and better things.'

I smile gratefully. 'Yeah, me too.'

And then we wave at each other as she scooters off down the street, her figure disappearing down the road in my rear-view mirror.

Of course I'm lying.

Angling the mirror towards me, I peel a rogue piece of packing tape out of my tangled hair, before corralling it back into its dishevelled bun and turning the ignition. With the engine running, I pause to look across at the house, with its SOLD sign in the front garden. My eyes flick upwards and I gaze at the bedroom window, imagining myself drawing back the curtains, remarking upon the weather, like I've done every morning for a decade; and I'm hit by such a wave of grief that it physically hurts.

My life doesn't feel like it's going to get bigger and better. It feels like it's over.

And, looking straight ahead, I pull out into traffic and drive away.

Lost and Found

Still, it's hardly breaking news, is it?

Husband leaves wife for another woman. It's the biggest cliché in the book. We've all heard the story so many times we've become numb to it. As one of my students, Kieran O'Conner, once said when I caught him cheating in an exam, 'What's the big deal? This shit goes down all the time, Miss.'

Which, come to think of it, was the only thing Kieran ever got correct in an exam. But that doesn't make it any *less* shit. And just because you've heard it all before doesn't make it any less painful when it happens to you.

Thing is, I never thought it *was* going to happen to me. I'm not one of those people who love drama and scandal, and have exciting lives filled with fascinating anecdotes and conversations that start breathlessly with, '*Guess what?*' I was happily married. I had a steady job, paid holidays, a nice house and a mortgage. There was no guessing what.

Growing up, I was always 'the sensible one'; it was my sister Josie who got to be wild and reckless. Despite being two years younger, I was always looking out for her, making sure she didn't get into trouble and fixing things when she did. Apart from a rather half-hearted attempt to be a goth as a student, I never pushed any boundaries. Too afraid of taking risks and making a wrong decision, I always stayed resolutely in my comfort zone. I dated unremarkable men. I had unremarkable sex. And then I met David and everything changed. Last year we celebrated our ten-year wedding anniversary.

I was in my forties and life felt sorted. I had good friends and a good social life. I loved my husband. I worked hard and went to the gym (though not nearly as often as I should, considering that I once divided the membership fee by the number of classes I went to and realized my last yoga class cost forty quid, which is an awful lot for *Namastes*). I had a kitchen shelf full of celebrity recipe books that promised to make me thinner, and a wardrobe full of dresses and high heels that could still make me look half decent. Plus enough hair products to start a salon. I've got my mum's thick, dark curls, which often take on a life of their own and are both a pride and a pain. Especially when it rains.

I was a normal woman leading a normal life. Admittedly on occasions I'd read one of those magazine articles about people having these incredible life-changing adventures and briefly think, *Is this it?* But then I'd look across at David sitting next to me, sharing the sofa, a bottle of wine and a takeaway and he'd smile at me; older, familiar, but still just as handsome, and the feeling would pass just as briefly. I felt content. Secure. *Lucky.*

After everything that had happened in my childhood, my life now was pretty uneventful and that's how I liked it. No big surprises. No chaos. No heartache. Everything was trundling on.

And then, suddenly, it wasn't.

'*After the initial shock and disbelief, you will begin a journey that will take you through a series of complex emotions . . .*'

The distinctive voice of a famous Oscar-winning actress is playing on the car stereo. She's narrating an audiobook I'm listening to, in an attempt to stay awake. Stifling a yawn, I roll down the window to let in some cold, fresh air. I've been driving for hours. Darkness has long since fallen, and my headlights pick out the cat's-eyes reflectors, guiding me down the narrow country roads in the Yorkshire Dales. I'm used to a city's light-polluted skies, but above me now the skies are dark and vast and London seems a long, long way away. Skeleton trees loom towards me, while on either side of the drystone walls it's open fields, wild moorland and sweeping valleys. There's nothing to see for miles around.

That's if I could see properly over the drystone walls. I've rented a Fiat 500, which seemed cute and nippy in the capital's traffic, but now seems ridiculously small and vulnerable in the dark, open countryside. I switch on the full beams as the road curves and steepens, and hunch forward over the steering wheel, bleary-eyed and exhausted. Hopefully I'll be there soon. Surely it can't be much further.

What's that?

I swerve sharply as something shoots across the road. It's gone before I've even had a chance to register it, but it looked like some kind of wild animal. With my heart pounding like a drum in my chest, I brake sharply as the wheels hit a grass verge. The car stalls. And now anxiety starts up like percussion.

This is the first time in ages that I've driven anywhere. Living in London, I always used public transport and, whenever we went abroad, David always drove the rental car. I take a few deep breaths. I used to be such a confident driver when I was younger. But then I used to be more confident about a lot of things.

Shakily I start the car. The engine springs to life. And, with it, the stereo.

'. . . *denial, pain, guilt, anger, depression, loneliness* . . .'

Great, lots to look forward to then.

Quickly I go to turn it off. I'm jackknifed across the road. If something comes round the bend, it will crash right into me. I need to concentrate. Only I'm not familiar with the stereo system and accidentally turn up the volume instead.

'. . . AND FINALLY ACCEPTANCE . . .'

Her distinguished voice blares out.

'. . . HOPE AND EVEN JOY.'

Oh, for crying out loud: shut up with your hope and bloody joy!

Panicked, I jab at the controls, until finally I hit the right button and the car falls silent. Relieved, I quickly straighten up. Then, feeling slightly guilty about shouting at the famous actress – well, she is a national treasure – I set off driving again.

The thing is, everyone's divorce is different. I've heard of women leaving their marriages with a sense of joy and relief. They're out there celebrating their new freedom by throwing Divorce Parties with penis-shaped *piñatas* to whack and *All the Single Ladies* bunting strung up across their dining room.

Meanwhile I'm out in the middle of nowhere, in the pitch-dark, with no phone signal. And now Google Maps has stopped working. I glance at my phone for directions, but it's simply whirring around. For so long my life had a clear direction, but now I have no idea where I'm going. How do I get from my old life to my new life? Even Google doesn't know, and Google knows everything.

So not at the Beyoncé stage *just* yet.

With no road signs, I take a random right turn. Even now, months later, I still can't quite believe this is real. I feel like I'm living someone else's life – not the one belonging to me, Liv Brooks, wife, teacher, stepmother. Except now I'm none of those things. Which begs the question: *Who am I?*

Truly I have no idea any more, but at least I still have my name. I never changed it when I got married. It seemed an outdated tradition, unless you're going to have children, and David didn't want any more. He was upfront about that from the very beginning. David already had a son, Will, from his first marriage, and one set of private school fees was enough, he'd joked on one of our early dates.

To which, quick as a flash, I'd replied that wouldn't be a problem as, being a teacher in a local state school, it would be over my dead body before any child of mine would be sent private. But joking aside, David was serious. And joking aside, I was madly in love with him. So when he proposed after six months, I happily gave up the fantasy of a baby that I wasn't sure I wanted, for the reality of a husband that I most certainly did. In the words of Jane Eyre: *Reader, I married him.*

But there was another reason why I didn't take David's surname; I didn't want to give up Dad's. We lost him just months after he'd managed to walk me up the aisle of the register office. He'd been a heavy smoker all his life. My sister Josie furiously smoked roll-ups at his funeral. Well, why the fuck not? she swore. She was so angry, whereas I was so sad. A tearful newly-wed who'd now lost both her parents. I was so thankful I now had David by my side.

Now I'm completely lost.

I pull over. Luckily I've brought a road map and, flicking on the overhead light, I turn to the correct page. David and I used to have so many rows about directions. Apparently he didn't need directions, especially not from me. So ten minutes later I can't help feeling a small victory when I see the signs for Nettlewick. Not bad for someone who can't read a map, *apparently*.

My phone beeps up a message. I've got service. I listen. It's from the removal company, saying they've already unloaded and left. Followed by another message from Mr Hardcastle, the estate agent, saying he met the removal men with the keys and the office is now about to close.

'But not to worry,' he adds cheerfully, 'I've left the keys under the plant pot on the windowsill.'

Oh, well, that's all right then. Because of course no one would ever thinking of looking there.

Trying not to stress about how everything I own is in that house, I drive over the ancient stone bridge and up the hill. Not much seems to have changed since those childhood holidays, and I head up the main street that leads into the village with its small, cobbled square, around which sits an assortment of bow-windowed shops, past the local pub, the cafe and the tiny post office.

Though, of course, so much has changed. Our grandparents are long gone, as are our parents, and we're all grown-up now. Josie, always so creative and free-spirited, became a photographer and began travelling the world. I, always the sensible one, became a teacher, moved to London and got married. But now all that's changed too.

The cottage is on the outskirts of the village, down a narrow cobbled lane that makes me grateful for my tiny Fiat, which niftily manoeuvres around the bends. I pull up outside and cut the engine. It looks more dilapidated than I remember, and anxiety and doubt rise up inside, like acid reflux. Quickly swallowing them down, I remind myself what Naomi said about fear and excitement being basically the same thing. I glance up at the tatty net curtains at the bedroom window. I'm not convinced. I remain seated in the warmth of the car. Despite the long journey I'm not ready to go in yet. I turn the stereo back on.

*

Even with the keys, it takes three hefty kicks before the door finally swings open to reveal a narrow hallway crammed with packing boxes. The removal men must have dumped them all here and left. Flicking on the overhead bulb, I step over a pile of junk mail and pull my coat around me. The temperature gauge on the car said minus two, and even inside I can see my breath. Shivering, I close the front door behind me.

When I first announced I was leaving London and moving to the country by myself, there were a few raised eyebrows, but people were mostly enthusiastic. 'Oooh, lucky you! Getting away from this rat race! What an exciting new adventure!! Just think, you'll be able to grow your own vegetables!!' After all, who doesn't watch *Escape to the Country* and dream of a return to nature and raised beds? Though of course dreaming of a life off-grid is always more appealing when you're watching it on a flat-screen TV while eating a Deliveroo. A couple of my friends even called me brave.

Except for me, it seemed less of a choice and more of necessity. This wasn't about me growing heirloom tomatoes, it was about trying to save my life. Which I know sounds dramatic to those who have never suffered the crushing despair of a broken heart, but that's how it felt to me. I was drowning in London. I needed to escape. I wanted to run away from it all and disappear. But now, faced with the stark reality, it's overwhelming. This doesn't feel like an exciting new adventure; it feels scary and bewildering.

A mouse darts across the floor, making me jump, and I let out a scream. I quickly pull myself together. It's late. I'm exhausted. I need to go to bed. Only it turns out my actual bed has been dismantled and lies propped against the wall in the hallway. Instead I make do with the sofa, which I find in the living room, and use my puffa coat as a duvet. It's midwinter and there's no central heating, so the house is freezing. Curling up wearily against the cushions, I lie alone in the darkness, listening to the unfamiliar sounds of the house and the wind whistling in the chimney.

So this is it. My new life.

I feel anything but brave.

Then I remember something. Reaching for my handbag, I pull out the photograph of Josie and me and angle it to the shaft of moonlight coming in through the bare windows. I peer at her face, grinning out at me, and am instantly comforted. Suddenly I don't feel so alone. And, placing the photograph on the empty mantelpiece, I curl back up on the sofa and, for the first time in months, fall straight asleep.

Stanley

On. Off. On. Off. On.

From the window in his attic bedroom, Stanley, kneeling at the end of his bed, peered through his telescope at the house in the distance. Far away on the other side of the graveyard, he watched as the lights flicked on and off in the distance.

Bottom window: On. Then off. Bottom window on the other side: On.

He still couldn't tell his left from his right. Everyone else in his class could do it, but he could never remember. Some of the other children made fun of him, but Dad told him to ignore them. Dad said he was in the big school before he knew left and right, and that was *miles* older than he was now. The teacher said an easy way to remember was, 'Right is your writing hand', but he used his other hand to write with, so it got him all mixed up.

It didn't make sense, thought Stanley, as he continued peering through his new telescope, which was a present from Santa at Christmas. But lots of things didn't make sense; that's what made them so scary. Santa did not make sense. On Christmas Eve, Dad had said Santa was going to come into his bedroom when he was asleep and leave presents at the end of his bed, but he'd got frightened. He didn't want a strange man coming into his bedroom when he was asleep, even if he was magic.

Upstairs window: On. Bottom window still on = two lights on.

It was like the house was telling him something. A secret code spelled out in lights. Clambering off his bed, careful not to bang his head on the low, slanting attic ceilings, Stanley picked his way through the railway set that was laid out neatly all over the floor. He was wearing his special pyjamas and his feet were bare, so he didn't want to step on anything. It wouldn't just hurt his feet, it would upset the order of everything. The order was very important. Everything had to be done in a certain way. *The right way.* If it wasn't, he couldn't sleep.

Once Dad came in to kiss him goodnight and knocked over a level crossing and broke it, and Stanley was awake for hours worrying about it. In the end he had to wake Dad up and ask him to fix it with his special glue, but he got mad. He said it was the middle of the night and told him to go back to sleep. Stanley remembered crying. Then Dad started crying. It was just after Mummy became a star in the sky. But in the end Dad got up and fixed it, so he must have been really worried about it too.

Stanley knew he was supposed to be fast asleep now. But he couldn't sleep. For months the house on the other side of the graveyard had been in darkness, but then suddenly, a few days ago, he'd seen a light go on. Now he watched it every night. Finding the torch he kept hidden behind the stationmaster's house, he climbed back onto the bed. Aiming the torch at the window, he flashed it off, then on. Then waited expectantly.

Mummy being a star didn't make sense, either. How could she disappear into the sky one day when he was at school? And did that mean it could happen to anyone? Could Dad just disappear too? Stanley didn't want his dad to become a star. He got scared thinking about it, even now with his new telescope, so he chose not to gaze at the stars, but to stare at the lights instead.

The house answered. Off. Off. On . . . Off.

As the whole house fell into darkness, Stanley put down his torch and wriggled back underneath his Spider-Man duvet. Somehow he didn't feel so scared going to sleep, knowing the house was sleeping too. He closed his eyes. Tomorrow he would count the lights again. Maybe the house was trying to give him a message.

Maybe it was from Mummy.

A Charitable Act

'So how's it going?'

'Great . . . really great . . .'

Saturday. Two weeks later. And I'm on the phone to Naomi.

'See! I *told* you! God, I'd love to get out of London – all that fresh air and open space. Ellie would love it. Have you been going for lots of lovely long walks?'

'Sort of . . .'

Pushing my trolley up and down the endless aisles of a big DIY store probably isn't what Naomi has in mind by 'lovely long walks', but I don't want to disappoint her.

'Lucky you. I bet the scenery's stunning, isn't it?'

I pause by the display of matt emulsion, lit by the flickering overhead fluorescent lights.

'Stunning.'

Since moving to the countryside I've discovered that I can't get a mobile-phone signal inside the cottage; according to my network provider, I'm in a 'black spot'. Translated, this means I have to stand right at the top of my garden where it borders open fields, almost freezing to death, while waving my phone around like a demented lunatic to get even half a bar. Meanwhile I still don't have any Internet, due to a delay with the engineers.

Which is why I'm multitasking. While Naomi fills me in on some gossip at school, I gaze upon the vast array of paintbrushes – all different sizes, varieties and prices. I pick one up, running my thumb over the bristles and trying to decide whether I should go for the 50mm synthetic hollow-fibre or the 75mm cutting-in and framing with the raw timber handle, before spotting a whole section dedicated to rollers and feeling even more overwhelmed. I only wanted to paint the front bedroom.

'So, have you met any hunky farmers yet?' she asks, finishing telling me about an argument in the staffroom over mugs. Teachers can be very territorial over their mugs, and apparently the new deputy head and supply teacher had nearly come to blows over a 'Keep Calm and Carry On' mug.

'Er, hello, what Catherine Cookson novel are you living in?'

Naomi laughs throatily. 'Well, you never know.'

'No. Trust me, I do. And that is the *last* thing I'm looking for.'

I chuck in a few brushes and a roller.

'Look, I better go.'

'Yeah, me too, I've got to get Ellie to football. Enjoy your weekend!'

'I will – you too.'

Hanging up, I shove my phone in my pocket and eye the bucket of white emulsion. If only Naomi knew the real truth. And being careful not to put my back out, I squat down, grab the handle with both hands and, with a loud grunt, hoist it into my trolley.

OK, so the real truth is that, since moving in, I've not even had a sniff of fresh air or scenery. Rather I've been pulling up moth-eaten carpets and taking them to the local tip. It was a gruesome job – God only knows how long they'd been down, but there were enough mouse droppings, spiders (dead and alive) and silvery slug slime to give *I'm a Celebrity . . . Get Me Out of Here!* a run for its money.

I've also been busy getting quotes from local building firms and wading through all the necessary paperwork, plans and permits needed to do the renovations. I've had an architect draw up plans, involving knocking through to create a more open-plan living area, adding a new kitchen extension and downstairs loo and installing a log-burner, while upstairs, although the bedrooms are a decent size, I need to somehow transform the poky bathroom.

Unfortunately it's turning out to be a lot more complicated and expensive than it looks in all those glossy house magazines. That will teach me to buy a Grade II-listed cottage that's over three hundred years old. Thankfully, I had the damp in the front bedroom fixed before I moved in, so now instead of the giant mushroom, I have smooth, fresh pink plaster, all ready to paint. According to the advice I've read, it's very important to have one room in your house that you can live in while the building work is going on.

I dig several pages of my list out of my bag and with a pen check off PAINT. The list keeps growing longer and longer, like the time the fax machine in the staffroom had some kind of glitch and started spewing reams of paper all over the floor. That's showing my age. No one has fax machines any more, do they? I bet David's new girlfriend has never even *seen* a fax machine.

'Excuse me, where are the doormats?'

'Sorry?' I look up from checking things off my list to see a man staring at me.

'I'm looking for a doormat.'

Literally, *right* at me.

'Um . . . I don't work here.'

'Oh, OK.'

36

As the man moves briskly away, I feel my cheeks burn. Except, he didn't get the wrong person, did he? If anyone knows about doormats it's me. I *was* one. My husband ran off with someone young enough to be his daughter and what did I do? *His ironing.*

Still. At least I was the one who filed for divorce. Feeling like a doormat is one thing. Being the victim is quite another.

Face flaming, I negotiate my way towards the checkout. It's busy and there's a long queue. It was a mistake coming at the weekend. I edge slowly forward. In fact this whole thing was probably a huge mistake. I mean, seriously, if I'm going to uproot my life and try making a fresh start, shouldn't I be gadding about Bali on a spiritual journey? Or renovating a Tuscan farmhouse in the sunshine and meeting lots of handsome Italians? Isn't that what divorced women of a certain age do in the movies?

Except I'm not in the movies. I'm in Homebase.

Grabbing the shopping divider, I begin unloading my over-flowing trolley onto the conveyor belt. I didn't buy a farmhouse in the rolling Tuscan hills, but a damp, mouldy wreck of a cottage in the Yorkshire Dales. All those self-help books I bought talk about fresh starts and new projects – why didn't I learn a new language or take up baking my own sourdough? Why didn't I just rent and stay in London? It's not like there was much risk of bumping into my ex, as he's living on the other side of the city, and I could have avoided certain mutual married friends.

Actually I didn't need to avoid them – they've already avoided me. That's the thing with divorce. Married people fear it's contagious, like the measles. If David and Liv could split up, who might be next? When David first walked out, my girlfriends were brilliant and rallied round. There was lots of David-bashing and wine being drunk. But after a while the texts and the WhatsApps and the phone calls trickled away. Once the shock is over, friends get on with their own busy lives and assume you're getting on with yours.

But here's the thing: shock and disbelief don't simply disappear overnight. Worse still, you don't want to disappoint or burden anyone by admitting you're *still* not over it. That last weekend you weren't really busy; you just couldn't face getting dressed. That the future, which used to seem so secure, now scares the living daylights out of you.

So you go quiet. Delete all those social-media apps on your phone. Quit your job and move hundreds of miles to try to rebuild your life. Because I could cry in my pyjamas, wake up in the middle of the night having a panic attack and celebrate my birthday surrounded only by packing boxes, but one thing I was certain of: I hadn't got this far to give up now.

'That'll be three hundred and fifty-seven pounds, eighty pence.'

'*How much?*' I feel myself blanch.

Crikey. It would actually have been a lot cheaper to go gadding about Bali. I dig out my credit card. That reminds me: I must drive into town and put an ad in the main news-agent's about tutoring work. At this rate, I'm going to be running low on savings sooner rather than later.

Wordlessly the sales assistant turns the credit-card machine towards me and taps at the digital display with her fingernail. I notice she has impressively long, bright-orange fingernails. I curl my own, split and broken from ripping up underlay, into the palms of my hands to hide them.

I peer at the total.

'Right, yes,' I nod, though I can't see a thing. I've forgotten my reading glasses. I insert my credit card and punch in my code. It must be accepted, as a long receipt spews out. She hands it to me.

'Thanks for shopping with us today.'

'Thanks.' I smile, but she's already lifted up the divider and moved on to the next customer: an old man with a potted hyacinth. It begins making its way down the conveyor belt towards my items and, hastily finishing packing, I lift my bags into the trolley and head briskly for the exit.

Outside, the skies have turned grey and sullen and the temperature has dropped. February in London was never this cold. Here it gets into your bones. Putting on my gloves and hat, I begin pushing the trolley towards the car park. I've driven to a retail estate on the edge of town. I extended the agreement on the rental car for a couple of weeks, but I've got to return it soon as it's costing a small fortune.

'Would you like to make a donation?'

I pass a girl with a collecting box. She's wearing a hi-vis vest with some kind of slogan, but I don't read it.

'I'm sorry, I don't have any change.'

It's the standard answer. All I can think about is getting in the car and putting on the heater.

'Even if it's just a few pence, every little helps.' She smiles. She has pink hair and a silver nose-ring. She's a lot younger than I first thought. Probably only a teenager. I notice she's not wearing gloves and is pulling down the sleeves of her sweatshirt, trying to warm her fingers, which are red-raw with the cold.

'It's for our local dog-rescue shelter.'

And now I feel guilty. I pause to dig in my pockets. Finding nothing, I look in my purse.

'Do you have a dog?'

'Um . . . no.'

Damn. I've only got a twenty.

'Have you ever thought of getting one?'

'No, not really.' I shake my head, 'I'm not really a dog person.'

'I don't believe that.' She grins, wrinkling up her nose.

I feel conflicted. I'd like to make a donation – it's for a good cause and she seems like a good kid, standing out here on a weekend in the cold – but I can't really afford to give twenty pounds.

'Well, if you ever change your mind, we've got lots of lovely dogs looking for a loving home.'

She offers me a leaflet. On it are printed various photographs of dogs, their sad faces looking at me beseechingly.

'Here.' I pull the twenty out of my purse.

'Oh, wow!' Her face lights up, before doubt appears and she frowns. 'Sorry . . . I don't have any change – it's all in the collecting box.'

'I don't want any.'

'That's sick! *No way*,' she exclaims, and then claps her frozen fingers to her mouth. 'I mean, for real? Wow, thanks so much!'

'Well, it's for charity,' I smile.

I begin moving off with my trolley before I can regret my generosity. It's starting to sleet and I pull up my hood as I head across the car park.

'Hey!'

A voice calls after me and I turn to see the girl with the pink hair and collection box waving at me.

'See, I was right. You're definitely a dog person!'

Valentine

By 'eck, he was jiggered.

Halfway up the hill he had to stop to catch his breath. Whoever said age was just a number must never have been seventy-nine. Putting out his hand, he leaned against a stone wall, feeling his chest rising and falling. It was quite a walk from the bus stop up the hill, and it seemed to get steeper every day. He couldn't get enough air in his lungs. It's like they'd shrunk, somehow. His legs weren't what they used to be, either. In fact he might have to sit down for a minute.

Valentine eased himself onto the wall, lifting each buttock to free his overcoat and pulling at his hem to straighten it. It seemed like only yesterday that he used to cycle up streets as steep as these, doing his paper-round. He used to fly up them, the wind in his coat tails. Now they loomed ahead of him like bloody Mount Everest.

He banged his chest with the end of his fist. Shouldn't have smoked all those years. Silly bugger, he was. Thinking he was the bee's knees. Still, everyone did in those days. Even Gisele.

After a few minutes' rest he resumed his walk up the hill. The wind had dropped a bit and soon the familiar red-brick building came into view. Clifton Court Residential Care Home. He still couldn't get his head around it. He'd been making this daily pilgrimage for the past six months, yet each time felt like the first time. His sense of loss was still

41

acute and, drawing closer, he felt a familiar wave of grief and disbelief. How had it come to this?

Walking down the paved path towards the entrance, he trailed his hand lightly along the metal handrail. Valentine looked at the thin gold band on his wedding finger. 'Till Death Do Us Part.' Isn't that what the vicar had said? And yet here they were, fifty-nine years later. Death hadn't parted them. Something else had. Something that was, in many ways, much worse.

Reaching the entrance, he pushed open the doors and walked into the brightly lit reception. There were several plastic potted plants and some bland prints on the walls. Both these things vexed him. At least they could have got real plants and some nice pictures. It was little things like that that were important. Maybe they thought the residents wouldn't notice.

But Gisele noticed. It was one of the first things she commented upon when she arrived. A memory of her stooping down to stroke the feathery leaves of a fern between her fingers, and her expression when she realized it wasn't real, still pained him. Gisele always loved plants and flowers. 'Green fingers', that's what he used to call her. She could grow anything on their little front patio. Windowboxes of pillar-box red geraniums and multicoloured swirls of trailing petunias, pots filled with clambering clematis, spectacular dahlias and lacecap hydrangeas.

Now all the windowboxes and pots were empty.

'Hello, Mr Crowther.'

As usual, he was greeted by the receptionist, who sat perched behind the large desk like a big colourful parrot. She smiled widely. She was wearing that funny frosted lipstick she always wore. Even without his glasses, he could see that she'd got a bit on her front teeth. Valentine found her cheerfulness annoying. What was there to be cheerful about?

'Morning,' he replied gruffly, removing his flat cap.

'How are you today?' she continued brightly.

Angry. He was so angry at the bloody unfairness of it all. Sometimes he didn't know what to do with all the anger.

'All right,' he shrugged.

Still, it wasn't the receptionist's fault. It was nobody's fault. The staff at the nursing home weren't to blame. They were always so nice to him. So kind to Gisele. Some of these places were awful, you read about them in the newspapers – all sorts going on, terrible things – but he couldn't ask for a more wonderful home. They'd been lucky, if you could call it that.

'And it's "Valentine" – how many times have I told you?'

And now he felt remorseful. Silly old bugger, taking it out on other people; he needed to watch his temper. What would Gisele say?

'I know, sorry, but those upstairs told us we've got to greet the guests by their proper names.'

'Well, tell them upstairs that *is* my proper name.'

The receptionist made a face and nodded. She reminded him of his daughter, Helen, when she was younger. She used to pull that face too.

'I've come to see our lass. How is she?'

'She's just had her breakfast. You'll be pleased to know she managed two boiled eggs *and* a slice of toast. She made soldiers with it apparently.'

Valentine felt a lump in his throat as he remembered his wife making soldiers for their daughter when she was little. She would call them *mouillettes* – Gisele often spoke to their daughter in her native French – as she dipped them in the runny yolk and marched them into their daughter's mouth, to the sounds of childish laughter and demands of 'More *mouillette*, Mummy!'

'Aye, she always made the best soldiers.' He nodded, clearing his throat. He mustn't be sad. He mustn't ever let Gisele see him looking sad.

The receptionist beamed. 'She's in the recreational room watching TV. Go on through.'

The recreational room was accessed through the double fire doors and was at the end of the corridor. Part conservatory, it was a pleasant enough room, with large windows, which let in a lot of daylight and gave a view of the gardens. Even on a dull February day like today you were able to see both the sky and the grass; heaven and earth – what more could you ask for?

Valentine removed his overcoat and scarf. It was always so hot and stuffy in here. When Gisele had first moved in, he'd asked if they could open a window, let in some fresh air, but he'd been told they kept the windows closed and turned the thermostat up high to keep the residents warm. More like keep them half asleep, he'd grumbled.

He never wanted this for Gisele. They used to talk about it, before she got poorly. 'Never put me in one of those,' she'd say with a shudder, whenever a report about care homes came on the news. They'd watch footage of rooms full of old people nodding off in their armchairs, heads flopped backwards, mouths wide open, and both look at each other with horror.

'Just give me a cyanide pill and finish me off,' he'd say. To which she'd laugh, that tinkly, high-pitched laugh of hers, and say with her thick accent that had never lessened over the years, 'Oh, Valentine, you've watched too many of your war films. Now where am I going to buy cyanide, eh? At the Co-op?'

He spotted her immediately. She was sitting in an armchair by the window, staring out into the garden, her hands clasped in her lap. From a distance she looked the same as always. He could almost kid himself he'd come to pick her up and take her back home. That the doctors had got it wrong, and she was well again. When she caught sight of him, she'd tut sharply and click her tongue and tell him off for leaving her.

'Hello, love.'

Walking over to Gisele, he smiled and went to sit beside her. It was still the hardest thing not to lean over instinctively and give her a kiss on the cheek. He'd done it his whole life, ever since their first date all those years ago, but then several months ago he'd gone to kiss her as usual and she'd recoiled and become distressed. The doctor at the care home said not to get upset, or take it as a personal rejection. That it was common for patients to become unsettled or agitated when relatives tried to kiss them.

'It would be like a stranger coming up to you and giving you a kiss,' Dr Khan had explained.

'But I'm not a stranger, I'm her husband,' Valentine had protested.

'But she doesn't always remember,' she'd replied gently.

Gisele turned to him now, her bright-blue eyes running over his face. The carers had dressed her in one of her favourite cerise sweaters and applied her make-up, just as she liked it, but up close, it was as if the light had gone out of her face.

'It's Valentine. Your Valentine,' he prompted.

She smiled, but he wasn't sure if it was out politeness rather than recognition.

'Is it Valentine's Day?'

'Not yet, love,' he shook his head, 'but every day is Valentine's Day when you're married to me – isn't that what you used to say?' he joked feebly, searching her face for a flicker of memory.

It had started innocently enough; he thought she was being forgetful, getting confused. 'Well, aren't we all? It's called old age,' he'd soothe, when she couldn't recall where she'd put her glasses or got lost on the way back from town. Except it wasn't. When they got the official diagnosis of Alzheimer's, he put his arm around his weeping wife in the doctor's surgery and told her not to worry. She'd looked after him for years, so now it was his turn.

At first they'd managed just fine. They even went on holiday to the South of France, driving in their camper van like they'd done every year. But as the disease continued its grim march through his beloved wife's brain, it was like having to stand aside and watch helplessly as thieves broke into your home and stole the things that are most precious to you. It robbed Gisele of her quick-witted sense of humour, her uncanny ability to recall any date or recipe, and her joy of gardening. Instead her behaviour became more erratic: getting out of bed in the middle of the night and putting on her coat to go to the supermarket, becoming angry and impatient, when all her life she'd been so calm and kind.

Worst of all was watching her sobbing uncontrollably in the fleeting moments of lucidity when she realized what was happening to her. Trying to comfort her and failing. He managed for as a long as he could, but even with the help of carers, in the end it got too much.

'Acqua di Parma.'

'Sorry, love?'

'Your cologne,' she said, leaning forward to smell him. 'I bought you that cologne one Christmas.'

'Yes . . . yes, you did, love.'

It was like getting his wife back again for a few brief, wonderful moments and Valentine felt his heart soar as he reached for her hand. Just like he did all those years ago when he first asked her to dance at the Palais. Her teenage skin was firm and smooth then; now it was tracing-paper thin, but it was still the same hand that had held his as they jived around the dance floor.

'Is Helen coming?'

Gisele was looking over his shoulder, her expression hopeful, as if at any minute she might see her daughter walking through the door.

'No, she's gone to stay with your sister Agnès, in Paris.'

Disappointment flashed across her face and she said something in French that Valentine couldn't understand. She spoke French more and more these days. One time he visited, she refused to speak any English and he had to try get by with what little French he knew.

'Are we in Paris?' she said finally in English.

'No, Helen is.'

Gisele seemed agitated now, as if trying to process this information, and then said, 'Can we go home now?'

'Maybe tomorrow,' he soothed, stroking her hand with his thumb. He hated lying to her, but he'd learned it was the kindest thing. She asked this every time he came to visit her, and at first he tried to be truthful and explain that she was living here now, but she would grow too upset.

So now he lied. He lied to his own wife.

'I've got you a gift.' Hoping to distract her, he reached into his shopping bag and pulled out a potted hyacinth that he'd bought on his way here. The DIY shop at the local retail park had a large gardening section and it was right where the bus dropped him off, at the bottom of the hill. 'They're your favourite.'

'*Jacinthe.*' Gisele's eyes lit up.

'Aye,' he nodded now, smiling. 'I know how much you love the smell.'

47

He held it for her as she dipped her nose into the purple flowers and took a deep inhale. Its effect was magical. Closing her eyes, she appeared instantly calmed as she drew in its fragrance.

'I had them as my wedding posy.' She spoke in hushed tones, as if the memory was being coaxed from her mind and to speak any louder might scare it away. '*Jacinthes pourpres* . . . deep-purple ones, tied with an ivory ribbon. It was the most beautiful thing I'd ever seen.'

'You certainly were.' Valentine smiled and nodded, enraptured by his wife. These few precious moments when she remembered were becoming more and more rare. 'Most beautiful bride I'd ever seen.'

She frowned then and, opening her eyes, turned to face him.

'Do I know you?'

He fought back tears.

'Yes, it's Valentine, love, your husband.'

He should be used to it by now. She didn't know what she was saying. She didn't mean it. And yet, every time, it broke his heart a little bit more.

Gisele looked at him, her expression blank. Nothing. A whole lifetime together and there was nothing there.

He sniffed sharply. 'Well, let's see if we can put it in your room, eh?' He eased himself up from the armchair. No point sitting here feeling sorry for himself. That wasn't going to help anyone. 'I'll go and ask the nurse if we can put it on your bedside table. Then, when you go to bed, it'll remind you of your wedding day.'

He smiled cheerfully, but she'd already turned away from him and was gazing out of the window, her hands twisting agitatedly in her lap. She had retreated into a world that he couldn't reach. Holding the hyacinth in his hands, Valentine watched her helplessly.

'Right, well, bye then, love. I'll come see you tomorrow, as usual.'

It was only when he walked away that Valentine finally allowed the tears to fall. Sixty years married this summer, and he couldn't even kiss his wife goodbye.

Online Dating

Turning on the tap, I hold the paintbrush underneath it to clean the bristles, separating them with my fingers as the water sends swirling silvery ribbons of emulsion down the plughole of the old metal sink.

It's Sunday night. I've spent the whole weekend painting the front bedroom. In London we always got the decorators in. Tomasz and Basek, a local two-man team who drank gallons of sugary tea and listened to really loud, thumping house music.

Thing is, Tomasz and Basek made it look really easy, but it's not easy at all. Before I could even start painting, I had to do all the prepping and sanding and filling in of cracks. Of which, in a three-hundred-year-old cottage, there seems to be an alarming amount. I had a survey done when I bought it, but I chose the basic one to try and save a bit of money.

'If it's been standing all these years, it's not going to fall down now,' reasoned the estate agent cheerfully.

Which will teach me to listen to estate agents.

Dumping the paintbrushes in the sink, I turn off the tap, then notice the open bottle of red wine on the side. Pouring myself a large glass, I go to put the bottle back, then change my mind and take it with me into the living room, along with a bar of my favourite dark chocolate. People talk about the Divorce Diet, but after the initial shock of discovering David's affair had worn off, I gained weight. It's all the comfort-eating I've been doing. Though, frankly, I don't know why they call it comfort-eating; all my clothes are now so *un*comfortable.

Unbuttoning my jeans, I flop on the sofa. I've bought several of those oil-heaters you can plug in, but it's still chilly. The cottage has a centuries-old inglenook fireplace, but it takes forever to make a fire in the grate, twisting strips of newspaper and carefully stacking kindling and logs. It seems silly to go to all that effort when it's just me. Grabbing a blanket, I pull it over my legs to keep warm and take a large sip of wine.

It feels strange to be lying on the sofa drinking Malbec on a Sunday night. Usually I'd be getting ready for Monday morning and the week ahead. The TV screen flickers animatedly in the corner, like a chatty friend who never draws breath. I'm not watching it; I have it on in the background for company. When I was married I would often find myself wishing for a bit of peace and quiet – some time alone that didn't involve marking homework or doing laundry, or being asked 'What's for dinner?' the moment I walked through the door.

Now no one greets me. When I close the front door there's no one to talk to or share things with – be it a pizza or the sofa, or discussing the crap day you've had at work. It's true what they say: be careful what you wish for. Feeling my thoughts darken, I reach for my bag, pulling out its contents to find my phone. The engineers finally showed up to install my Internet, so now at last I have Wi-Fi; it will be good to hear a friendly voice. I scroll through my WhatsApp contacts and pause at Josie's number. I hesitate, then dial Naomi instead.

It goes to voicemail, so I leave a message. I try to make it sound cheerful and upbeat. About how busy I've been. All the plans for the house. I don't want her to know how lost and lonely I am. How during the day I distract myself but, come the evenings, how depressed and afraid I can feel. Hanging up, I notice a leaflet on the sofa that's fallen from my handbag. It's the one the volunteer in the car park gave me. Unfolding it, I read about all the dogs needing homes. Perhaps she was right; perhaps I should get a dog. It would be good company and good exercise and I could offer one a home, even if the roof is leaking.

There's a link to their website, so I look it up on my phone and begin absently scrolling through the photos of all the dogs that are up for adoption, reading their profiles. It's a bit like online dating. *Sociable, easy-going and energetic. Loves going on long walks in the countryside and cuddling up on the sofa in front of the fire.*

It's a match!

Well, perhaps not the energetic bit; I'm exhausted after spending all weekend decorating and I haven't actually *gone* on any long walks yet, unless you count up and down the aisles at the DIY store. I haven't been very sociable, either. In fact, since moving here I've felt like hiding away and have barely spoken to a soul, though in fairness it is the middle of winter and the cold makes you want to hibernate. That said, I did say hello to my neighbours, but they were only here for the weekend, as most of the cottages in my row appear to be either second homes or holiday lets.

Clicking onto the next page, I read the section entitled *Things to Think About When Adopting a Dog.* Underneath there's quite an exhaustive checklist; owning a dog is a lot of responsibility, including a bit about 'dogs needing a routine'. I think about my own life, and how everything's such a mess right now. Actually, on second thoughts, perhaps I should wait.

'Please, Dad. Please can we get a puppy?' I suddenly hear Josie's voice in my head and glance across at the mantelpiece, at the photo of the two of us as children. After Mum died, we used to beg and plead with him, but we were always moving around and our various landlords would never allow it. It wasn't until I got married that it would have been a possibility, but David was against it. 'I'm allergic to cats, and dogs are too big a commitment,' he said dismissively.

Marriage too, as it turned out.

Returning to the screen, I exit the page, but the one underneath is still open and my attention is caught by a photo of a litter of puppies needing homes. I look at their little faces gazing out at me, then check the address; it's not far from here. Maybe I should pay a visit. After all, there's no harm in looking, is there?

Maya

'Don't you pull that face at me.'

'What face?'

'You know exactly what face I'm talking about. The one that never smiles any more but just scowls instead.'

'That's not true!' She scowled at Simon, her stepfather, across the kitchen island. 'I smile all the time when I'm with my friends.'

'Exactly, but not when you're at home with your own family!' He slammed his mug onto the counter top, causing his tea to spill onto his paperwork. 'Now look what you've made me do!'

'I didn't make you do that!' She was indignant. Why was everything *always* her fault?

The sound of the front door slamming interrupted their argument and they both fell silent as a policewoman appeared in the doorway. As she took in the scene, her face fell.

'Mum, tell him!' Maya was the first to speak. Relieved her mother was home from work, she swiftly made her appeal. 'Dad won't listen to me!'

As PC Neesha Sharma, her job was to keep the peace in the community, but now she seemed to doing it at home all the time as well.

'Can someone please tell me what's going on?' Heaving a weary sigh, she sank onto the dining-room sofa and kicked off her shoes. It was the sigh of a woman who'd just done a ten-hour shift dealing with a traffic accident, the owner of a missing cat and a fifteen-year-old boy who was injured in a gang-related knife attack. A woman who simply wanted to come home to some peace and quiet, but instead was faced with trying to calm the situation between her husband and teenage daughter. Maya saw all that in her mother's face and felt guilty for involving her.

'It's Maya, she's being completely unreasonable.'

'Simon, please,' her mother reasoned, but he wouldn't listen to her, either.

'Neesha, leave this to me. If you hadn't allowed Maya to take time off school and go on those silly marches, this would have never have happened.'

'They're not silly,' interrupted Maya furiously. 'Black lives matter! Climate change matters!' He was like all the rest of the stupid politicians.

'She does have a point, Simon.'

Maya threw her mum a grateful smile.

'Well, you would say that, wouldn't you, Neesha? Why is it you always have to take her side over mine?'

Sitting with her mum on the sofa, Maya knew he felt excluded and didn't care. Simon wasn't her real dad. Her parents split up when she was still a baby and her real dad moved to America and had another family. He didn't keep in touch apart from birthday cards, though she followed her half-siblings on Facebook.

When her mum remarried, she got to be a bridesmaid. She was only six and didn't remember much – just how excited she was about getting a new dress and a new dad. They were like a proper family now, and theirs was such a close relationship. 'Thick as thieves,' that's what her mum used to call them. Now he just got angry all the time and shouted.

'Simon, for goodness' sake!'

Her mum too. Maya wished she was still at Zac's, where she'd been all afternoon bunking off sixth form. She wished she'd kept her mouth shut, like he told her to. 'You don't need to tell your parents; you're practically an adult. It's your life – you do what you want.'

But then Zac could always do what he wanted. He wasn't seventeen and studying for his A-levels and still living at home. He was twenty-one and lived in a squat and whenever anyone asked him what he did for a job, he said he was an activist. She was glad she'd never told her parents about Zac. They'd freak.

'Well, in that case I'm sure you'll be happy to know our daughter has informed me she's going to quit the sixth form to go and save the planet instead.'

Her mum looked upset. 'Oh, Maya, it's not long until your exams in the summer, don't give up now.'

Maya hated disappointing her. It seemed to happen a lot these days.

'But what's the point of A-levels when the planet is being destroyed?'

'Well, if we take that opinion, what's the point of me being in the police? Should I quit doing my job too?'

'No, of course not.'

'Well then, why is it different for you?'

'Because . . .' Maya felt a familiar rush of frustration. Why was it that whenever she tried to explain how she felt to her parents, it always got so muddled up inside? Like she couldn't get the right words out. Yet with Zac, she never had to explain. He just understood. 'It's a waste of time. I'm not going to get the grades to go university anyway.'

'That's because you barely study for them,' exploded her stepfather. 'You're always on that bloody phone instead!'

'That's not true,' she yelled back. Maya was more like

her stepfather than she would like to admit; they were both hot-headed and prone to outbursts. 'And anyway, why is it never about what *I* want? Why's it always about what *you* want?'

'Because I'm your father.'

'No you're not. You're not my real dad!'

It flew out like a slap across his face. Maya saw him blanch.

'Well, I'm the only dad you've got here,' he replied. 'And you're not leaving school. That's final.'

'We just want you to make the most of your opportunities in life – that's all, sweetheart,' her mum implored.

'But it's my life, not yours.'

There was a beat.

'You'll thank us in the end.'

Maya's jaw set as she looked at her parents. So that was it. The argument was over and the decision had been made. She didn't even get a say.

'Can I go to my room now?'

Without waiting for an answer, she left the kitchen and went upstairs, making sure to stomp on the stair carpet and slam her bedroom door. Throwing herself on her bed, she pulled out her phone and hit 'Recents'.

'Zac?'

'Hey, babe, what's up?'

'I fucking hate my parents.'

Rescue Me

Now I know why they call it puppy love.

Two days later I find myself sitting on the floor while five squeaking bundles of wagging tails, pink noses and soft, velvety ears crawl and tumble all over me.

'So what do you think?' Brenda is looking at me expectantly, her eyebrows raised. Brenda is one of the full-time staff who greeted me when I first walked in. Apparently the girl I met in the car park was just a weekend volunteer.

I think I'm about to become an even bigger cliché. I can hear Naomi now, teasing me about Meno-Paws. Well, who hasn't read one of the many articles in those magazines you find at the hairdresser's?

LOST & FOUND
My husband left me, so I got a puppy
and I've never been happier!

MENO-PAWS
Meet the middle-aged women swapping
their HRT patches for puppies!

'Gosh, I can't choose between them.'

'Maybe you don't have to,' she smiles. 'I think that little one has already chosen you.'

She motions to the little ball of golden fluff that's fallen fast asleep in the crook of my arm.

'You're in luck. Puppies go quickly, but she hasn't been reserved yet.'

I feel my heart melt. Who cares if I'm in Meno-Paws?

Brenda beams with satisfaction. 'If you want to follow me through to the office, we can fill in a reservation form.'

Carefully putting the puppy back with the rest of the litter, I dust myself off and follow Brenda past the row of kennels and the cacophony of barking into the office, where she sits down at her desk and offers me a seat opposite.

'Just be careful of our newest arrival,' she says as I pull up a chair.

It's then I notice a dog basket on the floor. Curled up inside, sound asleep and snoring raspily, is a scruffy black dog. I notice his muzzle is greying and covered in scars. I can see his ribs, he's so thin.

'He came into the shelter yesterday, but we can't put him in a kennel by himself, as he howls.'

'Howls?'

'Yes, the old boy doesn't like being alone.'

Brenda looks across at him, her face sympathetic.

'Plus it's warmer in here. He's got bad arthritis in one of his back legs. By the looks of things, it's from an old injury that was never treated properly. Shame, as now he's quite lame.'

'Oh no, the poor thing.'

I'm watching as he begins to dream, making little excited barks and yelps, his front paws moving as if he's running.

'What's his name?'

Tapping away on the computer, she doesn't look up. 'We don't know.'

'You don't know? Why?' I say surprised. 'What happened to his owner?'

She turns away from the screen, taking off her glasses to look at me. 'We don't know that either as he hasn't been microchipped and there was no collar. He was found up on the moors. By the looks of it, he'd been dumped.'

'*Dumped?*'

'I'm afraid so.'

'How could anyone abandon a dog?' I ask, shocked.

Brenda shrugs. 'He's some kind of lurcher, so it's likely he was used for hunting when he was younger. Sadly, when they get old and can't hunt properly any more, they're often found abandoned, or worse.'

'So they just throw them away, like rubbish?'

She nods, her face resigned. 'This one seems a really sensitive soul. He didn't deserve such cruel treatment. No animal does.'

I look across at the dog without a name. He's woken himself up with all that dreaming and as he lifts his grey muzzle, his chocolate-brown eyes meet mine. I don't think I've ever seen a dog look so sad. I'm used to seeing all the ones in parks in London, with their happy waggy tails and shiny pedigree coats.

'How could anyone do that to him?' I say quietly.

Getting up from my chair, I bend down to stroke him, but he turns his head away and stares fixedly at the wall.

'He's shut down,' she explains. 'Not surprising, considering.'

Gently I stroke his back, feeling his ribcage beneath his fur. Not wanted any more and dumped by his owner. I know how he feels.

'You and me both,' I whisper, tickling his ear.

'The hikers who brought him in said he was very disorientated when they found him. I doubt he would have survived another night up there.'

'At least he's safe now.'

'Yes.' She finishes typing and stands up to get something

from the printer and, when she looks over at me, her face is a picture of resignation. 'But it won't be easy. It's hard to find someone willing to take on an older dog with issues.'

I feel something warm and wet brush against my hand and turn back to see the old dog gently licking it.

'Anyway, if you just want to check and sign this reservation form.' She passes it across to me.

'Actually I need to change something.'

She frowns. 'Is there a mistake?'

'Here.' I point to the section where it asks for a description of the dog being offered a new home. 'Can you cross out "puppy" and instead put "Harry".'

'Harry?'

I look down into the chocolate-brown eyes staring up at me.

'Well, he's going to need a name.'

STAGE 2

Keep Calm
(and go for a walk)

Faith

They say things come in threes. Even impulsive decisions. So if the first was quitting my job and the second was buying a cottage deep in the Yorkshire Dales, then my third is deciding to adopt Harry.

After filling in the necessary paperwork and undergoing a home check, which I was nervous I would fail, as the cottage is barely fit for habitation – by a human *or* an animal – Brenda calls. It's good news. I have somehow managed to be deemed fit enough to be his new owner.

Which is how, a week after first laying eyes on a big, scruffy dog with no name, I find myself driving back to the rescue centre to collect Harry and bring him home. I'm excited but apprehensive. I've never owned a dog before, or any kind of pet, so I've been doing lots of reading up about what to expect, especially with Harry being a rescue. I also spend an absolute fortune in the local pet shop. I had no idea how much stuff you need. Still, I'm someone who likes to be prepared, so I'm feeling quietly confident as I park the car at the rescue centre and go in to collect him.

Plus, as I sign the paperwork, Brenda points out that today's date is 14th February. I'm not one to care much about Valentine's Day, but surely that's got to be fortuitous.

Except ours is not exactly what I'd call an immediate love affair.

First off, Harry refuses to get into the car. After a real

struggle, I succeed, only to get half a mile down the road before he throws up all over the back seat. Then, when we stop at the traffic lights, he suddenly transforms from old and docile to completely ballistic, barking his head off and body-slamming himself against the window, trying to get to a ginger cat sitting on a wall. Finally, on reaching home, he refuses to *get out* of the car.

I think it's when I'm standing in the pouring rain, trying to coax him into the house and getting soaked through, that it begins to dawn on me that the reality of rescuing a dog isn't going to be quite how it appears in all those jaunty, heart-warming shows on TV. Me and my new buddy, bounding joyfully around in the garden, playing fetch with a ball or cuddling up together on the sofa, a picture of contentment.

In fact when I eventually manage to get Harry through the front door and close it behind the both of us, I fully realize how completely naive I've been. Fearful and anxious, he's unable to settle and paces around, whining. It's distressing to witness, and obviously deeply distressing for Harry.

'Come on, boy.' Patting his new basket enthusiastically, I wave some of his organic chicken treats to try to tempt him. 'It's delicious – look, it's the breast, all white meat.'

He barely even sniffs it as he limps around in endless circles. I watch helplessly, my spirits sinking. He hasn't eaten a thing since we got back from the shelter, and that was hours ago now. Still, that's not surprising, considering the journey home. I wince at the memory of him being carsick. Poor Harry. Poor Fiat. Despite scrubbing it for hours when I got home and spraying it with an entire bottle of the expensive perfume David got me every Christmas, that uphol-stery is never going to be the same again.

Still, I never liked that perfume; it gave me a headache, so there's a silver lining of sorts.

'How about some TV?'

In desperation I grab the remote. I once saw a funny video of a dog watching TV and being really engrossed in a wildlife programme by David Attenborough. I turn it on and start scrolling through the channels.

'*Love Island*?'

It's the new winter series. OK, so it's not quite David Attenborough, but it's a wildlife programme of sorts.

Busy sniffing the sofa leg, Harry looks up and starts barking at the screen.

'Not a fan?' I keep scrolling. 'The news?'

Harry begins howling.

But honestly, who can blame him? That's mostly how I feel these days when I watch the news. I quickly turn the channel over.

'OK, how about a movie?'

As I put on Netflix I'm reminded of when David and I would do a film night at the weekend. After a hard week at work I used to love ordering a takeaway, opening a bottle of wine, snuggling up on the sofa . . . Tears prickle my eyelashes and I blink them back furiously. I can't start crying in front of Harry.

But it's too late. He looks at me and starts whining again, and as the music swells and the title credits roll, he resumes his pacing. Despair beats. I've tried everything but I can't get him to settle. He's going round and round in circles.

Just like you did when David first left.

My mind suddenly casts itself backwards and, remembering the tears and snot and desperation, I wince at the memory. I was pitiful. Pathetic, really. But at the time I didn't care. Shock and heartache do that to you. Pride doesn't get a look-in. For weeks I was in a daze. Pacing up and down, stomach churning, my mind going round in circles. Disbelief congealing into devastation that we were over, and we could never go back.

I don't believe it. Harry's lain down.

I stare at him in astonishment. I was so distracted by my thoughts that I didn't notice him lie down on the rug. Stiffly curling his big, black body into a circle, he tucks his long legs underneath him and buries his grey muzzle into his tail. After a few moments I hear his breathing deepen and he begins to snore.

Watching him sleeping, I feel a sense of relief. More than that, I feel a glimmer of hope. Discovering my husband was in love with someone else broke my heart, but it was the betrayal of my trust in him that truly broke me. But if this scared, defenceless dog can trust me, after everything he's been through, then maybe one day I'll be able to trust someone again too.

Valentine

Every morning he had a routine. That's the first thing everyone tells you when you retire. Apparently it's very important.

'You must keep up a routine, Mr Crowther,' his GP had warned him when Valentine went to see him about his water-works, though to be honest, he wasn't sure what a routine had to do with having to get up half a dozen times in the night to pee.

Still, he didn't want to take the risk. Rumour had it that's what finished off Cyril at number forty-two. Poor bugger had only been retired six months when he keeled over one afternoon while watching cricket on the telly. According to someone at the post office, he was still in his pyjamas.

So every day Valentine woke up just before 7 a.m. After sixty-four years of getting up for work, he didn't need to set an alarm. After putting on his dressing gown and slippers, the first thing he did was go into the kitchen and put the kettle on. He made it in the teapot, with tea leaves. None of this putting a teabag in a mug, like Helen.

'Oh, Dad, I can't do all that faffing around with a teapot – it's only me,' she'd said when she first moved into her own student flat and they bought her a teapot as a house-warming present.

It's only me.

Valentine stared at the teapot now as he ladled in a single teaspoon of loose tea, just enough for one person. There was no Gisele to share it with him, to ask whether she was in the mood for Lapsang Souchong or Darjeeling this morning. The kettle boiled and clicked itself off. He reached for it and poured the water onto the tea leaves, replacing the lid to let it brew for a few minutes.

Who'd have thought it? Him, drinking posh tea. His old army mates would rip him to shreds if they could see him now. Back in those days, they used to brew up Tetley so strong it could take the varnish off the handle of your rifle. It was meeting Gisele that changed his taste in tea. But then she changed a lot of things.

Putting the knitted tea cosy over the pot to keep it warm, he set it upon the small table by the window, along with a china cup and saucer. The table was one of those with extending leaves, though he couldn't remember the last time he'd needed to use them. Gisele used to love to entertain; she'd go to town, whipping up soups and soufflés and delicious-smelling casseroles, all polished off with a fresh *tarte tatin* and baked Camembert. He could see her now, standing at the stove like a conductor in charge of her beloved orchestra of orange Le Creuset pans, wooden spoon in hand, as they bubbled and steamed and browned under the grill.

They'd moved to Nettlewick when Valentine retired, away from the city and their pre-war semi on a busy main road, with exhaust fumes and lorries that shook their pictures on the walls. It had always been their dream to live in the countryside one day, but it was still a wrench to leave behind the home in which their daughter grew up and which held so many memories. Fortunately they found their new home warm and welcoming and soon made new friends, inviting them over for barbecues and dinner parties. It felt like a fresh start, in more ways than one.

But it was a long time now since they'd had people over.

Long before Gisele got ill. He'd tried to suggest it – even offered to cook, Lord help them – but she'd just patted his hand and said maybe later. That's the thing about later, though. It never really comes, does it? Instead you always seem to skip right past it without noticing and then, before you know it, it's not later – it's too late.

Toast. Two slices with butter and jam.

Putting the bread in the toaster, Valentine put the butter dish on the table along with the strawberry jam. His GP had warned him about his cholesterol, but he wasn't going to switch to that spreadable stuff.

'Over my dead body,' he'd told Dr McDermott at his last appointment.

'And well that might be, if you don't change your diet,' Dr McDermott cautioned, giving Valentine a pamphlet about saturated fats and a list of foods to eat.

Nuts and seeds? What did he think he was? A bloody sparrow?

That reminded him, he needed to fill up the bird feeders. Reaching for the jotter pad that he kept on the side to make daily lists, Valentine turned the page to start a new one and wrote in his spidery handwriting:

monday 10th February

1. Fill bird feeders

He'd shoved the pamphlet in a drawer, along with all the other stuff that he didn't want to read. Endless circulars and flyers about getting his guttering cleaned and his drains rodded. Bills in brown envelopes with cellophane windows. They all went into the deep dresser drawers in the hallway. When they were filled up, he'd move on to the ones in the sideboard.

Before Gisele became poorly, he used to take pride in dealing with it all, opening the post every morning and filing everything neatly away. It was a husband's job. Now he hid it all away out of sight – out of sight, out of mind. If only he could do that with all the regrets and the guilt and the memories that woke him in the middle of the night, his heart beating so hard he feared it was going to burst right out of his chest. With all the anger that still raged inside. Just shove it in the drawer and close it and that was it: all gone.

He turned on the radio.

Too much thinking never did anyone ever good. He tuned it to the jazz channel and glanced at the library books on family history and military records on the side. He'd been doing his family tree for years but not getting very far. Gisele was forever teasing him. 'Can't you get a faster hobby?' 'It's not a hobby,' he'd grumble, 'it's genealogy.' 'Well, can't you get a different -ology?' she'd reply, like that advert on the telly.

The toast popped up.

Putting the slices on a plate, he went to sit down at the table. He poured his tea, added his milk, buttered his toast and smeared on the jam. He made sure to use a different knife for the butter – Gisele was very particular about that. A lump appeared in his throat and he swallowed it down with a mouthful of tea. He gazed out of the window. At the whole day stretching ahead of him.

He'd looked forward to retirement. To all the things he and Gisele would do together when he finally gave up painting and decorating and hung up his ladder. Lots of blokes he knew down the pub dreaded retiring. They eked work out for as long as they could. 'What are we going to do all day?' they would groan into their pints, fearful of being stuck at home under their wives' feet.

But not Valentine. Every morning over breakfast he and Gisele would look out of the window at the weather and eagerly plan their day. He liked to go for a drive. 'Look at that view: God's own country,' he would marvel as they set off in their ageing camper van to take in the sweeping ghylls and valleys across the Dales. Gisele liked to visit garden centres. 'Just look at the flowers on that *Clematis montana*,' she'd exclaim with an equal amount of joy and wonderment.

He used to love their day-trips. They'd always stop somewhere nice for lunch. The cafe at the abbey was a firm favourite. They did lovely home-made scones there and you got a fabulous view of the ruined abbey. He went once by himself after Gisele left, but it wasn't the same. He sat outside in the sunshine and watched children paddling in the river.

He liked to watch kids playing; there was something so innocent and carefree about them. One of them, a little girl, reminded him of Helen when she was that age, and he told her Helen's favourite 'Knock, knock' joke – the one about the penguin – and it made her laugh, a giggly, girlish laugh. But then the mother came rushing up and pulled the little girl away. Caused quite a scene. He left soon after that and never went back.

Valentine buttered a second slice of toast and looked out of the window of the bungalow. There wasn't a soul about, just a field full of cows. It was situated right at the top of the lane that led onto a public footpath, and he rarely saw anyone passing except the odd hiker. As for friends, they'd drifted away, after the diagnosis. Last year Gisele had shouted at one of the neighbours further down the lane, accusing them of stealing from her, and the police were called.

Then there was the time in the post office when she insisted on paying with coins, counting them out, one by one. Some customers in the queue got impatient and started saying things, so he tried to pay with his card, but that only made Gisele upset and angry and everyone stared. In the end they stopped going out – it was easier that way. Most people in the village had been kind, but he'd retreated into himself. Caring for Gisele had been hard, but harder still was the guilt Valentine felt for not being able to look after her properly. Now he kept himself to himself.

The central heating was coming on.

As the radio played in the background, Valentine listened to the radiators gurgling and cracking as they expanded. Peace and quiet. That's what they'd liked the most about the bungalow. 'I can hear a pin drop,' Gisele had marvelled with delight. Valentine sipped his tea and looked out of the window. Now it felt suffocating.

Bugger! His hand slipped, spilling tea down the front of his dressing gown. Tutting, he reached for his jotter pad:

2. wash dressing gown

He looked at his to-do list. Two things already. Once he'd finished this piece of toast, he'd best make a start on those bird feeders.

First Steps

The next morning dawns crisp and clear and, after feeding Harry, I clip on his new lead and step out of the front door. It's deepest February and there's a sharp wind, but the sun is shining brightly and its cheerful resilience buoys me up.

Harry seems perkier too, despite keeping me awake half the night with his howling. I'd put his basket in the kitchen, but in the end I surrendered and let him come upstairs, immediately breaking the 'first and most important rule of setting boundaries', according to all the dog behaviourist books I've bought. But I didn't care about rules at three in the morning. All I cared about was getting some sleep.

Still, it was probably just first-night nerves. I'm sure he'll soon get used to the sleeping arrangements. It's going to take a few days, that's all.

'That's right, isn't it, Harry?'

I look down at him as both of us stand on the doorstep, Harry sniffing the air expectantly. He looks up at me as I say his name and I feel a beat of anticipation. So this is it. *Our First Walk*. It feels quite momentous.

'Come on then, boy.'

When I'd envisaged getting a dog, I'd pictured long hikes across the Dales, but Harry and I are only going on a short walk around the neighbourhood. Locking the door behind me, I set off walking slowly, with Harry limping beside me. We make an odd couple. Harry seems anxious and unsure of his new surroundings, while I hold his lead nervously. It's quiet. On the other side of the street someone with a Labrador walks past and nods. I nod back, feeling a bit like an imposter. They think I'm one of them.

My grandparents lived in a large, rambling old farmhouse that overlooked the river, but my own, much smaller house is at the end of a cobbled fold of traditional stone cottages at the opposite end of the village. Even in winter, it's picture-postcard pretty. Tiny front gardens, in which the first snowdrops are already peeking their heads, lead out onto the narrow lane that runs alongside the graveyard. We begin making our way towards its entrance, Harry stopping every few minutes to sniff various trees and fence posts. It's a slow process.

A sign on the gates says that dogs are allowed on leads, so Harry and I continue inside. After my initial unease at over-looking a graveyard, I've actually grown rather fond of seeing it from my bedroom window – if you can be fond of a grave-yard, that is. I like watching people coming and going with their bunches of flowers. Some sit quietly in reflection on the benches; others are industrious, weeding and tidying, armed with small trowels and bedding plants.

We do a short loop past the primary school down to the river, crossing the narrow wooden bridge and walking along its wide grassy banks. Just long enough for Harry to stretch his legs, but not overtire him, and for me to learn that he does not like tractors, ducks or children on scooters racing towards him on the pavement. It's like being in a video game. They come at us from all angles and, after trying to dodge them, with Harry barking in fear or attempting to chase them, he isn't the only one whose nerves are fraught.

Heading back, I decide to take a quieter footpath through the patchwork of fields. I remember it from when Josie and I used to run along it as children and, as we pass through the stile, memories come flooding back. Endless hot, sticky summer days by the river, Josie, brave and undaunted as always, jumping straight in, while I paddled safely in the rockpools.

Up ahead I see a three-bar gate: Whistling Gate, that's the name we gave it one Christmas, when the fierce gales blew through its holes, making it whistle. I fasten it carefully behind us as we carry on past the patchwork of allotments, where my granddad used to grow funny-shaped carrots and big, fat tasteless marrows that grandma would stuff with mince and onions and nobody wanted to eat.

The warm syrup of nostalgia runs through me as the cold wind continues to blast across the fells. 'Blowing away the cobwebs' – that's what my grandparents always used to say. Enlivened, I pause to look out across the valley, feeling the fog of lethargy that I've had for months lifting. Just look at the landscape. The space. The vast skies. London felt so claustrophobic, but now I feel as if I can finally breathe.

I take in a deep lungful of fresh country air—

And nearly gag. *Shit! What's that awful smell?*

Hearing the rumble of a tractor, I spot a farmer in the field below and realize he's muck-spreading. Literally squirting the fields with exactly that: *shit*. Which abruptly makes me laugh; that will teach me to start waxing lyrical and getting carried away. The countryside is beautiful, but it's also a lesson in keeping things real. And covering my nose with my scarf, I tug Harry's lead to hurry him along.

It takes a further twenty minutes to reach the end of the footpath. It's not very far, but Harry likes to pause frequently to sniff things. A gatepost. The drystone wall. A cowpat. One things for sure, he isn't squeamish or bothered by smells.

Strangely, he's a lot fussier about exactly where he wants to 'go'. So it's a relief when he finally decides on a small grassy verge in front of a bungalow. I don't remember the house being there as a child, it must be quite new. I study its exterior. It's perfectly nondescript, but for the plethora of terracotta pots on the small front patio. All different shapes and sizes, they fill the flagstones, but what strikes me is that every single one of them is empty. I stare at them, idly wondering if anyone lives there as the place looks so bare and neglected, when the front door opens and an old man suddenly appears in his dressing gown and slippers.

It's too late to look away.

He seems surprised to see me. Well, I doubt he was expecting to find someone standing in front of his house, gawping while their dog takes a dump. It's barely even light.

'Morning.' I smile politely.

There's a brief moment when I think he might ignore me, but then he gives a curt nod of his head. 'Morning.'

He looks both grumpy and embarrassed to be caught in his dressing gown and slippers, and pulls the belt tighter.

'I was just waiting for my dog.' Feeling the need to explain, I gesture towards Harry.

'I hope you're going to clear that up,' he replies gruffly.

'Yes, of course.'

'Because I trod in some the other day – right mess it was.'

'Oh dear, that's awful.'

'Not the dog's fault, mind. It's the owner's.' He stares at me accusingly and I feel myself wither under his stony glare.

'Totally inconsiderate.' I nod in agreement, and then turn my attention back to Harry, who seems to have one thing in common with my ex-husband in the extortionate amount of time he takes to go to the bathroom; David used to be in there for hours.

'By 'eck, you're hungry buggers, aren't you?'

The old man's voice interrupts my thoughts and I turn back to see him pull a packet of birdseed out of his dressing-gown pocket. Talking to himself, he carefully unwraps the packet and unscrews the lids from the empty bird feeders hanging from various hooks around the patio. I notice they're made out of plastic bottles.

'Do you make those?'

He looks up from filling them with seeds, to cock his hand behind his ear. 'What was that?'

'The bird feeders,' I repeat.

He looks at me as if I'm a complete moron. 'Aye, it's called recycling.' Then, seeing my expression, he adds, 'You young ones think you invented it.'

Despite his grumpiness, I can't help but smile.

He resumes filling them up and I turn back to Harry. Having finally finished, he's kicking up clods of grass verge in an attempt to bury it, and I quickly clear it up before the old man has cause to complain.

'You put two holes here, see . . .'

I look up to see that he's taken down one of the bottles and has brought it over to show me, holding it over the low wall that separates his small patio from the path.

' . . . and push a stick through the holes. There should be a couple of inches left on either side for the perches.'

'Wow, yes – how clever.' I smile, fascinated. It really is quite ingenious.

'Then just cut a feeding hole with some scissors.' He gestures with his thumb. 'You have to be careful not to leave any jagged edges, as their feathers can get caught. You need to make them as smooth as possible.'

'And do the birds really come?'

'Oh, aye, you get all sorts, especially this time of year.

Sparrows . . . blue tits . . . chaffinches . . . nuthatches . . . Even got myself a family of robins. The ones that don't migrate need feeding up to survive the winter.'

As he speaks a few brave ones come swooping to the bird feeders he's already filled, while the others sit twittering and fluttering on the sidelines, perched on chimney pots and telegraph poles, waiting impatiently. I don't remember seeing so many birds in London.

Suddenly Harry notices them and starts barking.

'Who's this old fella then?'

'Harry.'

I try shushing him, as he's scaring away the old man's birds.

'Sorry,' I apologize, trying to calm Harry down and not having much success. Despite his limp, he's lungeing and pulling on his lead.

'What's wrong with his leg?'

'Arthritis,' I gasp, struggling to keep hold of him. He's really quite strong, considering.

'Poor bugger. Me and him both.'

The old man smiles for the first time and bends down towards him.

'Oh! Be careful . . . He's a bit nervous.'

'Hello, lad, got a poorly leg, have you?'

Too late. Ignoring me, he reaches his hand over the low wall and I freeze, with visions of him being bitten, or worse, but unexpectedly Harry stops barking and goes to sniff it.

'There, there, lad . . . '

And now he's licking the old man's hand and letting him stroke his face and rub his ears. I watch, amazed. Even more incredible is watching Harry's tail make its first smallest and bravest of wags.

'Did you think he was going to bite me?'

'No. Of course not,' I protest, but I feel a bit guilty.

'Turmeric.'

'Excuse me?'

'It's supposed to do wonders for arthritis. Helps the inflammation . . . There's something in it – I forget the name, but it's powerful stuff. Better than ibuprofen, for the pain and stiffness. You can have it with honey or make a paste with it—' The old man breaks off, as if embarrassed to be caught over-sharing. 'My wife was always into all that kind of homeopathy stuff.'

Was. I notice the wedding ring still on his hand. He must be a widow.

'Well, I must get on and finish these before I freeze to death.'

With a grunt he raises himself stiffly to his slippered feet. I notice the fleecy hems of his pinstriped pyjama bottoms, like the ones my granddad used to wear. See, he's a sweet old man really.

'Thanks for the tip.' I smile and he nods.

'Bye, Harry.'

He gives Harry a little wave as we walk away.

'And think on,' he calls after me, and I turn to see him gesturing at the poop bag I'm holding. 'Don't be chucking that dog shit in my dustbins.'

Hey you,

Guess what? I got a dog! He's called Harry and he's from the local rescue shelter. He's a big black scruffy thing with a little white patch on his chest that looks a bit like a star, and he has this really long, bushy tail, though I've only ever seen it wag once as he's so nervous and scared. But it was love at first sight. He's got these big brown Disney eyes, and last night when he gently nuzzled his soft wet nose into my lap and looked at me, it was like he understood what it's like to get your heart broken.

Though I'll be honest, the first few days have been a bit of nightmare. I even wondered if I'd made a mistake. In fact there were a few tearful moments when I thought maybe I wasn't a dog person. Maybe I didn't have what it takes to rescue a dog. I mean, seriously. Harry moults hair every-where, digs holes in the garden, destroys all his toys and howls if he's left alone. I've been trying to get him to sleep downstairs, but without much luck. Last night he chewed up his dog bed and wouldn't go to sleep until I let him sleep on *my* bed. And I still can't get the smell of sick out of the rental car, from when he threw up on the back seat.

But then this morning I took him for his first walk and we met this old man, and it was only when I got home that I realized I had the first real conversation with someone since moving here – and it happened because of Harry. And it got me thinking. Maybe it's not me rescuing Harry, but the other way round. Maybe Harry's the one rescuing me.

x

A Moment of Truth

'This car smells funny.'

'Really? I can't smell anything.'

A few days later I drive into town to the local branch of the rental-car company, to return the Fiat and lie through my teeth.

'Hmm . . .'

Ajay has the distrustful air of a sales agent who has seen, heard and *smelled* it all when it comes to customers and the lengths they will go to in their subterfuge to conceal dents, scratches, missing wing mirrors and worse. Unbuttoning his suit jacket, he pushes his glasses onto the bridge of his nose and ducks his head further inside the car.

I watch with trepidation as he takes a deep inhale of the upholstery.

'It smells like . . .' He pauses, searching for the right word.

'A floral fragrance with citrus top notes,' I jump in, smiling broadly. What's that saying: smile and the world smiles with you?

Ajay, however, does not appear to know that saying and re-emerges grim-faced.

'Vomit.'

'Oh.'

This is excruciating. I should have told the truth, but I can ill afford to lose my deposit.

He glances down at the clipboard in his hands, which has my paperwork. 'Mrs Brooks.'

'It's Ms . . . but, please, call me Liv.'

'Ms Brooks,' he repeats again, firmly, 'have you had a dog in this car?'

It's less an accusation and more of a statement.

I clutch my chest theatrically. 'A dog? No, whatever gives you that idea?'

As if presenting an exhibit in court, he holds up a rubber bone in his left hand and squeezes it. It gives a loud squeak.

I'd wondered where it had gone. I'd taken it for Harry when I went to pick him up from the rescue shelter, but he completely ignored it. It must have got wedged between the seats.

'Because, as you will see by the terms of your policy, no animals are allowed in any of our vehicles without prior consent, and an excess fee being paid. Furthermore, to do so would invalidate your policy and result in a cleaning fee, plus the forfeit of your deposit.'

'I bought it as a present for a friend. She just got a new dog.'

You know that feeling when you're digging your own grave but keep on going, regardless? I simply can't afford to lose my deposit.

'In that case, let me rephrase the question.'

I recognize Ajay's weary tone. It's the one I would use with pupils when their homework was late and they would come up with weird and wonderful excuses.

'Was your "friend's dog" sick on the back seat of this car?'

He says it like a question, but we both know the answer.

I sigh in defeat. 'Ajay, can I level with you?'

He gazes at me steadily. 'I wish you would, Ms Brooks. It would save us a lot of time.'

'You're right, there was a dog in the back seat.'

His shoulders visibly square.

'And yes, he did throw up.'

And now his jaw sets in vindication.

'But, you see, I can explain. His name's Harry. He was dumped by his owner, who didn't want him any more – a bit like me, really.'

'Ms Brooks.'

'My husband left me,' I blurt, before poor Ajay can stop me. 'We just got divorced and I moved here for a fresh start, but I didn't realize how lonely I'd be and how lost I'd feel . . .' I sense my eyes welling up. 'So I adopted a dog from the local rescue shelter, but he was carsick on the way home – he couldn't help it, the poor thing was probably traumatized by everything that had happened . . .'

'I don't think that's entirely relevant.'

'Well, it is to Harry!' I cry. 'You've probably got no idea what it's like to be rejected, to have your heart broken, to have the person you love and thought you would spend the rest of your life with throw you away like a piece of rubbish – to know how devastating that feels. I mean, look at you; what are you: like, *twenty*?'

I jab my finger at his clipboard and Ajay steps backwards.

'You've no concept of what it's like to be my age and feel like you've been thrown on the scrapheap. To have to start over again . . . Trust me, it's terrifying!'

I can hear my voice getting more and more shrill. I'm no longer talking just about Harry.

'My life is a mess. I've lost my husband, my home, my job. I'm depressed. I feel old. I can't sleep. My jeans don't fit. And now you want to punish me by being an officious little jobsworth prat and stealing my deposit!'

I break off, my heart pounding. With my sleeve I wipe away the tears that I suddenly realize are streaming down my face.

Ajay looks at me, his face unreadable. No doubt stunned into silence by having some angry, weeping, perimenopausal woman on his forecourt. I suddenly feel acutely embarrassed by my outburst. And mortifyingly repentant. It's not his fault. What on earth am I doing? Yelling at some poor car-rental salesman and pouring my heart out? He must think I've gone mad. *I think I've gone mad.*

'Look, I'm sorry.'

'My girlfriend dumped me two weeks ago.'

We both speak at the same time. I look at Ajay in surprise.

'Trust me, I know completely how you feel.' He pulls out a small pack of tissues from his pocket and passes it to me. 'Here.'

'Thank you.' Taking one, I wipe my eyes and blow my nose. 'I'm sorry . . . about your girlfriend.'

'It's all right. Afterwards I found out she'd been sleeping with one of my mates behind my back.'

'Jesus, that's awful.'

He shrugs. 'He wasn't much of a mate, was he?'

'No, I suppose not.' Sniffing, I pass the packet back.

'By the way, for your information I'm twenty-nine.'

My face flushes. 'Oh God, I'm sorry. And I didn't mean what I said, about the other thing . . .' I trail off, not wanting to finish the sentence.

'You mean about me being an officious little jobsworth prat and stealing your deposit?'

Then he smiles, which makes me smile.

He closes the door of the Fiat. 'OK, Liv, I think we're done here. Now if you'd like to follow me into the office, we'll settle up your paperwork.'

Ajay lets me off with solely the cleaning fee. He really is a nice man, and not an officious jobsworth prat at all. He even gives me his tissues and tells me to take as many of the complimentary mints as I'd like.

Afterwards I walk to the main newsagent's in the high street to put a notice in the window about private tutoring, then on to the supermarket to buy a few things I can't get at the local shops in the village.

As usual I completely overestimate how much I can carry. It looks fine in the trolley, just a few bits, but once it's packed into bags it seems to quadruple in size. Without a car, I set off towards the bus stop, lugging the heavy shopping bags, but it starts to rain. It does that a lot here. So by the time I reach the bus stop I'm soaked.

Luckily it has a shelter, but it has no sides and the rain is now coming down in icy diagonal sheets. Standing underneath, I peer up the road, willing a bus to appear. I've got a new building firm coming over to give me a quote. When I called before, they were fully booked, but they've had a job fall through and are now available to work on the cottage. Apparently they're the best in the area, so I don't want to be late.

I wait.

Fifteen minutes later I'm still waiting when a van slows down. I step back, so as not to get splashed by the large puddle of water that has formed next to the kerb.

The window rolls down and the driver leans across the steering wheel.

'You're wasting your time,' he calls out cheerfully.

'Excuse me?'

'The bus only runs once a day to Nettlewick, and you've missed it.'

'Once a day?'

For a moment I think he's joking, then I look at the time-table behind the scratched plastic. Sure enough, he's telling the truth. I let the reality sink in for a moment, along with the rain into my sodden trainers. I wriggle my toes. They squelch against the fabric.

'OK, well, thanks for letting me know.' With frozen fingers, I dig my phone out of my pocket. 'I'll call an Uber.'

The driver laughs. 'I take it you're not from round these parts then?'

Opening the app, I go to book a car . . . only there aren't any. Of course. I'm forgetting where I am. I look up from my screen to see the van still there, with the engine running.

'Hop in, I'll give you a lift,' offers the driver. 'I'm going that way.'

I waver at the thought of getting a lift from a complete stranger, but it's pouring down, I'm cold and tired, and I can hardly walk the ten miles home with my shopping.

I reach for the door handle. 'If you're sure you don't mind, thank you.'

The dashboard is stuffed full of rubbish. Old receipts. Parking tickets. Coffee cups. Chocolate wrappers. Sitting in the passenger seat, I let my eyes sweep across the detritus to try and get a better look at the driver. He looks about my age, but it's hard to tell. Between his beanie, which he's pulled down over his ears, and his beard, I can only see a narrow, rectangular letter box of face. His eyes are crinkled around the edges and he has one of those noses with a bump that looks like it was broken once. I once read somewhere that men's noses and ears keep growing, the older they get, but it looks a fairly decent size, so no clues there.

'I didn't know rain was forecast,' I say, as we continue out of town, the windscreen wipers on full speed.

'This is Yorkshire. Don't you know we've got webbed feet?'

His accent is strong and he glances across at me, his mouth twisting up in amusement. He's wearing a thick checked flannel shirt, the sleeves of which are turned up to reveal tattooed forearms.

'It wouldn't surprise me.' I find myself smiling. 'I think it's rained pretty much every day since I moved here.'

'Don't worry, we get a few weeks off in summer for good behaviour.'

Despite being soaked through, I can't help but laugh.

'So what brings you to these parts? Apart from the glorious weather, of course.'

Indicating right at the roundabout, we leave the town behind and head out into open countryside.

'My grandparents used to live in Nettlewick. In the old farmhouse that overlooks the river.'

The windows are steaming up. He rolls down his window a little, to let in some fresh air, and leans forward to wipe the windscreen with his hand. I notice his wedding ring and instinctively curl my bare fingers into my lap.

'Oh, I know the house.'

'You do?'

'Yeah, I did some work there a few years back. They have a big oak in the back garden.'

'Yes, that's the one! Me and my sister used to climb it.' Suddenly reminded, I feel a beat of joy. 'One summer we built a treehouse in it, and Granddad made us a swing.'

The driver takes his eyes off the road to stare across at me and I shift uncomfortably.

'Sorry, did I say something?'

His face breaks into a grin. 'Well, I'll be damned. *Livvie?*'

I feel a jolt of surprise as he calls me by my old nickname.

'Don't you recognize me?'

'Should I?' I search the letter box of face for clues, then quickly gesture to the temporary traffic lights ahead. 'Watch out!'

He brakes sharply and, as we come to halt, he takes the opportunity to swivel his full body towards me and peer at me. 'It really is you!' He looks triumphant. 'I can't believe it! Little Livvie!'

Oh God. Abruptly it dawns.

'Ben Armstrong,' I say flatly, trying to keep the dismay out of my voice.

'Yep, that's me.' He's grinning at me even more broadly now and I feel slightly frozen. I'd forgotten all about him. Or, more likely, I'd deliberately blanked him out. Now here he is, sitting right next to me.

A car honks behind us. I notice the lights have turned green.

'All right, hold your horses,' he yells, gesturing rudely at the driver out of the window, before cranking the van into gear and setting off again.

'I see you haven't changed,' I mutter, turning my head to look out of the window and hoping he doesn't hear me.

'What was that?'

'I said nothing's changed.' I gesture to the sweeping valley and endless fields that flash past us on either side of the van.

'That's the Dales for you,' he nods. 'Must be . . . what? Thirty years since you were here last?'

'Yes, something like that.'

Every summer Josie and I used to hang out with a gang of local kids, playing games and swimming in the river. Ben was a few years older than me and a bit of a troublemaker. Forever getting drunk and into fights, he was your typical bad boy. Good-looking, unapologetic, fearless. Sexy as hell. As a teenager I had a secret crush on him, but he fancied my sister Josie and was always showing off, trying to get her attention. I think the only time he spoke to me was to make fun of my flat chest and braces.

'It's so great to see you! After all this time,' he's saying now, shaking his head from side to side in disbelief. He doesn't remember. To him it was nothing, just harmless teasing. To my thirteen-year-old soul, it was crushing. 'How are you?'

'Wet.' I wipe away a strand of hair that's dripping down my forehead.

He laughs. 'How's your sister – what was her name?'

'Josie.'

Ben was forever flirting with her and now he doesn't even remember her name? I feel oddly offended on her behalf.

'Josie, yeah, that's right,' he nods, smiling.

'She's good,' I say tightly. 'What about you? I see you got married.' In an attempt to change the subject, I say the first thing off the top of my head.

'Oh . . . yeah.' His eyes flick to his wedding band. Flexing his fingers, he grips the steering wheel tighter. 'I'm a dad now, too.'

'That's great.'

'What about you?'

'No, no kids.' I quickly sidestep the issue of marriage. Not that I care what he thinks, but my teenage self in braces and a trainer bra still does, and somehow admitting that I'm single and divorced feels like a failure.

'Though I used to have thirty-one thirteen-year-olds,' I add and then, seeing his confused expression, I explain, 'I'm a teacher. Well, was. I'm taking a bit of a break.'

'That doesn't surprise me – you were always the brainy one. Not like me. I hated school. "He'll either end up in prison or a millionaire," it said on a school report once.'

'So you're a millionaire?'

'Not yet,' he laughs, and I decide not to ask him about the other option.

Luckily his phone rings, interrupting our conversation. He apologizes: sorry, he has to get this. I hear him talking about work. I zone out, turning to look out of the window as the countryside flashes past. As we slow down to cross the bridge that leads into village, he hangs up.

'So how long are you visiting for? We should catch up properly. I only live behind the Crooked Billet pub.'

'To be honest, I'm really busy,' I fib, cutting him off before having a drink together for old times' sake is suggested. As we enter the main square, I gesture for him to pull over. 'Actually I can walk from here.'

'Are you sure?'

'Yes, it's only two minutes.'

He stops the van and I clamber out.

'Well, thanks again for the lift.'

'Bye.'

Relieved to be out of the van, I slam the door behind me and walk briskly across the cobbles. I want to put as much distance as I can between us. It's still raining and I keep my head down as his van rumbles past me. Ben Armstrong. Of all the people to run into. Still, I suppose it had to happen sometime. Nettlewick's a small place.

Lugging my heavy shopping bags, I turn up the small lane that runs alongside the graveyard. Almost home, I dig out my house keys, and I'm just thinking about warm, dry clothes and a hot cup of tea when I notice there's a van already parked outside my cottage. I get closer. Wait a minute, that looks like—

'*Ben?*'

He's standing on my doorstep ringing my doorbell, which doesn't work, while inside I can hear Harry barking like crazy.

At the sound of his name, he turns and we both look at each other in astonishment.

'*Livvie?*'

'What are you doing here?' I pause at my gate.

He's rolled his sleeves down to cover his tattoos. 'I've got a meeting with the new owner about some building work—' He breaks off and frowns, noticing the keys in my hand. 'Hang on. What are you doing here?'

My eyes dart to his van and for the first time I notice the logo painted down the side.

'*You're* Nettlewick Building Contractors?'

At which point my plastic bags finally decide they can't hold it together any longer and choose that moment to split, scattering loo rolls, tins of baked beans and a crushing sense of inevitability all over the wet cobbles. It's the perfect end to the day.

Anger and Letting It Go

When I discovered my husband's affair, everyone told me I needed to get angry. Naomi, friends, self-help books, even the therapist I saw for a while after David left. Apparently anger is a healthy emotion, whereas crying in the toilets at work is not. It's one of the stages you need to go through.

My therapist seemed almost disappointed by my lack of fury. And I tried, really I did. I managed flashes of anger, usually fuelled by wine and late nights, but try as I might, I couldn't keep hold of it. It would slip through my drunken fingers and I'd go back to feeling sad and scared.

But since Harry came to live with me, things have started to change. For the first few weeks after he arrived home from the shelter, he was completely shut down. He couldn't even wag his tail or look at me, and whenever I made a sudden movement he would shy away in fear. And for the first time I stopped feeling sad and scared and started feeling angry – angry towards the people who had treated him so badly and tossed him away like a piece of rubbish. Furious. Indignant. Outraged.

And it started to rub off on me.

By getting angry about what had happened to Harry, I started feeling angry about what had happened to me. Only I got angry at the wrong people. I got angry at poor Ajay. And I got angry at myself. So last night I wrote an email: *To David, the Man Who Broke My Heart*. A furious, ranting, punching bag of an email, into which I poured out every single drop of rage and betrayal. Long, rambling sentences without care for the punctuation. Me, an English teacher. Until I was left purged and exhausted at my keyboard and it was long past midnight.

Then I pressed 'Delete'.

And it was all gone and, with it, most of the anger too. Because I've realized that while anger might be healthy and liberating for a while, I only have to watch a certain scruffy black dog happily sniffing around the overgrown bramble bushes that are my garden to see that healthier still is letting it go. Who knows what Harry went through before he was dumped on those moors, but he's not angry or bitter about what happened in the past. It's in the past.

'C'mon, Harry, dinner time.'

Putting his food bowl on the kitchen floor, I open the old stable door and call him in from the garden. He's started to recognize his name and, as he limps his way towards me across the patch of grass, he slowly wags his tail. Not big, sweeping excitable wags, just small, tentative ones, as if he's feeling his way. Like me, really.

I smile. I'm beginning to think I can learn a lot from Harry.

The Boy

After the awkward run-in with Ben Armstrong, my first impulse is to go with a different builder. However, after giving it some thought, it seems foolish. His company has by far the best reviews of anyone in the area; plus everyone I call for references provides a glowing one for Ben.

So in the end I decide to put aside any childhood grievances and go ahead as planned. Signing the contracts, I email them back, pay my deposit and agree on a start date of the beginning of April, with 'works estimated to take six months'.

'Thanks, Livvie. Can't wait to move in the lads and get started!'

'Great. Looking forward to it.'

And I try not to think about how living with builders in my house now effectively means living with Ben Armstrong.

In the meantime I register Harry with the local vet. Being in *All Creatures Great and Small* country, I imagine a cosy encounter with a hunky James Herriot type and even put on a bit of make-up for the appointment. Sadly, as is often the case, the reality is very different. Mr Jenkins, one of the partners, must be well into his sixties and completely bald, apart from a pair of fierce eyebrows that make him resemble an owl.

He is, however, an extremely good vet and checks Harry over thoroughly. He says Harry seems in good health, apart from his arthritis, and advises joint supplements and gentle lead-walks. He's also very kind and generous and doesn't ask me to pay for any of the damage Harry inflicts on the waiting room, when he lunges at man with a sick ferret on his knee. Mr Jenkins says it's just Harry's hunting instinct, and not to worry about the overturned display cabinets and broken chair legs. Luckily the owner was really understanding too, and the Fred the ferret was none the worse for wear.

So every morning, on the vet's advice, we do our same walk, only each time I notice something different. The way the light appears, catching on the stone roofs of the village like brushstrokes. The stillness. The bright-green moss on the drystone walls. The shapes of the clouds (whoever knew clouds could be so beautiful? Before moving here I thought they were just grey, fluffy blobs). The smell of wood-smoke, The rumble of the farmer's tractor.

Yet one thing is always the same. The old man. I always see him sitting in the window, but I only spoke to him that once. The first few times I smiled and waved, but he never waved back, so in the end I stopped.

In the afternoon I take a different route and follow a series of narrow alleyways – or 'snickets', as they're known here – that lead out onto a cul-de-sac overlooking a green. Usually we don't see anyone much. Being February, most people choose not to brave the weather, but it's on one of these afternoon walks that I first see the little boy.

Well, I hear him first. A distant thumping and squeaking as we turn the corner out of the alley and Harry stops to sniff the street sign.

Thump . . . squeak . . . thump . . . squeak . . .

It's rhythmical. I listen harder, trying to figure out what it is. It's a peculiar sound and I can't tell where it's coming from. I notice Harry's ears prick up too. We set off walking again. It sounds like it's coming from up ahead. As we pass a few houses the thumping and squeaking grow louder . . . then suddenly I see a head. It pops up from behind the garden fence, only to disappear again. It has dark curly hair and is wearing large yellow headphones. It reappears, flying up in the air. Only a few seconds, then it's gone again. But it's long enough to see that it belongs to a little boy.

He's on a trampoline. I catch sight of it now in the front garden of a pebble-dashed semi. Wedged into the corner, it's still taking up nearly all the space on the small patch of grass. As we pause by the garden gate, Harry barks at the strange object, but the boy can't hear him and continues jumping. I notice his face is turned to the sky as he bounces higher and higher. It's almost like he's trying to take off.

Harry barks even louder.

'C'mon, boy.'

I go to pull Harry away, when the boy suddenly glances in our direction. Immediately he stops jumping and stares at us, his face appearing frozen in shock.

'It's OK, he's friendly,' I reassure him quickly – and pointlessly, I realize, as the boy can't hear me.

I tug on Harry's lead, but he's taken root and is refusing to move.

For a few moments the boy continues to stare at us, before climbing off the trampoline and carefully making his way down the garden path. He's wearing his school uniform and yet, despite the freezing temperatures, he isn't wearing a coat. Or shoes and socks, I notice as he tiptoes carefully in his bare feet on the paving stones towards us, his face a picture of concentration.

Reaching the gate, he takes off his headphones.

'He just got a bit scared by the noise,' I reassure him, gesturing at Harry, who has stuffed his nose firmly through the metal swirls of the garden gate and is taking deep sniffs, as if trying to inhale the little boy.

'Does he want to wear my ear defenders?' The boy holds them out.

'Oh, thank you, but no.' I smile, touched. 'I'm sure he'll be fine now.

'That's why I wear them, because I get scared by noises too.'

Standing a few feet away from the gate, he studies Harry, his brow furrowed in concentration.

'Noises can be a bit scary,' I nod in agreement, 'but they're only noises.'

He doesn't answer. I'm not sure he's really listening to me. He seems completely enthralled by Harry, his expression a mixture of fear and fascination.

'Do you want to stroke him?'

'I'm scared of dogs.'

'Harry used to be scared of people.'

He eyes Harry curiously.

'Why isn't he scared now?'

'He still is sometimes, but he's trying to be brave.'

'Daddy tells me I need to be brave sometimes.'

I nod sympathetically. 'Me too.'

He hesitates, then reaches through the gate and tentatively touches Harry's head with his fingertips. As good as gold, Harry allows himself to be touched without shying away. It's as if instinctively he knows the little boy is scared.

'He's all soft.'

I notice how small his hand is against Harry's big bear of a head. The boy must be only about seven or eight. Harry tries to lick him, and he suddenly lets out a squeal and quickly retracts his hand, jumping back behind the garden gate.

'He licked me!' He seems unable to decide whether to be delighted or scared.

'That's because he really likes you.'

I give Harry a reassuring rub around his ears as a reward for being so good. I'm fast learning that's one of his favourite things.

'Stanley!' A woman's voice calls from inside the house. 'Tea's ready!'

The little boy looks at me, then pulls a small laminated card from deep inside his pockets and squints at it. 'I have to go. Look, it's number seven.'

He thrusts the card at me, and I can see it's some kind of list:

1. *Get home from school*
2. *Wash hands*
3. *Empty backpack/lunchbox*
4. *Have snack*
5. *Do homework*
6. *Play outside*
7. *Teatime*

'Stanley!' yells the voice, louder this time.

And before I can finish reading it, he snatches the card away, runs deftly up the garden path on his tiptoes, making sure to miss all the cracks, then disappears into the house, slamming the door behind him.

The Teenager

Nursing a cappuccino, I try to eke out the last remaining bits of froth. It's long since gone cold. I look at my watch for the umpteenth time.

They're almost twenty minutes late.

It's Friday afternoon and I'm sitting in the small cafe in the village where I've arranged to meet my first student, after getting a reply to my tutoring ad. Outside it's grizzly, but inside is warm and welcoming, with old-fashioned flowery wallpaper and shelves filled with a collection of old teapots. A fire burns in the grate, while wedged into the corner is a pine dresser laden with home-made cakes displayed under glass domes. Filled with butter and cream, the slices are the size of doorsteps. No gluten-free brownies here. It's a world away from the trendy cafes in London with their chalkboards, vintage lighting and hipster baristas. And I love it.

The bell on the door goes and I look up, expectantly, only instead of a teenager, it's another hiker.

'Do you want another coffee?'

One of the two ladies who run the cafe bustles over in a tomato-red apron, her cheeks flushed, balancing plates of toasted teacakes. The cafe is busy with cyclists, in training for the Tour de Yorkshire, and she's rushed off her feet.

'Actually, I'm OK, thanks . . . maybe in a minute.'

'No worries, dear, just give me a shout.' She smiles generously and weaves away through the tables.

Harry stirs under the table. The cafe allows dogs, so I've been able to bring him, which is lucky, as he still hates being left alone. In fact his separation anxiety seems to be getting worse, not better. Yesterday I only popped to the postbox and found him tearing up yet another squeaky toy. He rips them to shreds until they stop squeaking and then buries them in the garden. Kind of like some Swedish crime series.

I glance at my watch: twenty-five minutes. Not exactly the best start to my glittering new career as a private tutor. On the table my phone pings. That's probably them texting to say they're not coming. Wishing I'd told them there was a cancellation policy, I pick up my phone to text back – only it's from Ajay at the car-rental company instead. I've been chasing him about the return of my deposit. It's been almost a month and it still hasn't been paid back onto my credit card. I've given up emailing and have begun texting him directly.

'Are you Olivia Brooks?'

Before I have chance to read his text, I look up to see a figure bundled up in a beige furry coat and a bright-yellow bobble hat, standing by my table. So this must be my long-awaited pupil.

'Hi, yes,' I smile, taking in the young teenage girl. 'You must be Maya.'

I was expecting to meet her with her parents – the arrangement being that they would drive her over, as they live a few miles away – but the plans must have changed.

She doesn't smile or apologize for being late. Instead she stuffs her hands in her pockets, her expression unreadable.

'Nice to see you. Please, sit down.'

Deciding against getting off on the wrong foot, I make no mention of her keeping me waiting and motion her to the chair opposite me. She sits down wordlessly, her hands still in her pockets.

'So, tell me . . . your mum gave me a little information on the phone and told me you're studying for your A-levels and that you might need a bit of help with some of the set texts. So is there anything in particular you'd like to start with?'

'This is a total waste of time.'

'Oh.'

'I don't need a tutor.'

She glares defiantly at me across the salt and pepper, as if willing me to challenge her.

'Not according to your parents.'

Her jaw sets, but she doesn't argue. I look down at my notes.

'I understand you're studying *Macbeth* and *Wuthering Heights*.'

'If you say so.'

When teaching, I often think of the opening line of *A Tale of Two Cities*: 'It was the best of times, it was the worst of times.' I swear Charles Dickens must have had teenagers in mind when he wrote that. They can be wonderful, but oh God, they can equally be awful.

'So how are you liking those?' I persevere.

'They're OK,' she replies, dismissing two of the most important works in literature with a mere shrug of her shoulders.

'I just moved here from London, so it's exciting to be in actual Brontë country.' I try to galvanize her with my own enthusiasm. 'We could visit the parsonage where Emily lived and wrote, see her inspiration at first hand.' I smile brightly. 'Is that something you'd be interesting in doing?'

'Not really.'

The trick with teenagers is not to take it personally.

'So what *are* you interested in?'

She averts her eyes, choosing instead to stare at the sugar packets. She picks one up and begins tearing at the corners.

103

'Stuff that matters.'

'And this doesn't?'

She looks up at me then, her dark eyes flashing.

'What have books and plays, written hundreds of years ago, got to do with what's happening today?'

'Well, from where I'm sitting, I'd say the universal themes of love and death, and joy and tragedy, are still pretty relevant.'

She seems caught off-balance by my reply. 'But what about climate change?' she argues, quickly finding her voice. 'What about the threat to our wildlife, and women's rights and how black lives matter?'

'Well, Shakespeare is all about human nature and the world at large. You might not realize it, but his stories and ideas shape and influence who we are, even today.'

As I look across at Maya I'm reminded of that confused teenager inside me once, struggling to make sense of anything and finding salvation within the pages of books loaned from my local library.

'Look at all the popular phrases we use. Do you know that you're quoting Shakespeare when you say, "cruel to be kind", "a brave new world" or "the lady doth protest too much",' I add, smiling.

But just as quickly as I have her attention, I lose it again. With a bored expression, she pulls her phone out of her pocket and begins scrolling.

'OK, well, I can see this isn't going to work.' I shut my notebook. 'You're right: it's a waste of both of our times, and your parents' money.'

'Told you,' she mumbles, kicking the table leg with her trainers.

'And if you don't mind, I'd rather you didn't do that. My dog won't like it.'

As if on cue, Harry gives a nervous little bark from underneath the table.

'*Dog?*'

Abruptly her expression changes and she quickly scrapes her chair back, ducking her body underneath the table to take a look.

'*Oh, wow, look at you – you're gorgeous.*'

Instantly dropping to her knees on the floor, she begins fussing over Harry.

'He can be quite nervous.'

'It's OK – I volunteer at the local rescue, I'm used to the shy ones . . . But you don't seem that shy, do you?' she coos, smiling.

The transformation is remarkable.

'Wait a moment . . .' She stops tickling Harry to look up at me. 'I remember this dog.'

'And I remember you,' I say, as it suddenly registers. 'From the car park: you were collecting money for the charity.'

'That'll be me.' She grins proudly and her whole face lights up.

'You're the reason I adopted Harry.'

'I am?' She looks pleased, then frowns, knitting her perfect eyebrows together. 'Hang on, were you the woman who said you weren't a dog person?'

I smile. 'Yes, that was me.'

'So what happened?'

'I saw Harry and changed my mind.'

There's a pause as she takes this in.

'I suppose we could try one lesson.' She shrugs. 'See how it goes?'

'OK,' I nod casually, but I want to punch the air. 'Let's see how it goes.'

Text Message: Ajay, Car Rental Man

Good news. Accounts have finally responded regarding your deposit and the refund was actioned this morning, so it should be in your account by the end of the day. An extra £25 has been added as a gesture of goodwill. I want to extend my apologies regarding this matter and hope this conclusion is satisfactory.

Furthermore, on a personal note, I wondered if you would you like go for a drink with an officious jobsworth twat sometime?

Ajay x

Only a Number

'You've been asked on a date!'

It's Friday evening and I'm on the sofa again in front of the fire. I've ordered some logs from a local delivery place and started making the effort of having a fire every night. I wouldn't go to the trouble just for me, but I know Harry likes to warm himself in front of it. Plus I've discovered a certain satisfaction that never came with simply flicking a switch on the gas fire in London.

'Don't be so ridiculous!'

'Why is it ridiculous to go on a date?'

'It's a drink, not a date.'

I'm on the phone to Naomi, while nursing a glass of wine. It's not even six o'clock yet, but I'm taking the approach that it's six o'clock somewhere. Harry's already zonked out for the night. I think about how Friday nights in London used to involve dinner in a restaurant, meeting friends for drinks or tickets to the theatre. It feels like another lifetime.

'What's the difference?' she demands.

'A date is between two people who could potentially be in a relationship. A drink can be between anyone.'

'Is that an actual dictionary definition?'

Curling my feet up underneath me on the sofa, I take a large mouthful of wine and slosh it around my teeth like mouthwash. I don't know why I feel so thrown. It's only a text.

'Well, no, but . . .'

'But nothing!' Naomi sounds triumphant. 'Besides, you two could potentially be in a relationship.'

'Now you're *really* being ridiculous.'

I'm beginning to regret telling Naomi. I'm still not convinced it's not a joke.

'Didn't you hear the bit where I told you he's only in his twenties?'

'Yes. *So?*'

In the background I can hear the familiar noise and bustle of the city I called home for so many years. Naomi must be on her daily commute home on the bus, just like I used to do. I feel a strange mixture of homesickness and disconnection. I look across at Harry, dozing contentedly by the fire. At least I'm doing something right.

'I'm twice his age.'

'No, you're not – that would make you . . .' she quickly does the maths, 'fifty-eight and you're only forty-five,' she points out.

I'm not sure when we got to prefix forty-five with *only*, but I let that slide.

'He's still far too young for me.'

'It didn't seem to bother your ex-husband.'

'Is that supposed to make me feel better?'

'Sorry,' Naomi sighs, 'but what I'm trying to say is that no one cares about age gaps any more. Look at Madonna.'

I look at myself, lolling on the sofa in the bombsite that is my living room, with a bottle of wine. 'Trust me, I'm hardly Madonna.'

When I was married I never used to give my age much thought. Apart from moaning about the odd wrinkle, I was grateful to leave behind my angst-ridden twenties and thirties. Relieved that all the uncertainty was behind me.

Oh, how naive I was. Now, after the events of the past year, I'm supremely conscious of it. Going through my divorce felt like being in one of those time-lapse videos where you start out young and end up feeling about a hundred years old.

'You know what I mean,' Naomi is saying now. She sounds frustrated, and I suddenly feel guilty.

'I do, and I'm sorry: you're being sweet and I'm being grumpy. It's just, well, even if Ajay was asking me out *on a date*' – merely saying the words out loud seems vaguely ludicrous – 'I don't want to go. Not with him, or anyone. And it's not that he's too young, or because I'm too old, it's because there's no point. I was married to someone for ten years and now it's over. I don't want another relationship. I don't want to go through all that again. That's it. I'm done!'

I take a declarative swig of wine.

'But did you fancy him?'

'Naomi!' I gasp. 'Didn't you listen to anything I said?'

'Liv, sweetie, you're divorced, not dead. And you're not done until they're lowering your coffin into the ground—' She breaks off. 'Hang on, this is my stop.'

There's the beeping sound of the doors opening and I can hear Naomi getting off the bus, 'Excuse me'-ing her way through the other passengers, the noise of traffic and rain on wet tarmac, wheezing brakes and the rumbling engine as the number seventy-two pulls away.

'Liv, can I ask you something?'

'Not if you want to know the answer.' I attempt a joke at my own expense. If there's one thing I've learned, it's that when everything falls apart, it shakes the very foundations of your own judgement. You realize you can't be certain of anything.

'Why did you leave London and move two and hundred and fifty miles away?'

I don't know what I was expecting her to ask, but it wasn't this.

'You know why.'

I think about all the lunchtimes and breaks she spent with me in the staffroom over the past year, being the supportive girlfriend.

'Humour me,' she persists, her footsteps loud on the pavement.

'I wanted to run away from everything,' I say simply. 'I wanted to disappear. To leave it all behind and make a new life for myself.'

'Exactly.' Naomi sounds slightly out of breath from the briskness of her walk. 'So what's the point of moving halfway across the country if you're going to take your old self and fears with you? If you're not going to take a few risks, try something new? You might as well have stayed here, in that case.'

I listen, feeling slightly defensive.

'You're wasting an amazing opportunity, Liv. How many people get the chance to cast off everything from their old life and start over?'

'But that's just the thing,' I protest. 'I didn't want to start over. I liked my old life.'

'I know you did.' Naomi's voice is sympathetic. 'But there's no point looking back. You're not going that way.'

I fall silent. She's right. Of course she's right. And yet . . .

'I'm scared,' I hear myself say quietly.

'It's good to be scared. If you aren't scared, you're not doing it right.

'Doing what?'

'Life.'

There's a pause on the other end of the phone and I gaze at the ribbons of flame making shapes in the fireplace, letting her words sink in.

'We need to do the things that scare us – that get us out of our comfort zone. That's how you know you're alive.'

'I wish I had your confidence.'

'I get scared too. Remember when I was pregnant with Ellie? I frightened myself to death most nights, lying awake, thinking about the future, about being a single mum . . . but I also knew I had no choice, because the alternative of never being a mum was even more terrifying.'

I think back to all those talks we had in the staffroom together when she'd made the decision to go ahead. She was so determined, so brave, so open about it all; and yet sometimes I'd catch a glimpse of how scared she really was.

'Mummy!'

There's a girlish cry in the background.

'You're busy. I'll let you go – say hi to Ellie for me.'

'OK, but I'm not letting you off the hook. You can't sit in that cottage by yourself all day and night.'

'I'm not, I've got Harry to keep my company.'

'A dog isn't going to keep you warm at night.'

'Actually that's where you're wrong.' I glance over at Harry snoozing by the fire and think about our nightly bedtime routine. 'Anyway, I wouldn't know what to text back.' I dismiss the situation. 'It's been so long since anyone asked me out for a drink, I'm completely out of practice.'

'Oh, that bit's easy,' replies Naomi cheerfully. 'Just say yes.'

Back to the Future

Of course, I didn't always feel like this.

Back in my thirties I was desperate to meet someone. I wasn't done; I hadn't even started. I'd been single for a while, after another short-lived romance with yet another man who didn't want to commit to a proper relationship. London was full of such men. Good fun, easy-going, confused thirty-somethings who weren't ready or not there yet. And, like most women in their early thirties, I finally grew tired of going nowhere except the pub, and wanted more.

David promised to give me more. Divorced with a young son, he was more mature, more driven and more serious about me. We met online and for our first date he took me to see a play in the West End, followed by dinner in a swanky restaurant, where he expertly navigated the wine menu and asked me questions about myself. Used to dates with men where I made small talk over a pint and a packet of crisps, this was a revelation.

And it didn't stop there. For Valentine's Day he sent the most beautiful bouquet to the staffroom. For my birthday it was a five-star hotel in Vienna and tickets to the ballet. While summer was spent in London because of his heavy workload, it was a London that I had never experienced before: one of evenings spent at gallery openings, rooftop bars in private members' clubs, open-air opera in Holland Park.

I was completely swept off my feet. David was good-looking and successful and I couldn't quite believe he was interested in an impoverished supply teacher with henna-red hair and a student loan that she still hadn't managed to pay off. It turned out I wasn't the only one.

Born into a wealthy middle-class family, David grew up on a sprawling country estate that had been in his family for generations. When he first took me to meet his parents, I remember giving his mum a hug when she offered to take my coat. I was so nervous, and I thought she was lovely.

Only it turned out that wasn't his mum; it was Lydia, the housekeeper. Well, how was I to know? I'd never met a housekeeper before. I didn't even know they existed, except in *Downton Abbey*.

His mother, on the other hand, was polite but cold, and didn't hide her disapproval. Still I was undeterred. So what if we had different backgrounds? Everyone knows opposites attract, and we couldn't have been more opposite. A Range Rover-driving, golf-playing, Harley Street dentist and an incense-burning, disco-dancing, comprehensive-school teacher in possession of her own Oyster card.

Nor could we have been more attracted to each other.

'I could stay in bed with you all day.'

'So let's stay in bed.'

It was one morning, soon after we'd met. I'd taken to staying over at his flat most nights, rather than at my house-share.

'What about my pupils and your patients?'

'This is more important.'

'Tell that to the poor sod with toothache.'

He laughed. David had a great laugh. He would throw back his head and really *commit* to a laugh. I've always been attracted to people who laugh out loud when watching something funny on TV, or in response to a joke. Envious of those big belly-laughs that seem to erupt effortlessly and confidently out of nowhere. My sense of humour feels more discerning, more self-conscious. I'm laughing on the inside, I always used to protest, whenever David would tease me about it.

'It's their own fault – people need to floss more.'

'I love it when you talk dirty to me,' I grinned.

Still laughing, he rolled on top of me, pinning me down.

'Hey!' I pretended to protest. 'You're going to make us both late.'

'I rather like getting into trouble with you.'

'I'm the teacher – I'm supposed to set a good example.'

'You know this was a boyhood fantasy?'

'What? Being late for work?'

'Sleeping with a teacher.'

We were dancing with words; back and forth, it was our form of foreplay.

'I thought you went to a boys' boarding school and all the teachers were men.'

Reaching for my hands, he interlaced his fingers through mine and pressed them into the pillow.

'Didn't I ever tell you about Miss Laurent, our French teacher?'

'*Non.*'

Then he said something to me in French that I didn't understand, but I didn't need a translation. I knew how he made me feel, and that was enough. I was like Dorothy in the *Wizard of Oz* when her world turned Technicolor, and I couldn't have been happier.

Years later I would come to realize what most wives realize about their husbands: that the men we fall in love with aren't wizards; once we get to see behind the curtain, we discover human beings with fallibilities and fears like the rest of us. But in the beginning I was in awe of David. Nothing seemed to faze him. He approached life with a sense of ownership, instead of something to be scared of. He rarely apologized, whereas my default setting was always 'Sorry', even when it was someone else bashing into me on the Tube.

He was competitive, even at Scrabble, and would use two-letter words with triple-letter scores that I, as an English teacher, still have a sneaking suspicion don't exist.

Meanwhile I couldn't have been more different. Forget rules and tactics – my adrenaline high came from the dance floor. I love dancing, though now I'm older I never get the opportunity to do it nearly enough. I love the freedom it brings when you forget about everything and everyone and lose yourself on the dance floor. It doesn't matter what kind of music. Salsa. Disco. Jazz. Big Band. Dancing is like mindfulness set to music.

David hated dancing.

'Oh, c'mon.'

'I can't. I have two left feet.'

We were at a friend's birthday party. It was at their house and they'd hired a DJ and a barman to make these funny purple cocktails, of which I'd had three. We'd been dating for about three months. We were both exhilarated, yet still uncertain of each other's feelings. No one had mentioned the L-word yet, but I already knew I was in love with David.

'Nobody has two left feet. It's a misnomer.'

'Trust me, I do.'

'Trust me, it'll be fun.'

Laughing, I looped my arm through his and pulled him towards the dance floor. The party was in full swing. Disco lights flashed. Justin Timberlake began playing.

'It will not be fun, not for anyone. People have been known to run for cover – seriously, I can clear a dance floor quicker than "The Birdie Song".'

'I love "The Birdie Song"!'

Grinning, I flapped my elbows.

'You're crazy.'

'I know.'

'I love you, Crazy.'

Boom! Just like that.

His words seemed to hang in the air for a few moments, suspended above us as I raised my eyes to meet his. Until then he'd always seemed so self-assured, but for the first time I saw an uncertainty reflected back at me.

'I love you too.'

I can't remember if I was still flapping my elbows as I said it. Or as he pulled me towards him and began kissing me. But I will never forget the surge of exhilaration and happiness that blew right though me as I kissed him back. He tasted of those funny purple cocktails and canapés, and of my future.

We never did make it onto that dance floor.

Not a Date

March in the Yorkshire Dales brings with it the promise of longer days and finer weather; the clocks go forward, spring is on the horizon and soon it will be lambing season. It feels like new beginnings are just around the corner. In lots of ways.

'OK, fingers crossed this works.'

The following weekend I finish rigging up the video camera and open the app on my phone. I've been forced to take desperate measures. Since Harry came to live with me I've barely left him home alone, for fear of what he might chew. The first couple of times it was the kitchen skirting boards, but then a few days ago I returned to find what shall forever be referred to as 'The Scatter-Cushion Massacre'.

In the time it took for me to pop out for a pint of milk he'd managed to rip apart every cushion and pillow on my bed, strewing feathers everywhere. Returning home was like entering a soft-furnishing crime scene. Apparently chewing is a classic sign of separation anxiety. I'm sympathetic. After David left I suffered from it too – only instead of eating cushions and skirting boards, I chose the contents of my fridge.

So having followed all the advice from dog behaviourists, without any success, I've bought a doggy-cam, which – according to the thousands of reviews from desperate dog owners on Amazon – is a 'lifesaver'. Frankly, I don't want to save my life, just my cushions. Now, through an app on my phone, not only will I be able to watch Harry, but I can talk to him, 'to offer comfort and reassurance' if he becomes agitated. As a plus, the video cameras can also be used to catch burglars, though considering I've removed every single item Harry could chew ahead of my drink with Ajay this evening, my living room looks like I've already *been* burgled.

'Hurrah, it works!'

Beaming, I look at my phone to see an image of me sitting on the sofa, which I've covered with an old blanket. I've also brought in Harry's water bowl and tuned the radio to Classic FM, as studies have shown that classical music helps to soothe stressed animals. Chopin's fifth nocturne is playing.

From his position by the TV, Harry stares at me unblinkingly. He does not look soothed.

'OK, so I'm leaving you a little treat in case you get hungry . . .' I wave a dog chew. 'But don't worry, I won't be back late.'

Harry looks worried. Head tilted, ears down, he's got that anxious look in his eyes.

Rubbing his soft, velvety ears, I try to reassure him, but part of me is trying to reassure myself. I'm having second thoughts – not only about leaving Harry, but about agreeing to meet Ajay. Earlier I nearly cancelled, but something inside me said that I need to go.

'You're going to be just fine, I promise,' I tell us both.

And, kissing Harry's head, I ease myself up from my haunches.

'Just please try not to eat the sofa.

We've arranged to meet in the Crooked Billet, the low-beamed sixteenth-century pub tucked away at the top of the village. Clad in ivy, it commands sweeping views across the valley and is only a ten-minute walk from my house; more like five, if you're wearing flat boots and walk briskly. Which I do, as I didn't want to wear a heavy winter coat, and it's still chilly at night.

Ajay is already waiting for me. I spot him the minute I duck my head underneath the doorway that leads into the flagstoned bar, which has thankfully escaped the gastro-make-over that has afflicted every pub in London and still has its old range, decorated with horseshoe brasses and copper kettles. He's sitting in an old armchair in the corner of the snug, next to the roaring fire, reading his phone and drinking a glass of red wine – a quiet presence amongst the rowdy locals who are congregating at the bar with their pints of ale and familiar banter.

'Hi.'

Shaking out my hair, I walk over to his table. He looks up and sees me and immediately stands up. He's taller than I remembered, and he's not wearing his glasses.

'You came.'

He looks relieved and breaks into a smile. He really does have the loveliest smile – that bit I do remember. I berate myself for having second thoughts about coming. What was I so worried about?

'Of course.' I try to act surprised, as if there was never any doubt I would come. Taking off my jacket, I hang it over the back of a chair.

'You look nice.'

'Thanks. You too. You look different,' I add, then realize how that might sound and wish I hadn't.

'Contacts,' he explains, gesturing to his eyes.

He's wearing jeans and a jumper. Out of his suit, it's immediately noticeable that he works out at the gym. I feel suddenly intimidated.

'I like your top.'

119

'Oh, this old thing.'

I make a pretence of having casually thrown it on, rather than the reality of the last few days spent yanking things off hangers in a desperate attempt to find something that fits. All my dresses and nice trousers are too tight. Since moving to Yorkshire I've been living in my old dungarees, which are dangerous as they have no waistband. It's given me a new respect for Felicity Kendal in *The Good Life*. How on earth did she manage to make dungarees look so sexy? I do not look sexy.

In the end I gave in and ordered something online in a bigger size.

'Here, let me get the chair.'

'Oh . . . thank you.'

Ajay pulls out a chair for me.

'Hang on – I need to do something.'

He reaches towards me unexpectedly. Instinctively I jerk backwards, but his fingers are already brushing against the side of my neck.

'You left the tag on.'

My face flushes with embarrassment. 'Oh . . . thanks.'

'I have lots of old things in my wardrobe with the tags still on them,' he smiles, putting me at ease. 'So, tell me. What are you drinking?'

I smile back gratefully. 'Whatever you are.'

Ajay goes to the bar to order me a glass of wine, and I nip to the loo to check my hair hasn't gone frizzy in the rain; and the app on my phone, to see that Harry isn't destroying the house. Relieved to discover both are fine, I return to the bar feeling more relaxed and discover Ajay has got us a bottle.

'Well, it seemed easier. And cheaper,' he adds sheepishly.

'Great,' I smile as he pours me a glass, but feel a bit worried. Now I can't escape after one drink, if I want to.

'Cheers.' We chink glasses.

And I pull myself together, because being stuck sharing a bottle of wine with a handsome man wouldn't exactly be the worst thing in the world, now would it?

'. . . so that's how I ended up renting out cars.'

We've spent the last twenty minutes filling each other in a little about our lives: where we grew up, our backgrounds, families. After my outburst at the car-rental office, we already knew the spoilers in both our relationships, so neither of us mentions my divorce or his break-up. Instead I find myself speaking mostly about my childhood spent here in the Yorkshire Dales, and how both strange and yet familiar it is to find myself back again, while Ajay tells me about the severe bout of anxiety that caused him to drop out of criminal law – much to the horror of his parents – and how his job is only temporary until he figures out what he wants to do.

'Still, it's much less stressful than defending,' he finishes.

'Now you only have to deal with vomiting dogs,' I add, and he laughs.

'Sorry, that was all probably a bit heavy for a first date.'

'Who said this is a date?'

'Ouch.'

'Sorry. I didn't mean . . .'

Feeling bad, I fiddle with my beer mat. Ajay watches me, his expression serious.

'Would it be so awful to go on date with me?'

'No, of course not, it's just . . . Well, I'm a lot older than you,' I point out, stating the obvious.

'You don't look it.'

'Are you sure you didn't forget to put your contacts in?' I attempt a joke, but he doesn't laugh this time.

'You shouldn't put yourself down, you know. You're gorgeous.'

I look down at my wine glass, flattered and oddly upset by his observation.

'You know, I deleted that first text to you twice.'

I glance up, his honesty disarming me.

'What made you change your mind and send it?'

'Why not?' he says simply.

I don't know what I was expecting him to say, but it wasn't that.

'Why did you say yes?' he asks, throwing the question back at me.

I look at him across the table, and it strikes me that I've been so caught up in worrying about the difference in age I haven't stopped to consider that we might have more in common than I realized.

The thought makes me smile. 'Why not?'

So we start again. Only this time it feels a lot more comfortable. Something has shifted and, with it, there's been a release, like when you finally manage to pop the airlock on the lid of a jar that refuses to open. Ajay is intelligent and articulate and refreshingly honest. And now I've stopped over-thinking everything, I realize I'm enjoying myself for the first time in months. We order a second bottle of wine.

'So, how's Harry?'

'You remembered his name? I'm impressed.'

'I tend to remember names when they're yelled at me across a car park.'

I groan with embarrassment and cover my face with my hands. When I emerge, he's looking at me with amusement.

'Do you want to see?' I pull out my phone and shift my

chair around so that Ajay can see my screen, then tap on the app. 'Look, I can check up on Harry.'

The Wi-Fi is sketchy and it takes a moment to connect.

'What? You can see him?'

'Yes, it's brilliant. It's a remote camera. When I checked on him earlier, he was fast asleep.'

The camera suddenly goes live. Except instead of seeing Harry curled up fast asleep on the sofa, he's disappeared.

'Where is he? I can't see him.' Ajay squints at my phone.

'That's odd – hang on, let me turn on the volume.'

Suddenly there's the sound of howling coming from my phone.

'Whoa! What's that noise?'

My chest tightens. 'Oh no, that's Harry.'

'It's a dog making that sound?'

Ajay looks at me in disbelief. The howling is really quite loud. In the bar one of the walker's dogs starts barking, causing a few of the locals to look over. I quickly avert my eyes and glance back at the camera.

'Is he OK?'

'I don't know.'

Trying not to panic, I stare hard at my phone, willing Harry to come into view. My mind is flicking through a Rolodex of worst-case scenarios, imagining Harry in all of them.

'I'm sure he's fine.'

'Yes, I know. I just wish I could see him, so I know—' I break off as Harry suddenly appears on-camera. 'Oh, phew!' I joyfully thrust my phone at Ajay to show him.

He frowns. 'What's he got in his mouth?'

'Huh?' I turn the screen to see Harry has an object between his teeth and is shaking it violently, like he's trying to kill it.

'Oh no, he's got my handbag.'

'You know there's something I've always wondered,' ponders Ajay. 'Why is it women have so many handbags?'

But now is not the time to start discussing a woman's complicated relationship with her handbag. I get a sudden close-up as Harry swings mine in front of the camera in his jaws and my chest constricts. *It's my Gucci handbag.*

'Harry, no, put it down – that's a good boy.'

Pressing the voice-activation button, I try to remain calm and speak to him through the phone, and in what I hope is a soothing, reassuring voice. Of all my handbags, he had to choose my only designer one. It was a fortieth birthday present from The Ex. I'll say one thing: Harry has great taste.

'Harry. No!' I say sternly. 'Drop it.'

He ignores me and starts flinging it around the room with his teeth, the contents flying everywhere as he shakes his head violently.

'Drop it! Harry! DROP IT!'

He drops it. I feel a burst of relief. Before, flopping to the floor, he starts to chew it.

'No! Stop it! NO!'

'Is everything all right over here?' demands a gruff voice.

I snap back to realize that the pub has fallen silent and everyone is staring at me, pints in their hands, mouths agape.

'Um, it's Harry . . .' I mumble, feeling slightly mortified and turning to the figure standing behind us. 'Oh, hi.'

It's Ben Armstrong, still dressed in his builder's overalls and holding a pint.

'So, Harry, what seems to be the problem?' He steps towards Ajay accusingly.

'Do you mind?' Ajay jumps up, biceps curled.

'Yeah, I do mind all that shouting and bawling, actually.'

'No . . . wait . . . What are you both doing?' I try quickly to explain.

Ignoring me, they square up to each other.

'Look, this is all a misunderstanding.' Visions of Ben as a teenager getting into fist-fights come flying back to me and, seeing the scene unfolding, I try again. 'Please, I can explain.'

But Ben isn't listening. 'It's OK, Livvie. I'll handle this.'

Ajay looks back and forth between us. 'Hang on a minute. Do you two *know* each other?'

'Ajay, this is Ben – Ben, this is Ajay.' I make a desperate and rather tardy attempt at an introduction.

Ben frowns. 'Who's Harry then?'

'My dog.' I gesture to the designer-bag horror video that's still playing on my phone. 'Speaking of which, I think I'd better go.' And, grabbing my coat from over the back of the chair, I race out of the pub with a sense of relief and leave them both to it.

The Old Man

He's not in the window.

Early the next morning I take Harry out for his usual walk. My head throbs and I spend most of the walk nursing my hangover. It's not just the red wine making me wince. Later Ajay texted to check I was home safely and everything was OK. I sent him a reply apologizing and thanking him for a lovely evening.

'I'll call you,' I added. But I won't. I enjoyed last night, but in the cold, sober light of day I know I'm not ready to start dating again. Even if it wasn't a date. And Ajay was a nice guy. It's not fair to waste his time. It's best left as it was.

I glance over at the old man's bungalow. As usual we're passing it on our walk. I only spoke to him that once, but I still always look for him in the window. It's become a habit now. But today I stop dead in my tracks. I feel a beat of worry.

There's no one there.

'Morning.'

A loud voice makes me jump and I turn to see a figure appearing from the garage. It's the old man, only this time he's properly dressed in a flannel shirt and old brown corduroys, worn smooth at the knees. A flat cap is perched firmly on his head.

'Oh, hi.'

Caught staring, I don't have time to feel embarrassed before Harry spots him and limps over, his long bushy tail circling wildly.

'Someone's pleased to see you,' I say as the old man walks down his driveway towards us. I'm surprised by how relieved I feel to see him.

'Hello, lad.'

Joining us on the pavement, he bends down to pat Harry, who rubs his body against the man's legs, almost knocking him over. I've never seen him so excited.

'Harry, be careful,' I caution, but the old man bats away my concerns.

'Oh, it be right,' he says gruffly, but he seems genuinely pleased to see Harry.

'We walk past your house every morning. I waved for weeks. You mustn't have seen me.'

'No, 'appen not.' He gives a small shake of his head and continues to stroke Harry. 'So how are you then, lad? Being a good boy?'

'Not last night, he wasn't.' I smile ruefully. 'He likes to chew things when I go out.'

Tickling him behind the ears, the old man tuts good-naturedly. 'Now then, lad, you can't be doing that.'

'It's not his fault. He doesn't like being left alone. He gets separation anxiety.'

'Aye, well, I know how that feels.' He nods sympathetically as Harry gives him a gentle lick on his hand. 'It can be tough being left on your own.'

I suddenly realize how insensitive I've been and quickly grope around for something to say. I notice something bulky in the pocket of the old man's anorak and see the end of a plastic bottle sticking out.

'Are you putting up another bird feeder?' I gesture to his pocket.

Seeming to remember it's there, he pulls it out and holds it towards me. 'It's for you.'

'Me?'

'Aye. I made it for you.' He shifts uncomfortably. He looks embarrassed now and unsure, as if deeply regretting his actions.

'Oh, wow, thank you so much.'

I'm surprised and touched. I wasn't expecting this at all. To be honest, when he didn't wave back, it crossed my mind that he might be simply ignoring me.

'If you don't want it, it's all right.'

'No, I love it,' I say quickly, taking it from him and turning it round in my hands to inspect the small wooden perch and the holes. 'Where do I hang it? To attract the birds?'

'Oh, anywhere'll do – on a tree branch, or you can put a nail high up. I've made the holes small, so the pigeons won't eat it all . . . their beaks are too big . . . Just try keep it away from the cats.' He glances at Harry, who's staring up at the bird feeder as if it might hold food for him. 'But I reckon you don't have to worry about those, with this one about.'

'No, I don't,' I agree, the memory of Harry body-slamming the window of the rental car to try and get to a ginger tom still etched in my mind.

'Fill it about half full, then sit back and watch the birds do the rest.'

'That's really kind, thank you.'

'Ah, it's nothing.' Batting away my thanks with his gnarly bear of a hand, he looks down at his feet uncomfortably. 'Right, well, best get on.' With a shrug of his shoulders, he starts to move away.

'I'm Liv, by the way.'

He pauses, then raises his eyes to mine. He looks tired, with heavy bags beneath his eyes and deep creases etched between his unruly grey eyebrows.

'Liv? What kind of name is that?'

I smile. 'It's short for Olivia.'

'Oh, right,' he nods, and then, 'Valentine,' he adds gruffly.

'Pleased to meet you, Valentine.'

But he doesn't reply. I feel as if I've been dismissed and, assuming the conversation is over, I say my goodbyes and begin walking away.

'You know you can always leave Harry here with me,' he calls after me.

I turn round. He's still standing on his driveway, hands stuffed firmly in his pockets.

'If you want to go out, I mean . . . It'd be no trouble. I'd be glad of the company.'

I'm a bit taken aback, but try not to show it. 'OK. Thanks. I might take you up on it.'

'You do that.' He gives a sharp nod.

'And thanks again for my bird feeder!'

But he's already retreating back into his garage. I watch as he disappears, then set off walking. Despite my hangover I suddenly feel quite cheered up.

I hug the bird feeder to my chest all the way home.

STAGE 3

Woulda, Coulda, Shoulda

The Bombsite

I can think of lots of words in the English language to describe how it feels to be living in a nightmare. Different adjectives to describe terror and fear and horror. As a teacher, I used to tell my creative-writing students to imagine that sinking dread you feel in the pit of your stomach. The sickening clutch of anxiety in your chest. That feeling of panic.

However, come the beginning of April, I learn four new words: *Got. The. Builders. In.*

They arrived first thing. The peace and quiet of a morning in the Yorkshire Dales was broken by the sounds of the van pulling outside and the radio blaring. Ben was first through the door, all smiles and cheerful banter, followed by two younger men in overalls, whose names I didn't quite catch as they were eating bacon butties, which immediately endeared them to Harry. Some guard dog he'll be.

Still, I was trying to be positive. Fresh start, and all that. The plans had finally been passed and the cottage was going to be amazing when all the work was done. So I busied myself making them cups of tea, while trying not to fuss about their muddy footprints through the living room as they brought in their tools, dumped them all over the place and cranked up the radio. I was a bit nervous, but I told myself not to worry. Not even when Ben pulled out a massive sledgehammer. After all, in London people were always getting the builders in. My old street used to be full of skips and scaffolding. It was going to be fine.

It is *not* fine.

It's a nightmare.

Several hours later and I'm hiding upstairs with Harry in my bedroom, which I've now renamed the Panic Room. Not only because it's the sole safe sanctuary in the house away from all the banging, crashing and thumping downstairs, but it's also the room where I've gone to panic. As the cottage shakes, I can't stop myself wondering what I've done, while my brains tries to wrap itself around the alarming fact that this is going to be my reality for the next few months.

When, after several hours, I finally pluck up the courage to venture downstairs, the first thing I notice are clouds of dust and a layer of dirt over everything. The second is there now appears to be a gaping hole, and I can see straight into the kitchen from the hallway.

'Um, hello.'

Music is blaring from a badly tuned radio and someone appears to be singing to it, off-key. Tentatively I peer my head around the doorframe, to be greeted by a scene of chaos and rubble. I can't quite believe this used to be my kitchen. It's already unrecognizable. Ben spots me and stops whacking the wall with a sledgehammer.

'You all right?'

He reaches over and turns down the radio.

'Yeah, fine.' I look again at the gaping hole. 'I see you made a start. Everything OK so far?'

'Yeah, smashing.' He smiles, showing no awareness of the incongruity of his adjective. 'Hopefully we'll get this wall down by the end of the day, and then we can get the RSJs in.'

'RSJs?'

'Reinforced steel joists.'

'Right, OK.'

A huge lump of plaster drops from the ceiling.

'Stops your house falling down.' Ben calmly reaches for a mug of tea on the kitchen counter. 'Any chance of any biscuits with this cuppa?'

'Um, yes, I think they're in that cupboard.'

Slightly dazed, I break off as I realize the kitchen cupboard has been ripped from the wall and is now propped up against the fridge, its door at a jaunty right-angle to its bashed-in casing.

'Oh, you've pulled it off already.'

'Yup,' he nods, taking a satisfied sip of his tea.

'And most of that wall with it, as well,' I add, looking at where the tiles lie in a broken heap. I don't know what I was expecting, but it all seems a bit brutal. I feel a twist of anxiety. There's actual daylight coming through the brickwork.

'Well, that's the thing with these old houses – you never know what you're going to find, until you start. There was a house up the Dale: all the back collapsed when they took out a window.' Ben grins delightedly and shakes his head, as if this is an entertaining story, and not one that is turning my insides to ice.

As well as my outsides. Every single door and window is open and it's freezing in here.

'God, yeah, remember that, boss?'

One of the builders appears carrying a huge box of tools, which he dumps unceremoniously on the stone-flagged floor with a loud clatter.

'It went down like a pack of cards,' laughs the other builder from the garden, where he's smoking a roll-up in a trampled flower bed.

I've since learned these are two brothers called Darren and Paul, though I still don't know which is which; and listening to them constant yelling instructions at each other, they appear to go by the names of 'Fetch Me' and 'Carry Me'.

Crouching down, I yank open the door of the cupboard and reach inside for the packet of chocolate digestives. I hand them to Ben.

'I hope you like broken biscuits.'

'Love them,' he grins, missing my sarcasm.

I turn back to go upstairs to panic in the Panic Room.

'Thanks, Livvie. And don't worry. That's not going to happen to this house.'

Behind me, I hear the kitchen door blow shut and the crash of something breaking.

'Trust me. You're in safe hands.'

Two Weeks' Notice

A few days later I'm woken by the chime of a WhatsApp message. Still half asleep, I grab my phone from my bedside table. It's Naomi. We haven't caught up properly since I filled her in on the fallout from my drink with Ajay. Life, as ever, has got in the way. Surprisingly she didn't try to persuade me to change my mind, which I'm grateful about, and we ended up laughing about Harry instead.

'The Handbag Massacre!' she'd snorted, tears rolling down her cheeks as she told me to stop before she peed herself. Naomi always could make me see the funny side of things, as if her laughter gave me permission to laugh too; and now, with the benefit of hindsight, I suppose it was quite hilarious. Mortifying, but hilarious.

Blurry-eyed, I reach for my reading glasses:

What are you doing for Easter?

Eating too much chocolate – why?

Any chance I can still take you
up on that invitation to visit?

Yes, of course!
Would love to see you!

Great! Ellie will be so happy;
she says she wants to see a cow.

I think I can arrange that ☺

Thanks Liv, you're a superstar.
Can't wait to see you and
have a proper catch-up.

Me too. Can't wait!

It's still dark outside and, propping myself up on my pillows, I turn on my bedside lamp, pleased by this unexpected turn of events. I've really missed Naomi and our daily conversations in the staffroom; not just the big stuff, but the small, inconsequential, random stuff that makes up a life and a friendship. It will be great having her and Ellie to stay.

'Our first guests. What do you think of that?' I ask Harry, who's sprawled across the bottom of the bed, like an old fur coat. He doesn't stir. I know he's ignoring me. Harry has selective hearing. He can hear the jingle of his lead or the rustle of a biscuit wrapper from the bottom of the garden, but when he's doing something he shouldn't – like digging holes in my flower beds or sneaking onto my bed in the middle of the night – he suddenly goes completely deaf and pretends he can't hear me.

Which, now I think about it, reminds me a lot of my ex.

'Well, don't get too excited,' I tut.

But *I am getting excited*, and my mind begins running through all the things we can do when they visit . . . until I suddenly remember I am living in a building site. Not to mention that the guest bedroom, which I haven't even started on, is currently piled high with boxes of junk; or the avocado horror that is my bathroom; or the fact that I no longer have a kitchen, but a sort of makeshift campsite in the corner of my living room, with a camping stove and kettle, along with my fridge-freezer.

Feeling a slight panic, I look at the calendar on my phone. Since moving to Yorkshire I've completely lost track of the days. Unlike in my old life, where I was ruled by the calendar. Back then life was so busy, if it wasn't 'in the diary', it wasn't happening. It's a wonder I didn't have 'Husband Walks Out' scribbled there too.

I scroll through the dates. Oh, shit. Easter is less than two weeks away.

The Snowman

Overnight the world outside my window turns into a snow-globe and I wake to see thick, fluffy flakes swirling from a heavy woollen sky, covering the graveyard in a deep white blanket and muffling everything in a quiet stillness.

The house is silent. The builders have stopped work for the weekend and I pick my way through the dust and debris to put the kettle on. All the mugs are dirty and piled up in the sink, its plughole blocked by a pile of old teabags, some still attached to their spoons. For some reason I'm reminded of the time I went to Pompeii and saw a city frozen in time after the volcano eruption. Not that my cottage is a Roman city, but finding anything does involve something akin to an archaeological dig.

Donning rubber gloves, I clear up as best I can, then feed Harry and let him outside. Despite his arthritis, Harry likes to charge full pelt into the garden every morning to chase his nemesis, the grey squirrel who lives in the old apple tree and likes to taunt him. Only this morning, when he dives out of the back door, he dives head-first into a snowdrift, before reappearing with two large white eyebrows, looking completely bemused.

Meanwhile I check my bird feeder; it's still untouched. I filled it up and followed all of Valentine's instructions, hanging it from the large silver birch, with the intention of watching the birds from the window, except no birds have come. Not a single one. Concerned, I told Valentine when I passed by his bungalow a few days ago. Maybe I was doing something wrong? Perhaps I'd hung it in the wrong place? Maybe it was too high or not high enough? Perhaps I'd used the wrong birdseed?

But he told me not to worry. 'Just be patient. It'll happen. Give it time.'

After a few hours the snow finally stops falling, and Harry and I venture out for our walk to discover the village and surrounding landscape have been transformed into a winter wonderland, with glittering white fields, bright sunshine and a spotless blue sky. Fresh air fills our lungs and the views are so clear you can see for miles. Bundled up against the cold, we do our usual route along the footpath that runs alongside the edge of the fields. Normally they're filled with cows and sheep grazing, but they must have been taken in by the farmers to shelter inside the barns, as today the fields are bursting with local children sledging, their shrieks of delight and laughter piercing the frozen air.

We stop for a while to watch them, Harry straining at his lead and barking as they whizz past on bright plastic trays, as if wanting to join them. I don't blame him. They're all having so much fun. *Fun* – God, how I've missed that. The concept gets a little lost when you're trying to rebuild your life, buried underneath all the other practical stuff. I let Harry off the lead and play fetch with him, throwing his ball gently so as not to overtire him. And yet what's more important than having fun?

We pass Valentine's bungalow, but it's later than usual and he's not there. On the way back I call in at the post office to pick up a package. The driver left a card to say no one was in. Which isn't true; I was hiding upstairs and the builders were downstairs, but I can't have heard anyone knocking.

Which isn't surprising, considering that I can barely hear myself think, with all the deafening racket they're making.

Sheila, the postmistress, is forthright and friendly, as usual. Since moving in, I've had to pick up quite a few deliveries. At first it was all brisk hellos and brief exchanges about the weather, until one day she saw me tying Harry up outside and insisted that I bring him in.

'It says "No dogs", but I'll make an exception for this old boy. Far too cold for him to be tied up outside in this weather. What's his name?'

Now our visits to the post office are never complete without her coming out from behind the counter and fussing over him. Apparently Sheila's son is stationed with troops overseas and loves dogs; 'Wait till my Peter meets you,' she always says, as if somehow fussing over Harry brings her closer to him.

But it's not just Sheila. Since beginning our daily walks around the neighbourhood I've started noticing the effect that Harry seems to have on people. When I lived in London, striking up a conversation with a random stranger would probably have got you arrested, but here people often stop me in the street to ask after him, or wave and say hello. Like Nigel, the local window cleaner, who recently shimmied down a ladder to tell me about his hip replacement and suggest hydrotherapy for Harry's arthritis – 'It works wonders'. Or the street sweeper in the graveyard who lost his English bulldog, Dolly, last year and always lights up when he sees Harry. 'Dolly used to sleep on a velvet cushion – like royalty, she was; my wife used to give her all the best bits of the Sunday roast, whereas I got left with the scraps.' Funny how I soon know everything there is to know about Dolly and the state of his marriage, but we've never got round to knowing each other's names.

*

After collecting my package we come upon the local farmer on his tractor, clearing the lane and gritting, so instead we take a detour home. Walking through the housing estate on the other side of the graveyard, I immediately spot him in the front garden. Bundled up in a thick coat and yellow headphones, he's building a snowman.

'Hello, Stanley.'

He stops what he's doing and eyes me suspiciously.

'I like your snowman.'

He spots Harry and immediately his face brightens. With his gloves full of snow, he makes his way over to the gate to see us, careful to step only in his previous footprints. I notice he's wearing Spider-Man wellies.

Harry wags his tail to see Stanley and pushes his nose through the gate.

'Does Harry like snow?'

'I'm sure he does, yes. He wanted to go sledging.'

Reminded of all the other kids playing together, I feel sad that Stanley's on his own.

'Didn't you want to go sledging?'

Busy stroking Harry's head, Stanley says nothing, but just shakes his head.

'Where's his nose?' I point to the snowman, who's missing one.

'We don't have any carrots.'

'Maybe you could use something else?'

Stanley frowns. 'It has to be a carrot.'

I look at Harry, who's carrying his tennis ball in his mouth. 'Harry will give you his ball, if you want.'

Stanley studies it and I can tell he's trying to decide what to do. At that moment his mum appears from the house.

'Oh, hi.' She looks surprised when she sees me and Harry.

'He's very friendly,' I gesture to Harry, hoping to re-assure her quickly. 'Stanley was showing us his snowman. I wondered if he wanted a green tennis ball for his nose. Be a bit different.'

'I suggested a parsnip, but it has to be a carrot.' She rolls her eyes. 'His dad's gone to get some.'

'Probably better,' I nod, catching Stanley's eye and smiling.

'This is Harry,' he says, proudly showing off his new friend to his mum. 'If you tickle him here, he likes it. Harry gets scared too,' he adds, and I notice how animated Stanley is around him.

'Stanley is always asking for a dog, but it's a lot of respon-sibility. Bit too much right now,' his mother adds, lowering her voice.

She looks harassed, and I nod and say yes and glance at Stanley, who seems so different from the boy we met five minutes ago.

'OK, well, you should come inside now – time for your lunch. Remember what it says on your list,' she adds, as disappointment flashes across his face.

'Bye, Harry.'

'Bye, Stanley.'

And I smile and wave as he reluctantly follows his mum inside.

It's only later, when we get home, that I realize we must have left Harry's ball in Stanley's garden, so the next day when I'm walking past, I stop to get it. Only there's no sign of Stanley – just his snowman with his brand-new nose.

Only it's not a carrot; it's a bright-green tennis ball.

Heathcliff

The snow melts and disappears as quickly as it arrived, and a few days later I arrange to meet Maya at the Brontë Parsonage Museum in Haworth for our next tutoring session. As dogs aren't allowed, I take Valentine up on his kind offer and drop Harry at his bungalow, then catch the local bus to the small village of Haworth.

It's been years since my last visit. I came with Josie and my grandparents and, as I walk up the steep cobbled high street, memories flood back. Granddad giving me a piggyback because my legs were tired; Grandma telling us off for climbing on the moss-covered headstones in the graveyard; pressing my face against the glass case to squint at the miniature books made by the Brontë sisters as children.

Josie and I promptly went home and painstakingly made our own, creating stories and filling the pages with our minuscule handwriting. I still have them somewhere. So much of the stuff from our childhood was lost or thrown away every time we moved, but somehow I managed to hang on to those. They were the first stories I ever wrote, and mine were always filled with dreams of Happy Ever Afters, whereas Josie's were always much darker. Even then we seemed set on a different course.

'You're here already.'

I discover Maya waiting for me at the top of the hill. Sitting on the stone steps that lead into the parsonage, her hoodie pulled up, she's texting furiously.

145

'Well, I didn't want to be late. After last time,' she grins, looking up from her phone.

I smile and stop to rest for a moment against the wall. I'm a little mortified to realize I need to catch my breath after the climb up the main street.

'I don't remember it being that steep.'

'Have you been before?'

'Years ago, as a child. Have you?'

'No, never. There was a school trip here once, but it was the same day as Mum and Simon, my stepdad, got married. I was a bridesmaid, so I didn't get to go.'

'Oh, well, I'm sure you had a lot more fun being a bridesmaid.'

'My stepdad's a dick.'

Right. OK.

'Shall we go in?' I suggest, deciding to ignore that comment and gesturing towards the entrance.

Standing up, she pulls down her hood. Her pink hair is scraped back into a high ponytail, and she's wearing large hoop earrings and what looks like the entire make-up counter of Boots.

'I think Heathcliff's a bit of a dick too,' she adds and, throwing her backpack over her shoulder, she follows me inside.

Looking around the Parsonage Museum is like stepping back in time. In the parlour is the table around which the Brontë sisters would pace while reading out their stories, while the creaky wooden staircase leads to their bedrooms, where mannequins are dressed in their original gowns with the full-skirted petticoats, tiny shoes and bonnets they wore to walk on the windswept moors.

'Wow!' marvels Maya, peering into the glass cases with fascination.

Standing next to her, I nod in agreement, while feeling thankful that wellies and waterproofs have since been invented.

We continue on through the various rooms and, despite my initial reservations, I'm pleasantly surprised by Maya's enthusiasm. She spends ages poring over the various artefacts and mementoes, at one point even putting her phone away to study a manuscript of *Wuthering Heights*. Which, as anyone who knows a teenager will tell you, is something of a miracle.

Finally, we exit through the gift shop, where I buy the customary tea towel and Maya buys several postcards, plus a leather bookmark, which I feel quite happy about, as it shows she's reading something other than her smartphone.

'That was really cool, thanks.'

'I'm glad you found it useful.' Standing outside the parsonage, I'm pleased by the success of the visit. 'So shall we head back to the bus stop?'

'What's Top Withens?' As we turn to leave, she points to a sign for a footpath.

'I think it was inspiration for Wuthering Heights.'

She looks incredulous. 'You mean it's actually a real place?'

'Well, I should imagine it's a ruin now.'

'Can we go?'

'What? *Now?*' Our trip to the museum has already gone on for much longer than our allotted hour for the tutorial lesson. 'Don't you have to get back to school this afternoon?'

'No, it's a free period.'

I look at my watch, then at the signpost again.

'It says it's six miles there and back.'

'So?' she says eagerly. 'It's still only lunchtime – we've got ages before it gets dark.'

'And it looks like it's going to rain.'

As I gesture towards the dark clouds I watch Maya's face fall with disappointment. I feel a beat of regret. She's so keen, I don't want to dampen her enthusiasm. Still, I need to collect Harry and was planning on spending the rest of the afternoon trying to find more tutoring work. I should be sensible and go home.

As opposed to following in the actual footsteps of the Brontë sisters and seeing the actual farmhouse which, legend has it, was the setting in Emily's mind when she wrote her famous novel. Really, Liv?

'OK, you're on.' Turning away from the moors, I set off walking in the direction of the village. I still need to be a *little* bit sensible. 'But first we're going to need an umbrella.'

After calling Valentine's house to check on Harry – 'Oh, he's grand, we're getting on famously, no need to rush back' – and arming ourselves with a huge golfing umbrella that I find in a gift shop, 'just in case', we set off, following the signs for Brontë Waterfall.

'I don't understand why Heathcliff's supposed to be this big romantic hero,' Maya's saying now, as we make our way along a rough track that leads towards the moors.

'Brooding, tortured, passionate. What's not to love?' I quip, remembering my own teenage crush.

'But he's so fucked-up.' She catches my eye. 'Sorry, but he is.'

'Bad boys usually are.'

'And that's *attractive*?'

Climbing over a stile that leads out onto open moorland, I turn to see Maya looking at me with genuine incomprehension. She seems a lot more savvy about boys than I was at her age. I think back to my younger self, lying awake at night, crying hot, salty tears over idiots like Ben Armstrong.

148

'Normal boys of my age seemed so immature and dull. Whereas Heathcliff was so tragic and misunderstood,' I say. A blast of cold wind makes me shiver and I wrap my scarf tighter. 'I wanted to save him . . . to be loved as much he loved Cathy.'

'You wanted to date someone who would dig up your corpse?'

'Well, now you put it like that . . .' I laugh, pulling a face at the grisly thought and feeling slightly embarrassed by my admission. 'It must have been all those teenage hormones,' I add, and Maya shoots me a withering look.

We carry on walking, Maya striding ahead while I follow behind, trying not to slip on the muddy pathway and wishing I'd worn sturdier walking shoes. I look enviously at her Doc Martens and down at my own suede boots, which are already covered in mud.

'I know what you mean about boys my age, though,' she says a few moments later. 'They're just stupid and childish. Zac says girls mature a lot quicker.'

'Who's Zac?'

'My boyfriend. He's twenty-one.'

'Oh, right.'

'My parents don't know about him, though,' she warns quickly. 'They'd say he was a bad influence on me.'

'And is he?'

'No. But I know they'd blame him for me not wanting to go to uni. He thinks it's a waste of time. He says you don't change the world by getting a degree in English Literature.'

'And what do *you* think?'

My question seems to catch her by surprise.

'The same,' she says defensively. 'And you can't change my mind, you know.'

'I'm not trying to.'

149

She seems to relax then and looks satisfied. 'So do you have a boyfriend?'

I consider telling Maya that's none of her business, then decide that would be hypocritical, considering I've just asked her about hers.

'No,' I shake my head. 'I was married for a long time. I just got divorced.'

'I'm never going to get married. It's a waste of time. Everyone gets divorced.'

'Well, not everyone.'

I feel a raindrop and look up at the leaden skies.

'One in two marriages fail. I've read the statistics.'

She's so absolute. Was I so black-and-white when I was Maya's age? I feel oddly envious. Now everything seems to be so many shades of grey.

'No one gets married thinking about the statistics,' I reason, as we carry on towards the waterfalls. 'It's a leap of faith.'

A memory of David's proposal flashes through my mind and I feel a sudden lump in my throat.

'And it looks *so* boring. All Mum and Simon do is talk about what's for dinner, whose turn it is to empty the dishwasher, and watch TV.'

Which is so funny and relatable it cheers me up. 'Maybe if Emily Brontë was writing about Heathcliff and Cathy now, they wouldn't be running around on the moors, they'd be arguing over the dishes and watching Netflix,' I joke. 'Not sure it would be such a classic, though.'

Maya laughs and I pull out the pamphlet I got from the museum and begin reading.

'Apparently the Brontë sisters used to do this walk often . . . Do you know "wuthering" is an old Yorkshire word for stormy weather.'

'Look at that rock,' she cries, scrambling up to a large boulder shaped like a seat.

'That's the Brontë chair,' I continue. 'Legend has it they sat here and told each other stories.' I stop reading to gaze upon it. 'Wow, isn't that fascinating?'

'Cool,' she says, pulling out her phone and, without further ado, she promptly sits down and takes a selfie.

We continue on, me reading bits from the pamphlet, Maya taking endless photos and posting them to Instagram whenever she can get a signal, and we arrive at the Brontë Waterfall as the heavens open. Grateful for the huge golfing umbrella, we huddle underneath it as we cross the small footbridge, being careful not to slip. They obviously have a lot of tourists here, as I've noticed all the signs are written in Japanese, but today it's just us. Nobody else would be barmy enough to come out in this weather.

Up on the tops, the skies darken as the storm moves in. The wild moorland is bleak and windswept and, despite the umbrella, we're both getting completely soaked through.

'This was a mistake,' I say. 'We should turn back.'

'Look. There!' Maya almost has to shout to make herself heard above the wind. 'That must be Top Withens.'

She points ahead and then I see it. Far in the distance, the dark shape of a ruin brooding on the horizon. We can't turn back now.

Ducking our heads, we brace our bodies against the elements and for a while we both fall silent, concentrating on negotiating the footpath, until finally we reach what's left of the farmhouse, perched on top of the moor. Now just a ruin, it's completely open to the elements, with trees gnarled and twisted by the force of the wind.

'It's like being on top of the world.'

My voice catches in my throat as, beneath us, the valley sweeps away and I take in the dramatic scenery. It's so powerful, it feels almost supernatural.

'Look, there's a sign.' Maya points to a stone plaque on the wall that's been placed there by the Brontë Society.

'I get it now. The story, I mean. Why she wrote it. It's so wild up here, isn't it?' Turning away from the sign, she's gazing out across the moors, spellbound. 'Even Heathcliff makes sense now – well, sort of,' she adds, glancing sideways at me, the corners of her mouth twisting upwards.

I smile and together we find a place to rest on what's left of one of the walls. Then for a while we sit there, lost in our thoughts, taking in the views that stretch for miles. This wasn't a mistake at all. Not even in the driving rain and bitter cold, and the wind that whips the hair around our faces. Coming up here has taught Maya more than I ever could.

And maybe she's right; maybe Heathcliff does make sense now. Maybe that's where it all started: under those bedcovers with a torch in my teenage hand; my belief that if I tried harder, loved deeper, then I could save someone I loved. That I could fix them.

I don't know how long we sit there, but after a while I notice it's stopped raining and, putting down the umbrella, I lift my face to the skies. They're brightening and I close my eyes and breathe it all in.

'*Petrichor.*'

'What's that?'

I open my eyes to see Maya studying me, her brow creased.

'It's that smell you get after heavy rain. That special fragrance of clean air and wet earth.'

Without speaking, Maya takes a deep inhale and exhale. 'It's like you've cleared the air.'

I think about being a child, coming here with my sister – about everything that's happened between us since. How I'm finally beginning to realize that you can't save someone by loving them, or fix a relationship that doesn't want to be fixed. And I'm not just talking about my marriage.

'Yes,' I nod, as I think about Josie. 'It's exactly that.'

'I think that's my new favourite word.'

I stand up, beckoning towards the shafts of sunlight breaking through the clouds on the horizon ahead. 'Come on,' I say, 'let's head back.'

Valentine

'C'mon, lad, it's time for *The Archers*.'

It was 2 p.m. Switching on the radio, Valentine put down his cup of tea and settled himself on the sofa. Harry followed him through from the kitchen and paused at the doorway, staring at him. Waiting. Valentine frowned. He'd been given strict instructions not to let him up on the sofa. His owner, Olivia, was trying to train him out of bad habits apparently

'I won't tell anyone, if you don't.'

He patted the empty cushion and immediately Harry jumped up, curling himself up next to Valentine.

'We all need a few bad habits, don't we?' he said, ruffling the dog's fur as Harry rested his muzzle on his knee and closed his eyes, letting out a deep sigh of contentment.

Valentine couldn't remember the last time he had shared the sofa. He and Gisele had always used to listen to the episodes together, side by side with a cup of tea and a slice of something, but since she'd been gone, it had just been him on his own. On the radio the familiar opening bars of the soundtrack began to play, and Valentine sipped his tea – a classic Assam – and enjoyed the simple joy of a warm body next to him.

'Bloody hell, lad,' he grumbled, wafting his hand.

Even if it did let out farts that stank to high heaven.

*

He'd pretended not to see her. He liked to keep himself to himself. He didn't have any friends; it was much better that way. And at first he thought she'd go away, but she didn't. She kept walking past his bloody window every morning and she kept waving. Day in, day out, rain or shine. And she was always with Harry.

Valentine missed having a dog. He and Gisele used to have Haggis, their little Scottish Highland terrier. She would go everywhere with them, sitting between them on the front seat of their camper van. When she died, at the grand old age of sixteen, Gisele had been so heartbroken that she wouldn't consider getting another dog. And now Valentine was too old. It was too late.

But then he met Harry. And with each passing day he found himself looking forward to seeing him limping past. Watching him sniffing around, his nose set to the wind like the arrow of a weathervane; the comical way he wobbled when he cocked his leg. Watching Harry became the favourite part of Valentine's day, and more and more he wanted to go out there and give him a tickle behind the ears.

Only now he was stuck. He couldn't simply start waving, after ignoring her. She'd think he was barmy. Which is how he came up with the idea of making her a bird feeder. It was just an excuse, really, to see Harry. Only he hadn't reckoned with how much he'd enjoy making it. He used to make things for Gisele all the time, and for Helen; little gifts for birthdays and Christmas. Or with how much she would love it. It was only a bird feeder, but she seemed genuinely delighted, and her delight rubbed off on him.

'You've got a spring in your step,' remarked Ruth, the receptionist, when he next visited Gisele. He couldn't wait to tell Gisele all about Harry and his offer to dogsit. Helen, too, when he spoke to her on the way home. Still, to be honest, he wasn't sure if Harry's owner would take him up on his offer, so he was a bit taken aback when he got the knock on the door the very next day and there she was, standing on his doorstep, asking if she could drop Harry off for a couple of hours next week while she taught. When he said yes, she tried to give him a hug, which was a bit awkward as he didn't go in for all that, but he was chuffed nonetheless. As soon as she left he got his jotter pad and turned to a new page:

Tuesday 10th April
1. Looking after Harry

It was the best thing he'd written in the longest time.

There was a knock at the door. It woke him up. He must have nodded off.

'Hi, Valentine, it's Liv – I've come to collect Harry.'

'Oh, is it that time already?'

She was smiling broadly as he opened the door and he felt the pressure to smile back, but inside he felt only dread. How had the time gone so fast? He'd looked forward to this all week, and now it was over. Harry was fast asleep on the sofa inside. He felt a slight panic at the thought of Harry waking up and leaving.

'I've brought you a cake to say thank you.' She held out large white cardboard box. 'Don't worry, I didn't make it myself – it's from the bakery in the village. It's chocolate.'

Taken aback by her kindness, he stood, frozen, on the doorstep.

'Oh dear. You don't like chocolate. I knew I should have gone for the Victoria sponge.' Her face fell and Valentine felt a stab of guilt.

'Victoria sponge? Over chocolate? Never!' Swiftly he took the box from her. 'Come in, I'll put the kettle on.'

He blurted out the invitation before thinking. He hadn't had any visitors since the care workers came to move Gisele into the home. But it was too late now.

'Oh, thank you.'

Stepping inside, she closed the door behind her as Harry appeared in the hallway, bashing their legs with his bushy tail.

'Hello, have you missed me?' Dropping to her knees, she began kissing and hugging him. 'I know you're not supposed to make a fuss at first, but I can't help it.'

'Neither can he, by the looks of things.'

Leaving them to their reunion, Valentine continued through to the front room. A few moments later they followed him.

'I see he's made himself at home.'

Bugger. She'd spotted the sofa with his blanket on it. He felt himself colour up. There was also evidence of biscuit crumbs. Valentine had discovered that Harry shared his fondness for custard creams.

'He didn't care much for his rug.'

As if to prove a point, Harry jumped nimbly onto the sofa and settled himself down.

They both pretended not to notice.

'So what tea would you like, Olivia?'

He wasn't going to call her by that silly nickname; no one ever called him Val.

'Oh, I don't mind – whatever you're having, thanks.'

Valentine took the cake through to the kitchen and set about busying himself boiling the kettle, filling the teapot, finding teacups and saucers and side plates. His hands trembled. It was so long since he'd had guests and he felt absurdly nervous. He located a cake stand, stuffed in the back of a cupboard. He wished he'd got fresh flowers. Giselle always used to have them on the table. He made a note to put them on the list.

When he came out of the kitchen holding a tray, he found Olivia reading the back of one of his library books from the large pile on the side.

'I'm doing my family tree,' he offered in explanation. 'Well, trying to.'

'Genealogy is fascinating.' She began flicking through the book and he felt pleasantly surprised by her interest. 'I love that programme on the TV – what's it called?'

'*Who Do You Think You Are?*' said Valentine, putting the teapot down on the table, along with the cake.

'Yes, that's it!' She looked up then, her face filled with enthusiasm. 'I love how they always discover such interesting stories about their ancestors – like their great-granddad was a highwayman, or they're descended from Charles I.' Putting the book back on the pile, she turned her attention to him. 'What have you found out? Don't tell me you're related to royalty too.'

He gave a small laugh of embarrassment.

'Well, to be honest, I've been doing it for years and not getting very far.'

'Oh, really?' She looked disappointed now. 'Have you done one of those testing kits?'

Pausing from getting out the place mats from the dresser, Valentine frowned. 'What are those?'

'You know – the DNA tests, where you can trace your ancestors.'

Valentine had heard about them; the librarian had mentioned it to him once when she restamped his books, but he preferred to do it the old-fashioned way, trawling through archives and records and censuses, going back to

158

the library, month after month. It was laborious and time-consuming and involved lots of painstaking research. One day it had struck him that perhaps he didn't really want to get anywhere, because what would he do then, when it was finished?

'Too expensive.' He shook his head dismissively and began setting the table.

'I got a test for Christmas a few years ago – not exactly the most romantic of presents, but . . .' She broke off, shrugging. 'Can I do anything?'

'No, you're fine.'

He wished she'd sit down. Relax. Valentine didn't feel very relaxed.

'Is this your wife?'

He looked up to see Olivia peering at a small silver-framed photograph on the dresser. He nodded.

'That's Gisele with our Helen, when she was just a baby. We'd gone on a day-trip to the seaside at Whitby.'

'I've always wanted to go to Whitby, ever since I read *Dracula*.'

'Well, we didn't find any vampires, only buckets and spades,' he said and Olivia smiled.

'She's beautiful. They both are.'

'Aye.'

His voice was gruff and he turned back to the table to finish laying the cutlery. 'Oh, bugger!' A fork fell on the floor. 'It's too small . . . the table.'

'Is it one of those that extends? I can help.'

'No, it's all right.'

But before he could say anything, she was crouching down next to him, pulling out the folding leaves and dusting them off. He watched helplessly, feeling a rising panic. He didn't want her to touch things. He wanted them left as they were.

'There. See, much better.' She grinned when it was finished and the table was set and they'd both sat down. 'Don't you agree?'

And, much to his surprise, Valentine did. He poured the tea, while Liv offered to cut the cake and Harry joined them from the sofa, settling himself underneath the table to wait patiently for crumbs. Valentine felt much better. Things weren't meant to be folded away and not used, he realized. Like people, really.

'Gosh this is delicious. What kind of tea is it?'

Fifteen minutes later they were on their second cup. Olivia looked impressed when Valentine told her.

'I only drink builder's,' she confessed, digging into a large slice of cake. She'd cut them the size of doorsteps. 'You must think me such a philistine.'

On the contrary; Valentine thought her completely fascinating as she chattered away, complimenting him on his bungalow and the view, while telling him how she'd recently moved here on her own from London. *From London* – imagine that. Valentine couldn't. He'd once been on a coach trip with Gisele to see *Les Misérables*, and that was enough. Too many people. Too much noise and traffic. How did anyone hear the birds?

'So, no fella?' he asked and then, seeing her expression, added hastily, 'Or lady friend?' Well, he didn't want her to think *him* a philistine.

She smiled then, like he'd said something funny. 'It was a fella . . . now it's just me.'

She had such a lovely smile. Wide and generous, it creased up the corners of her dark eyes. And yet he couldn't help noticing it never quite reached them.

'And Harry, of course.'

There was movement underneath the table and Harry's nose emerged from below the tablecloth, ever hopeful. They both laughed.

'What about you?'

'My wife Gisele wasn't well . . .' Valentine trailed off. 'Now it's just me, too.'

'What about your daughter? Does she live locally?'

'No. Paris,' he added, after a pause.

'Lucky her.'

'Aye. Lucky her.' He nodded and speared a large chunk of chocolate cake on his fork. He tried to swallow it down, but it felt dry and stuck on a lump in his throat. In the background Valentine became aware of the radio and the sound of loud trumpets. With everything that had been going on, he'd forgotten it was still playing.

'Sorry, I'll turn that off.' He stood up, his chair scraping loudly.

'No, please, keep it on. I love Tommy Dorsey and his orchestra.'

'You know them?'

Valentine was surprised. They were a big swing band from the 1940s. Young people didn't listen to that kind of music. They listened to loud, thumping stuff that he could hear even through their headphones when he sat next to them on the bus to the care home.

'His band was one of my grandparents' favourites.'

'Mine and Gisele's too,' he nodded, 'we had all his records. We used to go dancing together at the town hall and they'd play all his tunes; that and later swing, and jive and rock-and-roll . . . She was such a good dancer, so light on her feet.'

'You must miss her.'

'I do, though I still get to visit her every day at the home.'

'Oh, I thought—' she broke off, looking embarrassed, and it suddenly dawned on Valentine.

'That I'm a widower?'

'I'm sorry – I didn't mean . . .'

'Nay, don't be,' he reassured her. 'Sometimes I wish I was one.'

It just came out. He didn't meant to say it, but he'd thought it many times. But if Olivia was shocked, she didn't show it.

'I know that's a wicked thing to say, but often my wife doesn't recognize me. Worse still, I don't recognize her.' It was the first time he'd said these things out loud and, as guilty as he felt, telling someone brought a sense of release. 'She's got Alzheimer's, and it stole her from me. That bloody disease – it stole my wife, and I miss her. I miss growing old with her.'

He was so full of anger and sadness and regret that he didn't know what to do. It was all stuffed inside of him. So tight and all tangled up. Sometimes he felt like he couldn't breathe with the unfairness of it.

'We had all these plans for when I retired. We were going to travel. We were going to see the world together . . .'

And for a moment he was back there: Gisele excited, with her arms full of glossy brochures from the travel agent's in town. Him with his maps spread out over the very table they were sitting at.

'Now she's in a world that only she can see.' He scratched his cheek, roughly brushing away the tears that threatened to fall. 'I'm sorry, I don't know what's come over me.'

He snapped back, mortified. Honestly – pouring his heart out like a silly old fool. What must Olivia think?

But if Olivia thought anything, she didn't say a word. Instead she did the most remarkable thing. She put her cup down onto her saucer and reached across for his hand. And

162

while Valentine's instinct was to pull away, he let it be held by this kind-hearted young woman that he barely knew, who had come into his home bearing chocolate cake, and conversation and friendship. And who, for a brief while, had made him feel normal again.

'Sometimes I just feel so lost,' he said.

'And that's why Harry and I are here to find you,' she replied.

Which made him smile, because really it was a lovely thing to say to a silly old fool like him, and that made her smile too. And this time Valentine noticed it reached her eyes.

Hey you,

It's late. Sometime after midnight. I need to turn out the light and go to sleep, but I was thinking about you and dreaming about summer. Being here brings back so many memories of summer holidays and rocket-shaped ice-lollies, and running around barefoot in bathing costumes from dawn to dusk. And that feeling of being carefree.

You know, sometimes it's hard to remember that feeling. I think the last time I felt truly carefree must have been the summer I turned eight. Do you remember? That was the really hot year when the river nearly dried up and the tar on the telegraph poles melted. We would pick it off with our fingernails while we listened out for the chimes of the ice-cream van. It was so hot Grandma refused to cook, so it was sandwiches and crisps for tea every day – and salad cream with everything. I remember we used to fight, but on this we were in agreement: it was like being in heaven.

Back then Granddad still worked for the council and every day he would return home at five thirty on the dot. I used to wait for him at the end of the lane and wave when he appeared. He drove a denim-blue Morris Minor with cream hubcaps and knitted covers on its seats, remember? That would be the car I'd later learn to drive in, and that you'd have your first kiss in, but for now it was just Granddad's car. His pride and joy.

I remember how every Sunday he would hand-wash it, soaping it down with a bucket and a giant sponge, working methodically in circles, back to front. And how, for two sisters watching this ritual that hot summer, it seemed to

164

take an eternity. We were desperate for him to finish because, at the end, Granddad always let us hose it down. Of course it was simply an excuse for us to play with the hosepipe before they introduced the ban. You knew how to do this thing with your thumb, pressing it against the pipe to make the water spray out – you always knew how to do all the cool stuff – and I would run through it, shrieking with laughter, while Grandma would come out of the house, yelling for us to mind her windows.

'Can you recall a time when you felt truly happy and carefree?' It was the therapist who asked me that question. I'd gone to see her after David left, to talk about him, but the funny thing was, I ended up talking about you instead. You see, at first I assumed it must have been on a recent holiday, or celebrating my birthday or even my wedding day. After all, isn't that supposed to be the happiest day of your life? But it was only when she really made me think about it that I realized it was none of those times. Despite the happy occasions, I didn't feel *carefree*. There's a difference.

I needed to go further back. Back to those long, hazy and bleary-hot days when we were running around in the driveway with the hosepipe, getting soaked. Back to the innocent sounds of shrieks and laughter; the sensation of ice-cold water on warm suntanned skin and the pure, unfiltered, not-a-care-in-the-world carefreeness. Back to the summer before Mum died. Before everything changed. Before two little girls grew up way too fast.

OK, that's the church clock chiming. It's one o'clock in the morning. I'll sign off now.

x

PS: I hope me talking about the past doesn't upset you but you're the only one who understands and ever will.

Father and Son

They say a year in a human's life is equivalent to seven years in a dog's life. Which means, according to Harry, he's already been living with me for over a year. And in a funny kind of way it feels like that, as already I can't imagine life without him. We're like an old married couple. Only in this case one of us isn't having an affair with the yoga teacher.

I've also discovered there's another way to measure time: builders. Since Ben's firm started work on the cottage I've learned that 'A Builder's Week' is a normal person's month, as everything takes infinitely longer than the builders say it will. Sort of like 'A Baker's Dozen', only there are no free loaves; just two more weeks of waiting and an extra headache. Their ability to make time elastic is also reflected by how long they've been in your house, as they completely take over. It's only been three weeks, but it already feels like a decade.

That said, living with builders does mean that life's never dull. Fetch Me and Carry Me are like a comedy duo and are forever cracking jokes, most of which are too rude to repeat, but I probably don't have to, as I'm sure everyone in the village can hear them, because they like to yell at each other from one end of the garden to the other. There's also a constant stream of new faces: Sparky the electrician, Flood the plumber, Beanz the gas man.

As for their interesting – and, in the case of the plumber

– rather worrying names, I don't like to ask. I do, however, draw up some house-rules after Fetch Me blocks the toilet for what feels like the millionth time. Well, we are sharing a house and I've heard too many horror stories of people falling out with their builders. Hopefully this will stop me falling out with mine:

Builders' House-Rules

1. *When listening to the radio, check the volume. Windows rattling are a good gauge that it might be too loud.*
2. *If singing along to aforementioned radio, please try to be in tune.*
3. *The crack of dawn is not the best time for the noisiest, messiest jobs.*
4. *Kindly remember that, after the mix-up with the Portaloo, we are sharing one toilet and the walls are thin. So I would prefer it if you didn't drink ten pints and eat a curry the night before.*
5. *PS: Striking matches in the loo does not work.*
6. *If outside, please don't clear throat of phlegm, release gas or use expletives before looking over the fence to check if the guests in the holiday cottage next door are relaxing in the garden with a bottle of wine.*
7. *A handy tip: while getting rid of extra grout down the sink or loo might look like the best option, Dyno-Rod assures me it is not.*
8. *Please use the sweeping brushes provided and don't simply pick up the hose and flush everything into the guttering and drains.*
9. *Teabags: while I appreciate the technical skill involved in building a skyscraper that resembles London's*

Walkie Talkie building, I would prefer to have a plughole that water can flow through freely.

Thank you.

But in the end I decide against giving it to them. After all, I'm trying to avoid falling out with them, aren't I? And the first rule is probably not to give them a list of house-rules. So I buy them more biscuits instead.

I look at Ben now, leaning against a half-demolished wall in the bombsite that used to be my kitchen, a mug of tea in one hand and a chocolate digestive in the other. Of all the kitchens in all the world, he had to demolish mine.

'How was the walk?'

I've just come in from walking Harry and am peeling off my waterproof layers. No surprise, it's raining again. I feel slightly irritated by his presence. The walls of the entrance hallway have been knocked down, so the moment you come through the front door you walk straight into a building site. And Ben, who seems to be constantly on a tea break.

'Wet,' I grumble, trying to grab Harry and dry him off before he shakes everywhere. Not that it would make much of a difference, considering the mess. 'How's the tea?'

'Wet,' he says, putting down his mug and handing me a towel from the hook in the corner.

'Thank you.' I smile gratefully and feel guilty for being grumpy. Crouching down, I begin drying off Harry.

'Oh, by the way, I believe this is yours.'

I look up to see Ben pulling something out of his pocket. It's a green tennis ball, although less green and more muddy-coloured.

'Well, Harry's.'

I frown. 'Where did you find that?'

'The snowman didn't have much use for it any more.' He

raises his eyebrows, a faint air of amusement playing on his lips. 'Stanley thought Harry might want it back.'

I look at him in surprise. 'You know Stanley?'

'I'm his dad.'

'Stanley's your son?'

'Well, that's how it usually works.'

I colour.

'Stanley has been talking about it being Harry's ball, and I finally put two and two together. Took me a while. Like I said, I didn't get your brains.' Ben grins and I smile, though mostly out of embarrassment.

'We see him on our walks . . . I didn't realize that was your house.'

'Well, no – you never wanted to go for that catch-up, did you?'

Reminded, I shift awkwardly.

'He's a lovely little boy,' I say, changing the subject.

'Thanks.' He gives a small nod of pride. 'He loves Harry – Stanley talks about him all the time.'

'The feeling's mutual. Harry loves him. They hit it off right away.'

Ben smiles. 'Stanley seems to find it easier to connect with animals than with humans. We did think about getting a dog after . . . well, everything, but it's a lot and I'm out at work all day.'

'Stanley can come on a walk with me if he likes. Have a play-date.'

'Thanks, but Stanley doesn't do play-dates.'

'Not even with his friends?'

Ben sighs and looks down at his mug of tea. His hands are covered in dust and dirt and he rubs his wedding band with his thumb, making the gold shine. 'Well, that's the thing: he doesn't have any friends.'

There's a beat and he falls silent. I can see this is difficult for him. I can hear the other builders banging and clattering, erecting the scaffolding that's going up to the roof, but inside the house there's a stillness.

'Kids at school think he's strange. Stanley's special – he has his little ways. When he was born we could tell he was different from other friends' babies; his speech was delayed, and he would get fixated by things . . . I remember him sitting for hours watching the garage door open and close, like it was the most fascinating thing in the world.'

As Ben breaks off, remembering, I suddenly see him in a totally different light. Beneath the tattoos and swagger and the cheerful banter, there's a vulnerability and seriousness; he's a concerned father who loves his son.

'It was actually a bit of a relief when he was finally diagnosed. Being on the autism spectrum, that's what the doctors call it. It helped us understand why change makes him anxious, why he likes everything a certain way.'

'He showed me his list,' I nod, and Ben smiles.

'He likes lists – they make him feel safe. It's the routine. He likes everything to be in order.'

'I'm with Stanley on that one.' I pull a face at the mess of the kitchen. It makes Ben laugh, and I feel pleased to be able to lighten his mood.

'He's a brilliant little boy and he's been through such a lot. He's just different, that's all; and the other kids don't like different, at that age.'

'Well, if there's anything I can do to help . . .'

'Thanks.'

I gesture towards Harry, who's pounced on the ball and is now chewing it enthusiastically, trying to rip off the green furry coating.

'Don't tell Stanley that Harry ate his snowman's nose.'

'I won't.' Ben smiles and shrugs. 'Anyway, I'd best get on.'

'Yeah, me too.' I pick up the towel. 'I've got my friend and her daughter coming up from London to stay at the weekend and I've so much to do. I haven't sorted out the spare bedroom, so I've no idea where they're going to sleep.'

'Well, I might be able to help you with that.'

I look at him with interest. 'Really?'

Ben pulls out his phone. 'Hang on, let me make a call.'

The Castle

'Oh, Liv, this is wonderful!'

Naomi and Ellie have just arrived and are standing hand-in-hand in a patch of dappled sunlight in my back garden, surveying the large white bell-tent strung with candy-coloured bunting and lanterns that has been erected underneath the giant sycamore tree, which has seemingly burst into leaf overnight.

She turns to me, her face a mix of delight and astonishment. 'How did you do it all by yourself?'

'Well, I had some help,' I admit, pleased by her reaction.

In truth, I had a lot of help. It was all Ben's idea. His friend has a company that provides bell-tents for local festivals. At first I hadn't been sure at all. A tent? In this weather? But Ben had been convincing; it always rained at festivals and these tents were waterproof, plus – by some divine miracle – they'd forecast good weather for Easter.

'And let's be frank: where else are your friends going to sleep?' he'd asked, eyebrows raised, looking at all the junk piled up in the back bedroom. 'In your mouldy bathroom?'

The tent had arrived yesterday, and Ben and his builders downed tools and spent all day in the garden putting it up – luckily the garden's quite big, so we could position it far away from the cement mixer, which didn't quite go with the festival vibe. And Ben was right. By lunchtime the drizzle had stopped and, as if by magic, the sullen grey skies

172

disappeared and the sun made its entrance like a long-lost friend, bathing everything in sunlight and drying up my sodden lawn.

'What do you think, Ellie?'

Seven-year-old Ellie, who's normally a chatterbox, has suddenly gone all shy on arrival and is clutching her mother's hand.

'It's like being in a circus,' she says, breaking into a grin. Unable to resist any longer, she lets go of Naomi's hand to run across the garden. We follow her, stepping over the tent posts and lifting up the front flap. Inside, it's not just a tent, but something far more impressive, with a proper floor, patterned rugs, and duvets and pillows.

And Harry, who's already made himself at home on one of the rugs.

Ellie's face lights up as soon as she sees him. They only met a few minutes ago when Harry greeted them at the gate, his tail wagging furiously – as if now that he's discovered how great it feels, he can't stop. Naomi grins and throws her arms around me in a hug.

'I love this place!'

'Really? I wasn't sure . . . I know you're such a city girl.'

'Are you kidding me? All this space and fresh air! And the scenery on the way here on the train was amazing. It's no wonder they call it God's own country.'

I feel a sudden burst of pride. That's how I feel when I'm walking Harry and I look out over the Dales, but hearing someone else say it about my new home gives me a real feeling of gratification

'I mean, look at this garden.' Naomi has already stepped outside the tent and is stomping around the garden in her Birkenstocks. 'It's about twenty times the size of my tiny one in London.'

173

'And about twenty times more overgrown,' I point out, my pride quickly vanishing and being replaced by embarrassment at the state of my patchy lawn and wild tangle of plants and trees. I'd imagined moving here and creating this beautiful cottage garden, but in truth I can barely keep a houseplant alive. 'I haven't got a clue where to start.'

'I can help you while I'm here, if you want. It just needs a bit of a tidy-up. We can cut back some of those bushes and clear those brambles. You've got some real hidden gems sprouting . . . Look at those gorgeous clumps of primroses and crocus under those crab-apple trees.' She flings her arms around, pointing at things and making the stacks of bangles on her wrist jingle. 'That's a camellia . . . those are rambling roses and jasmine – lucky you, their scent will be incredible when they bloom . . . This is a gorgeous honeysuckle.'

I listen to her in astonishment as she lists plants like an encyclopaedia. I knew Naomi had green fingers, but I didn't realize she was this much of an expert.

'Since when did you turn into Monty Don?' I ask, and she laughs and points to the broken-down shed tucked away at the bottom of the garden.

'What's in there?'

'To be honest, I don't know,' I confess.

'You don't know?' Naomi turns to me, incredulous.

'Well, I did have a bit of peer in the window when I first moved in, but it looked like a load of old junk and garden tools, and there was this huge spider – you should've seen the size of it.' I give a shudder. 'It's on my list,' I add sheepishly.

Pushing her sunglasses onto her forehead, Naomi puts her hands on her tiny hips. 'Well, we'd better get cracking on that list while I'm here then, hadn't we?'

'Don't be silly – you're a guest,' I begin to protest, but she bats away my objections.

'It'll be good to keep myself busy, take my mind off things.' She glances towards Ellie who's now playing on the grass, making sure she's out of earshot. 'I've had a big fight with Danny.'

'Why? What happened?' I feel a beat of concern.

'Mummy, can we go to the castle?' Ellie runs over.

Naomi shoots me an apologetic look, 'Sorry,' she hisses, 'I told her there was one near here, and it's all she's been talking about on the way up. I did try to explain it wouldn't be like Arandelle Castle.'

At the mention of the castle, my memory flicks back to me and my sister as children, playing hide-and-seek in its ramparts. It catches me off-balance.

'*Frozen*,' she adds, mistaking my expression for confusion.

'It's fine,' I say quickly, as much as for my own benefit as hers. 'Let's go. It'll be fun.'

After checking with Valentine that it's OK to drop Harry over at his house, I drive us all to Raven Castle in my new car. I bought it a few days ago, after getting more replies to my tutoring ad. I've now gained three more pupils, all doing their eleven-plus, all living in nearby villages, and with transport links not being like those in London, I need the car to get around.

That said, the Trade Descriptions Act might take issue with the words 'new' and 'car'. After my experience with the rental car, I needed to be able to see over the drystone walls and have seats that I could wipe down easily, but after several weeks of searching fruitlessly for cars online, I was beginning to think I was never going to be able to afford anything suitable.

That was until I bumped into the local farmer at the weekend. I'd actually been taking photos of the trough that he used for his cows – a rusty old claw-foot bath – in order to show Ben what I had in mind for my bathroom, when he drove by in an old Land Rover with a 'For sale' sign taped on the window. Apparently he'd just bought it for his wife, but she was having none of it, having set her heart on 'one of those newfangled electric cars'.

Which is why, after offering me it for a price I couldn't turn down, his wife is now the proud owner of a sporty red Honda Jazz and I'm rattling along the country lanes behind the wheel of an ancient olive-green Land Rover Defender, with Naomi next to me and Ellie on the back seat; she's insisted on wearing her glittery blue Princess Elsa dress and bringing her wand, complete with its mini snow-globe on top.

'Because I might need it to cast magic spells,' she says gravely, bouncing up and down in the child safety seat that I found being offered for sale in the post-office window.

'I wish adults got to carry wands,' I confide as we pass over the eighteenth-century packhorse bridge, silently saying my prayers that we don't meet anyone coming the other way.

'We get iPhones instead,' remarks Naomi.

'They're not quite as magical, though, are they?'

As we climb higher, the blue skies widen and sun streams in through the windscreen. I roll down the windows, letting in the fresh air.

'Oh, I don't know,' says Naomi, 'one of the filters makes me look about twenty years younger. I'd call that pretty bloody magical.'

'Mummy swore!' giggles Ellie.

Which makes us all laugh as, hair blowing around our faces and hands surfing the warm winds, we continue towards the top of the world.

*

Perched at the top of the hill, and more than a thousand years old, Raven Castle might not look like something out of Disney movie, but with its huge turrets and drawbridge, it's still almost as impressive. Ellie doesn't look disappointed, either. With our tickets in our hands, I watch her – wide-eyed with wonder as she charges ahead through the turnstiles – remembering my own and Josie's reactions when we first came here. I couldn't believe the castle was real.

'So Danny wants us to move in together,' says Naomi as we follow Ellie into the Tudor courtyard; it's exactly the same as I remember it.

'That's great,' I react, as one does to good news, then sense something's wrong. 'Isn't it?'

She sighs, then bites her lip and frowns. 'I don't know.'

'But you said you wanted him to show more commitment.'

'I do. I did. It's just . . .'

Normally so articulate, she breaks off and shoves her hands deep in the pockets of her dungarees, as if she might find the right words in there.

'So what did you say?'

'I said I wasn't sure; that I had Ellie to consider and it was a big step . . . Of course Danny completely took it the wrong way and saw it as a rejection, and it turned into this great big row.'

We climb the stone steps that lead into the grand dining hall. A huge barrel-vaulted roof soars above us like a cathedral. We crick our necks and gaze upwards.

'Mummy, look!' Ellie points to two members of staff dressed in suits of armour. Several children are gathered around, as they do some kind of show-and-tell. We walk over to join them.

'*Are* you rejecting him?' I keep my voice low.

'No!' Naomi hisses.

Barely able to contain herself with excitement, Ellie pushes her way to the front. We stand with the rest of the adults and watch the poor souls sweating in their heavy costumes as they re-enact one of the sieges.

But I can't have looked convinced by Naomi's denial, as a few moments later she leans in. 'Danny said I didn't let him in. And OK, I admit there's probably some truth in that,' she confesses, looking guilty. 'But I've done everything by myself for so long. It was always just me; and then it was me and Ellie. I've had to be independent, to not need anyone, to put up the barriers and go it alone.'

'But you're not alone any more.'

'I know. But in my head, I don't know how *not* to be.'

She turns to me with an anguished expression and I look at my wise, brave friend and think how hard relationships can be to navigate as we get older. Not only the ones we have with our partners; but the ones we have with our friends and parents and siblings. Or is it us that makes them harder, with our layers of stuff that we accumulate? Like old clothes that we haven't worn for years and no longer have any use for, but which we drag around with us in heavy suitcases.

The boyfriend who dumped you, the dad who criticized you, the kids at school who bullied you, the mum who abandoned you – all the ghosts of our pasts. The memories. The traumas. The triggers. Those feelings weigh heavy, and we pack them away out of sight, but never truly out of mind; they're always with us, wherever we go and whomever we meet. If only we could clear out those emotional suitcases, like we clear out our wardrobes. Get rid of all that stuff that doesn't fit us any more. Make space for the exciting new things in the future.

'Danny loves you,' I say simply.

'And I love him,' she shrugs. 'But I don't know how to need someone without feeling needy.'

'Talk to him.'

'I've tried.'

'Keep trying,' I urge. 'Maybe if David and I had talked more, instead of assuming we both knew what each other was thinking . . .'

Naomi's face falls. 'Oh God, I'm sorry. I'm being tactless. Going on about Danny.'

'Don't be silly. I want you to tell me. Though I'm not being very helpful.'

'You are. Just by listening.'

'Well, I'm not sure you should be asking a divorced woman for advice about relationships,' I shrug, with a smile. 'Though I have learned you can only be in a relationship with someone who really wants to *be* in that relationship.'

She's studying me, her dark eyes serious.

'And it sounds to me like Danny really wants to be in your relationship.'

Naomi smiles gratefully, then glances around her. 'So you used to come here with your sister?'

'Yes, all the time.' My eyes dart around the familiar surroundings. 'But it's the first time I've been back since we were kids.'

'It must bring back some memories.'

I nod, casting my mind back. 'We used to play hide-and-seek here. We'd catch the bus and sneak in. Josie always used to win. She'd go down the stairs that were roped off and hide in the dungeon. I could never find her, because I'd be too scared to look there. I remember once walking around crying, thinking I'd lost her forever—' I break off, feeling a lump in my throat.

Naomi brushes my arm. 'You OK?'

'Yeah.' I force a smile. 'Big sisters, huh?'

'I wouldn't know – I'm an only child. Which is why I worry sometimes about Ellie having just me.'

Her face turns serious and we both glance over to where Ellie's still huddled with a group of children.

'Though perhaps I should worry more about the fact that she's utterly transfixed by those knights in shining armour,' she adds with a rueful smile.

'Don't burst her bubble yet,' I say and we both start laughing. Because sometimes, when you can't solve things, that's all you can do.

Courage

From a distance they look such a part of the countryside setting, it's like gazing upon a Constable painting. The old man with his flat cap, sitting outside the village pub with his pint, while next to him his old dog lies on the cobbles, basking in the late-afternoon sunshine. Heading up the high street, on my way to collect Harry from Valentine's, I look at the pair silhouetted against the golden backdrop of the Dales. It's only as I draw closer that I realize this picture of contentment *is* Valentine and Harry.

I feel a beat of surprise. Since moving here, this is the first time I've seen Valentine out in the village. When he isn't visiting Gisele, he seems to confine himself to his house.

'Fancy seeing you here!'

Valentine looks up when he sees me, as if caught doing something he shouldn't, while Harry lifts his head and gives a few lazy thumps of his tail.

'It was too nice a day to stop in. I thought I'd take Harry out for a breath of fresh air while you were at the castle.' He looks over my shoulder. 'Where are your friends?'

'They've gone back to the house so Ellie can have a nap. She's only seven – she gets tired.' I sit down across from Harry on the wooden bench.

'Don't we all. I thought I'd sit here and rest my legs for a bit.'

'I didn't know you liked a pint.' I smile and gesture to his half-empty glass. 'I thought tea was more your thing.'

'First one I've had in years.' Wrapping his fingers around it, he takes a swig. 'No fun drinking on your own. But it's different with Harry.'

He smiles then, and we both look at Harry dozing next to us. I feel pleased that Valentine found the courage to get out of the house and come to the pub.

'How do, Valentine.'

We both look up to see a broad-shouldered man with an impressive handlebar moustache. I recognize him as the pub landlord, from my disastrous date with Ajay.

'Nice day for it.' He begins cleaning up glasses around us. The good weather has brought a rush of day-trippers and the village has been busy. 'Not seen you for a long time.'

I feel Valentine stiffen, and he nods and mumbles something.

'We've missed you at quiz night.'

'You have a quiz?' My ears prick up. If it's one thing I love, it's a pub quiz. Some of the teachers at the comprehensive formed a team and we used to take part in a weekly quiz at the local pub near the school. We had so much fun. Though once I made the mistake of taking David along and he was so competitive that he demanded a recount when an opposing team won. 'When is it?'

The landlord points to the poster on the door.

'Every Sunday. Seven thirty sharp,' he says in his deep baritone voice. 'Valentine and Gisele used to be a winning team.'

I glance sideways at Valentine, worried that might have upset him, but he nods proudly. 'We were that.'

The landlord pauses by our table, his hands full of glasses. 'We're all sorry to hear she's not been so well.' His voice is gruff, but matter-of-fact, and I'm reminded of my grandparents and how they used to show their concern without making a fuss, in the way Yorkshire folk do. 'Make sure to send her our love, won't you?'

'Aye, I will.' Valentine gives a brief dip of his head, but I can tell he's touched.

Satisfied, the landlord nods to himself.

And how in a world that is constantly talking, tweeting, liking and posting, such a brief exchange between these two men conveys so much.

'Think on – about that quiz.' He pauses in the doorway of the pub. 'It would be good to have you back.'

As he disappears inside, I look across at Valentine.

'We should get a team together.' As I suggest it, I'm fully expecting to have to persuade him. So I'm surprised when he drains the rest of his pint and sets the glass back on the table.

'Aye, you're right, lass. Who do you know that's good at sport?'

Easter weekend is spent hanging out with Naomi and Ellie: exploring the village, playing board games, watching films and making numerous trips to the tiny hole-in-the-wall fish-and-chip shop next to the pub.

'I'm so sorry about not having a kitchen,' I apologize for the umpteenth time, as we unwrap the vinegary newspaper and sit in a patch of dappled sunlight in the garden to eat from our knees.

'Stop saying "Sorry". Ellie's in heaven, aren't you, Ellie?' admonishes Naomi, to which Ellie, covered in ketchup, nods happily and declares that chips are her favourite food.

We talk about anything and everything, as old friends do, picking up and putting down threads of conversation as if we're browsing through racks of clothes in a shop. We unfold topics like sweaters, trying some on and turning

183

this way and that in the mirror – my need for a haircut, that new show on Netflix, random school gossip, the state of the world, the state of our necks – while discarding others, like my ex David, who was quickly picked up and put down, a sweater that *definitely* doesn't suit me.

At some point one evening, after several glasses of wine, Naomi gets all determined to find me a new man and suggests doing some 'Boyfriend shopping', and so I play along and we scroll through various dating apps, 'just to see'. After all, I met David online. Only it all looks a bit different now that I'm older, and so do the men. But then so do I, even with Naomi's magic phone filter. Which is depressing and funny all at the same time, as things always are, when accompanied by a bottle of something dry and white and your oldest friend.

My garden also gets a makeover. Naomi is as good as her word and attacks the brambles with gusto, while, under her watchful eye, I make a start on the weeding, and together we fill endless wheelbarrows until our backs beg us to stop. She also bravely helps me clear out the shed, which turns out not only to contain so many spiders that I nearly die of arachnophobia, but to be a treasure trove from the past.

We unearth several dusty boxes of original Victorian glazed tiles; rolls of hand-painted wallpaper, carefully stored in a trunk and in perfect condition; half a dozen lovely old paintings; antique mirrors with their original mercury glass; and a couple of Art Deco lamps with kaleidoscope-glass shades wrapped in hessian. It's a miracle they're not chipped.

'All they need is rewiring and bulbs,' Naomi says, giving them a wipe-down, 'and they'll be as good as new.'

Excitement flickers. I haven't been able to see beyond all the building work, but now I glimpse the light at the end of the tunnel – no pun intended – and the fun part of decorating the rooms with lamps and rugs, hanging pictures and choosing paint colours.

'Damn! This one has a crack.' I point to the hairline fracture in the tip of one of the shades.

'That's where the light gets in,' Naomi grins. 'It's the imperfections that give something its character.'

And I smile too, because I know she's not just talking about the lamps.

With the rise in temperatures, spring seems to appear overnight in an explosion of colour. Roadsides and river banks are transformed by golden daffodils, woods are filled with a magical carpet of bluebells, and the village is awoken like Sleeping Beauty rousing from her slumbers, after winter had cast its spell.

Meanwhile I'm now woken by the dawn chorus and find myself rising early. When I lived in London I noticed the change in seasons by the clothes in the high-street windows, but here I feel like part of nature itself. Despite sleeping less, I feel more energized than I have done in months, as if it's not merely the countryside that's bursting into life.

Harry can feel it too. On our walks he has an extra spring in his step and seems to be able to walk that little bit further, his nose tipped towards the unmistakable smell of wild garlic, and his ears cocked for the distinctive whistling sound of the swooping curlews that the Brontës used to write about.

On Monday, Naomi and Ellie accompany me and Harry on a walk down to the river. They're due to catch the train back to London later that afternoon and Naomi is keen for 'a last blast of nature'.

'So do you miss it? London, I mean?' she's asking now, as we walk along the footpath so Ellie can see the sheep and cows grazing in the neighbouring fields.

'I miss the green curry with tofu from our local Thai restaurant,' I confess. 'And my favourite bookshop in Marylebone – I used to drop by for five minutes when I was in town and end up losing all track of time . . .' My mind scrolls back. 'And I loved cycling through the parks.'

'You could cycle here.'

'True,' I nod, 'but have you seen the hills? I'd need thighs of steel.'

She laughs.

'You know I used to take London for granted – all the restaurants and bars and cafes and shops; getting last-minute tickets for the theatre or a concert; grabbing a pint of milk at nine o'clock on a Sunday evening; jumping in a cab; *sushi* by Deliveroo.' I smile as I reel off the longlist. 'There's always something open. Something happening. When I came here it seemed so quiet and sleepy, it was a shock. Plus it didn't help that it was the middle of winter. It was like everyone was hibernating.'

'That's what we used to do when I was growing up in Scotland,' Naomi nods. 'It was so cold and dark in winter . . .' She gives a little shiver, remembering. 'Beautiful, though.'

'Well, that's the thing.' I nod. 'It's forced me to slow down, to stop rushing about, to look and listen. To really notice things. And I've realized that actually the countryside is far more alive and invigorating than any city. I mean, just look at that landscape.' I gesture across the sweeping valley. 'It's much grander than any of London's skyline.'

We both pause for a few moments to stare at it, before climbing over the stile and descending the grassy bank to where the river deepens and widens, forming a small pebbly beach. Immediately Ellie runs onto it gleefully, followed with a little agility by Harry.

'What a gorgeous spot.'

'Josie and I used to swim here in the summer. Well, Josie did. I used to paddle,' I add as an afterthought.

'You were ahead of the times – wild swimming's all the rage now.'

'Wild swimming, what's that?'

'Don't you look at Instagram?' she laughs, and I frown.

'I deleted all my apps, remember? So I wasn't tempted to look at photos of David's new girlfriend.' Squatting down, I pick up a pebble, rubbing my thumb along its smooth edges. 'She's a yoga teacher. Can you imagine? It would be like self-harming.'

'They call that a social-media detox.'

'I call it a means of a survival.'

'*Self-care*,' she corrects firmly. 'You're practising self-care.'

'Self-care,' I repeat, skimming the pebble into the river. It makes a splash as it hits the surface – once, twice – then disappears.

'Anyway, it basically means swimming outdoors in natural places – you know, like rivers, lakes, the sea . . . I've been a few times with Danny; it's supposed to be a really good way to de-stress, and great for the metabolism—' She breaks off and her face lights up. 'We should go wild swimming here.'

'*Here?* But it's still only April – the water will be freezing.'

'That's why it's so invigorating.'

'And we don't have any swimming costumes.'

'That's another reason why it's wild.' Naomi flashes her wide, white smile.

'What? You mean . . . *naked*?'

'Well, you can keep your underwear on, if you're prudish.'

'I'm not prudish,' I rebuke, while at the same time feeling less than enthusiastic about getting my naked body out into the open. 'But what if someone sees us?'

187

'You said it yourself: this is a little hidden spot, and no one ever comes down here.' Putting down her backpack, she sits on the grass and starts pulling off her trainers and socks. 'Come on.'

'What? Now?' I look around, somewhat alarmed.

'Why not? No time like the present.' She looks across at Ellie, who's playing with Harry on the small stretch of pebble beach alongside the banks of the river. 'What do you say, Ellie?'

Without further ado, Naomi strips off and jumps in, accompanied by Ellie, who is as daring as her mother. Barking gleefully at this sudden exciting turn of events, Harry needs no persuasion and follows them.

'It's not bad, once you get in – it's really refreshing,' Naomi calls out, to the sound of shrieks of laughter and splashing.

I take off my clothes but keep on my underwear, then hesitate on the river bank. Memories of being a child, and of Josie jumping straight in the deep bit while I would remain paddling sensibly in the rockpools, flood back. I remember saying I was fine, I didn't want to swim; but now, looking back, I wonder if I mixed up being sensible with being scared.

I strip off naked and jump in.

My breath feels like it's being sucked out of my body. *It is freezing.*

'Yay, you're in!' grins Naomi, as I swim, splashing and gasping, towards her. 'Isn't it fab?'

I can't answer, as my voice seems to have disappeared along with my breath, but as I start to splash around I feel the strangest of sensations. My body begins to rapidly acclimatize, the shock quickly disappears and I'm suddenly filled with exhilaration at how amazing it feels to be swimming around in nature, surrounded by nothing but blue skies and green fields. And it strikes me that while I might have moved physically, it's as if I've still been stuck in my emotions, unable to move forward properly.

'Woo-hoo.' Splashing around with Naomi and Ellie and Harry, I whoop and laugh. Because now I suddenly feel free.

After about fifteen minutes Naomi reluctantly reminds us of the train they have to catch back to London and swims to the river bank with Ellie, to dry off and get dressed. Further upstream, I take a few more minutes and am just about to start clambering out across the slippery rocks when a figure suddenly happens upon us.

'I thought I heard a commotion.'

He's immediately recognizable in his flannel shirt and jeans. Ben. What's he doing here? I plunge back into the water.

'Oh, hi.' I try to wave casually, only I probably look like I'm drowning, as he hurries off the footpath and down to the bank.

'Livvie! You all right?'

'Yes, fine,' I bluster, trying to remain fully submerged while willing him to stay back. 'I'm wild swimming.'

'I can see that,' he says, and his face splits into a wide grin.

Despite the freezing-cold waters, I feel my cheeks flame. Until now I didn't realize boobs floated. It must be the natural buoyancy. 'These are my friends.' Trying to strap my boobs down, by folding my arms while frantically doing doggy-paddle, is not an easy manoeuvre. I motion towards Naomi and Ellie, who are along the bank and now fully dressed. They both smile and say their hellos.

'Ben's my builder. He put up your tent.' I continue with the introductions as if I'm at a cocktail party in Mayfair, not naked in a freezing-cold river in the Yorkshire Dales.

There follows a flurry of thank-yous and a discussion

of bell-tents versus yurts, which I'm sure is all very interesting, but I've been in the river so long I can no longer feel my legs.

'Well, I'd best be off. Just heading up to see the farmer about a quote for converting a barn.'

'Super!'

My teeth are beginning to chatter and I'm physically numb from the neck down. I say physically, because emotionally I am completely and utterly mortified.

'Bye then, see you tomorrow.' He waves. 'And safe travels,' he adds to Naomi and Ellie, before giving Harry a rub around his ears and heading off up the fields.

As soon as he's out of earshot, Naomi turns to me, goggle-eyed.

'You never told me about Bob the Builder!' she hisses.

'It's Ben,' I correct, relieved to be able to finally get out of the river. My legs are dead weights, and Naomi has to give me a hand as I stumble onto the pebbly beach.

'Now I know why you don't miss London. And to think I fell for all that stuff about dramatic landscapes,' she snorts, as I dive onto my clothes.

'He's married,' I cry, fumbling at my underwear with numb fingers, 'and even if he wasn't, I would not be interested, trust me.'

She makes a little noise in her throat and nods her head in that infuriating way Naomi has of pretending to agree, when really she doesn't. Quickly pulling on the rest of my clothes, I put Harry on the lead and we start to walk back to the house. For a few minutes nobody says anything, and I relish the feeling of the warmth returning to my limbs. Naomi walks beside me as Ellie runs ahead. I can feel Naomi looking at me but steadfastly ignore her, until finally she can't bear it any longer and elbows me in the ribs.

'Still – now I know what you mean about the scenery.'

And flashing me that wide Naomi grin that never failed to set me off in the staffroom, we both burst out laughing.

STAGE 4

Hang in There

Hey you,

So you'll never believe it: I went wild swimming in the river! Yes, me! The scaredy mouse who would never go further than her ankles. And you were right all along – it was freezing, but truly amazing. I wish I'd found the courage years ago; still, now I've found it, I'm not planning on letting it go. I remember once reading about the difference between courage and bravery: being brave is having no fear, but having courage is doing something despite being afraid. And I've decided that courage is a lot like swimming; you've just got to practise it.

Something else you're not going to believe. Ben Armstrong is my builder. Yes. *That* Ben Armstrong. He's changed a lot. Married with a little boy now, called Stanley, and owns a building firm. A really successful one too, by all accounts. I've hired his firm to renovate the cottage – but, oh my, I had no idea what it's like living with builders.

The renovation is coming along, though we've had to alter a few things, as some of the original plans weren't passed. At first I was disappointed, but now you know what? I'm actually pleased. My friend Valentine is always saying you never want to erase the past, and it's made me look again at what I saw as negatives and view them as positives. To stop beating myself up about its imperfections, and celebrate them. A bit like life, I suppose.

What I need now, though, is someone with an artistic eye. I wish you were here to give advice. You're so amazing at all that. I need help on the colours. When I first moved in, it was so dark I wanted to paint it all white, but now I've completely changed my mind and want colours and prints and fabrics. What do you think of Hippo Pink? Isn't that a great name for a paint? Or what about Silhouette for the skirting boards?

OK, I'm getting carried away. It'll be weeks until I get to that stage. It's currently a building site! Still, you know me: I like to be organized. ☺

Miss you. x

Sleeping Arrangements

He snores. And he farts. And he kicks me when he dreams. Quite hard sometimes. I've even got a few bruises. He takes up all the bed, so I wake up to find I'm teetering on the edge. He tosses and turns all night long. I don't get a wink of sleep and wake up feeling exhausted.

I swear it's like being married.

'Right, that's it.'

After yet another sleepless night, I prop myself up groggily against my pillows and eye Harry sternly.

'Something's gotta give.'

Stretched out full-length across the duvet, Harry briefly raises his head and looks at me drowsily, before letting out a huge yawn and flopping back down again to fall straight back to sleep.

After dropping Harry at Valentine's, I drive into town, ten miles away, the plan being to buy Harry a new basket – one he'll hopefully sleep in, rather than eat. We've been living together for several months now and it's time to stop making allowances and feeling guilty about telling him off. I need to start being firm and laying down some proper ground rules, otherwise I'm never going to get another wink of sleep.

On arrival, I discover it's market day and people are out in droves. May has brought with it some warmer temperatures, and the high street is busy with stalls selling an array of locally made things: hand-carved wooden bowls, wool blankets from the neighbouring mills, soy-wax candles and divine-smelling soaps, plus the most gorgeous sheepskin rugs, in all shapes and sizes. I decide to buy one for Harry. They're so big and warm and fluffy – this will be a perfect alternative for him. Much nicer than a basket. He couldn't possibly *not* want to sleep on it.

Talking of sleep, I'm about to head back home when I pass a bed shop on the high street. It's the window display that catches my eye; pride of place is one of those gorgeous French beds you just want to sink into, with plumped-up pillows and crisp white linens. Staring at it, I think about my own bed. It's the one I shared with my ex-husband. We bought it when we first moved in together, a big wrought-iron thing that cost a fortune from an antiques shop and weighed an absolute ton. David loved it, but it was never really my style. Plus the mattress must be at least ten years old.

That said, it came with a lifetime guarantee. Being practical about it, there's nothing wrong with it. I turn away from the window. But psychologically and emotionally, everything is wrong with it. Pushing the door, I walk inside. Harry isn't the only one who needs a new bed.

Derek, the salesperson – or 'sleep consultant', as he introduces himself – quickly swoops upon me and I spend the next half an hour choosing a bed frame and trying out mattresses.

'Have you thought about a Tempur-Pedic?' he's asking me now, eyebrows raised, as – in true Goldilocks style – I discount the orthopaedic ones for being too hard, the double-pocket sprung ones for being too soft, and the Vispring for being too expensive. 'They're very popular. How about a test drive?'

A few moments later I'm flat on my back again, wriggling around under his watchful gaze as I try to stimulate sleeping.

It's actually the most bizarre thing buying a mattress: trying to re-create a very private act in a public showroom, while other shoppers mill about, rolling around on mattresses next to me. Earlier, I even spotted a couple spooning.

'Are you a side-sleeper?' Derek stands watching me, clipboard in hand, ticking off boxes.

'Hmm, sometimes.'

'Or do you like to sleep on your back?'

'No, my stomach,' I muffle, rolling over.

'And your partner?'

Face down, I feel suddenly uncomfortable – and it's not the mattress. The last few months have been spent rebuilding my life, getting used to being on my own, and now it suddenly hits home again.

'Is he or she a front-sleeper too?'

'Actually he tends to sleep at the foot of the bed,' I reply, swallowing down the lump in my throat and thinking about Harry, which makes me smile.

There's a pause, and I sense Derek is confused by an answer that is not in a box he can tick.

'Right, well, if you want to see how you feel, I'll be back in a few moments.'

I turn my head sideways to see him attend to a young couple, their arms wrapped lovingly around each other: much less confusing. I'm sure they tick all the boxes.

I lie still. In truth, this one's really quite comfortable. Closing my eyes, I spread my arms and legs out, starfish-wide, imagining that I'm asleep and Harry's snoring next to me on his new sheepskin rug. Wait a minute. *Someone is snoring next to me.*

I snap open my eyes and get quite a surprise. Ajay is standing next to the bed, an amused expression on his face.

'Sorry, I couldn't resist.'

'What are you doing here?' I sit up quickly and get a sudden rush of blood to the head.

He rubs his chin, pretending to think for a minute. 'Hmm, buying a bed?'

I suppose I did ask for that.

'I'm joking.' He smiles, and I'm reminded of what a lovely smile he has. 'I saw you in the window, when I was walking past to get a sandwich for lunch. Quite some window display.'

I feel my cheeks colour. God, this is awkward. It's a couple of months since our disaster of a date and my promise to call Ajay back.

'Look, about that drink – I know I said I was going to call.'

He puts up a hand and shakes his head. 'You don't have to explain.'

I smile gratefully, relieved he's being so nice about it. 'Thanks,' I say, only now I feel bad. I should have called back. How many times did I berate men for not doing that, when I was younger?

Yet, in reality, what could I have said? I didn't want to lie – I've been lied to and it sucks, as Maya would say, but that left only the truth. And the truth is that once I'd got over my hang-up about our age gap, I hadn't expected to like Ajay as much as I did; that he was interesting, and interested in me; that he was far too handsome and I was intimidated; that I was flattered and vaguely embarrassed, and still suffering the aftershocks of my divorce, when I would be fine and trundling along and then, every once in a while, I would catch myself and my situation and think: how could it be that everything I knew was gone, and I'm single and starting over?

Exactly.

Just the kind of fun, flirty phone call that a man wants to have after a first date. Ajay would have hung up and run a mile, and I wouldn't have blamed him. And so it was decided: it was all too scary and too uncertain; I don't like uncertainty, it makes me anxious. And Ajay brought with him a whole bunch of uncertainty.

'So, did you make a decision?'

We're interrupted by the salesman who, having finished with the other couple, circles back.

'Yes, I think so.' I nod, and Ajay gives me a look.

'Well, I'll leave to you it. I just wanted to say hi.' He takes his hands out of his trouser pockets and gives me a little wave. 'And bye.'

'Bye,' I nod, raising a hand.

'OK, wonderful. Well, if you'd like to follow me to the payment point, we can start taking all your details . . .'

The salesman is talking and leading me away and I follow him, only now I feel all discombobulated. Because I had certainty, didn't I? I got married, we made promises to each other, and I thought it was forever. I watch Ajay leave the shop and disappear down the high street. Only it turned out that love – unlike mattresses – doesn't come with a lifetime guarantee.

Stanley

'Come on, son, time for school.'

'I don't want to go.'

Friday morning, and Stanley was sitting on the edge of his bed, staring down at his new school shoes. He'd grown out of the old ones, and last night it had taken him ages to thread his laces. He wanted them to go straight across – that was very important – and also quite hard, as the laces had to end up equal lengths and they never did. It meant doing it lots of times until you got it right.

Tricky, that's what his mum had called it. Stanley liked that word. Much better than the words his dad used. His dad got impatient and swore a lot, and said what was wrong with laces being criss-crossed? Laces were always criss-crossed.

But Stanley knew that wasn't true, as he'd seen them laced in a shop when his mum had taken him to buy the last pair. The laces definitely went straight across. He remembered the sales assistant threading them through. It had been fascinating. He'd watched her carefully, committing it to memory. Which was lucky, as this time he didn't go into a shop. Instead they ordered his shoes from a website on the computer and, when they arrived, all black and shiny in the box, they weren't laced up and there wasn't a nice assistant called Fatima to do it for him.

So he did it himself. After his dad sent him to bed with the criss-crossed laces, he'd got out his torch. Patiently doing it again and again until he got it right. Because it was very important that he made the new pair like the old pair. They had to be the same. Everything had to be the same.

Even when it wasn't.

'I've got to work, even if I don't want to go,' his dad was saying now.

Stanley raised his eyes from his shoes. Above him, his dad was peering down at him, frowning. He had that deep line that went between his eyebrows, which he always had these days. Once when his dad had fallen asleep on the sofa watching telly, Stanley had run his finger across it and was surprised to realize it was a proper groove. Since then he often rubbed the bit between his own eyebrows with his thumb and wondered when he'd get one.

'Why don't you want to go to work?' asked Stanley, frowning and trying to copy his dad.

'Because sometimes I don't want to face the world.'

And now his dad was bobbing down next to him, and brushing the hair out of his face. His hands were rough, like sandpaper, but Stanley didn't say anything. He didn't like people touching him, but with his dad it was different.

'Look, Stan, it's going to get easier, I promise.'

Stanley chewed the inside of his lip and looked down again at his laces. They really were very straight. He'd even used a ruler.

'Can I come to work with you instead?'

'Yes, but not today.'

'I want to see Harry.'

When he'd learned that the house his dad was working on was where Harry lived, Stanley couldn't believe it. He learned a new word: *coincidence*.

'You'll see him after school, I'm sure.'

It was true. Every day after school Harry walked past with

his owner, and Stanley always made sure he was there, waiting for him. His owner probably thought it was also a *coincidence*, but Stanley knew it wasn't that at all. In which case, Stanley wasn't sure he believed in coincidences. He needed another word. Could you make up words? His teacher, Miss McCleary, would know, but that meant having to go to school to ask her.

'Do you promise?

His dad look thoughtful. 'If you promise to go to school, I'll promise to have a word with Harry. I'll lift up one of his big ears. Make him promise to pop round and see you after school.'

That made Stanley giggle. 'Dogs can't talk.'

'Says who?'

'I do.'

His dad was smiling now. 'Happen not, but they can listen, and that's more important.'

Stanley thought about that for a moment, twisting and turning it around in his mind, looking at it from different angles. He did that a lot with new ideas.

'Like people in heaven?'

His dad breathed in then and didn't exhale for five seconds. Stanley knew because he counted them. 'Exactly,' he nodded, then glanced down at Stanley's shoes and let out a low whistle. 'You did your laces! Well, aren't you a clever lad?'

Stanley felt a burst of pride.

'Now come on, let's go show them off.'

'OK,' he said and stood up from the bed.

Peeling Back the Layers

In my spare bedroom the radio is playing golden oldies in a futile attempt to drown out the noise of the building work downstairs. Valentine is hard at work up a ladder, armed with a scraper; I'm on the ground with a steamer.

Welcome to Operation Woodchip.

It had been Valentine's idea. Following my trip into town to buy a new bed, I went round to his bungalow to collect Harry, where I told him my plans to put my old bed in the spare bedroom.

'Problem is, it needs redecorating.'

'Well, why didn't you say?' he cried, his back straightening and his chest appearing to visibly inflate as he poured me a cup of Darjeeling. 'I was a painter and decorator for over sixty years. Fully booked, I was, months in advance. Nobody could hold a paintbrush to Valentine Crowther. My skirting boards were legendary.'

So, like a rock star coming out of retirement, he turned up yesterday with his ladders, which he informed me were 'aluminium and light as a feather' as I fussed around him. Though he did finally allow me to help with his paint pots and tool bag, grumbling incessantly as we carried them together up my narrow staircase.

'I've never needed any help before.'

'That may be, but we all need help at some point.'

'I can manage.'

'It's ten litres of paint.'

'And you a woman too,' he puffed, his breathing laboured.

'I didn't have you down as sexist, as well as stubborn.'

'It's not sexist – it's how it should be.'

'Since when did we time-travel back to the last century?'

'Gisele never carried anything. I did all the heavy lifting . . . Oof! Bloody hell.' Forced to rest on the step, he hung on to the bannister. 'That's heavy.'

'What did I tell you? It needs two of us.'

Which makes me think how it's not only a ten-litre pot of Dulux Trade that's too heavy for one person – it's so many things in life. So we managed it together, each holding the handle, shifting the weight between us. We all need to help sometimes; the hardest part is accepting it.

And so for the last two days we've been attacking the woodchip, a type of textured wallpaper that, in the past, was used to cover up a multitude of sins and is a complete nightmare to remove. The cottage is covered in it, and it's become my nemesis. Still, it has to come off before Valentine can start to work his magic with his paintbrushes. So we have a system. He uses the edge of the scraper to scour the paper, making a diamond pattern on the walls, while I follow with the steamer, holding it for a few seconds over the marks to let the steam penetrate. We started at the bottom, as the steam rises, and are working our way slowly upwards.

It's hard and messy work. Years of wallpaper and wood-chip, and coats of nicotine-stained paint. Slowly we chip away at the layers, peeling them back, revealing what's under-neath. And we talk.

'So how did you and Gisele meet?' I'm asking him now, aiming the steamer at a particularly stubborn patch.

'At a dance at the Plaza,' he informs me from halfway up

the ladder. 'She was with her friend Betty. Took me ages to get up the courage. And then she said no.'

'She did not!'

Valentine nods and continues scraping at the woodchip. It floats down like confetti. 'So then I asked Betty.'

'Valentine!' I look shocked.

'Tactics.' He laughs and taps his nose. 'Of course, once she'd seen me jiving, Gisele couldn't refuse.'

I laugh then and put down the steamer. 'That's a good bit,' I point to a large piece of wallpaper that's bubbled up from the wall.

'I'll say.'

With a swift piece of professional wrist action, Valentine neatly slips his scraper underneath and a large piece peels off. It's hugely satisfying. Less satisfying is the state of the plaster underneath.

'My ex-husband preferred golf to dancing.'

'Hitting a little ball into a hole?' Valentine tuts and shakes his head. 'What's the point of that?'

'He'd probably say the same about dancing.'

'He doesn't know what he's missing.' Pushing his flat cap back from his forehead, Valentine wipes his brow and peers down at me. His face softens. 'And I'm not talking about the dancing.'

I bash his compliment away and return to blasting the walls with the steamer. Yesterday I'd told Valentine I was divorced. I didn't go into details – Valentine didn't want any. He wasn't interested in the whys and wherefores. 'That's just background noise,' he dismissed it with a shake of his head. 'I'm here to listen to the main act.'

'OK, that should do it.' I turn off the steamer.

'Once when we were courting, we went to Paris to go dancing,' he continues, chipping away at a stubborn layer of paint. 'We rode all the way there on my scooter.'

Honestly, this is fascinating. Is it my imagination, or was dating then so much more romantic than it is now? '*On a scooter?*'

'Well, there was no Eurostar in them days.'

Putting down his scraper, Valentine pulls out his wallet from his trouser pocket and slips out a small black-and-white photo he keeps inside. Climbing down a few rungs, he passes it to me. It's of a young couple on a Lambretta in front of the Arc de Triomphe. She's wearing a gingham dress nipped in at the waist and a headscarf, knotted under her chin; he's in a white shirt, sleeves rolled up at the elbows, and braces, with a thick quiff of dark hair.

'Is this you and Gisele?'

Valentine nods. 'Over sixty years ago. She was eighteen, I was nineteen.'

I turn it to the light to examine it. 'Look at your hair. And her waist. It's so tiny!

'I used to be able to get my hand right round it when we were jiving.' He gives a little jig, and I grab the ladder as it sways.

'Be careful!' I cry, but he seems unconcerned.

'I remember we went to these underground cellar clubs playing jazz and bebop – nothing like we had here. It was like a different world . . . Saint-Germain.' He smiles at his terrible pronunciation. 'Gisele is French, of course, but I couldn't understand a word, although I didn't have to, as nobody was talking. We all just danced and danced till we couldn't catch our breath and our feet had blisters.'

Holding the legs of the ladder, I look up at Valentine; only he's not seventy-nine years old and in my spare bedroom peeling back woodchip; he's nineteen and in that club in Paris with Gisele, dancing up a storm.

'It was dawn when we finally left. The sun was coming

up over Notre-Dame.' As he turns to face me, his eyes are shining brightly.

'It's a lovely photo.'

'I wish I'd taken more. Now everyone takes so many photos. I see the young ones with their phones, snapping away.'

'Yes, but how many are they going to look at, sixty years later?'

I pass him back the photograph, and Valentine looks at it again.

'I never thought she'd agree to marry me, you know. We met and then I had to go away to do my National Service. I imagined she'd meet someone when I was gone, that she'd forget all about me.'

'But she didn't,' I prompt.

'No, she didn't,' he nods, slipping the photograph back into his wallet. 'Not then, at least.'

His face falls and I feel my heart ache for him. He's so sad and trying so hard to be brave. He goes to pick up his scraper and we both turn back to the job at hand when 'Shake, Rattle and Roll' starts playing on the radio. Valentine starts to whistle to himself.

'You should teach me.'

'What? Painting and decorating?'

'No,' I laugh. 'How to jive.'

'Oh, I'm long past that now.'

'Rubbish! Look at you, up and down that ladder.'

But he shakes his head. 'Nay, I'm not as fit as I used to be.'

Ignoring him, I reach over to the radio and turn up the volume. Bill Haley and His Comets blast out. 'How does it go?'

Valentine hesitates, but the pull of the music is too much and he puts down his scraper and descends the ladder.

'You know I learned to dance with a chair.'

'You did not!'

'I did that, as there weren't enough girls to go round. Me and Brian Hattersley had lessons every Sunday – I'll never forget it.'

'Well, I'm not a chair at least,' I say and he laughs.

'Right, well, I'm a bit out of practice, but you put your arm here, like this, and you just follow me.'

Sliding his arm around me, he starts stepping from side to side, with unexpectedly deft footwork. Harry watches us suspiciously from the corner, where he's curled up on a pile of old dustsheets.

The music is infectious and I try to follow Valentine, being careful not to trip over the decorator's sheet spread out across the floorboards.

'There, look, you're getting it.'

We sidestep together, Valentine's hips seeming to loosen up as he sways to the music.

'And now for the twirl,' he instructs, spinning me around. I laugh and stumble backwards, but he catches me with surprising strength, and for the first time I see the man he used to be, before he was diminished by age and grief and guilt.

'Now, see, this was the part where I'd spin you over my shoulder,' he jokes. At least I hope he's joking.

'I think we might draw the line at that, Valentine,' I protest as the song comes to an end and I realize I'm quite out of breath. 'This isn't *Strictly*.'

'Oh, that used to be mine and Gisele's favourite.'

Wiping his brow with a handkerchief, he props himself against the rung of the ladder to rest his legs.

'Mine too,' I grin, 'but my ex refused to watch it.'

'Well, that's enough reason for a divorce right there,' he smiles, and I can't help but smile too.

'How about this year we watch it together?' I suggest.

Valentine nods. 'I'd like that.'

We take a break to eat lunch and get our breath back, before Valentine climbs back up the ladder and I pick up the steamer. The last few feet of woodchip come off like a dream and we're left with bare, naked walls. And a day that I'll look back on forever as one of the most fun I've had in years.

Because it's only later that night, when I'm lying in bed, that it strikes me that the best times in life are never those special dates you circle in your calendar. It's a random, nameless day spent stripping woodchip with my seventy-nine-year-old neighbour, when I learned to jive and he learned to let go – just for a little while – and, more and more, the future seemed to hold something for us both to look forward to.

Regret

Everyone knows that regretting things is a complete waste of time. The legendary Edith Piaf famously sang 'Je ne regrette rien' and, as a woman who suffered many personal tragedies, she certainly knew what she was talking about.

Alas, I am not Edith Piaf, and I regret a lot.

No one ever mentions it when they talk about the stages you go through after a great loss, but it seems to me that regret is always to be found lurking at the end of any relationship, piping up with its 'woulda, coulda, shoulda', taking you on a journey down a road of reflection, playing the blame game.

Regret is heartbreak's unhelpful friend. They go hand-in-hand, like a comedy duo, only no one is laughing. Least of all me.

When my marriage fell apart, my regrets would keep me awake at night. I'd lie in the darkness, forensically running over old conversations, looking for clues and signs that I must have missed. Examining all the decisions taken and mistakes made. Second-guessing and doubting myself. Playing the blame game, and losing every time. It was a nightly ritual. As soon as I closed my eyes, the grim autopsy would begin.

Now I fall asleep as soon as my head hits the pillow. I don't know if it's all the fresh air and exercise, because when I'm not walking Harry, I'm pushing a wheelbarrow between my freshly dug raised beds, discovering muscles and a joy in gardening that I never knew I had. Or whether it's because deep in the Dales there are no street lamps or car alarms or planes flying overhead, to keep me awake. On a clear night here there's just the planets and the constellations twinkling above me in the vast, dark skies and the hoot of the owl that lives in the graveyard.

That, or Harry snoring.

Unlike me, Harry has no regrets to keep him awake at night. Harry is a walking, limping, barking affirmation. *Live in the moment! Today is a new day! Don't look back!* Harry never looks back (unless it's for a squirrel). He's *carpe diem* in canine form, and I love him all the more for it. He's not brooding about the time he threw up in the back of my rental car, or worrying I'm still upset about him chewing my Gucci handbag. He's out there digging a hole in the garden and having the best time of his life.

Sometimes, when I'm having a bad day, I look at him and can't help but feel inspired. And amazed that I'm the age that I am and it's taken a scruffy old dog to teach me lessons I should have learned years ago. To teach me how to be human. Because while I don't believe the scars of his mistreatment and abandonment will ever completely disappear, he's not dwelling on the past; he's all about living in the present. I don't know who came up with the phrase 'dumb animals' because, from where I'm standing, they're the smart ones. They've been practising mindfulness long before it became a buzzword.

So I've decided: from now on, I'm going to try my hardest to follow Harry's example and start living in the moment. To stop beating myself up with the endless 'what if's and 'if only's, and all the other regrets that haunt me.

And I'm going to start by calling Ajay.

The Village Idiots

'No-Brainers?'

There are groans around the table.

'I thought that was funny,' protests Ajay, reappearing from the bar with a round of drinks.

'Too corny,' Maya tuts dismissively. 'How about "Nettlewick's Got Talent"?'

'Only if I get to be Simon Cowell,' he laughs, putting down the drinks and crisps and sliding onto the stool next to me. 'You get the golden buzzer.' He winks and I feel myself blush.

Reaching for my pint of cider it suddenly comes to me. 'Hang on, I've got it! The "Not So Great Expectations"!'

I feel a beat of triumph. Though I say it myself, that's actually really good.

'Huh? I don't get it.'

Ripping open a packet of cheese-and-onion crisps, Maya wrinkles up her nose. It makes the stud in her nose twinkle.

'Charles Dickens!' I admonish, shooting her a look. She looks suitably sheepish, as she should for an English Literature A-level student.

'No, too literary.' Ajay shakes his head and takes a sip of his wine.

I glance across at him, rather miffed by his betrayal, and drink my cider.

We all fall silent.

*

It had been my idea to get a team together for the pub quiz. Ever since the landlord of the Crooked Billet had mentioned it at Easter, it had sounded like fun, and what better way to meet more people and get involved in the local community? Plus Valentine seemed energized by the project. Every time I walked past his window or dropped Harry off, he would appear from his bungalow with a leather-bound volume of the *British Encyclopedia* and reel off some fact or figure. I've never seen him so enthused.

'I bet you didn't know that, did you?' he would declare, before regaling me again with the story of how, when he and Gisele first married, they saved up each month and sent away for each illustrated volume until, over the course of several years, they had collected the complete set. 'Everything you'll ever want to know is in here,' he would say proudly. And I would say 'Wow!' and look impressed and resolve never to tell him about Wikipedia or Google.

Our only problem was our lack of team members. Normally never one to brag, Valentine threw his modesty out of the window and assured me that when it came to general know-ledge, he couldn't be beaten. 'One advantage of being an old bugger like me is I've lived through a fair amount of history and politics . . . and it's all up here,' he added, tapping his temple with his large forefinger. Valentine, I must mention, has the biggest hands I've ever seen. Literally the size of shovels. Apparently they're the reason for his boxing success when he was younger. 'I was never that good,' he admitted, 'it was just hard to miss my opponents.'

My speciality was literature, of course. But that still left music and sport. Luckily, when I mentioned it to Maya in our next lesson, she immediately volunteered to act as our expert in pop culture. 'Absolutely! Count me in!' Her exams are only a few weeks away and we've been making good progress.

Despite her initial reluctance, she's worked hard at her studies, though she's still determined not to go to university. The quiz would be welcome relief from both her revision and her parents for a few hours. Having recently passed her driving test, she'd even asked if she could borrow her mum's car.

With her mum being PC Neesha Sharma, this meant answering a few questions first – and confirming that no, I wasn't being used as an alibi so Maya could attend an illegal drug rave; and yes, she really was going to be spending the evening drinking Diet Coke and answering quiz questions with a bunch of old people and a flatulent dog – before Neesha was satisfied and lent Maya the Mini.

Which only left sport.

'I know it's not a traditional second date,' was how I phrased it to Ajay, when we were making arrangements to see each other again. Determined to let go of the past, I'd called him a few days after bumping into him in the bed shop. I was nervous of what his reaction might be, but I needn't have worried.

'Well, considering it was never a first date, I think we're OK,' he said, and I knew he was smiling on the other end of the phone. 'But does this mean you only want to see me because you know I'm massively into sport and can tell you which football team has won the Champions League the most?'

'That's not the only reason.' I smiled into my phone too. 'But it helps.'

'OK, great. I'll see you on Wednesday at seven. Oh and, Liv.'

'Yes?'

'The answer's Real Madrid, and they've won it thirteen times.'

*

216

So now here we all are, on Wednesday at seven. Actually it's nearly quarter past, as the last fifteen minutes have been spent trying to come up with a name for our team, and what started out as fun is now rapidly disintegrating into bruised egos and indecision. I hope this isn't a sign of things to come.

'We're the village idiots.' Valentine, who this whole time has been sitting in the corner sipping his pint and not saying anything, suddenly pipes up.

'Hey, who are you calling an idiot?' protests Ajay.

'It's the name of the team, you daft bugger. *The Village Idiots.*'

'It's tongue-in-cheek. *Obviously.*' Maya rolls her eyes at Ajay.

Valentine catches her eye and winks. She flashes him a grin and offers him her crisps. I watch them across the table. Despite the age gap, they share the same deadpan humour.

'OK, are we all agreed?' I ask. There's a nodding of heads. Picking up a pen, I write our team name across the sheet of paper. '"The Village Idiots" it is then.'

The landlord's son, a rather fierce figure in a Sex Pistols T-shirt, is going round selling raffle tickets. We buy several, more out of fear than for the cash prizes. The pub is packed; every table is filled with various teams, and there are even several people sitting up at the bar on stools.

I recognize a few familiar faces: Gary the postman, who kindly rings my doorbell and pops my mail inside on my windowsill to stop Harry ripping open the envelopes; the couple who run the local cafe and always let me have the table tucked away in the corner by the range, to tutor Maya; the local farmer and his wife, who always beams at me gratefully from the heated seats of her Honda Jazz. There's even Sheila from the post office. It's funny how quickly it's beginning to feel more and more like home here.

'Right then, teams, are you all ready for the first question?'

217

booms the landlord who, with his deep baritone, has no need for a microphone. Before he was married he used to sing with a leading national opera company in Leeds; local rumour has it that he once sang with Alfie Boe.

A hush descends over the chatter of the pub; I'm almost expecting the lights to go down and the thudding theme music of *Who Wants to Be a Millionaire?* to sound. Heads draw together, as teams confer with grave expressions. And there was I, thinking this was going to be a bit of light-hearted fun. Instead everyone is taking it very seriously.

On the table my phone beeps up a WhatsApp. Picking it up, I glance at the screen to see it's from Naomi.

'No mobile phones!' snarls the landlord and I almost drop mine. 'If I see a phone, you're out on your ear.'

Crikey. I quickly put it away without reading the message and glance across at Maya, who shoots me a rather scared look across the table. I see her smartphone in her hand, the illumination of her screen giving her away.

'I was only looking at TikTok,' she mutters as a disbelieving jury of locals throw her accusatory looks. I think that's the quickest I've ever seen her put her phone away.

As expected, Valentine excels in the general-knowledge round, while Ajay is an expert when it comes to sport. There are not many questions on literature, but still I'm relieved to know the answers. It's really quite nerve-racking. When Maya correctly answers a history question, Valentine tells her to keep her voice down.

'Ssshh! We don't want to be giving away the answers!' he hisses, looking over his shoulder to see if anyone's listening.

By half time we're all rather exhausted and grateful for the free food put on by the pub. It's like being in an exam, and not quite the fun event I had planned.

'Sorry – I had no idea,' I say to Ajay as we're handed free plates of Yorkshire pudding and gravy. 'I thought it would be a bit more relaxed.'

'It's cool,' he smiles and slips a hand onto my knee under the table.

I feel a prickle of anticipation. Earlier, when Ajay asked if he could stay the night at mine, so he could drink and not have to drive, I'd made it clear he'd have to sleep in the spare room.

'I like a bit of competition.'

'Oh, you do, do you?' I flirt back unashamedly.

Several drinks later and of course we both know he isn't going to be in the spare room. Like I said, I'm determined to throw caution to the wind and start living in the moment.

'In that case, they're the ones to watch out for,' interrupts Valentine, returning from the bar with a round of drinks and pointing to a table of three curly white heads, over by the dartboard. 'The Three Degrees.'

'Seriously?' Ajay looks intrigued and passes him his plate of food.

'Don't be fooled,' Valentine nods, lowering his voice. 'Gladys used to set the cryptic-crossword questions for the *Yorkshire Standard*, Janice was a local magistrate and Evelyn's a retired head teacher.'

All of us turn our heads to look over, at exactly the same time as they look at us. There's lots of nodding and raising of glasses in acknowledgement. I notice one of them is drinking a pint of Guinness. I watch her say something to her friends, then get up from her chair and come over.

'Valentine, how nice to see you back at the pub quiz.'

'Don't talk rubbish, Evelyn.'

She lets out a cackle of laughter. 'Aha, it's true – I'm horrified really.' She beams, evidently delighted. Evelyn, I notice, has quite a glint in her eye. 'This man here is one of my arch-rivals,' she informs the table, before turning back to him in his armchair and lowering her voice. 'Now, I'm not going to nag, but I know you got my cards and notes, because I delivered them myself.' Resting a hand on the arm of his armchair, she fixes him with a firm gaze that is a world away from the patronizing head tilts and sympathetic platitudes. 'And I know what it's like to be too proud to ask for help, as it was the same for me when my Charlie fell ill.'

They share a look. Valentine nods but doesn't say anything. He doesn't need to.

'But you know where I live, so I'll leave it at that.' Satisfied she's got the message across, Evelyn turns to the rest of us with an authoritative air. 'Now, may be the best man win.'

'Or woman,' I add and she registers me with approval.

'Wow – it's packed,' says Maya, returning from outside, where she'd gone to check her messages, away from the watchful eye of the landlord.

'I've never seen so many people,' I agree, watching Evelyn weaving her way back to her table.

'Well, it's one of the few places we can go these days; what with the village hall being closed, it's either this or the church,' says Valentine, catching my eye. I make a mental note to ask him more about Evelyn later.

'Why's it closed?' Ajay reaches for the salt.

'Council cuts. They said it cost too much to run and let it fall into disrepair. Now there's so much work needs doing to it. It needs a new roof, for starters, after last year's storm blew holes in it.'

'So does my cottage,' I groan.

'It's always a new roof.' Ajay shakes his head, along with the pepper.

'You should set up a crowdfunder,' suggests Maya.

Valentine frowns. 'What's that, when it's at home?

'It's a way of raising money on the Internet,' I explain. 'You ask for a small amount of money from a large amount of people.'

'What people?' Now Valentine looks really bewildered.

'All kinds of people,' shrugs Maya. 'People who live locally, friends of friends, strangers, businesses. People from all round the world.'

'You're telling me a complete stranger from the other side of the world would donate money to fix the roof on our village hall?'

Maya nods. 'If it goes viral, yeah.'

'Well, I never.' He shakes his head.

'That means if lots of people see it,' says Ajay helpfully, but Valentine tuts impatiently.

'I know what going viral means,' he says impatiently, turning back to his Yorkshire pudding. 'Why do you think I have my flu jab every year?'

The Three Degrees win, followed by Emergency Brexit. We come a respectable third. Our prize is a round of free drinks. As I'm collecting them from the bar, I spot Ben walking in. He doesn't notice me and goes straight to the other end of the bar. He orders a drink and I watch him talking to the girl serving him. He's being very friendly. Some might say flirty. The girl is laughing and flicking her hair. I look away and walk back to our table. It's none of my business.

'Fancy seeing you here.'

A few minutes later I glance up, to see Ben standing next to me. He's smiling and I get the sense this isn't his first pint.

'Ah, of course. The Quiz. I should've known – you always were brainy.'

He seems a little unsteady and his cheeks are flushed. He

rocks backwards slightly on his feet and his beer spills over his glass.

'Hi, Ben, how are you?'

He's drunk, and I feel a slight beat of concern.

'I think you've all met . . . Ajay, Valentine, oh, and this is Maya, one of my pupils.'

Ajay nods, while Valentine says, 'How do' and there's some small talk about plastering and painting. Maya, now reunited with her phone, smiles politely, then continues scrolling furiously. God only knows how many posts and likes she's missed during the hour it was turned off.

'I should have asked if you wanted to be on the team,' I continue brightly, trying to head off any potential awkwardness. Absently I wonder who Ben's come to the pub with or if he's on his own.

'Oh, no, I'm not clever enough.' He shakes his head dismissively. It seems to roll backwards on his shoulders. 'Make sure you study hard. You don't want to end up like me,' he warns Maya, laughing as he raises his pint to his lips.

No one else laughs, and I feel looks flying around us. I get a sense of other people in the bar glancing over. Wedged in behind the table, I resist the urge to get up and have a quiet word, make sure everything's OK. Like I say, it's none of my business. If Ben wants to go out and get drunk on a Wednesday night, he can. He's my builder, not my husband. I think about his wife. I wonder if they've had a row.

God, this is uncomfortable.

'Well, you look a bit busy, so I'll leave you to it.' Seeming to get the message finally, Ben raises his pint. 'See you tomorrow, Livvie.'

'Yeah, see you tomorrow, Ben.'

I feel a beat of relief, and watch as he stumbles away.

'Someone's going to have a sore head tomorrow,' jokes Ajay.

'Yes, you,' I snap, feeling unexpectedly protective towards Ben. Ajay looks hurt. And now I feel guilty. 'Sorry, I didn't mean it.' I reach for his hand and he interlaces his fingers through mine, but I still feel unnerved.

'It can't be easy for him,' mutters Valentine. 'His wife used to work behind the bar, before . . .' He trails off and doesn't get any further.

I turn to look at him. 'Before what?'

Valentine peers at me from underneath those shaggy grey eyebrows of his. 'Before the car accident.'

'Oh, I had no idea.' I glance over at Ben propping up the bar. 'Is she OK now?'

I turn back to Valentine, but when I see his expression I already know the answer.

'Ben's wife died a couple of years ago.'

The Morning After

Ajay stayed the night. Nothing happened, apart from a bit of hand-holding as we walked home together, and some drunken kissing on my doorstep. He barely made it up the stairs before he crashed out on my bed, still fully clothed – the result of drinking several large glasses of house red and a couple of celebratory whiskies for coming third in the quiz.

When I came out of the bathroom, where I'd gone to freshen up and steady my nerves, I found him face down and snoring. After all that build-up I should have been disappointed, but if I'm honest, I felt relieved. Not because I didn't find him attractive, because who wouldn't find Ajay attractive? Or because it was such a long time since I'd slept with anyone who wasn't my husband.

But because of Ben.

Hearing the news about his wife had completely thrown me. I felt shocked, upset and confused. He wore a wedding ring, and I'd assumed the woman I'd met was Stanley's mum. His wife. But now I didn't know what to think. On the way back from the pub, when I was supposed to be flirting with Ajay, I was thinking about Ben. Scrolling back through all our conversations, trying to remember what we'd talked about – what he'd said, what I'd said. Looking for clues, but not finding any.

How could I not have known? I kept asking myself. How could I have known? I kept telling myself.

Guilt gnawed at me. I thought back to when he'd first given me a lift home in his van; my dismay at seeing him again after all this time; all my preconceived ideas and prejudices against him. Born of what? Teenage hurt feelings and Ben's troubled past? I'd judged him and I'd been so very wrong. All this time I'd assumed his joking and his flippant remarks proved that he didn't take life seriously, when all along life couldn't have been more serious for him.

Let that be a lesson to you, Liv: who ever knows what's going on in someone else's life? And yet I'd been so quick to form opinions. I felt ashamed. And then I thought about Stanley, and my heart broke for him.

So not exactly the kind of lustful thoughts that should have been running through my head as I headed home with a gorgeous man who clearly intended to get me into bed. And yet the last few days had been spent looking forward to exactly this possibility. I'd dug out the expensive scented candles I'd been saving for a special occasion, swapped my comfy unflattering undies for the kind of lingerie you have to hand-wash, and had done some serious preparation with various body-scrubs and creams.

People always assume that if your husband has an affair and leaves you for a younger woman, he's 'not getting it at home', which is as glaringly sexist as it's so often untrue. David and I had a healthy sex life, whatever that is; it was the glue that kept us together. Even when we fought and didn't like each other very much, we were attracted to each other. In a way, it would have been easier if we hadn't been, as that would have made it simpler to understand. If he wasn't looking for sex, then what was he looking for? It was less straightforward, more complicated than that.

But then things always are, aren't they?

Ajay finding me attractive had made me feel good about myself again. My divorce had killed my libido, but now it stirred back into life. Which seemed to be at odds with how I should be feeling, according to all those magazines aimed at women of my age. Only the other day I'd flicked through a few at the supermarket while looking for ones on interiors, and there seemed to be an endless stream of articles about baking your own sourdough or taking a ceramics class. And nothing at all about sleeping with a man ten years younger than you – which seems a lot more interesting than getting your dough to rise, frankly.

But maybe it's just me. It'd been so long since those feelings of excitement and anticipation, and I relished them. But then I heard about Ben's wife and everything changed. Of course Ajay wasn't to know, and he continued flirting and flattering, while I kept trying to behave as if everything was normal. Later, as I left him undisturbed and went to sleep in the spare bedroom with Harry, I thought about how this wasn't as I'd imagined it would be. And then I thought about Ben – and how so much of life never is, is it?

I wake up early and, slipping on my dressing gown, go and check on Ajay. He's still sound asleep, so I leave him and come downstairs to make tea and feed Harry. I've got used to living in a building site now and I pick my way through the construction work.

The sun is streaming in through the windows and I open the kitchen door and let in some fresh air. It's going to be another lovely day. I check my phone and reply to the WhatsApp that Naomi sent last night. She's trying to get a few people together for her birthday:

Naomi

It's not until July but it's a Big One.
I feel I should do something, especially
since I'll probably be single ☹.

We haven't spoken since she got back to London and we're
due a proper catch-up, but obviously things have not gone
well with Danny.

Whatever you decide, count me in!

I get a thumbs up and start typing her a message about last
night, before realizing this is a group WhatsApp. That'll
teach me not to wear my reading glasses. Thankfully I manage
to delete it.

As I wait for the kettle to boil, I do a cursory check of the
bird feeder. Still untouched. It's been hanging there for months
now; it'll be summer soon. Despite Valentine's advice to have
patience, I'm fast losing hope the birds will ever find it.

'Is there enough water in the kettle for two?'

I turn round. Ajay is standing in my half-finished kitchen
in the shaft of sunlight. He looks rumpled and bemused. He
scratches the stubble on his chin.

'How do you take your tea?'

'Milk, no sugar.' He smiles sheepishly.

'Coming right up.' I reach for another mug.

'Look, about last night,' he begins, but I don't let him finish.

'It's fine, don't worry.' It strikes me that the roles are
reversed and now it's my turn to say it.

He slides onto a stool and rests his forehead on his elbows,
scraping his fingers through his thick dark hair.

'I don't remember anything.' His voice is muffled and he's
hugely embarrassed.

'There's nothing to remember.'

227

'I crashed out.' He raises his eyes to meet mine.

'I know.' I put the teabags in the mugs and pour on the boiling water.

'Did I snore?'

I can't resist. 'A little bit.'

He groans loudly. 'I had this whole big seduction planned.'

As I grab the milk from the fridge, we both look at each other and grin.

'I'm sure it was wonderful,' I pass him his tea and lean against the counter top, opposite him. 'Maybe you shouldn't drink a whole bottle of red next time.'

'Is there going to be a next time?'

He raises an eyebrow, but as we look at each other, we both know the answer.

'Listen, it's not you—' I begin.

'That's normally my line,' he interrupts with a rueful smile.

I laugh and put down my tea.

'See, I made you laugh at least.'

'Don't say that. I had a good time last night,' I protest.

'Me too.'

'It's just . . .'

'I know.' He nods. 'It's like we keep missing each other, right?'

'Yeah, it's exactly like that.'

Putting down his mug, he reaches out and strokes Harry, who has somehow managed to wedge himself under Ajay's stool.

'Keep in touch?'

'Absolutely,' I nod.

'I'm available for pub quizzes and bar mitzvahs.'

I laugh and he gets up off his stool and comes over, sliding his arm round my waist to give me a hug. It strikes me how different this feels to when Ajay held me last night on my doorstep.

I hear the key in the lock. It's the builders arriving. As the door opens we break apart, but Ben has already seen us.

'Morning.'

'Morning,' I say brightly. For some reason I didn't want this to happen. 'Ajay was just leaving,' I add quickly, then wish I hadn't. Why do I feel the need to explain?

Ben is carrying a large container and he steps aside to allow Ajay to pass. Briefly they say hello and I follow Ajay outside, bumping into Fetch Me and Carry Me, who look very surprised to see a man leaving my house so early in the morning. I ignore the looks flashing back and forth between them. Why do I get the feeling this is going to be discussed *very* loudly across the back garden later?

Outside, I offer to give Ajay a ride to the station. 'If you wait five minutes I can throw on some proper clothes, grab my keys.' But he refuses, saying he needs to walk off his hangover, so I wave goodbye, then turn back and walk up the path, trying to rehearse what I'm going to say to Ben. There are so many questions, so much I want to say, but I don't know where to start. How do you bring up the subject of someone's dead wife?

I walk back inside to find Ben with the other builders, clustered around the Aga. He looks up when he hears me.

'Livvie, if you've got a minute, do you want to look at these tile samples for the splashback?'

'Yeah, sure,' I nod.

Answer to my own question: You don't.

Maya

It was just after they'd left the theatre and were walking across the city centre towards the car park. Liv, her English tutor, had got tickets for a production of *Macbeth* and they were discussing the performance. Exams were only a couple of weeks away and the play was one of her A-level texts.

'I thought it might be really helpful to see it onstage,' Liv had said, all enthusiastic. 'It's in Leeds – an hour's drive away – so I'll pick you up.'

Maya liked Liv. She was cool. Much cooler than her parents, although she was probably about the same age. Plus she'd adopted Harry and was into sustainable fashion, though she really needed to have a word with Liv about all that fleece. She was also a good teacher. She made things fun and interesting and her enthusiasm rubbed off.

That said, not even Liv could make Shakespeare less boring. Because, sorry: his plays were *so* boring. All those long soliloquies and iambic pentameter that were so difficult to understand. Maya hated having to study him. Like Zac said, why was she wasting her time studying some old, dead white guy? He had no relevance to what was happening today. Saying that, old white guys seemed to be running the world these days.

Maya said as much to Liv when they were sitting in the audience, waiting for the curtain to go up, but Liv had simply smiled, like she was in on some secret. Maya wished she was at Zac's. She hadn't heard from him all day; he was busy updating the protest group's website and trying to organize a new rally. He'd wanted her to help, but she told him she had to stay home revising. She felt bad lying, but Zac said the theatre was just for luvvies and the bourgeoisie. Thing is, the woman next to her in a hoodie and trainers didn't look like a luvvy. She looked quite normal. In fact most people in the audience did.

The first scene was the one with the witches. Maya tried not to roll her eyes. Seriously, were they supposed to be scary? *Hasn't anyone got Netflix?* The first twenty minutes dragged on forever and she tried not to fidget or look at her phone to see if Zac had texted back. But then something weird happened: she totally forgot they were actors dressed up onstage, and somehow the words they were saying, which had never made sense when she read them in class, suddenly seemed to make perfect sense and the play immediately came to life for her.

It was the strangest thing. She'd expected to sit there for two hours being bored to tears, but instead she found herself gripped and on the edge of her seat. The time flew by. It was like she was right in the action. It was epic.

Why had no one ever told her that Shakespeare's plays weren't meant to be read, that they'd been written to be performed? No wonder she hadn't got it. But watching it onstage was a game-changer. Lady Macbeth was a badass. And the whole bit about Macduff and the C-section. That was sick.

Maya couldn't believe how wrong she'd been. Talk about being relevant today. It was all about the corruption of power – about people being motivated by greed and ambition, and jealousy and revenge. All the flaws of human nature. She'd been blown away. Seriously, it was better than anything she'd seen on Netflix. The end was so shocking and gruesome; when they appeared onstage with Macbeth's severed head, she'd had to hide behind her hands. Who would have thought it?

Well, Liv – because she whispered when it was safe to look again.

Wait till she told Zac! Maya hadn't told him she was going to the theatre, after he was so dismissive about it. She didn't want an argument, but now she couldn't *not* share her experience. So as soon as they left the theatre, she called him as they were walking through the city centre. Across the street were several bars and they were a bit rowdy, so she held her phone to her ear to hear it ringing.

And that's when she saw Zac. Across the street. Standing outside the Brasserie, with his arms around a girl and his tongue down her throat. Saw him pull his phone from his back pocket, look at the screen to see who it was and decline the call. A moment later a text popped up:

Working late. Call you later babe. x

And, just like that, she saw Zac for who he really was, and her teenage heart broke.

Things Left Unsaid

Often, when things are such a mess, you can't imagine they can improve. Deep in the thick of it, it's so easy to feel as if you're taking two steps forward, only to take two steps backwards; that everything is so uncertain and nothing will ever change.

Yet ironically, change is the one thing we can be certain of – nothing can ever stay the same. And while at first these shifts can be so small they're imperceptible, gradually, day by day, little by little, they grow and build. Until one day you catch yourself in the mirror and notice that you've somehow lost those extra pounds. Or a date on the calendar reminds you it's your ex's birthday and you realize that you haven't thought of him for weeks. Or you wake up to find that suddenly, as if by magic, the house seems to be taking shape.

It's the beginning of June. After two months of seemingly constant setbacks, we've started to make progress. Years of watching fraught owners on *Grand Designs* had warned me about spiralling budgets, but no number of spreadsheets could protect me from the various unforeseen issues I've so far encountered.

If it wasn't the discovery of woodworm or rising damp, it was a family of common pipistrelle bats roosting in the attic. Despite Ben's assurances that everything will be fine, there have been many nights when I've lain in bed worrying about expensive surveys, different treatments and specially designed bat-boxes, and wondering if there would ever be an end to all the problems and delays.

But gradually each hurdle has been overcome and, slowly but surely, it's taking shape. The main shell of the extension has been built, and the kitchen has been knocked through to create a large open-plan space. It's still a long way from being finished – one end is still open to the elements, and there are wires everywhere and rubble for the floor – but the cottage is now flooded with light. Best of all, I can see directly out into the garden, which, after a lot of hard work, is starting to really come together.

Upstairs, with the help of Valentine, the spare bedroom is almost finished. In the end I decided to go with a lovely pale yellow that catches the morning light, while on the wall with the chimney breast, Valentine expertly hung the Victorian hand-painted wallpaper I found in the garden shed. And it's true what he said: he really is the cat's miaow, when it comes to decorating. Seriously, I've never seen anyone so handy with a plumbline, lining paper and wallpaper paste.

Still, there's a lot of hard work ahead. There's the mouldy bathroom to tackle, floors to lay, walls to plaster and the log-burner to install. Plus a million other things on my to-do list. But sometimes, when I walk through a doorway and catch the evening light streaming through a window, or run my fingers over an old oak beam that's been stripped back and oiled, I think how far we've come and I feel excited. Because it's not just this old house that's slowly been rebuilt and transformed over the past few months – it's its owner as well.

*

'So I've gone over the measurements and I've got a suggestion.'

Two weeks after the pub quiz I find myself standing next to Ben in my bathroom. It's past six o'clock and the other builders have left, but he's been looking at the plans and wanted to share an idea with me.

'You can't do a proper loft conversion – with this being a conservation area and not being able to raise the roofline – but you could still make a third bedroom underneath the eaves.' He shines a torch into the open loft hatch, illuminating the dusty attic, which, thanks to my new bat-boxes, is no longer home to a family of pipistrelles. 'It would perfect for when your friend and her little girl come to stay. Much better than a tent.'

'But they loved the tent!'

'They wouldn't love it so much if it was winter and raining – and it rains here a lot, trust me.'

I didn't have to trust Ben. I'd seen with my own eyes. There was a reason Yorkshire folk have so many words for rain.

'But how do we get up there?' I peer into the rafters.

'Easy. We add a staircase up to the attic.'

'Gosh, yes, I love that idea . . . But hang on, where do you put the staircase?'

I turn to look at Ben. He's been working outside on the extension and his face is tanned.

'Well, that's the only downside. You'd need take off this corner of the bathroom here, which would reduce its size.'

He reaches for the pencil that is permanently tucked behind his ear and draws on the plans to show me.

'But then how do I fit in a roll-top bath?'

I gesture around my bathroom, with its avocado bath suite, dark-brown tiles and cottage-cheese ceiling. I've been living with it patiently since I moved in nearly six months ago – it's the last on the list of renovations – but now I'm desperate to make a start on it.

At this point Ben does this thing where he scrunches up his face. And if there's one thing I've learned during these last few months, this scrunching-up is not a good sign.

'You don't.'

'In that case, no.' I shake my head firmly. 'I'd rather have a tent.'

'You could have a lovely walk-in-shower – much more energy-efficient,' he encourages me, but I'm steadfast.

'You know how much I've set my heart on having a proper cast-iron claw-foot bath, Ben. I've been dreaming of it for months, years probably. It's on my Pinterest mood board and everything,' I add jokingly, but he doesn't laugh.

'And you know you don't have the budget for one, don't you?' He pulls out a spreadsheet. 'They don't come cheap, those baths – not if you want an original one that's been restored and refurbished.'

I hate it when he reminds me about the budget.

'You're renovating a cottage, not opening a boutique hotel, you know.'

He's right, of course. The prices are ridiculous. Even the cheapest one I found on eBay was more than I could afford. I've been bringing in more money from tutoring, but I still need to be sensible.

'Stanley loves his attic bedroom.' Switching off his torch, Ben closes the loft hatch. 'And you could even have a wet room, if you wanted.'

'OK, you win,' I concede with a sigh.

Satisfied, Ben turns to leave the bathroom, and it strikes me that this is the first time we've been alone in the house together. I think about the speech I've been rehearsing in my mind ever since I learned the truth about his wife: how sorry I am for his loss; how I want him to know that I'm here for him and Stanley, should he ever need anything.

'Ben.' As he starts to walk downstairs, I quickly follow him before the opportunity is missed. 'I wanted to say something.' I'm abruptly nervous.

'Don't tell me. You've changed your mind about the mixer taps for the kitchen island.'

'No, it's not about the mixer taps.'

Our footsteps clatter loudly on the bare stone steps as we go downstairs.

'Because you know I wasn't sure about the brass fittings, either.'

'No, I like the brass fittings.'

At the bottom of the staircase, he turns. 'I did wonder if we should have gone with the brushed steel instead.'

'No, Ben—'

'But don't worry, I can change them tomorrow.' He reaches for the door.

'I know about your wife,' I blurt.

For a moment my words seem to hang, suspended in the air. Regret stabs. That's not how I rehearsed it. With his back to me, I watch his body stiffen.

'I'm really sorry, I had no idea.'

There's a silence. Ben doesn't speak or turn to look at me. Instead there's a pause as he raises his hand to his brow and tilts his head skywards, as if he's thinking how to reply.

'Shit.' He lets out a heavy sigh.

My chest tightens as I realize I've said the wrong thing. 'Oh God, I'm sorry. I didn't mean to be insensitive.'

Why didn't I keep my mouth shut? I'm intruding on his grief, and it's none of my business. I feel the urgent need to explain.

'I've thought about it forever – I wasn't sure what to say, but I couldn't ignore it.'

'This is all I need.'

In horror, I stare at his back. Ben's still turned away from me. He can't even look at me, he's probably so angry. I feel terrible. I've made everything ten times worse.

'I just wanted you and Stanley to know.'

'It must be coming from the new boiler.'

We both speak over each other, and it takes a second to register.

'Excuse me?'

'The leak.' Turning to me, he gestures above his head. For a moment I can't see anything . . . until there it is, emerging through the ceiling: a drip of water. He wipes it from his forehead. 'Something must have come loose or burst.'

'Burst?' Distracted from my speech, I step closer and together we watch as the drip slowly grows bigger and falls, before another appears. I don't know much about plumbing, but 'burst' doesn't sound good. 'So what do we do now?'

It's that inevitable moment when you can see it happening, but can't stop it. A split-second pause. And then the ceiling suddenly collapses and a deluge of water, mixed with messy chunks of lath and plaster, pours down from above us, completely soaking us both.

Hiding in Plain Sight

From my back garden you can watch the sun setting over the Dales: streaks of orange and red across the vast expanse of sky, illuminating the dark-purple ribbons of clouds. Ben and I sit side by side in a couple of old stripy deckchairs – another vintage find from the garden shed – watching as it slowly sinks into the horizon. Next to us, Harry lies stretched out on the grass, exhausted by all the commotion of the last few hours.

After my ceiling came crashing down, Ben managed to turn off the stop valve to prevent the boiler from refilling and creating any more damage, and called Flood, his plumber, who was busy but promised to come and fix it first thing tomorrow. At this point I reasoned it was probably too late to ask how Flood got his name. However, the water had already shorted all the electrics, so after we'd done our best to clear up, we decamped outside to wait for Ben's electrician.

'Sparky shouldn't be long,' he says now, checking the time on his phone again.

Stripped down to our underwear, we're both wrapped in towels. I've hung our clothes from the branches of the tree, hoping they'll dry a little before the electrician arrives. Thankfully, it's almost summer and the evening air is warm and syrupy. Thankfully also, to spare my blushes, dusk is falling and the only illumination comes from the soft amber glow of the solar lights strung in the branches of the old sycamore. I'd put them up for Naomi's visit and they were so pretty, I haven't taken them down.

'I don't know what I'd have done without you.'

Ben makes some murmur of rebuttal.

'Faulty valve on the boiler. It's just one of those things. Once that's replaced and the ceiling is patched up, it should be as good as new.'

'Thank you.'

He doesn't say anything. There's a beat.

'Sorry, I should have offered you a drink,' I continue awkwardly. 'I've got wine, and I think there's some beer in the fridge.'

'Thanks, but no. I've decided to stay off it, after the other night. Stan doesn't need a drunk for a father . . .' He trails off. He doesn't need to say any more.

'You know, you don't have to wait with me. It's late. I'm sure you want to get home – see Stanley.'

'He'll be asleep in bed by now.' Ben glances across at the rear of the houses whose long gardens back onto mine, then tuts. 'At least he should be. I can see his light's still on.'

'Where?' I ask, feeling curious. Until now I hadn't realized I could see Ben's house from mine.

He points beyond the line of silver birch trees at the bottom of the garden. High up, I see a small attic window and a tiny square of yellow light.

'Who's looking after him?'

'Holly,' he replies, then pauses. In the dusk I can't see his expression. 'Holly's Stanley's aunt. She's Janet's sister. Janet was my wife.'

I absorb his words for a moment. So that explains who the woman was that I talked to in their garden.

'I'm sorry,' I say simply. 'I had no idea. I saw your wedding ring . . .' I let my voice trail off into the shadows.

He doesn't say anything. Why should he? He doesn't need to explain to me.

'For a long time, after Janet first died, I couldn't get my head around it.'

His voice is so low I have to strain to hear him.

'How could she simply disappear from our lives like that and not come back?' He breaks off and there's a long pause. It's a question to which there is no answer. 'I kept thinking she was at work or seeing friends, and one day I'd walk into the kitchen and there she'd be. Just like with a sunset.' He gestures at the sky. 'The sun doesn't stop existing because you can't see it.'

We both watch as the last bit of sun finally disappears into the landscape.

'But I don't feel like that any more,' he continues. 'It's been two years, and I know she's not coming back. I still have conversations with her in my head, though. Mostly about Stanley, telling her about the things he's been up to, or asking her advice. Janet always knew the right thing to do, whereas I feel like I'm playing catch-up all the time.'

Listening, I notice his left thumb instinctively go to his wedding band. He notices me noticing.

'You know, there's all these rules about when you should take off your wedding ring – people tell you to put it on your right hand, or wear it on a chain around your neck.' He snorts at the idea, as if he finds it ridiculous. 'But I don't wear it because I still feel married. I wear it because sometimes, when I feel like I don't know what I'm doing with Stanley, when I feel like I'm getting it all wrong, it reminds me that someone believed in me once to get it right.'

He turns to me fully then, his eyes searching out mine in the dusk.

'Does that make me sound crazy?'

241

'No, not at all.'

He lets out a deep sigh, leaning forward in the chair and scraping his hands through his hair. I think it's the first time I've seen him without his beanie or a baseball cap, and his hair is dark and wavy, like Stanley's.

'The hardest part was telling Stan she'd died. How could I explain it to him when it didn't make sense to me? That you can get in a car one day and drive off like normal and never come back. That it can be nobody's fault. That if she'd set off a few minutes later, everything would be different; that truck would have finished turning, she wouldn't need to brake, the car wouldn't have skidded off the icy road.'

His voice chokes and I watch as Ben rubs his eyes with the heels of his hands. Instinctively I want to offer up some words of comfort, but just as instinctively I know there are none.

'Stanley asked me if she'd gone to heaven to be with Granddad – I think he must have got that from his grandma. At the time that seemed to comfort him, so I said yes. But now I don't know if I did the right thing.' He shakes his head, staring off into the middle distance. 'Stanley talks about her being a star.'

'You were trying to protect him.'

'But I can't protect him from the truth forever, can I?'

'You don't have to.'

He looks at me then.

'My mum died when both my sister and I were young,' I say softly. 'It was terrible, but the worst part was Dad never spoke about her any more. It was too painful for him. He never mentioned her again and we were too afraid to, because he would cry and we didn't want to upset him. If it wasn't for our grandparents, it would be like she'd never existed.'

'I never knew about you losing your mum – when we were kids, I mean.'

'We didn't talk about it,' I shrug. 'We felt like we couldn't, so instead we buried our emotions. But you can never truly bury them, can you? Loss and grief don't magically disappear; they just find a different outlet, whether it's drink or drugs or depression . . .' I trail off. 'You have to find a way to deal with it, and we dealt with in different ways.'

I look across at Ben, but his face is in shadow and I can't see his expression.

'As long as you keep talking about her with Stanley – letting him ask questions even if you don't know the answers, showing him it's OK to cry, to feel confused – it'll work itself out. There's no right or wrong. You just have to make it up as you go along.'

'Like life, really.'

'Yeah, like life,' I murmur.

As we both fall silent, absorbed in our thoughts, I think about how people with broken hearts are all around us. I think about Valentine, with his photograph of Gisele in his pocket; of Ben's wedding ring; of Stanley gazing up at the stars. I think about myself as a little girl crying over her mum, not knowing that when she grew up, her heart would break all over again at the loss of someone else she loved. And I realize it's no surprise my divorce affected me so badly; it triggered all those old, buried feelings of loss that I never dealt with.

We are everywhere, and yet we hide in plain sight: the barista serving you coffee; the checkout girl at the super-market; the man next to you on the bus – how do we ever know what's going on in people's lives? Who just discovered their boyfriend was cheating, or suffered a miscarriage, or was let go from their job. Or, moments ago, left the hospital after their loved one died. People whose worlds have fallen apart and are bravely carrying on.

Yet what I'm beginning to realize it that although we might feel alone, we're not. There are more than seven billion people on this planet, and heartbreak – like love – is universal. And while each of us may be on our own individual journey, right alongside us is someone else navigating those same stages of grief and loss. It's different, and yet it's the same.

And if we reach out – be it by knocking on a door, or picking up a phone, or waving hello to a lonely old man in a window, or talking to a little boy too scared to come out from behind the garden gate – then our fingertips will brush against each other and we'll make that connection. Because more and more, I'm learning that it's only by coming together that we grow stronger; like lifting that pot of paint that was too heavy for one person, but which, together, Valentine and I carried up the stairs.

'So tell me, is divorce any easier?'

Ben's voice interrupts my thoughts and I turn to him.

'I don't remember telling you I'm divorced.'

'You didn't have to. We live in a village.' He puts on an accent far broader than his own. 'Don't you know, she's from London *and* she's divorced. Rumour has it she's got a toy boy.'

'You did not hear that!' I gasp.

He starts laughing at my shocked expression. 'I was joking about the toy boy. At least I think so.' He shoots me a look.

'Ajay isn't my toy boy – we're just friends.'

He raises an eyebrow.

'I'm serious,' I protest. 'It's not how it looked.'

'M'lord,' he adds, and I can't help but laugh.

'As for divorce being easier, well, my husband's not dead, so there is that,' I shrug, 'but then your wife didn't leave you because she didn't love you any more.'

Ben looks unprepared for my answer.

'Sorry, is that completely insensitive of me?'

He shakes his head. 'No, it's the truth.'

There's a pause. 'I don't feel like I can talk about getting my heart broken, after what you've been through,' I say after a moment.

'Why not? It's not a competition. I don't get the gold medal for heartache. Though I did get a lot of Tupperware,' he adds.

'Tupperware?'

'Mountains of the bloody stuff. When you're a widower, women like to cook you food; they bring it round in Tupperware dishes, or leave it on the doorstep. I still have a chest freezer full of it.'

I start laughing, then apologize. 'Sorry, I shouldn't laugh.'

'What's the alternative?' He shrugs and smiles, that long, slow, lazy smile of his. It used to exasperate me, when it was in response to any problem we encountered in the building works, which I felt demanded urgency and immediate sorting-out, but now it has quite the opposite effect.

'Well, you don't get anyone cooking for you, if you're a woman and you get divorced, that's for sure,' I smile. 'Though your girlfriends bring you lots of white wine.'

'That doesn't sound too bad.'

'I think I would have preferred the Tupperware, actually.'

'You can have some of mine – I've cupboards full of it.'

'Do any of the lids match?'

'Ah, well, that's another story.'

The mood has lightened and the conversation drops for a few moments, as we sit in the comfort that comes from shared truths and allowing yourself to be naked – not physically, though we are in our underwear, but emotionally. We've known each other for more than thirty years, but

245

it's only now I feel like we're finally getting to truly know each other.

It's after ten at night, but there's still a glow across the Dales. Small fireflies dance around us, and the air is fragranced with the sweet scent of honeysuckle and jasmine. Despite the earlier chaos, it's one of those warm, fuzzy-around-the-edges kind of evenings when everything seems peaceful and at ease with itself. I'd forgotten how this feels.

'Oh, wow, look! See the bats.'

Ben points into the sky and I look up to see dozens of them, swooping and twirling in the night sky.

'Gosh, they're beautiful,' I gasp as we both watch, spellbound.

'So they should be – they cost you eight grand,' he replies. And I laugh and think how funny life is; how one minute something can feel like a disaster, and the next a delight. And how lovely it is sitting out here with Ben, and how I don't want the night to end.

The doorbell rings and I snap back to the present.

'That'll be the electrician,' Ben says and I feel an unexpected crush of disappointment. 'Well, best get dressed, eh? We don't want anyone getting the wrong idea.'

We both stand up, trying not to drop our towels as we grab our damp clothes from the branches of the trees.

'Yes,' I agree quickly. 'We wouldn't want that.'

STAGE 5

The Curveball

So Lucky

'Jaisalmer was awesome!'

'Where's that?'

I peer over his shoulder to look at the photo of an incredible sunset on his iPhone.

'Rajasthan in India. We rode camels out into the desert and camped overnight in tents. It was like being on safari. Only not full of old people in shorts with binoculars,' he adds with a smirk.

'Hey,' I protest, swatting him good-naturedly on the shoulder. 'Me and your dad weren't old when we went on that safari to South Africa.'

'That's open to interpretation.' Grinning, he puts down his phone, picks up his knife and fork and turns his attentions to his full English breakfast. 'Anyway, he definitely wore shorts and had binoculars. I've seen the photos . . . and there were *plenty* of them,' he adds, rolling his eyes beneath his thatch of blond hair.

'Oh yes,' I say, remembering. 'He did take rather a lot, didn't he?'

'I think it was after the millionth wildebeest that I lost the will to live.' He spears a rasher of bacon and groans with pleasure. 'God, I'm starving, this looks delicious.'

The visit from Will, my stepson, had come completely out of the blue at the beginning of July. I'd received an email a few days ago to say he was catching a flight back from Delhi

249

and could he come and stay for a couple of days? He'd gone travelling over a year ago and, apart from the odd text, I hadn't heard from him for months.

But now here he was, sitting at my kitchen table showing me photos of his trip and telling me how he thought his dad was an idiot.

'Don't call him an idiot.'

'Why not? He is.'

'Because he's your dad.'

'Why do you always feel the need to protect him? I'm grown-up now.'

It was true. At six foot three, with broad rower's shoulders and a scraggy beard, there was no denying Will was well and truly grown-up. And yet he would always be the shy little ten-year-old that I first met, who would still suck his thumb when he watched TV.

Best not remind him of that.

'So have you spoken to him?' I ask, then immediately wish I hadn't. Since the divorce was finalized, David and I haven't had any contact. There's nothing to say, and yet at the same time there are so many things left unsaid. Still, it's for the best. Water under the bridge. Clean break and all that.

'Briefly.' Scooping up the runny yolk of his fried eggs with his toast, Will pulls a face. He reminds me so much of David when he does that, it's startling.

'Does he know you're here?'

'No, and he's not going to.'

He puts down his knife and reaches for his mug of coffee. Fortunately it's the weekend, so we've got the house to ourselves; plus now it's much less of a construction site than when Naomi visited. Downstairs is entering what Ben keeps referring to as 'the final phase', which seems to be builder-speak for 'Will it ever end?' But at last there's been huge progress: I now have a kitchen actually *in* my kitchen, not a makeshift one in my living room, and it's hand-made of oak and really rather beautiful.

'Do you mind me being here?'

'No, of course not.' I hand him more toast. He might have lost weight while he's been away, but he certainly hasn't lost his appetite. 'It's lovely to see you.'

He smiles then. 'Any Marmite?'

I grimace. 'I don't know how you eat that stuff.'

'I don't know how you can't,' he replies.

I smile at our well-rehearsed exchange. I go to the cupboard and pull out a large unopened jar.

'First thing I went out and bought, when you said were coming.' I put it down on the table in front of him.

Will pounces on it, quickly unscrewing the lid and smearing large dollops on his toast. 'Lovely to see you too,' he says, grinning through a large mouthful.

'Don't eat with your mouth open,' I tell him off. But of course I'm thrilled to see him too.

When you tell people you're getting divorced, the first thing they say after, 'I'm sorry' is to ask, 'Do you have kids?' And when you say no, they tell you you're lucky. Because of course getting divorced when you have children adds a whole other level of complication and heartbreak.

Yet what people didn't realize is that I didn't feel lucky. Rather, I felt unlucky – not because David and I hadn't had children together, as I'd been happy with our decision, but because of Will. Families are built in many different ways; I might not have given birth to Will or be his 'real mum', as certain relatives liked to point out, but the love I felt for him was certainly real. When my marriage broke up, I was scared it meant I wasn't going to see Will any more. That by not being David's wife, I wasn't his stepmum any more. That legally, in fact, I wasn't anything at all.

And because I wasn't part of his family any longer, did that mean I wouldn't be part of Will's life any more, either? Last summer, after David left, I missed Will's graduation; I hadn't been invited. Too awkward, apparently. Of course I understood, but deep down I was terrified I was going to miss the rest of his future. This smart, funny, sensitive little boy, whom I'd cooked pesto pasta for on repeat, read *Harry Potter* with under the glow of his dinosaur lamp and cheered on from the frozen sidelines of a football pitch, was all grown-up now; he didn't need me any more to patch up his grazed knees or his crushed heart after Sienna Jackson turned him down for the prom. Losing David was one thing, but I couldn't bear the thought of losing my stepson as well.

No one gives you a manual on how to be a step-parent, but I'd found it both wonderful and challenging. I never liked the title 'stepmother', with its wicked connotations, but as Will's bond and mine grew, I stopped caring about labels. I worked hard at carefully navigating my way through the every-other-weekends and holidays, slowly and sensitively building up our relationship so that it existed independently of his father. The divorce threw that relationship into petrifying jeopardy.

But now, having Will here, those fears have been allayed. Our relationship is still intact; if anything, it's stronger than ever. We're still each other's family. That was never in jeopardy. A piece of paper is not going to change that. And it's made me realize that, ironically, all those people were right after all, only in a different way than they intended. Because it's true. I *am* lucky.

*

'Someone else is hungry.'

'Ignore him.'

Harry is on full begging alert. He's been sitting glued to the table leg all morning. Having been living with a vegetarian for the past six months, he's no doubt over the moon that Will has arrived, as it means having bacon in the house.

'Don't feed him at the table,' I instruct, as I catch Will sneaking food off his plate.

'I didn't know you were into dogs,' he says, quickly snatching his hand away as Harry nearly wolfs down his fingers along with the scraps.

'Neither did I,' I smile.

'Did you know Mum's got another cat? I think that makes five now.'

'No, I didn't.' I nod and smile respectfully. David was already divorced when I met him and my relationship with his ex-wife was polite but perfunctory.

'I told her she was turning into a crazy cat-lady, and she said thanks for the compliment.'

I laugh.

'She said to send her love by the way.'

I'd presumed she would be secretly gloating, and I feel surprisingly touched.

'Tell her thanks – same to her.' As Will finishes cleaning his plate, I take it from him and put it in the sink. 'So what do you want to do now?'

'I thought maybe I'd take a snooze.' He yawns widely, stretching out his tanned arms above his head, his wrists boasting the woven bracelets of a seasoned backpacker. 'Jet lag sucks.'

'I've got your room ready.'

'Thanks.' Pushing back the chair, he stands up. 'Nice place you got here, by the way.'

I smile, pleased by the compliment. Will wasn't known for noticing things, hence the plates of rotting food that I used to find in his bedroom.

'Good job I did the extension, otherwise you'd be hitting your head on the beams in here.'

'It looks great.' Looking around, he nods approvingly. 'I like your style. It's a lot different from the old house.'

'Yes, I suppose it is.'

My eyes sweep over the open shelving filled with its piles of mismatched crockery, some of it inherited from my grandparents; various framed photographs of me and Josie; and a few vintage flea-market finds. They all jostle alongside each other, like my books that line the oak bookshelves Ben has built for me along one whole wall. I like having all my things around me where I can see them. I find it comforting, like an extension of myself.

'Your dad liked everything put away neatly.'

'Out of sight, out of mind. Like his feelings, huh?'

A look passes between us, and I realize it's not just the house that's different. I am. I don't want things hidden away any more, whether it's in cupboards or hearts. I want everything out in the open. I want the unsaid things said.

Will joins me by the Aga; it took me weeks to clean and I've had it re-enamelled a bright cherry red. It was the one thing we managed to save from this kitchen and I'm so glad we did, as it's the heart of the home. He gives me a hug, towering above me. He must have grown another three inches since he went travelling. Either that or I'm shrinking.

As we break apart, he motions to his rucksack. 'By the way, any chance I could do some laundry?'

I roll my eyes. As a student he was forever coming home from university with bags of dirty washing, and I was forever moaning about it.

'Lucky for you I just got my new washing machine plumbed in.'

'Awesome.'

He goes to grab it and I watch as he begins emptying the rucksack's filthy contents all over the floor. I never thought I'd be so glad to see nothing has changed.

A Helping Hand

After the conversation with Ben in my garden I was apprehensive about seeing Stanley again. Ben's words weighed
heavily upon me and I worried that my emotions might get
the better of me. I thought constantly about his mum, Janet,
and it brought back painful memories of my own. Alone the
next night, I looked out into the garden and saw the light
on in Stanley's attic bedroom and I found myself unexpectedly sobbing, not just for a little boy who had lost his mum,
but for two little girls who lost theirs.

Luckily Harry had no such worries and behaved exactly
the same, stuffing his nose between the gate and wagging his
tail as Stanley ran out to greet us, so I followed his example.
When I watched them together, they were acting like nothing
had changed because nothing *had* changed. As soon as I
realized that, any awkwardness or concern about saying the
wrong thing simply disappeared.

Stanley and Harry have formed an undeniable bond.
Stanley knows what time we walk past now and makes sure
he's always there to see Harry. Recently he even added it to
his laminated list. 'Look – "Harry",' he pointed proudly,
showing the list to me as we stood on one side of the gate,
and he on the other. 'See, now it's not a coincidence, because
it's on the list.' For some reason Stanley seemed very pleased
about that.

Their friendship isn't the only one that's deepened. Neither

Ben nor I has mentioned what we talked about that night in my garden, but there's been a shift in our relationship. You think you know someone, but by both allowing ourselves to be vulnerable, it's as if I've been given an access-all areas pass. I've seen the heartbreak that lurks beneath the cheerful banter and the crushing grief behind a lost temper.

And while most of what we talk about has nothing to do with feelings, and everything to do with plumbing and electrics (including one discussion about the merits of underfloor heating versus cast-iron radiators, which went on for what felt like hours and I nearly lost the will to live), woven into our conversations are other things. More important things.

Like, for example, Stanley is deeply unhappy at school. Ben has known this for a while, but now he begins to open up more and tells me about an incident when Stanley locked himself in the toilets and refused to come out – 'It was PE, and he got overwhelmed by all the different games and noises'; and of a meeting with the head teacher to discuss his son's disruptive behaviour, 'which didn't end well,' Ben admitted. 'I lost my temper and she ended up calling me disruptive and saying that now she knew where Stanley got it from.'

It all comes to a head a week later, when we're in my newly configured and much smaller bathroom, having a discussion about walk-in showers. Ben's armed with a spirit level and tape measure, while I'm looking through his A4 file filled with various brochures, trying to drum up some enthusiasm for one with a minimalist contemporary design. I'm pleased about creating a third bedroom in the attic and yet . . .

'Are you sure we don't have room for a bath? Not even a small one?'

'Not unless it's the size of a bucket.'

'Ha-ha, very funny.'

I turn back to the folder, but I must look disappointed because a few moments later he adds, 'Showers are more hygienic anyway. Who wants to sit in their own dirt?'

'Speak for yourself. I'm not that dirty.'

A pamphlet falls out.

'What's this?' Scooping it off the floor, I glance at the glossy photograph of smiling children on the front: *Alderley Academy: A Bright Future.*

'Oh, it must have got mixed in by mistake.'

'Are you thinking of sending Stanley to a new school?'

'I'm just considering the alternatives.'

I unfold the brightly coloured pamphlet and quickly scan the prospectus about teaching and caring for children with autism. 'This is an independent school offering specialist teaching.'

Ben puts down his spirit level and turns to me.

'I thought you wanted him to stay in mainstream education?'

We'd talked about it previously. Despite Stanley's difficulties, Ben was keen for his son to stay at the local primary.

'I do, but I don't know if that's possible. Stanley's been in trouble again.'

'Trouble, why?'

'Oh, the usual.' Ben shrugs, his face resigned. 'Thing is, his teacher seems to think I'm making excuses for Stanley's behaviour, but he finds it hard in certain situations – like in groups and stuff. It's difficult for him.'

'I'm sorry.'

Ben flashes me a grateful look.

'I'm not making excuses, but it can be difficult for teachers too,' I admit sadly. 'There's so much pressure these days, what with inspectors and academic targets and a lack of resources. It's hard to meet the needs of every child when you've got a class of thirty-one kids.'

'I know it's tough for everyone.'

I look back at the prospectus. It does look like a lovely school.

'But Stan's my little boy,' Ben continues, 'and he's only seven, and he's so smart and funny and sensitive. I feel like I'm letting him down.'

'Don't be silly, of course you're not—'

'But I am.' He cuts me off. 'I want his differences to be celebrated, not seen as a problem. I want him to grow up to be happy and confident and independent. I don't want him to slip through the net and get left behind. I want him to reach his full potential. Janet was really passionate about that. She wanted Stan to have a brilliant life. Because he *is* brilliant.'

Ben's pride is palpable. As is his frustration.

'Let me try and help.'

He frowns. 'How?'

I gesture to the prospectus in my hand. 'This isn't your only option for Stanley – far from it. There's more than one primary school in the area and, with the right resources and support from teachers and staff who understand children like Stanley, it can make all the difference.' Tiredness is etched on Ben's face and I recognize that same feeling of being overwhelmed that I felt when I first moved here. 'It's a big decision and you know your son better than anyone, but it's also important you know what your choices are and what you're entitled to, so you can make the best decision.'

I hand him back the prospectus.

'And that's where I come in.'

259

Valentine

'I'm afraid we have a few concerns about your wife's health.'

Valentine sat across from Mr Richards, the senior manager of the care home, and one of his team leaders. They had called him in to talk about Gisele, although it was the manager doing all the talking.

'Lately she seems to have lost her appetite,' he continued, his face grave.

'Gisele's always been a fussy eater.'

'She's lost quite a bit of weight – my staff are concerned,' added the team leader, looking at her files.

Valentine shifted in his seat. He felt ambushed.

'No offence, but my wife's French. She finds the food here quite basic.'

Merde was how she actually put it, thought Valentine, but best not go into detail.

Behind his desk, which was filled with photographs of his family, the manager bristled.

'We might not have a Michelin star, Mr Crowther, but our catering staff are highly qualified to create meals that specifically meet the requirements of our residents.'

Specifically meet the requirements of our residents.

Valentine suddenly had an image of *Le rosbif* that Gisele would conjure up every Sunday. Crisp on the outside, rare and pink on the inside, accompanied by *gratin dauphinois* and a Béarnaise sauce. With the best will in the world, the

Sunday lunch he'd just witnessed would never come close to meeting Gisele's culinary requirements.

'And she doesn't like it when you put a bib on her.'

Earlier, Valentine had been quite upset to walk in and find his wife with a bib around her neck, as if she was a baby. Gisele wore silk scarves from Paris, not a plastic bib.

'We take the utmost care to preserve the dignity of our residents, but we have to balance this with the practicality of their needs.' The team leader spoke kindly, but firmly.

'It's not always an easy job. As I'm sure you're aware,' added the manager, fixing him with a pointed look.

And now Valentine felt guilty. He'd seen how hard it was looking after Gisele at home. Constantly spilling and, later, soiling. Dressing and undressing. He hadn't been able to cope. That's why she'd come to live here.

He felt his eyes well up, threatening to betray him, and he blinked hard. He wished Helen, his daughter, was here. She was so clever and always so calm in situations like this; people respected her. She'd know all the right things to say.

'I know you're doing your best.'

'Everything we do is in your wife's best interests, Mr Crowther,' said the team leader kindly, and the manager nodded.

It was as if the air was being let out of a balloon. Valentine felt himself deflate. He wasn't here to get angry or argue. Mr Richards was a nice enough man. Young, probably in his forties, with a wife and children, judging by the array of silver-framed photographs. His wife probably made him his tea when he got home, washed and ironed his shirts; kissed him goodnight after they'd made love.

Or maybe it was one of those modern marriages – maybe he ironed his own shirts and cooked his family's tea. Either way, Mr Richards had no idea of the horror that could be lying in wait ahead of him. That while his wife was booking a family skiing holiday at half-term, and he was wondering whether to increase his pension contributions, there might well come a time when she would have no recollection of that holiday. Or of him, in fact. That when he showed her those silver-framed photos of the kids, she'd smile and nod, then ask who they were. Or that he'd be spending his retirement alone.

But maybe he'd get lucky and it wouldn't happen to him. Valentine hoped it wouldn't. He wouldn't wish it on his worst enemy. Not that Mr Richards was his enemy. He just didn't have a clue. It didn't matter how many certificates he had hanging on his wall to show how qualified and experienced he was in dementia care, nobody really had a clue until it happened to someone they loved.

'Gisele told me today, she wants to see the sea again.'

'The sea?' Mr Richards frowned.

Valentine got a sense that he was losing patience.

'Mr Crowther. I was rather hoping our meeting today could be spent discussing the arrangements we've put in place for her to see a doctor to assess the current situation. On his recommendation, it might be that your wife needs to be referred for blood tests.'

Words. He used so many words. Valentine had never been a man of words; he left school at fifteen, and since then he simply got on and did things. What was there to discuss? His wife was suffering from a disease that no number of blood tests was ever going to cure. But somehow, in the growing fog of her mind, she'd glimpsed a memory of their trip to Whitby with their daughter more than fifty years ago. The feeling of sand between her toes. The salty smell of the sea. The sound of the waves. Talking about it had made her come alive again, and Valentine wanted to grab on to his wife once more before she slipped away.

Because of course she was slipping away. Valentine knew that. He wasn't daft. He didn't need Mr Richards and his team leader to call him in to tell him. Gisele didn't need blood tests. She was disappearing fast before his eyes – not only mentally, but physically.

'If you don't mind, I'd like to take her to Whitby first.'

The way Mr Richards's chest inflated in his neatly ironed shirt, it would appear that he minded rather a lot.

'Just for the day,' added Valentine, hoping to appease him.

'I'm afraid we don't recommend day-trips, not for the first six months, as it can upset their routine.'

'But you couldn't stop me.'

Valentine watched the looks fly between the senior manager and his team leader. Up till now, her role at today's meeting appeared to be more in a supportive, paper-shuffling, note-taking capacity. But now, judging by the look he'd thrown her, it would appear that her role was to rescue the manager from this cantankerous old man.

'No, of course not, Mr Crowther.' She smiled brightly. 'We're not here to stop families seeing their loved ones.'

Valentine felt himself relax. He didn't mean for it to come out like that; he was just upset and feeling frustrated.

'Now, how about I make us all a nice cup of tea and we can talk it over? Perhaps put a date in the diary for later in the year?' She stood up, watched by a relieved Mr Richards. 'How do you take it? Milk? Sugar?'

Valentine felt a flash of disappointment, followed by determination.

'Actually, no, but thank you.' He stood up and doffed his cap. 'I've taken up too much of your precious time already.'

Turning to leave, he smiled gratefully. Because really, at the end of the day, they were bloody saints, the lot of them. Keeping Gisele safe, looking after her and everyone else's loved ones too. He'd seen how kind and patient the care workers were, and he owed them all a great debt.

But that wasn't going to stop him taking his wife to the seaside to visit the sea.

'Forecast for Monday is sunshine. I'll see you both then.'

Hey you,

Wish you were here!

Thought I would send you a postcard from Whitby. I'm on a day-trip with my friends Valentine, his wife Gisele, Maya, who I used to tutor – oh and Will came too. Did I tell you he's staying with me for a few days? Anyway we all drove here this morning in Valentine's old camper van (thank God Harry's got over his carsickness). We took 'the scenic route', but really I think we just got lost, and when we finally saw the sea Gisele was so excited. As was Harry!

I think it's his first time at the seaside, as he went a bit crazy on the beach, barking at the waves and trying to catch them. He made everyone laugh, including Gisele, which was pretty special as she hasn't been very well. Valentine says it's the first time he's seen her laugh like that in ages. It's been great getting to spend time with Will again too. Wait until you see him again; he's grown so tall! He and Maya seem to have really hit it off – holiday romance, maybe??

Oh, to be a teenager again . . . it feels so long ago. Like being a different person. Makes me think about Ben. You know, I've been seeing a lot of him. No, I don't mean like that. He's working on the house and we've really got to know each other. Funny how you can get someone so wrong. He's nothing like he used to be. But then are any of us the same as when we were young?

Being here reminds me of that time we went to the seaside, and you got a rubber dinghy and I was so scared you were going to float away. Remember how you tied a piece of string to the dinghy, and I stood on the shoreline and held the other end to make sure you were safe and didn't disappear. Sometimes I still feel like I'm standing on that beach, holding that piece of string.

You know I'll never let go, don't you?

x

'See You Later, Alligator'

Sitting on my beach towel, I finish writing my postcard, then take out my phone and take a photograph of the front and back and email it. A very twenty-first-century postcard. This way, it'll get there much quicker; plus you don't need a stamp.

Or an address.

Taking a deep lungful of salty air, I straighten up and look out across the waves, watching their frothy peaks rolling lazily in and out; the way the light is catching on the water, making it glitter, as it stretches out to meet the horizon. It's a perfect summer's day. Blue skies. Plenty of sunshine. The warmest of breezes.

I turn and look over my suntanned shoulder to see Maya and Will on the sand next to me. They met a few days ago, when she came over to the house on the premise of returning some study aids now her exams were over, though I think it was more a case of wanting to talk about her recent break-up with Zac and to get away from her parents. They were still insistent she was going to university. Maya was still resolved not to.

Poor Maya. She put such a brave face on things, but I know how devastated she's been about Zac. When I drove her home from the theatre that night, she refused to cry and declared herself better off without him. Still, he was her first love, and we can all remember how intense that feels, even if it's unrequited. Look at me with Ben. It's more than thirty years ago and I can still conjure up those teenage feelings.

As it turned out, Maya didn't end up talking about Zac, but talking – nay, *flirting* – with Will, who'd woken from a mammoth four-day sleeping session and was pottering around my kitchen in nothing but flip-flops and a sarong. He's decided to stay a couple of weeks, and I couldn't be happier. I look at him now, stretched out on the sand, looking like something from *Love Island* with his tanned muscular frame and brightly coloured board-shorts he brought back from Thailand. Headphones in, he's scrolling through his phone and talking to Maya. I used to have to nag him a dozen times to do one thing, and now look at him. *Multitasking.* Who would ever have thought it?

Maya sits cross-legged next to him wearing a large pair of chunky headphones, sunscreen and an oversized T-shirt, scrolling through her own phone in tandem. Every so often they'll show each other their screens and laugh. There's also a roll-up being passed between them that smells quite suspicious. I don't ask – I'm just pleased to see them both look so happy. I'm strictly an old fart whose holiday romances pre-dated smartphones and Spotify.

What did they look like in Valentine and Gisele's era? I wonder, glancing over at them now. They're sitting side by side in their deckchairs, sharing a flask of tea. Lapsang Souchong, apparently. Behind them a row of brightly coloured beach huts lines the front. To look at them, you'd think they were just an old married couple enjoying a day out at the seaside, without a care in the world. I grab my phone and take a photo. Capturing forever a moment in time when that's exactly what they are.

*

'Want to go for a day out, hunting vampires?'

Having brought his old camper van out of the garage, that was how Valentine had put it when he'd asked me a few days ago. He'd remembered our conversation from before, and I jumped at the chance. I'd always wanted to visit the famous seaside town of Whitby; plus it was the perfect opportunity. With schools about to break up for the summer holidays, my tutoring work had slowed right down, so I had lots of free time.

But who knew for how much longer? I hadn't missed being in the classroom, but I had missed the salary. Being sensible about it, I knew I should probably return to full-time teaching, yet I'd kept putting off applying for jobs.

Plus this way it meant I finally got to meet Gisele. I'd heard so much about her, but Valentine hadn't wanted me to see her in the care home. 'She wouldn't like it,' he'd said, when earlier I'd suggesting accompanying him on one of his regular visits. 'She's such a proud woman. She always said first impressions count.'

If the truth be told, I also think Valentine needed an extra pair of hands on his day out. He would never say it, but it was a lot for him to manage. Gisele had her walking stick, but she could be a little unsteady on her feet, and it was easier if there was someone to help her in and out of the camper van. Although, as it turned out, there were three extra pairs.

'More the merrier,' Valentine had said, when I'd asked if Will and Maya could come along too.

Gisele was tinier than I'd imagined, with finely turned ankles and bright eyes the colour of hyacinths. She was dressed immaculately in a smart navy trouser suit teamed with a silk scarf, which she wore effortlessly around her neck – how do French women do that? And a wide-brimmed sunhat, which no doubt explained her beautiful skin.

She spoke French quite a bit, which, despite my O-level, I understood only sparingly. She seemed delighted to see me, hugging and kissing me on both cheeks; and even more delighted to meet Harry, to whom she responded immediately, stroking and petting him, even though he covered her navy trousers in endless dog hairs. Meanwhile Maya and Will waved from the back of the camper, which was surprisingly roomy. It had been stuck in the garage forever, but Valentine had given it a wash and hoovered the inside, while I spruced up the curtains by giving them a quick iron.

'Be good to get it out for a run,' he said as we busied ourselves with our buckets and mops and the ironing board. 'Blow away the cobwebs.'

And I said yes and nodded, as the radio played and the kettle boiled. But we both knew the cobwebs we were trying to blow away, and they weren't just the ones in the camper van.

'Argh, I can't believe it!'

Maya lets out a scream, waking up Harry, who's lying next to me. He jumps up and starts barking at some invisible danger.

'What's wrong?' I ask, trying to quieten him down.

She quickly scoots over, waving her phone underneath my nose.

'Nothing's wrong. Look!'

I squint at her screen, but the sunlight's causing a reflection.

'I can't see – what does it say?' Plus, if I'm honest, I need my reading glasses.

'It's the crowdfunding page I set up for the village hall,' she continues, excitedly. 'We've got our first contributions.'

'You set up a crowdfunder?' I look at her in astonishment. 'I had no idea.'

'Well, I thought I'd better not say anything, in case we didn't raise any money.' She breaks off with a grin. 'But look, we've already raised seven hundred and fifty quid.'

'Did I hear someone say "seven hundred and fifty quid"?'

A voice from the deckchair. Valentine's hearing seems suddenly to have improved considerably.

'Who donated?' I ask, amazed.

Maya scrolls through the names and begins reading them out. I recognize a few of the locals in the village.

'Well, I never.' Valentine shakes his head.

'Never what?' Gisele still has her French accent. I see her turn to Valentine. She looks troubled.

'We're raising money, love, for the village hall, so that we can go dancing again.'

'Dancing?' Her face visibly lights up.

'Aye, remember? Like we used to?'

But now she's looking worried again, and I can see her hands clasped tightly in her lap, her fingers rubbing themselves agitatedly over her knuckles. I get up from my towel and walk over to them both. As soon as she sees me, Gisele breaks into a smile and reaches up her hands to me.

'Helen. *Mon bébé*.'

I see the pain on Valentine's face as his wife confuses me with his daughter, but I simply smile back and let Gisele hug me. I've read that correcting someone who is suffering from dementia only confuses and upsets them.

'Isn't it a lovely day?' I say as we break apart, though she slips her hand into mine to keep hold. I squeeze it back and glance reassuringly at Valentine. He smiles gratefully.

'*Jour parfait*,' she says now. 'I came here once with my daughter and husband, you know.'

'That sounds like fun.'

'She was only a baby – she liked to crawl on the sand.'

Gisele peers at me then, as if trying to place me, and for a moment I worry I've confused her, but within seconds her mind has changed direction. 'You would have loved my husband. We used to go dancing at the Plaza. Oh, you should've seen us on the dance floor.'

Letting go of my hand, she begins beating out an invisible tune with her fingers on the arms of her deckchair.

'Do you want to borrow these?' Maya joins us and unloops her chunky headphones from around her neck and holds them towards Gisele. 'You can listen to music.'

'Thanks, but it's all right, love.' Valentine answers for his wife. But Maya isn't to be put off.

'What music did you dance to? I've got Spotify.'

'Eh?' He frowns, confused.

'Bill Haley and His Comets,' I tell her, recalling Valentine teaching me how to jive.

'OK, hang on.' With both thumbs she texts dexterously into her phone. 'How about "See You Later, Alligator"?'

'We loved that one, didn't we, Gisele?' Valentine turns to his wife.

There's no response. It's as if she's retreated somewhere and can no longer hear us; I see Valentine's crushed expression and feel my heart break a little. There are no miracles, like in the movies. This is real life. But then something quite remarkable happens. Crouching down in the sand next to her, Maya holds the headphones to Gisele's ear and, as the opening beats of the song begin to play, her reaction is as immediate as it's joyful. Her eyes suddenly widen and a delighted smile breaks over her face as she begins to move in time to the beat.

'See, she remembers,' grins Maya as I watch with amazement.

'Of course she does.' Valentine's face is overcome with emotion.

'I have an idea.' Quickly Maya calls over to Will. 'Hey, let me borrow your headphones.'

It only takes a few minutes to synchronize them, and now Gisele and Valentine are both wearing headphones as the song begins to play again. Only this time Valentine reaches out his hand, just like he did all those years ago in the Plaza in Leeds, when he was only nineteen years old. And Gisele takes it, as she did when she was only eighteen, and together they dance barefoot on the beach.

Two people lost in a happy memory, with only the sound of the waves washing against the shore. I don't know about a miracle, but if that's not magic, I don't know what is.

Running on Empty

Afterwards we leave the beach and go to get fish and chips on the beach front.

'What did I tell you? There's nothing wrong with your appetite that a bit of sea air wouldn't solve,' says Valentine cheerfully, sprinkling salt and vinegar on his wife's chips. 'Is there, love?'

He's not fooling anyone, least of all himself. It's apparent to us all that Gisele can only manage a few mouthfuls, but Valentine is determinedly upbeat. Dancing together again was an unexpected gift – nothing is going to spoil today.

We leave them sitting together on the front and walk up to explore the abbey set on the hill, Harry at our heels. The path weaves up to the soaring Gothic ruins, with their stunning sea views. No wonder Bram Stoker chose to set his horror novel here; it couldn't be more atmospheric.

Or ripe for trying to frighten the living daylights out of us, as Will larks around, jumping out from behind the ruins, doing a terrible Dracula impression.

We laugh and shriek and take too many photos, which they immediately post to Instagram. I send one to Naomi, who messages:

Fang-tastic!

Count me in!

This proves exactly why we're friends.
We're both a pain in the neck.

To which I reply with a funny vampire meme, as I'm with young people and they know about these things.

It's fun being with Maya and Will and, for their part, they don't seem to mind me tagging along, playing third wheel. They talk about bands I've never heard of and Will's backpacking antics, which, frankly, I *wish* I'd never heard about, while discussing summer festivals and future plans.

'I'm sure I failed.' Maya is still fretting about her exams.

'You're not going to fail them,' I tell her as we stop to admire the view. 'And anyway, I thought you weren't going to uni, so what does it matter what grades you get?'

'Why wouldn't you go to uni?' frowns Will. 'It was the best three years of my life.'

'Because I don't want to spend three years partying,' quips Maya. 'I want to change the world.'

'Oh yeah?' He looks at her with interest. 'And how do you plan on doing that?'

'By protesting and going on marches.'

'Do you really think that changes anything?'

'Ask Greta Thunberg.'

'She's probably too busy talking to world leaders.' He grins and I watch Maya loosen. 'I'm not saying marches don't work, but I think it's easier to change the world from the inside than protesting from the outside. That's why I did a law degree – I'm going to be an environmental lawyer.'

'You are?' Now it's Maya's turn to look with interest. Until now, a degree had seemed so pointless. Studying law isn't something she's ever considered and I can see it's a revelation.

'Yeah, I'm starting a paid internship with one of the big rewilding and climate-change charities in September.'

And just like that, without knowing it, Will does what nagging parents and private tutors could never do. He changes Maya's mind.

Later that afternoon we leave to head home, with the smell of the sea and fish and chips and sunshine clinging to us. It's a two-hour drive and we spend the journey sharing photos and funny moments, talking over each other and laughing, in the way old friends do.

'Look at the size of Valentine's ice-cream!'

'When you eat it in a cornet, there's no calories. It's a fact.'

'What's Dracula's favourite flavour of ice-cream?'

'Dunno. Garlic?'

'*Vein*illa.'

'Argh, that's so corny!'

'Did you see that man in his budgie smugglers?'

'I can never *un*-see it!'

'You shouldn't have been looking . . .'

'What about when Harry tried to eat that woman's sandwiches!'

Which was somewhat less funny, but still.

Only Gisele remains silent. I look at her now, sitting next to Valentine in the passenger seat. With her window wound down, she's gazing out as the scenery flashes past. I wonder what she's thinking. I wonder if she can remember any of their previous day-trips, or even today's. I think about how we're always told to live in the moment. Since getting Harry, he's taught me that more and more, but after spending the day with Gisele and Valentine it hits me even harder.

This time it's a straight shot home, as Valentine has agreed to let me do the directions. But after we've been travelling for an hour the van begins to stutter and cough.

'Is everything OK?' I ask.

'Aye, it's nothing.' Valentine bats away my concern.

We continue on for a few minutes and I'm thinking I probably imagined it, when gradually we begin losing speed. Followed by a few more hiccups. And then the engine cuts out and the camper van grinds to a halt. Luckily we've managed to freewheel into a lay-by.

'Is it the engine?' Will cranes his neck to try and see the warning lights on the dashboard, but having been built in 1967, there are only a couple of dials.

Valentine turns the engine. It doesn't start.

'Have we broken down?' Maya looks up from her phone.

I make a shushing sign and gesture at Gisele, who's looking alarmed.

'I want to go home,' she says now. 'Can I go home?'

'Of course you can, love, I just need to get her started.' Valentine tries to reassure his wife.

'Can I help at all?' I force a cheerful tone.

'Well, that depends.' Valentine pushes back his cap and scratches his forehead.

'On what?' Will shifts seats so he's nearer to the front. 'I know a bit about engines. I can take a look under the bonnet, if you'd like.'

'Well, you won't find much wrong there.'

'How do you know, before we've looked?'

'Because we've run out of petrol.' Pointing to the gauge on the dash, Valentine looks abashed. 'I forgot to fill her up.'

For a moment there is silence as this reality sinks in.

'I wrote it on the list and everything,' he continues. 'I don't know how I forgot, it must have been with all the excitement.'

'Are you a member of the AA?' asks Maya hopefully.

By the expression on Valentine's face, it's quite evident he's not, and he looks quite upset.

'Don't worry, I am,' I say, quickly digging out my phone and dialling them, but immediately I'm put on hold.

'I want to go home,' repeats Gisele, looking visibly distressed.

'Don't worry, it'll be fixed soon enough.'

When I finally get through to an operator, she tells me they're very busy. The good weather has meant there are a lot of people on the roads, which in turn means a large number of breakdowns to attend to. There's a current wait time of at least an hour for someone to attend our vehicle. I relay the message back to everyone.

'Please, I'm scared now.'

'You're safe, love, I promise.'

I can see the worry etched on Valentine's face as he tries, but fails, to console Gisele. Maya and Will attempt to help with words of encouragement, but nothing anyone can say or do seems to work. Instead she seems to growing more agitated and I feel a rising panic. How are we going to keep her calm until the AA arrives? There has to be something.

Then I notice Harry. He'd been curled under the back seat, fast asleep, but now he's woken up and is pushing himself between the seats, nuzzling into Gisele's lap in an attempt to comfort her. Absently she begins stroking his soft head in her lap, her fingers ruffling his fur, her mind visibly being soothed; the transformation is incredible.

When I finish giving the operator our details, I hang up and glance across at Valentine. He meets my eyes with a look of relief.

'Thank you,' he mouths quietly.

'Don't thank me.' I gesture towards Gisele; her eyes are closed in relaxation and she has a peaceful smile on her face. 'Thank Harry.'

Stanley

Red cars: fourteen. Blue cars: ten. White cars: six and a van, but that wasn't really a car.

Stanley counted how many vehicles they passed on the way there. He liked counting things – it made things neater and put them in order. Like when Auntie Holly got him to tidy up his bedroom. Only this wasn't his bedroom; it was the world outside. It also made him feel safer, because sometimes car journeys made him feel a bit scared. But today his dad told him not to feel scared because Liv and Harry were coming too.

At first he was going to count all the different car colours, but there were too many on the road, so instead he decided to only count red, white and blue because they were the colours of the Union Jack, which was the national flag of the United Kingdom. When they arrived, a lady came outside to meet them. She had really curly hair and smiled a lot when she shook his dad's hand. She asked him how their journey was, so Stanley told her about the red, white and blue cars and the Union Jack.

'And the American flag is called the "Stars and Stripes",' he added.

She seemed really impressed that he knew that flags had actual names, so he told her that his class had been learning about flags of the world this week at school.

'Do you like your school, Stanley?'

'Some bits.'

Because that was true. There were some bits he really liked. Like when he had to make a Second World War air-raid shelter in history class, out of papier mâché and poster paint, or when he got to do reading and making-up stories. Learning new words was his favourite. But there were other bits he didn't like, and he didn't want to talk about those because they could make him feel upset.

Luckily the lady with the curly hair didn't ask him about the bits he didn't like. Instead she asked if they'd like her to show them around the school, but it wasn't really a question. Stanley noticed adults did that a lot. Ask questions that weren't really questions. Anyway, he didn't mind this time, as she was really nice and she showed them lots of things – like the big, bright assembly hall with walls filled with lots of artwork, and the box they kept in the corner of all the classrooms, for if you were ever feeling sad or angry or cross.

She called it a 'calm box' and let Stanley play with it. It was really fun. He made a list in his head of all the things inside: playdough, bendy pipe-cleaners, a beanbag, a massage ball, and soft material like his comforter, which he still kept hidden under his pillow at home. His dad must have liked the box too, as he was smiling when Stanley was playing with it. Liv had left Harry in the van because dogs weren't allowed into the school, and she kept asking lots of questions. He kept hearing her talking about 'support' and 'adequate training' and 'keeping him in the mainstream'. Stanley didn't know what all those words meant, but he hoped Harry was OK.

When they drove home, his dad asked if he'd like to go to that school. Stanley didn't know if he would; he didn't like new things. But his dad said that Harry had been new, and now he liked Harry a lot. Which was a very good point, and one Stanley hadn't thought of before. So he said he would think about it and looked out of the window. This time he counted: Red cars: eight. Blue cars: eighteen. White cars: four.

Which made blue the winner, with a total of twenty-eight cars. Stanley was pleased about that, as blue was his favourite colour.

A Big Birthday

On a Saturday morning, two weeks after my day-trip to Whitby, I catch the train to London to celebrate Naomi's big birthday. This time I'm going to be away for the weekend. Well, technically it's only one night, but still. A whole weekend in the city! Back to where I used to call home for more than twenty years. It feels both strange and exciting, and a whole other bunch of complicated emotions that I don't want to think about right now, so I've packed them along with my underwear and toiletries.

Valentine has kindly offered to look after Harry. Apparently he's got plans to take him out for lots of walks, which is what the doctor ordered, though I have feeling most of them will end at the pub.

'Well, walking's thirsty work,' he says to me when I insinuate this. 'And the doctor told me it's very important to stay hydrated when you get to my age.'

'I'm not sure he meant with beer, though, Valentine,' I point out, but he pretends to not hear me.

Valentine's camper van is still in the garage – it turned out to be not just lack of petrol that caused it to break down on the way back from the seaside – so Ben drops me at the station. He's cheerful and much less distracted than recently. A weight of anxiety seems to have lifted after last week's visit to the new school. I'd learned about it after speaking to Evelyn, whom I'd met at the pub quiz. After Valentine had told me she was a retired headmistress I'd called at her house on one of my walks, in the hope that she might be able to help. Delighted to be of assistance, she'd put me in touch with a former colleague who was now head of a mainstream school in a neighbouring village that had great resources in place for children with support needs like Stanley.

The visit had been a huge success; now it was a case of waiting to hear if a space would open for Stanley in time for the start of the new term in September. Currently the school was fully subscribed.

The local train is busy, but I manage to find a seat as it pulls away from the station. I think back to when I first arrived here in the dead of winter, with my life in a total mess. Was it really only six months since I'd stood in that dark, poky bedroom of what was to become my home and looked out across the pitch-darkness of the graveyard?

It feels like a lifetime ago. I was so lost and lonely, so worried I was making a mistake, and desperate to find some kind of connection. A text pops up from Maya, wishing me safe travels, with a list of random emojis. I text a smiley face back. Now I've found that connection in spades. Even if sometimes it makes absolutely no sense.

Resting my cheek against the glass, I gaze out of the window. Gone are the skeleton trees and leaden-grey skies that greeted me when I first arrived. As we slowly rattle through the country-side, I take in the sweeping valleys dotted with sheep and criss-crossed with drystone walls. Summer is now blazing and the landscape is lush and green; it's hard to imagine the dead of winter when the Dales seem so glorious and alive.

The textile-mill chimneys herald the arrival of Leeds, where I change onto a sleek modern train that will take me to London. It feels symbolic. The speed increases, the colours blur, the fields and open space give away to urban sprawl. We stop at platforms; they get busier, as does the train. I see city clothes and smartphones. Once the passengers are in their seats, the texting and scrolling begin. Or did it ever stop? No one looks up. No one ever looks up. How did I never notice that before?

The final destination is King's Cross. It's a journey of more than two hundred miles and I disembark into a different world. The station is thronged with people, rushing back and forth, all in a hurry to be somewhere else. Life feels as if it has suddenly gathered pace. I look around me and, for the first time in months, I don't recognize a familiar face.

The Tube is packed, and I stand up all the way to Naomi's. She lives in a flat on the ground floor of an ex-local-authority building. From the outside it's nondescript, with a plain red-brick exterior and a bare forecourt that appears to be used only as storage for everyone's recycling bins. But walk through her front door and it opens out into a treasure trove of gold pineapple lamps, Frida Kahlo cushions and sixties prints. The style is unreservedly unapologetic; like Naomi herself.

'You're here! You're actually here!'

After greeting me with a shriek of delight that must have alerted all the neighbours, Naomi finally stops hugging me and ushers me past the wall of tropical-palm wallpaper and out into her courtyard garden, where there's a pitcher of something very alcoholic waiting.

'Of course I'm here – you invited me.'

'I know, it's just . . .' As she shakes her head, her feather earrings flutter back and forth. 'I didn't know if you'd be able to make it.'

'I'm not going to miss a party!' After the long journey I flop gratefully down into one of her rainbow-coloured chairs. Made of strings of wire rope, they are surprisingly comfy.

'They're called Acapulco chairs – isn't that the best name?' she says, pouring me a drink.

'It's like that song by Barry Manilow.'

'That's "Cocacabana",' she laughs, handing me a brightly coloured cocktail.

'Geography was never my strong point,' I grin and take a sip of my drink. 'Mmm, delicious.' Unsurprisingly, Naomi makes very strong drinks. I'm going to have to pace myself. 'Where's Ellie?'

'Having a sleepover, so Mummy can *par-tay*,' she whoops, shimmying her tiny hips and making me wonder how many of these cocktails she's had already.

'So how you feeling about your birthday?'

'A bit mental,' she admits, folding herself into the chair opposite. 'I mean, it's really kind of crazy. I remember my mum turning fifty. I was sixteen and got drunk on Malibu and pineapple. I thought she was so old.'

'It was different then. Fifty is the new thirty.'

'Try telling that to a thirty-year-old,' she says and I laugh.

'Well, I bet she wasn't wearing cowboy boots.' I gesture to them. 'Are they new?'

'They're a birthday present to myself. I always wanted a pair of cowboy boots with angel wings on the side.'

'Only you could pull them off.'

'That means you hate them.'

'No, I love them. They're fabulous. I just bought myself a pair of Crocs,' I grin.

Naomi looks appalled. 'You did not.'

'They're so practical,' I confess, and I can feel her eyes upon me.

'Fashion should never be practical,' she replies sternly, as if telling me a universal truth.

And she's probably right. But to be honest, I was never much of a fashionista, even when I was younger, and any last attempts at being fashionable ended the moment I got a dog and started living in a construction site in the middle of the countryside, somewhere it rains a lot. Even in summer.

'Don't worry. I decided if I'm going to a party in trendy bar in Soho, I needed a bit of a makeover, so I had Maya pick out my outfit,' I tell Naomi.

'Isn't Maya seventeen?'

'Soon to be eighteen, as she's forever telling me.'

'Don't tell me it's cut-offs and a crop-top.' She pulls a scary expression and I burst out laughing.

'It's like I said to my builder: it's a remodel, not a new-build.'

'How is Bob the Builder?' Crunching on the ice from her glass, Naomi raises her eyebrows.

I roll mine. 'He's pretty good. Nearly finished. A widow,' I add. It's like shoving something on a shelf because you don't know where to put it.

She almost chokes on her ice cube.

'He's a widow?'

I nod.

'So he's not married?'

It's not hard to see where Naomi is going with this.

'Well, that's usually what "widow" means.' To be honest, I feel a bit irritated by her insensitivity.

'Doesn't he have a little boy?'

'Yes, Stanley. He's seven.'

'The same age as Ellie.'

And just like that, all thoughts of potential matchmaking go flying out of the window and she suddenly sobers up. She's no longer the birthday girl getting into the party spirit, or the best friend trying to fix up her girlfriend; she's a mother imagining her worst fear. I see Naomi's expression and feel bad for judging her.

'It was a couple of years ago; it's been hard, but I think they're getting through it.'

'I can't imagine.' She shakes her head. 'I'm glad they've got each other. Are they close?'

'Very.' I can tell what she's thinking and wish I'd never mentioned it. 'I'm sorry, I didn't mean to spoil your birthday.'

'Don't be silly.' She quickly bats me away. 'It's life: part and parcel. Good and bad.' She forces a bright smile. 'People keep asking me how I feel about turning fifty. Bloody lucky, that's how I feel. Ageing is a privilege.'

'I'll drink to that.' Raising my glass, I think of my own mum. She was only thirty-four. She never even got close to fifty. 'So what's the plan for tonight?' I force myself to snap back.

'Danny said to be at the bar by seven thirty.'

Now it's my turn to look shocked.

'*Danny?*'

She nods, trying – and failing – not to look as pleased as she obviously is. 'We're back together. We're even talking about moving in together.'

'Naomi, that's great!' I cry, then reprimand her. 'When were you going to tell me?'

'I wanted to be certain before I said anything. These past few weeks we've been doing a lot of talking—' She breaks off. 'Thanks to you.'

'Well, it was hardly groundbreaking advice.'

'No, but it was.' She shrugs. 'It's so easy to imagine what's going on in each other's heads, and to have all these conversations with yourself, when really the conversation you should be having is with each other. Once we started talking, we both said things that neither of us had realized.'

'Like what?'

'Like all these years I thought it was the men who were the commitment-phobes.' She looks down at her summer

287

dress and picks at an invisible thread. 'But actually it was me all along.' She raises her eyes to meet mine.

'You really think so?'

'Yeah.' She says it quietly at first, then more firmly. 'Yeah, I do. And as soon as I was honest – not only with Danny, but with myself – it was as if all my fears fell away. Like they lost their power somehow.'

A look passes between us. Fears are such strange things, aren't they? We're so scared we don't confront them; yet it's keeping them hidden that makes them scary. Like monsters in horror movies, as soon as they're unmasked they're not so frightening after all.

'Turned out I was the one who didn't want to commit. How mad is that?'

I raise an eyebrow. 'You only just realized that?'

Naomi grins, leaning her head back and gazing up at the cloudless sky. 'I was scared of being trapped. Making a mistake. Needing someone. Scared of letting someone in, in case they let me down.' She takes in a deep breath, then lets it out. 'In case they broke my heart.'

'You'd still survive. Look at me.'

'You didn't simply survive it, Liv – you've thrived.' She looks across at me. 'You're my superhero.'

'Oh, I don't know about that.' I give an awkward laugh.

'I do. I saw how devastated you were when David left, how scared and brave you were being that day when you packed up and left London. Superheroes rescue people, and you rescued yourself. That's pretty heroic.'

I shrug. 'It happens to lots of people. I'm not special.'

'Just because what happened wasn't extraordinary, it doesn't mean that you're not.'

I fall silent, letting her words sink in. We grow up thinking we need lots of friends, but as I've got older I've realized all you need are a few who matter. Naomi has always allowed me to feel how I feel. She's never got mad or impatient with me, for not getting over my divorce as quickly as some people thought I should. And yet she's never allowed me to get stuck in my misery, either.

'If I told you I loved you, would we be veering dangerously into weepy, drunken "I love you, man" mode?' I ask and she grins.

'Probably. But it's my birthday, so I'm allowed to get drunk and weepy and tell you I love you.'

'What's my excuse?'

She laughs. 'You're going to be wearing an outfit picked out by a seventeen-year-old.'

The Surprise

Lots of things polarize people. Politics. Religion. Marmite. But there's something else that divides people into two camps: *surprises*. Either you love them or you hate them. I'm definitely in the second camp. In fact I'd go so far as to say that I live in fear of them. When people say, 'Oh come on, who doesn't love a good surprise?', I would stick my hand up and argue that, by its very nature, a surprise is never good.

It's being unprepared, it's the loss of control, it's the pressure to react correctly and quickly by looking thrilled and excited – and not how you might be feeling, which is most probably dazed and mortified. It's the very publicness of it all: by its very nature, when someone springs a surprise, they want to see your reaction.

It's everyone jumping out from behind your sofa shouting, 'Surprise!' when you've just got back from having a massage on your birthday and you're sporting scruffy joggers, oily hair and a face imprinted from lying face-down on a massage table. That happened one year and I was mortified.

It's finding a little red box in the back of a drawer.

Naomi, however, is definitely in the love-it camp. In fact as we catch an Uber across town to her party, she confesses to being a tiny bit disappointed that Danny hadn't kept it as a surprise.

'Not that I'm not really grateful to him for organizing it,' she adds hurriedly. 'It was really sweet of him to offer, and he's got his band to play and everything.'

'But that's brilliant.' I feel a swell of happiness, not only for Naomi, but for me too. I can't remember the last time I looked forward to an evening out as much. Getting over the loss of my old life, and feeling happy again, has taken a long time, but tonight I feel like I've finally turned a corner.

'Plus Danny is hopeless at keeping surprises, so I would've guessed anyway.' She grins and turns to rest her face against the open window, wound all the way down to let in the warm evening air, as we whizz through Hyde Park.

The venue is a private room above a stylish bar in Soho. The drummer in Danny's band is a friend of the owner, who has let them have it free of charge. It's accessed by walking through the downstairs lounge-bar area, which is so achingly hip it makes me feel about a hundred. And so deafeningly loud that my ears are still ringing as I climb the narrow staircase that leads to the upper floor.

We're the first to arrive and the big, empty space couldn't be more different from downstairs: bare, worn floorboards, cathedral ceilings and large sash windows, pulled wide open to give a great view of the busy cobbled streets below; a small bar is tucked in the corner and there's a makeshift stage at the far end.

Danny is still busy setting up and leaps over as we make our entrance. I watch him hugging and kissing Naomi, while she laughs and pretends to protest. I like Danny a lot. If you didn't know him, you might dismiss him as some ageing musician from Newcastle; too old still to be wearing a baseball cap and playing bass in a band that was never going to hit the big time. David used to say that Danny needed to grow up and act his age – which is a bit ironic now, considering.

But appearances can be deceptive and, behind the leather jacket and laidback attitude, Danny is twenty years sober and as solid as a rock. He's also something of a computer genius and recently sold a couple of apps to a US software company, which netted him a small fortune and afforded him the kind of stunning home that you see on the cover of *Architectural Digest*. But, most importantly of all, he completely adores Naomi.

'Wow, Liv, you look great,' he says, turning to greet me. Despite living in London for decades, he's kept his strong Geordie accent. 'The countryside definitely suits you. Love the dress.'

'Isn't she a knockout?' says Naomi.

'A total babe,' he grins, and I laugh and blush, because frankly Naomi is the knockout, in a red satin jumpsuit and killer heels.

But for the first time I don't bash away their compliments with a joke or the justification of 'What, this old thing?' because I *do* feel like a bit of a babe. Moreover I haven't felt anything remotely close to one in years.

Of course it's all thanks to Maya. To be honest, I was a bit nervous when she suggested a makeover. I thought she might want to dress me up in something whacky or bold, or just *not me*, but instead she'd rifled through my wardrobe and chosen an old Diane Von Furstenberg wrap-dress that I've had for years. Made of emerald-green silk with capped sleeves, it has a silver thread running through it and clings in all the right places, but I never wear it as it shows too much cleavage, so I have to safety-pin it.

Which Maya had called completely bonkers. 'You've got great boobs. Why are you apologizing for them?' she'd scolded, hands on hips in my bedroom as I tried it on. 'If I had such an amazing rack, I'd be showing it off!' Moreover, when I suggested a cardigan instead of the safety pin, our roles were reversed and she turned teacher on me, fixing me with the sternest of looks. 'If you're going to wear that dress, wear it how it's supposed to be worn, Liv.'

Suffice to say, I left the cardigan at home and threw away the safety pin. Being an English teacher, I'm sure there's a metaphor in there somewhere, because she's right: it looks so much better now. Funny how I was worried about her choosing something that wasn't *me*, yet in the end it took someone else to see what was me all along.

The party soon gets into full swing as guests arrive and the room fills up. Naomi introduces me to lots of new people; plus we share mutual friends and former work colleagues, so there's lots of hugging and kissing and catching up. I'd been slightly nervous about being back in London and seeing everyone again, and I have a bit of a wobble when I find myself on my own and having to talk to a group of strangers, but my unapologetic cleavage seems to be doing the trick at giving me more confidence. I should have asked Maya to help ages ago. Who knew that getting your boobs out was so much better than a brave face?

And yes, I've had a few drinks, so maybe that's helping. But I don't have time to think about it, as the band begins playing and Naomi and I are dancing and saying, 'Why don't we dance any more?' at the top of our voices, with big grins on our faces. And now Mr Bishop – 'call me Alan', and head of geography – has somehow shuffled into the middle of us and my radar might be completely off, but I think he's trying to flirt with me by telling me all about climbing the highest peaks in the Lake District while staring at my cleavage.

And now, thankfully, I'm being rescued by the arrival of the birthday cake and we're all singing 'Happy Birthday', and Naomi is blowing out the candles and I'm feeling all emotional, but in a good way. Because I love my friend and our friendship and how far we've come; and it strikes me that I might actually love my life again. And just when I think it can't get any better, Danny gets down on one knee, pulls out a ring and asks Naomi to marry him. And she says, 'Yes, of course, you silly arse' and everyone starts cheering and clapping.

And that's when I lose it. Turns out I like surprises when they're for other people.

'Naomi!' I shriek, throwing my arms around her in congratulations when I can finally reach her through all the well-wishers. 'This is amazing! The best news!'

'Really?'

'Yes, really!'

We hug each other, both of us teary-eyed. We have drunk quite a lot. I glance over to the bar, where an elated Danny is being congratulated by his band members, then turn back to Naomi. I'm expecting her to look elated too, but her eyes are anxious.

'What's wrong?' I lower my voice, suddenly worried. 'Don't you want to get married?'

As I said, surprises can be scary things – there's the pressure to react in a certain way. To say 'I do' when you don't.

'Yes, of course. I love him. Ellie loves him too.'

A wave of relief.

'I was worried about you.'

'*Me?*'

'You don't mind me getting married?'

'What? Because I got divorced?' I snort, then realize she's serious. 'No of course not, silly, I'm happy for you.'

But Naomi looks troubled. 'You're not just doing that thing where you're pretending to be really happy? Like I used to feel when women at work would announce their pregnancies. I'd be happy for them, but dying inside.' Her dark eyes meet mine.

'I'm really happy,' I repeat firmly. 'Truly.'

'Thank you.' She reaches for my hand and gives it a grateful squeeze. 'And I promise not to have a hen party.'

'Well, now I'm *elated*,' I say, and we both laugh and spend the next five minutes goggling at her ring, which is Art Deco and beautiful. Who knew Danny was such a traditionalist?

Or that, only six months ago, grief and loss threatened to swamp me. That I feared this heart of mine had been so bashed and broken, it would never heal. But watching Naomi and Danny together makes me realize that: you know what? My heart might still be a bit bruised and ragged around the edges, but it works fine. I still believe in love. And that makes me extraordinarily happy.

And now, after this revelation, I need a pee.

The toilets are downstairs. I leave Naomi and head down the narrow staircase, being careful not to trip in my high heels. I've spent the last six months in wellies or trainers, and more recently Crocs, so I'm woefully out of practice. Feeling rather pleased with myself for managing to navigate the stairs without stumbling, I make my way across the lounge-bar. It's a different world down here. Mood lighting. Expensive cocktails. Uber-fashionable couples. No one over thirty.

And then I see them.

Just a few feet away. Standing by the bar. A slim blonde in a minidress. A distinguished dark-haired man, his arm draped around her waist. He's whispering something in her ear. She's laughing and flicking back her hair. I notice the huge diamond on her finger. Watch his head turn, as he realizes someone is staring at them. See his expression when he recognizes it's me.

It all happens in seconds.

'Liv?'

I'm already in free-fall.

'Hello, David.'

Eighteen months ago

There's a basic rule when it comes to relationships: *Don't snoop*.

Because if you go looking for something, you're going to find it. And more likely than not, it's going to be something you really wished you hadn't found.

Only I wasn't snooping.

I was looking for something as mundane as a missing sock, when I found it tucked away at the back of the drawer. A small red box. It was nestling in David's sock drawer. Right at the very back. Underneath several pairs of rolled-up sport socks.

Hidden.

It was the day after Valentine's Day. Late evening. I was upstairs in our bedroom, putting away neat piles of clean laundry. We'd just got back from a weekend in Devon and I'd spent the last few hours feeding never-ending loads of dirty clothes into the washing machine and dryer. The weather forecast had said sunny, but it had poured down and everything had got filthy.

The place had been recommended on one of those glossy glamping websites. An amazing treehouse with all the trim-mings, in a picturesque spot on the coast. It was going to be super-romantic: all snuggling up beside campfires on the beach, stargazing far-away constellations in clear night skies and drinking the bottle of champagne that I'd hidden in the boot.

I'd also brought along a couple of champagne flutes, which I'd wrapped up in my underwear, because I once read an article written by a French expert about how champagne doesn't taste the same if you drink it out of plastic cups (*quelle horreur!*) – something about the way it affects the bubbles. And I wanted my bubbles to be perfect.

I wanted it all to be perfect.

The past few months we'd both been busy and stressed with work. Me with my new promotion as head of department; David with his partner retiring, and him having to take on their patients and restructure the dental practice. With the long hours, we'd hardly seen each other – David coming home late, me leaving early. We communicated over WhatsApp, and our conversations had lately become a list of reminders.

This was our chance to reconnect, spend time together, have some fun. Except that we didn't, not really. The weather didn't help. And we were both tired. But the treehouse was amazing, and we ate delicious food and swapped Valentine's Day cards and gifts. I gave him a gorgeous silver Art Deco cocktail shaker, which I'd found at an antique fair and knew he'd love; he'd been ridiculously generous and spent a fortune on a first edition of one of my favourite novels.

Still, it was nothing I could put my finger on, but something seemed off. Probably a bit like those champagne bubbles.

David was taking a shower. I could hear the water going. He never opened a window, so it would be all steamed up in there. I felt a beat of irritation, then closed the drawer. I never wanted to be the kind of wife who looked at her husband's private things. I knew of friends who looked through their partner's phone as a matter of course – 'Just a quick look, at night when it's charging,' one had reasoned. 'I never expect to find anything, it's merely a sort of habit. Kind of like an insurance.' But I didn't want that kind of insurance. If you didn't trust someone, then what was the point?

I turned my attention to putting away a pile of T-shirts, a few pairs of jeans, several pairs of my knickers, a couple of shirts. Putting them on hangers, I closed the wardrobe door and went to leave the bedroom to go downstairs and order a pizza. All done. Except for that one sock straggler, lying on the bed. *Bugging me.* I pulled open the drawer again and began scrabbling around determinedly. That missing sock had to be in there somewhere . . .

Aha, found it! Triumphantly I quickly bundled the socks together, then hesitated. My hand hovered over the small red box. Out of nowhere, I had a distinct memory of Naomi once receiving earrings from someone she was dating and telling me that the best presents came in small packages. It had to be jewellery. Yet David had already given me a Valentine's Day gift.

Somewhere inside me, a pulse started beating. As I picked the box up and pressed the small brass button to release the lid, I saw the distinctive gold logo of a famous luxury jewellers. David didn't skimp. Inside was a gold bracelet. Heart pounding, I turned it over in my fingers. He'd had it engraved. The words swam in front of my eyes and the walls seemed to warp in. I'd always thought nothing could be worse than finding out that the person you love doesn't love you any more. I was wrong. It's finding out they're in love with someone else that kills you.

*

So then I did what every woman does when the bottom drops out of her world. I looked at his phone and found the texts.

Brave Face

Thanks for such a fab party.

Was it? I can't remember!
Why did I drink so much?

**BECAUSE YOU'RE
GETTING MARRIED!!!**

Ah yes! Ha-ha. Love U!
Text when you get home.

Will do. Love you too xx

On Sunday I say my goodbyes to Naomi and catch the train from King's Cross back to Yorkshire. As the train pulls away from the station, I feel a wave of relief. Pretending everything is fine is exhausting. Grateful to finally be able to drop my brave face and be alone with my thoughts, I stick in my AirPods and stare abstractedly out of the window, replaying the night before.

I hadn't told Naomi about seeing David. I didn't want to spoil her party. We were supposed to be celebrating her birthday and surprise engagement, not talking about my ex-husband and his new fiancée. *New fiancée*. It had sent me reeling, but somehow I'd kept it together. Being introduced, saying hello.

*

'Liv, this is Hannah.'

'Hello. Nice to meet you.'

'Hi, how's it going?'

It was like all the air had been sucked out of my lungs. I nodded politely. Said something I can't quite remember, about the music being loud. Tried not to appear as awkward as I felt. She was so much prettier in real life. And younger than me. I hated myself for caring.

'I see congratulations are in order.' Well, I couldn't ignore it.

'Oh yes.'

I've never seen David look so uncomfortable. In different circumstances I might have enjoyed watching him squirm.

'Thank you.'

She glanced at her finger as if checking the engagement ring was still there. It was so unlike the one he'd bought me. Bigger. More flashy. I wanted to say something bitchy, but pride stopped me. I noticed she was wearing the gold bracelet I'd found in his drawer.

'You look well.'

I snapped back. I used to hear him say that to casual acquaintances at Rotary Club dinners. He was always so formal – I used to tease him about it. Now all that intimacy between us was gone, like it never existed. It felt surreal.

'Thanks. You too.'

She had amazing yoga arms. I suddenly regretted my outfit. Showing all this cleavage. I no longer felt like a babe. Or a knockout. I felt old and ridiculous.

'Well, nice to see you. I must go, there's probably a queue.' I gestured lamely towards the ladies' loos.

She smiled then and said something that I didn't quite catch because of the music, but I noticed her accent and that she seemed nervous. And it struck me then that she must think I hated her, which unexpectedly made me feel quite sorry for her. I didn't hate her at all; on the contrary, I didn't feel anything towards her.

Well, apart from wishing my arms looked like hers.

But then it was never about her. I raised my eyes to meet David's and, for the briefest of moments, the busy bar receded and all the background noise – all that grief and loss and hurt and anger – disappeared with it.

'Bye, Liv.'

'Bye.'

It was only ever about Us.

Of course the composure lasted only for the two minutes it took to find the ladies' loos and lock myself in a cubicle. At which point I burst into tears. I'm not sure how long I sat there, bewildered and blindsided by emotions I thought I'd dealt with months ago. But after a while I knew I had to pull myself together. I had a birthday party to go to. A best friend's engagement to celebrate. I couldn't sit there all night, sobbing and blowing my nose into the loo roll, feeling sorry for myself.

So I splashed cold water on my face, reapplied my make-up and I braced myself to go back outside. But David had gone, they must have left; and I went back upstairs like nothing had ever happened. And, really, what *had* happened? I'd just bumped into my ex-husband and his new girlfriend. Correction: *fiancée*. So what? It happens all the time. He'd moved on. I'd moved on. *Hadn't I?*

And that's what's floored me. I thought I was over it. All those stages of grief and loss they talk about in the self-help books – I'd pushed, stridden and dragged myself through them. Shock, disbelief, anger, depression, fear, hopelessness: the whole sorry mess. I'd waded through them all, done all the things they tell you to and had finally come out the other side.

Now, David is no longer the last thing I think about when I go to sleep, or the first thing when I wake up. In fact, the truth is, I haven't thought of him for months. It was deliberate at first, but now I can go days – even weeks – without thinking about our marriage. And when I do, it's only fleeting, some little reminder of my old life that's gone as quickly as it appeared.

But now it feels like I'm right back where I started. Which is as much of a shock as it is confusing. Why do I feel so upset? We're divorced; what does it matter if David's getting married again? Why do I care? Does it mean I'm not over it? That I still miss him?

That I'm still in love with him?

I catch a taxi home from the station. Earlier Ben had texted to offer to pick me up, but it was Stanley's bedtime, so I'd said thanks, but I was fine. *Fine.* That word should come with a warning. Even as I texted my reply I wondered how many people who used it actually were. Plus Ben would want to know all about my trip to London – ask for details of the party; I wasn't ready to put the brave face back on just yet.

I get the taxi to drop me outside Valentine's, so I can pick up Harry. If there's one face I do want to see right now, it's his. But when I knock on the door there's no answer, and it's then I remember that Sunday night is quiz night. Sure enough, I find them both at the pub. Valentine is sitting with the Three Degrees and, hearing my voice, Harry dives out from underneath the table, sending pints flying and tangling his lead around everyone's legs. It's quite some greeting, especially as they were in the middle of the bonus-points cryptogram round.

I'm invited to join them, but I just want to get home and, after much mopping-up and apologizing to the quizmaster,

I make my excuses and leave. The cottage is pitch-dark. Flicking on the hallway light, I dump my bag on the floor, unclip Harry's lead and busy myself by filling up his water bowl, flicking on the kettle, fussing over him and giving him a treat.

Waiting for the kettle to boil, I sit down at the kitchen table. Weariness threatens to overwhelm me. My new log-burner's finally been installed and I briefly think about making a fire and turning on the TV, but I have no energy or enthusiasm for either. I can't believe I'm back here. Depression lurks in the shadows, waiting for me, and I look at the clock on the wall. Eight thirty. Is it too early to go to bed?

The kettle clicks itself it off, but I ignore it and, leaving the teabag waiting patiently in its mug, turn off the lights and go upstairs. Harry loyally follows me, his soft body brushing against my legs as I head straight for the bathroom, where he flops himself down on the rug. His presence is comforting and I begin to get undressed. The walk-in shower has been installed. Ben was right: it looks great. The tiles and fittings that he suggested are sleek and stylish, and it's got this huge, rainfall shower-head.

And yet all I want is to run myself a bath and collapse into it. Soak it all away. Naked, I go to turn on the shower, then remember my dressing gown. It's hanging on the back of my bedroom door. I go to get it – and that's when I see it. Free-standing in the corner of my bedroom, its white cast-iron curves lit up by the moonlight streaming in from my window: a roll-top bath. Like I always dreamed of.

What the—?

For a moment I stand motionless in the doorway, before noticing a scrap of paper taped to the side. I pad barefoot across the floorboards and peel it off:

Stanley got into his new school! This is just a little thank-you from the both of us. The farmer let me have it. Don't worry, it's been cleaned and re-enamelled. now you get to soak in a long bath until the cows come home.

Ben

I stare at the note, then back at the bath in disbelief. No, it can't be. It's unrecognizable. And yet as the words slowly sink in, so does the realization that this is the same rusty old claw-foot bath that the farmer was using as a water trough for his cows – the one I used to walk past in the fields and photographed to show Ben. He knew how disappointed I was when I couldn't fit a new bath in my tiny bathroom, nor afford one. Somehow he's salvaged and transformed it, and plumbed it all in while I was away this weekend. He's even left a bottle of bubble bath.

Tears spring up. I suddenly feel quite emotional. I reach for one of the taps, marvelling as the hot water gushes out, before quickly putting in the plug and pouring in some bubble bath. Harry appears at the doorway, sniffing curiously at the scent of lavender, and I think how it's true what they say: sometimes not getting what you want can be a wonderful stroke of luck, because you end up with something so much better.

And, just like that, the black mood that has been following me all the way from London disappears. I'm going to have to change my mind about surprises.

STAGE 6

Love Your Mistakes

The Dales Country Show

'I would have punched her, then I'd have punched him.'

'You would not.'

'Actually, no, you're right,' Maya nods. 'I'd have punched him first.'

The following Saturday I arrange to meet Maya at the Dales Country Show, an annual summer event that attracts visitors from miles around. In celebration of the occasion, the weather has pulled out all the stops and it's a true scorcher of a day. Spotless blue skies. Twenty-eight degrees. Not a breath of wind. It's the rarest of combinations, and the crowds are out in force to watch all the different competitions, demonstrations and attractions.

Set over three fields, the show has so much to see and do, but as we haven't seen each other since I got back from London, all Maya's interested in is hearing about the party.

'I said "Congratulations".'

Now it's her turn to stare at me in disbelief. 'You did not!'

Weaving our way past a marquee, I shrug, shame-faced. 'It seemed the sensible thing to do.'

In hindsight, I'm now rather regretting being all middle-aged and adult about it. Pride and keeping your composure is all very well, but it doesn't sound quite as satisfying as Maya's reaction.

'What a head-fuck.' She kicks up a clod of earth with the toe of her Doc Martens.

'That's one word for it.' I nod as we pause by a stall selling waterproofs and wellies.

In fact, now I think about it, that's the *only* word for it. I've spent the past week replaying the events of last weekend. Seeing David again. Meeting the woman he left me for. Discovering he'd got engaged, and my physical reaction to it all. I've been trying to work out what it all means, or doesn't mean. How I should feel, or shouldn't feel. What is the appropriate reaction. The *healthy* reaction. Because I'm pretty sure it's not bursting into tears in the ladies' loos, then sinking deep into a depression.

'I really didn't think the Dales Show would be your thing,' I say, as we move away from the stall and head towards the exhibition of vintage tractors. When Maya had texted earlier that morning asking what I was doing and I'd told her I'd got tickets for the show, I'd been surprised she wanted to come too.

'It's not.' She pulls a face as, over the loudspeaker, they announce that the sheepdog trials are starting. 'But I wanted to tell you in person.'

'Hang on, what date is it?' What with everything else going on, I've lost track of the days and feel sudden alarm. 'You can't have got your exam results yet.'

'No, they aren't for a couple of weeks.' She grimaces, then holds out her phone. 'But look.'

I peer at her screen. It's all blurry as I don't have my glasses. 'What am I looking at?'

'The total!'

'Of what?'

She gasps in frustration. 'It's the crowdfunding page. For the village hall. How much money we've raised. We're reached our target!'

I squint at it again. Hang on, surely that can't be right.

'Forty thousand pounds?'

She grins then. 'Isn't it brilliant?'

'Maya, that's incredible!'

'Talking about me again, Ladies.'

We both turn round to see Ben standing behind us, grinning. Beside him is Stanley. Holding an ice-cream, Stanley is wearing ear defenders and a slightly anxious expression. His face lights up when he spots Harry at my heels, busy hoovering the field for any scraps of dropped food.

'Hi, Ben. Hi, Stanley.'

Harry launches himself upon Stanley, nearly knocking him off his feet. Stanley laughs delightedly and we watch them both making a fuss of each other.

'How's it going?' I turn to Ben.

'Great. I just bumped into the local farmer – he asked after your bath.'

'Did you tell him he's responsible for making one woman very happy?'

He rubs his chin. 'Well, he was with his wife, so I thought best not.'

I laugh at his expression. I've spent the past week thanking Ben profusely and insisting that I pay the cost of getting my bathtub re-sprayed, plus all the fittings and fixtures, which can't have been cheap, but he wouldn't hear of it. 'Don't be daft – it's me that should be thanking you. If it wasn't for you, Stan wouldn't be going to his new school. I can finally sleep at night, knowing I'm not letting him down.'

'So about the fund-raiser,' interrupts Maya, a little impatiently.

'Sorry, yes.' I shoot her an apologetic look. 'Maya set up a crowdfunding page to fix the roof and do all the work needed on the village hall, and it's amazing how much it's raised,' I explain quickly to Ben.

'Oh, someone shared that on Facebook. I gave a donation'

'Did you? Thanks.'

'My pleasure. It was always the heart of the village. We used to have parties there – wedding receptions, concerts, plays, you name it. When it closed, it was like something broke.'

'But now we can afford do all the stuff needed to get it open again,' points out Maya.

'That's great. Well done.' Ben looks genuinely impressed. 'So you'll be needing a good builder then.'

'Got any recommendations?' I tease.

'Well, now you're asking: I do know a really good building company,' he says, playing along. 'They're going to be finished on a renovation project next week. I'm sure I can get the owner to give me references.'

'You'll be finished next week?' Surprised, I stop joking. 'I thought it was going to be the end of the month.'

'Good news, eh? We've made real progress these past few weeks, so I reckon we'll be out of your hair by Friday.'

'Wow! So soon.'

'I knew you'd be pleased.'

'Yes. That's great news.'

Of course I'm thrilled. It's brilliant news. I can't wait for my house to be finally finished. It just feels a bit strange to think Ben will soon be gone.

'Daddy, can I get an ice-cream?' Stanley stops playing with Harry and tugs at Ben's hand.

'What? Another one?'

'Harry ate most of it.'

We all look at Harry. He can't defend himself, but by the sprinkles on his beard it's pretty obvious he's guilty as charged.

'OK, but don't tell Auntie Holly,' he winks and Stanley laughs conspiratorially. 'Well, see you both around.' Smiling good-naturedly, he takes Stanley's hand and dis-appears through the crowds.

'I've got to go too.'

I turn back to see Maya texting, her thumbs moving at lightning speed.

'Where are you going?'

'My parents are having some friends over for a barbecue. Do you want to come? I know Mum would love to meet you.'

'No, but thanks. I've arranged to meet Valentine in the competition marquee.'

'OK, well you're more than welcome. I thought I'd go home and give Mum a hand. Simon likes to wear the apron, but really Mum does everything – he just does the grilling. And lets everyone know about it,' she adds with an eye-roll, but this time it seems to be out of fondness rather than anger.

'Things sound a lot better now.'

'Yeah, they are. Thanks to you.'

'Oh, I don't know about that.'

'I do. If it wasn't for you, I wouldn't have had a clue what *Wuthering Heights* was about, or *Macbeth* – I didn't get any of it.' She shakes her head, looking embarrassed at herself. 'But you made it all real, taking me up on the moors and to see that play. Good job you did,' she adds, her lip curling, 'otherwise I'd still be going out with that idiot Zac.'

I have to give it to Maya. I really admire her for how she's dealt with the break-up, especially when it was only a week before her exams. I also love how once teenagers are over someone, they can be truly brutal.

'It's because of you I've decided to go through Clearing to study law.'

'Are you sure what wasn't Will's influence?' I ask and she reddens.

'No. I make my own decisions.' Maya shakes her head firmly. 'He just made me aware of my options. I'd never even considered a law degree before. Not that I'll get in anywhere – you need, like, straight As,' she adds, but I quickly shush her.

'OK, well, if you're sure you don't want to come and meet Valentine? They're judging the cakes.'

'Go look at a load of Victoria sponges?' She pulls a face. 'I think I'll give it a miss. Say hi from me, though.'

'Fair enough.' I smile. 'Oh, and Maya, I don't know if you're still in touch with Will . . . but if you are, I'd rather you didn't mention anything. About me seeing his dad.'

'Course not.' She nods and turns to leave, then pauses. 'You know, I'm sorry about your ex-husband and everything, but for what it's worth, I'm glad he ran off with another woman, otherwise I would never have got to meet you.'

'Thanks, Maya.' I smile, both touched and amused by her blunt admission. 'Me too.'

'Plus he sounds like a total dickhead and didn't deserve you,' she grins. And with that, she strides off in her crop top and Doc Martens, her pink hair tied up like a pineapple on the top of her head, bobbing through the crowds as she disappears.

I find Valentine in a large white meringue of a marquee, where the cake and flower-arranging competitions are taking place. I tell him all about the money raised for the town hall and he's both astonished and thrilled.

'Well, bugger me,' he declares loudly, which causes something of a ripple amongst the judges, who are in the middle of talking about soggy bottoms.

Hastily moving away from the Victoria-sponge exhibits, we make our way over to the flower displays.

'Gisele won second prize one year for her dahlias,' Valentine says as we watch the winner of the 'Romancing with Roses' class being awarded their rosette.

'Really? That's great.'

'Aye, she was delighted. Until she found out there were only two entries in her category.'

We both look at each other and start laughing.

'She called the judges all sorts. Luckily for them, they didn't speak French.' His eyes flicker wickedly. 'People used to mistake her for this sweet little French lady, but she had a feisty edge to her, you know. A real spirit.'

I feel his loss so keenly that I feel suddenly ashamed at how upset I was last weekend. And yet, it's like Ben said: heartbreak isn't a competition; there are no winners or losers – no one gets first prize or second.

'Here, I got you something.' I pull a small gift-wrapped box out of my bag and hand it to him.

'For me?' Valentine looks surprised. 'But it's not my birthday.'

'It's just a little something. To say thank you for looking after Harry when I went to London.'

'Nay, you shouldn't have.'

I quickly shush him. 'Aren't you going to open it?'

Turning the small box over in his hands, he tears off the wrapping paper to reveal a DNA-testing kit. His expression is unreadable.

'I thought it would help you with your family tree,' I say quickly. 'And don't worry, I can set up the account online and everything.'

'I can't accept this.'

'Don't be silly.'

'But these things aren't cheap.'

'You can pay me back when you find out you're related to royalty,' I joke and he finally stops protesting and laughs.

'Thanks, love.'

'Thank *you*,' I smile.

Reaching for my hand, he squeezes it and for a moment we stay like that until—

'Where's Harry?'

'I thought you were holding his lead.'

'No. I thought you were.'

Abruptly I have a feeling of alarm at the thought of losing Harry. And then I hear a panicked announcement over the tannoy: 'Will the owner of the large, hairy mongrel caught eating the prize-winning Victoria sponges please report immediately to Visitor Information. I repeat: *immediately*.'

The Teabag

'*A woman is like a teabag – you can't tell how strong she is until you put her in hot water.*'

Some people attribute that saying to Eleanor Roosevelt, and others to an old Irish proverb, but to be honest, I don't really care who said it. All I care about is that after many wobbles and doubts, highs and lows, one step forward and two very muddy steps backwards, I find myself, towards the end of August, finally beginning to feel like that teabag. Stronger. More resilient. Like I'm finally getting a handle on it all. Which, looking back, I think I always was, but it's only now that I've started to give myself credit for it.

And while on the subject of teabags, there is no longer a mountain of soggy ones left in the sink or staining the bottom of my mugs, because as of Monday the building work on my cottage is finally complete.

I can't quite believe it. It's a moment that, at many times, felt like it would never come; but when I did dare to conceive of it, I imagined it would be a bit like when you watch marathons on TV: all those athletes crossing the finishing line and sinking to their knees in gratitude, while being sprayed in champagne as the crowd erupts in cheers and applause.

OK, so perhaps I wasn't expecting champagne, but perhaps some prosecco and a bit of high-fiving. A celebration of sorts of how we've finally got there, and what an amazing job they've all done. Ben, Sparky, Flood, Fetch Me and Carry Me – the whole messy, infuriating, wonderful gang.

Instead the reality is very anticlimactic. Ben and his team simply clear up their tools, load the cement mixer into the back of the van and leave with a 'Cheerio'. Even the skip that's been a permanent fixture outside the house disappears. And then suddenly it's just me, Harry and total silence.

It's the strangest of feelings. Having been living in a building site for what feels like forever, I thought I'd be thrilled not to hear the radio blasting and the out-of-tune whistling, not to find plaster in my bran flakes, muddy footprints on my stripped wooden floors and grout down my toilet. I thought I'd feel elated.

Yet now it feels, well, a bit *too* quiet. And I'd never thought I'd say it, but it looks a little *too* tidy. That said, the cottage does look beautiful. In fact I can't actually believe it's the same one I walked into on that freezing cold, pitch-dark day last December. Downstairs the kitchen-diner is flooded with light. Full-length doors lead onto the garden, which is now bursting with colour, and when the sun shines you can push the doors right back. Even better, when it rains it's like being outside in nature and, if I look up, the large sycamore tree provides a canopy of leaves through the skylights.

And while the back of the house is open and airy, I've kept my traditional snug living room, where I first spent those evenings with Harry when both of us were getting to know each other. A log-burner now fits perfectly into the centuries-old inglenook; this way I get to have a real fire, only it's a lot less messy and more energy-efficient. Plus, with the new jewel-coloured walls, lamps and a brightly woven rug from a shop in the village, it'll be so cosy in winter.

Thanks to Valentine's amazing decorating skills, upstairs is unrecognizable, while the newly created attic room is fun and quirky. Ben was right. It works brilliantly. As for the avocado bathroom suite, it's now an ancient memory, and in my bedroom I've got the kind of stunning claw-foot bath you see in all those glossy interiors magazines; only mine's better, because it's been rescued from a field. Every time I take a bath, I'm reminded that just because something is old or dirty or falling apart, that doesn't mean it has no value. And, with love and effort, it can be transformed.

Because what I love most of all is that I can still recognize the old cottage underneath it's makeover. The history is still there, in the old beams and flagstones and fireplaces. Ben has restored the house but managed to keep its charm, the parts of it that made it special. It's the same house with the same history, the same bones, the same quirks that make it so unique, but it's much improved.

A bit like me, really.

I feel like, after all I've been through, I've been stripped back, polished and now have reinforced steel joints running right through me.

With the house finished, things can go back to normal. Only when I get up on Monday morning, I can't help asking myself: *What is normal?* After feeding Harry and letting him out into the garden, so that he can go through his morning routine of chasing his nemesis the squirrel, I stand in my brand spanking new kitchen and gaze out through my folding doors, which I've pushed right back to let the outside in.

It's early, but the sweet smell of fresh hay is already in the air. It's haymaking season and I can see right across to the open fields, and the local farmer already hard at work in the distance. I listen to the soft rumble of the tractor, watching it moving slowly up and down in the morning haze, my mind drifting.

Ever since moving here, renovating the cottage has been my focus, but now that Ben and his builders have gone, it's left a space. *A void.* I need to find a new project.

Turning away from the view, I fill the kettle and switch it on. On my counter is my laptop and I flick it open. On the screen are a couple of half-finished application forms for full-time teaching jobs. Great positions in good schools and the salaries aren't bad, either . . . And yet the honest truth is I don't feel any great passion for them. I love teaching, but I've been doing it my whole life and I don't want to go back into a classroom. I want to do something new and different – only I'm not sure what or how. So much in my life has changed, and I've changed with it; but one thing that hasn't are the bills that I still have to pay.

My mobile rings, interrupting my thoughts. The clock on the wall shows it's not even 8 a.m. Who on earth would call at this time? I look at the screen of my phone. It's Evelyn. We swapped numbers when she helped me with Stanley's school. I pick up.

'Olivia?' Evelyn is one of those people who sound surprised, and rather annoyed, that you've answered the phone, when it's your number they've called.

'Oh, hi, Evelyn, is everything OK?'

'It's about the village hall and the funds raised.'

'Isn't it amazing?'

'Marvellous,' she replies, before moving swiftly on. 'As head of the parish council committee, I'm in charge of the restoration works. The council has agreed to support the project, but I'm going to need some help in breathing life back into the place and coordinating a calendar of events. Which is why I'm calling you.'

'Me?'

The kettle boils and, as I reach for the tea canister, I discover a mouldy old teabag wedged behind it. Ben might be gone, but he's certainly not forgotten. Despite its revoltingness, I smile as I chuck it in the bin.

'Yes. I'm ringing to offer you a job.'

A Confession

'It's only part-time, and the money is horrible.'

'So what did you tell her?'

'That I'd be delighted, of course.' Pulling into a space in the car park, I switch off the engine and glance across at Valentine in the passenger seat. 'Evelyn is terrifying. I wouldn't have dared say anything less.'

It's a few days later and I've given Valentine a lift to the care home, as it was raining. Usually he'd catch the bus, but it's their wedding anniversary and he's made Gisele a bird feeder to hang outside her bedroom window so she can watch the birds.

Being a good half an hour's drive, I've spent the journey relaying my conversation with Evelyn. But while it's true – I am a little bit scared of her – the fact is I am excited by the opportunity to bring something to my community. The old, sensible me would have turned it down, as the salary is awful, there is no pension plan and it doesn't tick any career box, but the new me is getting much better at embracing uncertainty and I didn't think twice about accepting her job offer.

Plus these past six months I've realized I can survive on a lot less money. Living in London I would think nothing of takeout coffees, weekend brunches and Friday-night dinner reservations. I was always booking tickets for stuff

I thought I needed to see, shopping on the high street, buying things I didn't need; every month my credit-card bill was huge.

Now I spend my time walking Harry, talking to Valentine, laughing with Stanley. I wear old clothes, no make-up and spend time at home and in my garden. I've been inspired to start trying to grow my own vegetables and have sown rows of kale, spinach, carrots and beetroot. I've even got some quite impressive tomato plants that are loving the sunny spot beneath my kitchen window. Which makes me smile, when I remember all those comments about heirloom tomatoes that people made when I said I was moving to the country.

My life might be much smaller, but in many ways it's so much bigger.

'Evelyn can be very persuasive, I'll give her that,' says Valentine, undoing his seatbelt. 'She's roped me in to help decorate.'

'She has?'

We both climb out of the Land Rover and I pull forward the seat to let Harry out. I don't like him jumping out of the back with his arthritis, though it's improved dramatically since I started him on the turmeric that Valentine recommended.

'Though she called it *volunteering*.' He raises an eyebrow.

'On the phone she mentioned something about getting together an army of volunteers.'

'"Army" is the right word. More like bloody conscription,' he grumbles, slamming the door of the Land Rover. I catch his eye across the bonnet and he cracks a sheepish smile. 'Only joking. I'm more than happy to help get the place back up and running again. When it closed down, it was a real blow for a lot of folk.'

'She said works have already started.'

Valentine nods. 'Evelyn's not one to hang around. She

nursed Charlie for a long time; afterwards, it was if she had to make up for all the time she'd lost.'

The summer showers have stopped and we start walking across the car park, Valentine carrying his gift in a carrier bag, Harry trotting beside us. I think back to our phone call. Apparently the parish council invited local building companies to submit quotes for the work, but it was no surprise to anyone when Ben's company was the winning bid. Not only had his been the most competitive, and his firm had the best reputation, but like Evelyn said, 'This is a community project, and Ben and Stanley are very much part of the community.'

'What was Charlie like?'

'Shy and softly spoken, but she had Evelyn wrapped around her little finger.'

'She?'

'Charlie was Evelyn's wife. They were together for over forty years and married as soon as it was legal – their reception was held in the village hall.' Reaching the front door of the reception, he pauses. 'Like I said, it was special for a lot of people.'

His eyes meet mine and I nod in understanding. This isn't simply about fixing the roof of a village hall, it's about fixing the heart of a community, because that can be broken too.

'Well, I won't be long.' Valentine straightens his shoulders, as if bracing himself. 'Gisele gets tired easily these days.'

A look passes between us. The results of her recent blood tests have proved inconclusive, but the last few weeks she's been spending more and more time in bed.

I want to give him a hug, but Valentine isn't much of a hugger and stands awkwardly, hands by his sides.

I give him one anyway.

'Take as long as you need.'

*

324

While Valentine is inside, Harry and I take a walk around the grounds. I called ahead to make sure it was OK, as so many places don't allow dogs; but on the contrary, the senior staff nurse was very welcoming. 'Of course! Just as long as he's friendly and you keep him on a lead. Our residents love animals, especially dogs. We've found their presence brings a lot of benefits to those suffering from dementia.' Which comes as no surprise to me, because Harry has brought so many benefits to my life too, so why should the care home's residents be any different?

Now that the rain has stopped, the sun has come out and the temperatures are rising quickly; it promises to be another scorcher of a day. Everything looks freshly washed and bursting with colour. The grass is so green it's almost iridescent, and the swathes of rose bushes scent the air with a damp, sweet fragrance. The grounds are impressive. There are flower beds, a water feature and a sensory garden. A few residents appear to be gardening, while others are sitting on benches, chatting with visiting relatives or being accompanied on walks by the nursing staff.

Everyone seems delighted to see Harry and he gets lots of strokes and pats. Which of course he loves, wagging his tail and bashing their legs. Though it's as if he knows when he can be excited and when he needs to be calm, resting his soft head on the lap of one lady who stops hugging her teddy bear to tickle his ears gently. After a while we stop walking and I settle myself on an empty bench to wait for Valentine, lifting my face to the warm rays of sunshine and closing my eyes as Harry flops down beside me.

Valentine is subdued when he returns. Any excitement or anticipation at giving Gisele her gift has evaporated. I try to make conversation on the drive home.

'Did she love her present?'

'It's hard to tell these days.'

'I'm sure she does. It's a wonderful anniversary gift. How many years is it?'

'Sixty.'

'Sixty! Wow, that's amazing! Why didn't you tell me?'

'What's there to tell?'

'Well, it's a huge achievement!'

'Not when you love someone.'

There's a beat as he turns to look out of the window. Out of the corner of my eye I notice his hands in his lap, fingering his wedding ring.

'Isn't that your diamond anniversary?'

'Is it? Perhaps I should have bought her diamonds then.'

'Trust me, diamonds are totally overrated,' I reply, my mind flicking to the large rock on the finger of my ex-husband's new fiancée. 'I'd much rather have someone make me a bird feeder.'

Glancing sideways at him, I smile, but Valentine remains turned away, staring out of the window, so I don't press him. Instead I turn on the radio, but it wheezes and crackles in complaint, refusing to tune into a station. In the end I turn it off and we spend the rest of the journey in silence, winding our way across the Dales, lost in our own thoughts.

I drop him at his bungalow. Originally it was my intention to head straight home, as I've got some work to do, but instead I invite myself in for a cup of tea. As he goes to put the kettle on, I notice a few cards on his mantelpiece, wishing him a happy anniversary. There's one from Evelyn, another from the landlord at the pub, a couple more from people I don't know – most likely relatives or friends from when they lived in the city. But there's one that is distinctly absent.

When Valentine reappears from the kitchen we sit down

at the table by the window and he pours me tea. The bungalow is quiet, but for the soft ticking of the clock on the mantelpiece. A shaft of sunlight shines across the table, illuminating tiny sparkles of dust in the air. There's a stillness.

'Helen's not in Paris, is she?'

There's a pause. Valentine's face betrays nothing, but I feel a shift. As if we're about to cross a line and we can never go back.

'No, she's not.'

And then his shoulders collapse and he drops his head. When he finally raises his eyes to meet mine, the look that passes between us confirms what I've suspected for a long time.

'Helen died.'

Valentine

He never set out to lie to anyone.

Not to Olivia. Or the care workers. And certainly not to Gisele.

But he had no choice, you see. He couldn't bear to see her so upset. To watch her cry when she asked him where her daughter was and he had to tell her the truth. Over and over again. Because she'd always forget. And each time he broke it to her, it was like hearing the news for the first time. They say time is a great healer, but it's not, when you can't remember if it happened today or thirty years ago. For Gisele, the shock and the grief were as raw as the morning the police knocked on their door.

In the end he couldn't bear it any longer. He couldn't watch her break down every time she asked when her daughter was coming to visit and he had to tell her again and again what had happened. So he made up a story – about Helen being in Paris, visiting Gisele's sister Agnès and living life to the full. Living the life she never got to live. He filled it with laughter and red wine, and young men who would take Helen dancing. With all the fun and the fancy French fashions, and the pavement cafes and the walks along the Seine, that she should have had. He told Gisele how happy Helen was. How much she loved her. How she'd see her soon.

And he'd been telling it for so long that after a while he almost started to believe it himself.

Of course the reality couldn't be further from the truth. Helen never got to go dancing in jazz clubs, twirled around by some handsome French man, whom he would no doubt have disapproved of and declared not good enough for his daughter. Instead, while away at university, Helen had an asthma attack. It was nothing new, she'd had them before. She'd suffered from asthma as a child and always had to carry an inhaler. Except that night she'd gone to stay at a friend's house. When she woke in the night to find she couldn't breathe, she reached into her handbag only to realize that she'd left her inhaler at home. By the time her friend raised the alarm and the ambulance arrived, she'd already gone. Helen was nineteen years old.

For a long time Valentine thought they'd never get over losing her. She was their only child. They'd planned on two children, but when it didn't happen they weren't sad, because Helen was more than enough. It was like that saying 'You only get one life, but if you live it right, you only need one.' She was such a lovely little girl, never any bother, always bright, always smiling. She was the light of their lives and, when she died, it was like the light went out.

You never get over losing a child – it's not how it's meant to be – but they were lucky. It tears some couples apart, but with Valentine and Gisele it brought them even closer. Losing Helen reminded them, more than ever, that life was short and they were both determined to make the best of it. It's the reason why, when he retired, they decided to fulfil their dream and move to the Dales. They brought Helen's ashes with them.

This was going to be their forever home. When they moved here they both knew they were never going to leave, so Valentine asked the vicar if they could lay Helen to rest in the garden of remembrance in the churchyard. That way they could all be buried in the same place, and that gave them both peace somehow. Knowing they'd all be together again one day. Moreover it was a lovely spot, by the far wall where you got shade from the oak tree and the air was filled with the scent of rose bushes. There were no headstones there, so instead they'd put her name on a bench.

He liked to go visit, to sit on Helen's bench and talk to her. He often went after he'd been to see Gisele: to tell her how her mother was doing; about the birds; his battle with the neighbour's bloody cat; something interesting he heard on the radio. There was no one at home to talk to any more. These past few years Helen was the only person he felt he could confide in.

But then he met Olivia and Harry, and all that changed.

Valentine stopped talking and looked at Olivia sitting opposite him across the table. She hadn't said a word. Just listened while he spoke. He waited for her to say something.

'I'm so sorry,' she said finally.

'It's all right, love. It's a long time ago now. I'm the one that should be sorry. Not telling the truth.'

'Don't be sorry. You're a kind man, and you did a kind thing. Helen was very lucky to have you as her dad.'

Valentine had been fine up to that point. Over the years he'd learned to detach himself from it somehow. Like he was telling someone else's story. But now his eyes watered and he fought back tears.

'Silly bugger,' he sniffed sharply.

She reached for his hand across the table and rested hers upon it.

'Silly bugger,' she repeated and he smiled.

'How did you guess,' he asked, after a moment. 'About Helen, I mean. Was it because there was no card from her? I saw you looking at the mantelpiece.'

'It was your umbrella,' Liv said simply.

'My umbrella?' In confusion, Valentine glanced over at it drying on the radiator in the utility room.

'It was last December,' she began explaining. 'I'd come up from London to look at houses to buy and I walked into mine. It was such a mess back then, but so was my life. I didn't know what I was doing. I nearly called the whole thing off, said it was a mistake, caught the train back to London . . .'

She paused to shake her head.

'But then I looked out of the bedroom window, across the graveyard, and saw a flash of bright pink in the darkness – it was a bright-pink polka-dot umbrella. And it looked so bold and brave, so cheerful against the winter gloom; it was like a beacon of light amongst all those headstones . . . It was a sign of something good; that where there's grief, there's also joy.'

She looked at Valentine now and smiled.

'I put an offer in there and then and forgot all about that umbrella until after I moved in. Then I would often catch sight of it in the graveyard . . . when the trees have no leaves, you get a clear view from upstairs,' she added in explanation, reading his mind.

That had been the first thing Valentine had noticed when he'd gone to decorate. That she lived opposite. It had given him quite a shock. He'd stood at her bedroom window to try and see but, being summer, the large oaks had blocked him from making out anything.

'And one day I realized its owner was you.'

She raised her eyes to meet his.

'I used to observe you, come rain or shine; when it was fine, I'd see you sitting on the bench in the garden of remembrance. I presumed you were a widow.'

He shifted uncomfortably in his seat. 'I should've said. Explained.'

'Why? It was none of my business.' She dismissed the idea, batting away his guilt. 'Only when you told me about Gisele, I was confused. Still, I didn't want to say anything. I didn't want you to think I'd been spying on you.' She pulled her face. 'I mean, can you imagine?'

She looked so horrified that he had to smile then, which made her smile too.

'I looked for a headstone, but I couldn't see anything,' she continued. 'Then one day I noticed the plaque on the bench you always sat on. Saw it was dedicated to Helen . . .'

Her voice trailed off then and her eyes glistened.

'I'd wondered for a while about Helen – why she never called or visited, no mention of what she was up to . . . I wondered if maybe it was like my sister—'

At the mention of her sister, Liv suddenly looked upset and broke off. Valentine wanted to say something, but before he could think of the right thing, the moment had passed.

'I wanted to talk to you about her – about what happened – but I was too afraid. You see, my dad never wanted to talk about Mum after she died, he got too upset and I was so scared of upsetting you. And then, when you said she was in Paris, and Gisele mistook me for Helen at the beach . . .' She shrugged. 'I think I worked it out then.'

Liv fell silent and Valentine sat for a moment, absorbing it all.

'When we moved here, we didn't talk much about what had happened in the past,' he said finally. 'It wasn't a secret that we'd lost our daughter, but we didn't feel the need to publicize it, either. When you asked me if she lived locally, I couldn't bring myself to tell you the truth and, to be honest, I didn't want to.'

For so long he'd kept this stuff hidden inside, but Liv was drawing it out of him.

'That was Helen's umbrella, you know. She said it was so bright and cheerful it always made her look forward to the rain. She was like that, always seeing the positives in everything.'

Liv smiled. 'I'll always be grateful to her. If I hadn't seen it that day . . .'

She held his gaze across the table and Valentine thought how much she always made him feel *seen*, when for so long he'd felt invisible. 'I was planning on going to the churchyard this afternoon—' He broke off, unsure. He'd got so used to shouldering this alone.

'Do you want some company? I need to stretch my legs, and Harry could do with a walk.'

The sun had really come out now and shone through the window.

'Yes, I'd like that,' he nodded, feeling its warmth. 'I'd like that a lot.'

WhatsApp with Maya

Got my results! Straight As!!!!!!!!!

OMG!!!!!!

(See. I know how to text with a teenager. After six months of teaching Maya, she's taught *me* a few things.)

Got my first choice of uni too –
going 2 Manchester 2 read law.

That's amazing!

I couldn't have done it without you!

Rubbish!
You did all the hard work

☺ btw Liv

Yes?

I fucking love Heathcliff.

Snagging

I haven't seen much of Ben since the building work finished at my house. He's been busy working on the renovations at the village hall and although I'm now involved too, our paths don't cross, as most of my work takes place at my kitchen table. The lovely old farmhouse table I spent ages hunting for, and which I'd imagined friends and family gathered around one day, is now permanently covered in paperwork. It's less dinner party and more giant work desk.

Officially my new role started this week, and I've been busy doing lots of research into what the community wants and needs, from putting on plays and organizing cinema events, to after-school clubs, creative classes, local talks and Zumba. Evelyn was particularly insistent about Zumba.

'Have you tried it? It's very jolly, and good for the bones.'

When I admitted I hadn't, she was adamant that I try it.

'Oh, but you must! It used to be very popular with the older ladies. We had a marvellous instructor. Ronaldo from Colombia. I wonder if we could get him back?'

To which I replied that I'd look into it, though I can't help wondering if it's more Ronaldo from Colombia – rather than Zumba itself – that was very popular with the older ladies.

A couple of days ago one of my kitchen drawers started sticking and I also noticed a gap open up in a skirting board. And then last night the light switch in the bathroom stopped working. So I text Ben and he says he'll try to come over for a couple of hours the next day, 'to do some snagging'.

Snagging? What's snagging?

I pretend I know what he's talking about, then look it up, whereupon Google tells me it's 'the process of checking a new building for minor faults that need to be rectified. It is typically something damaged or broken.'

Which makes me realize that, according to that definition, I've spent most of my adult life 'snagging' my own self.

'So, how's it going?'

At lunchtime the next day I open the door to find Ben on my doorstep, his giant tool bag slung over his shoulder. For some reason I'd been expecting him after work and was therefore planning to change out of my work-from-home-wear: Gone are the days of the smart work suits that I used to wear teaching; now it's a shapeless T-shirt, no bra and a pair of old jeans that I've cut down into baggy shorts, and which are probably the most unflattering things known to mankind.

'Good.' I smile self-consciously, then remember I haven't yet cleaned my teeth. 'Oh, hi, Stanley.'

Emerging from behind his dad's large frame, Stanley looks up at me, his face serious.

'Where's Harry?'

'Pleased to see you too,' I smile, exchanging a look with Ben.

'Do you mind? With it being the school holidays, it's a bit tricky with childcare . . .'

'No, of course not,' I say, ushering them both in and closing the door. I check myself in the mirror and quickly try to do something with my hair. It's only Ben, but still, I'd rather not resemble a dandelion clock. 'Though I'm afraid Harry's not here at the moment.'

'Has he gone swimming?' asks Stanley.

'Swimming?'

As we head into the kitchen, Ben puts down his tool bag while Stanley clambers onto a bar stool.

'We just passed a few of Stanley's old classmates heading to the river,' explains Ben, looking up from inspecting the kitchen drawers. By his pained expression, it's obvious Stanley wasn't invited.

'No, he's gone for a walk with Valentine, but he should be back soon.'

Stanley stops spinning himself on the bar stool. He looks disappointed.

'You know, last time I went swimming the river was freezing,' I confide, pulling a face.

'Probably helps if you wear a bathing costume.' Ben raises an eyebrow and my cheeks flush as I'm suddenly reminded of him catching me skinny-dipping.

'Right. OK, so who's for cheese toasties?'

And, ducking my head into the fridge, I suddenly get very busy with a large block of farmhouse Cheddar and a wholemeal loaf.

As it turns out, I end up making rather more toasties than I envisaged, because not only does Valentine return with Harry – much to Stanley's delight – but Maya turns up unannounced with a bunch of flowers, as a thank-you for helping her with her grades. It's the first time I've had people, other than builders, in my new kitchen and as I quickly clear away my papers and put the flowers into a vase on the table, it feels almost like an impromptu house-warming.

Only with cups of tea, rather than prosecco; and with the host dressed not in a nice party dress, but in the first thing she found this morning, crumpled on the bedroom floor, and threw on. Still, at least I got to nip upstairs and put on a bra.

'Thanks, love.'

I take a cup now to Valentine, who's sitting in a deckchair in the garden. It's late summer and everything is beginning to fade and slow. Behind him the deep blue booms of the hydrangea bushes are turning pale green, while bumble bees buzz drowsily. Stanley is flopped next to him on the bleached grass with Harry, listening to Valentine pointing out all the different birds. He looks fascinated.

'None of them have ever used my bird feeder, though,' I grumble, looking at it hanging in the tree, untouched.

'They will. '

'But it's been months.' Unconvinced, I pass him his mug of Tetley's.

'Maybe they're scared,' suggests Stanley, who's taken off his ear defenders and has them resting around his neck. 'New things can be scary.'

'When they're ready, they'll come. You'll see,' reassures Valentine, raising his tea to his lips, before stopping to stare at it warily.

'Sorry, it might be strong,' I apologize. I know how particular Valentine is about his tea. It's bad enough that I only have mugs; I daren't even tell him it's not loose-leaf. Turns out I don't have to.

'There's something floating in it.'

Oh God, the teabag. I've forgotten to take it out. 'Oh. Sorry! I was distracted . . . here, let me get a spoon.'

But before I've finished, Valentine gamely fishes it out with his fingers.

'Don't worry. It's a smashing cup of tea.'

And, trying not to grimace, he takes an enthusiastic gulp. I take the offending teabag back into the kitchen, where

I find Maya at the Aga, making herself another cheese toastie in the frying pan.

'Sorry, do you mind? I'm starving.'

'No, go ahead.' Marvelling at a teenage figure who can eat three toasted-cheese sandwiches and still look like that in a crop top, I begin clearing up a bit. Four adults, one child and a dog make a lot of mess. 'So you must be over the moon about going to Manchester.'

She shrugs nonchalantly. 'Yeah, well, the parentals are pleased.' Taking her eyes off the pan, she shoots me a sideways look. I can tell she's completely delighted, but is desperately playing it cool.

'Have you told Will?'

She gives a little nod. 'He's stoked for me.'

'So you two are still—' I break off as Maya rolls her eyes at me.

'We're just friends, that's all.'

Now it's my turn to roll my eyes. 'OK, whatever you say.'

'Is that for me?'

Ben reappears from fixing the light switch in the bathroom, sniffing the air like a scent-hound.

'I thought you were working on the village hall,' says Maya, trying to barricade the frying pan as he makes a beeline for it.

'I am.'

'Ben popped round to do some snagging,' I explain.

She starts laughing. 'Excuse me?'

'That's with an s, not a sh,' says Ben, looking amused.

For the second time that day I feel my cheeks redden and shoot Maya a look, but she responds with one of her wide-eyed, innocent ones and hands Ben the toasted sandwich.

'Here you go – I'm not that hungry any more.' Smiling serenely, she grabs her Diet Coke and goes outside into the garden to join Valentine and Stanley.

Leaving me alone with Ben, feeling oddly agitated.

'Alone at last,' he jokes, and I feel myself relax a bit.

'Yes, it's a bit mad, isn't it? I didn't expect everyone to show up at once.'

Grabbing a sponge, I begin wiping down surfaces, while Ben makes a start on the kitchen drawers. From the garden I hear laughter and see Valentine with Maya and Stanley. He's telling some story and gesticulating wildly. I think back to the first day I saw him, sitting in the window of his bungalow. He's unrecognizable now as that lonely old man. Stanley is too.

I watch Stanley now, giggling, his freckled face creased up, and remember the little boy who was too scared to come out from behind the garden gate. While Maya, so angry and misunderstood, is lying chilled out on the grass, laughing and listening and texting all at once. I still don't know how she does that.

And then of course there's Harry – in the middle of it all in his shiny fur coat, panting in the hot September sunshine, but refusing to move into the shade; pink tongue hanging out, bright eyes constantly on the lookout for the squirrel, ears continually cocked, and ready for tickles. Who would have thought that the old, scared bundle of scruff I first met in the rescue shelter could change everyone's lives, mine included.

I'm distracted by the sound of the radio and turn back to look across at Ben. It's actually rather nice to have him back, pottering around the house with his screwdriver and spirit level. I realize I've missed his presence, if not the mouldy teabags. Even his incessant whistling along to the radio, which he promptly retunes from Classic FM.

'I didn't know you were a classical-music buff.'

'I'm not. I put it on for Harry.'

As soon as I say it, I know I shouldn't have. Ben looks at me, his eyes flashing with amusement.

'Harry listens to classical music?'

'It helps him relax.' I say, somewhat defensively.

'You've got to be pulling my leg.'

'It's been proven to help calm dogs down, if you have to go out. There are studies, and everything.'

'Interesting,' he nods, and I feel a slight victory. 'So was Harry listening to classical music the night I heard you yelling at your date in the pub then?'

He's smirking at me.

'It wasn't a date,' I protest, waving my sponge around. 'Well, not that night, anyway . . . And I wasn't yelling at him; I was yelling at Harry, trying to calm him down.'

Ben stops what he's doing, folds his arms and leans back against the counter top, trying to keep a straight face.

'And yes, he was listening to classical music that night. Chopin actually,' I add, rather haughtily.

There's a pause. At which point I stop waving the sponge and burst out laughing. Said out loud, it does all sound rather ridiculous.

Which gives Ben permission to start laughing too. And for a few moments we just stand there in my kitchen, facing each other, both cracking up. I look at him, his dark eyes creased up, his face so familiar. It feels so good to really belly-laugh – the kind that makes your sides ache. And I think how Ben's the first man I've really laughed with since my divorce. Since long before my divorce actually, when I think about it. And then I stop laughing and he does, and there's a pause when no one speaks, but it feels like there's a lot going on.

'You know, we never went for that drink.' Ben speaks first.

'No, we never did.'

I can hear everyone outside and I have the sense that we're about to be interrupted and the moment will be gone, if we don't grab it.

'I'm free on Friday,' I say. 'In case you're interested.'

Holding my gaze, he looks almost amused as he answers. 'Seriously, Livvie, has it taken you this long to know I'm interested?'

Hey you,

So I think I might be in trouble. I'm going out for dinner with Ben. Yes, I know what you're thinking. I've thought it too. But he's different now. I'm different now. I'm not thirteen years old with a crush on a bad boy who's going to break my heart.

And yet, I'm scared. Because while things might be different, what happens if the feelings are just the same?

x

A Different Kind
of Doorstep Challenge

By the time Friday afternoon rolls around I've got butterflies about my evening with Ben. I've tried not to over-think it. To live in the moment. Go with the flow. Just have fun.

Oh, who am I kidding? I've totally over-thought it.

The ability to compartmentalize will never be part of my skill set, and I've lost count of the number of scenarios that have run through my head about how the evening is going to pan out. About how I *want* the evening to pan out. This is Ben. My builder. My Teenage Crush. My First Unrequited Love. My Widowed Neighbour. Talk about 'it's complicated'. There's a lot going on there.

In the end I give up trying to untangle it all and pour myself a glass of wine instead. Not too large a glass, mind you. The aim is to calm my nerves and relax me, not get me drunk before he's even arrived. Tipping a bit back into the bottle, I head upstairs to get ready. Ben's booked a table at a rather fancy country hotel ten miles away that's famous for its French restaurant. It's a chance to get dressed up and, despite my nerves, I'm quite excited. Maya has offered to babysit both Stanley *and* Harry, and the plan is for Ben to pick me up at 7 p.m. and drop Harry off at his house. I glance at my watch. That gives me an hour and a half to pull it together. Plenty of time. *Just.*

So I'm taken aback when, in the middle of showering, I

suddenly hear Harry barking and realize someone's knocking at the door. Surely that's not Ben already? I ignore it and carrying on rinsing out the conditioner on my hair, but Harry continues barking. And now I can hear my phone ringing. Irritation turns to worry. Someone is obviously desperate to get hold of me. Quickly turning off the shower, I grab my dressing gown and hurry downstairs. Whatever it is, it must be urgent.

'Hang on, just coming.'

Calling out, I grab Harry's collar and fling open the front door. I'm half expecting it to be Ben telling me that Maya can't babysit and he's going to have to cancel. Or, much worse, Valentine with bad news about Gisele.

'Hello, Liv.'

It's David.

Lost for words, I stare at him in disbelief. He is literally the last person I ever expected to see standing on my doorstep.

'What on earth are you doing here?' I finally find my voice.

'Will gave me your address. Under duress, I might add.'

He shifts uncomfortably and pulls up his collar. I notice it's raining. Next door new holidaymakers have arrived at the rental cottage and are unloading several children and a dog. They catch my eye and I nod hello and make some cheery comment about the weather.

This is surreal.

'Well, aren't you going to ask me in?'

I turn back to David, who's woefully underdressed for the Yorkshire climate. He looks so out of place here, in his designer clothes and expensive shoes. I feel discombobulated. As if two worlds are colliding.

'Why should I invite you in?'

'I've been driving for seven hours.'

'It's only five and a half from London.'

'The directions were wrong.'

'You mean you got lost.'

Over his shoulder I notice a shiny silver Porsche parked outside my house.

'Did you buy a new car?'

'Yes, do you like it?'

'A sports car *and* a young blonde fiancée,' I quip, my voice dripping with sarcasm. 'Did you get a tattoo as well?'

I know. I'm being horribly immature, but it's all such a cliché. Michelle Obama's famous phrase flicks through my mind: *When they go low, we go high*. I love that sentiment. Only, standing in my dressing gown, with a towel on my head and my cheating ex-husband on my doorstep, I have never felt less like Michelle Obama.

'I heard you got a dog.'

Choosing to ignore me, he gestures to Harry, who is furiously trying to sniff David's crotch, despite my best efforts to stop him.

'Look, what are you doing here, David?'

Now that the shock of seeing my ex-husband turn up out of the blue is starting to subside, indignation snaps. How dare he just arrive uninvited like this? After everything he's done?

'I need to talk to you.'

'Don't you think that's a bit late?'

He's always been so entitled. It's that middle-class public schoolboy thing. It's infuriating.

'Please, Liv.'

He looks at me pleadingly and, despite everything, I feel a tugging inside. It makes me even more furious.

'For fuck's sake, David – I don't care what you have to say. I'm busy,' I snap. 'I'm going out and my hair is wet, and I have to get dressed. So if you don't mind,' I go to close the door, 'goodbye.'

'Hannah and I broke up.'

With my hand on the latch, I freeze.

'So? What's that got to do with me? We're divorced.' I try to steady my voice, but it threatens to betray me.

He doesn't answer, but stands there in the rain, looking down at his feet. 'That's just it,' David says finally, letting out a heavy sigh. 'It's got everything to do with you.'

And as he raises his eyes to mine, I feel a sudden weakness. A sense of my resolve wavering. My mind quickly races ahead, warning me: *Don't let him in. Don't let him back in.*

'I'm getting drenched out here.'

Curiosity. Closure. Our history. A chance for us to try and be friends. Call it what you want.

'You've got five minutes.'

I open the door.

I pour him a glass of wine, only a small one as he's got to drive back to London – I make that very clear – and we sit down at my kitchen table. Me in my blue fluffy dressing gown; David looking rather soggy and dishevelled. The situation feels both strange and yet crushingly familiar. Me and David, sitting across a kitchen table from each other. God, how many years did we do that? Only now it's not just the table that's different.

'I've been such an idiot, Liv.'

David is talking. Over this past year I've had so many conversations with myself in my head, rehearsed so many times what I was going to say to him. But now here we are and all those long speeches seem to have disappeared into thin air.

'Yes, you have,' I nod.

'I'm so sorry. I made a terrible mistake. I don't know what I was thinking.'

'You said you were in love with her,' I remind him. 'That you didn't love me any more.'

As I say the words that broke my heart, I feel strangely disconnected. As if they've lost their power to hurt me somehow. But not for David. His face crumples.

'You must hate me. *I* hate me.'

I look at him across the table. He's always been so charming and self-assured, but now, even with the designer labels, he cuts a sorry-looking figure. I feel a spasm of sympathy for him. It surprises me.

'You were a dick, but I don't hate you.' I shake my head slowly. 'I wanted to, but I never did, not really.' I shrug. 'I just hated all the lies.'

'I'm so sorry—'

'Don't.' I cut him off. 'You did me a favour.'

'I did?' He looks bewildered. 'How?'

I look down at my hands, stretching out my naked fingers on the smooth wood of the table, feeling its age and solidness. 'Because I thought I was happy – that we were happy – and when you said you were leaving, that you'd met someone else, I was so shocked. Devastated, really. I didn't see it coming.'

I raise my eyes to see him studying me intently. I've got his full attention. It strikes me that I can't remember the last time I had that.

'But it made me aware that if I hadn't seen that, what else had I been blind to? What else hadn't I realized? And once I started to look, I saw all kinds of things . . .'

'Like what?' David frowns, that deep, familiar crevice appearing between his eyebrows, and reaches for his wine. And yet he seems so nervous, it's like looking at someone else entirely.

'Like things I wanted to change – that I'd buried and never

dealt with – that weren't working.' My mind flicks from the past to the present. 'I discovered new things, new friends, a new career, new opportunities . . . That I like living here, in the countryside, that I don't miss London, that I love having a dog.'

I glance across at Harry. He's lying curled up on his rug, one eye open, watching us suspiciously, keeping guard. Somehow seeing him there makes me draw strength.

'That I'm more resilient, adaptable, *braver* . . . That I live in the moment more and I've learned how to have fun again; that I'm part of a community I love. That I like my life better now – I like *myself* better.'

Until now I've been so busy rebuilding my life that I haven't realized how far I've come or how I've changed, but – faced with a physical reminder of my old life and its dynamic – all these feelings come rushing to the surface and tumbling out.

'I was always so terrified of the worst-case scenario, but then the worst-case scenario happened and you know what?' As I look at David, I feel a sudden sense of empowerment. 'I didn't curl up and die, though for a while there I wanted to.'

David visibly winces and goes to say something, but I raise my hand to silence him. Because now I'm talking, I realize there's so much more I want to say. Out loud. For him to hear. For *me* to hear. Only it's none of those well-rehearsed speeches that were all about him and how he made me feel; this is all about me.

'You know, I was always trying to fix things, to make things right, to smooth things over. Not just between us, but at work, with friends, Josie . . . Nothing was going to fail on my watch. "Ask Liv, she'll sort it out."' I break off with a rueful laugh. 'And yet, you know, it's only now that I've realized it was *me* I was really trying to fix. I prided myself on being a perfectionist, but that was fuelled by anxiety, a fear of things being out of control, of trying to achieve certainty in an uncertain world.'

I feel a lump in my throat and swallow it down.

'I needed to protect myself, so my world would never collapse again, like it did when my mum died.'

I look around at my surroundings – once such a wreck and now completely transformed – remembering how I felt when I first walked in here, how I'd slept on the sofa, feeling so scared and alone.

'But I'm not scared any more. Now I know that, whatever happens, I'm never going to go back there again: to the feeling that my life is over. Because out of all of this, I discovered a strength I had no idea I had.'

I break off, my heart racing. The absurdity of me giving this speech of empowerment, in my fleecy bathrobe with a towel on my head, isn't lost on me, but, if anything, it makes me own it even more.

'I've changed, and I'm never going to change back.'

David is staring at me. He's listened and hasn't interrupted, and now he sighs and rests his eyes on the heels of his hands. I notice that he's drained his wine glass.

'But I didn't ever want you to change,' he says eventually, his voice muffled.

For a split second my mind flicks back to our first date in that restaurant all those years ago – to all that hope and anticipation – and I'm hit by a bittersweet wave of nostalgia so big it almost floors me.

'It was never about you, Liv.'

'Exactly. And now it is.'

And then David looks up at me, and finally I think he gets it.

*

Five minutes turns into forty-five. I end up putting on the kettle while David tells me about how, shortly after bumping into me in the club, Hannah accused him of not being over me – something that he realized he couldn't deny. They broke off their engagement and he moved out the next day. And yet, while the old me had dreamed of this moment, the new me gets no gratification. If anything, I simply feel a bit sad at how David blew it all up for nothing.

'She wanted to go clubbing and, you know, those clubs are so loud you can't hear yourself speak,' he's saying now as he drinks his tea, relieved that I've got real milk and not 'that awful oat stuff'.

'I don't think speaking is the point of clubs, David. I think you're supposed to be dancing.'

'You know how much I hate dancing.'

'And that's another good reason we're divorced,' I say with a smile.

A smile. *An actual smile.* Honestly, it's the most absurd thing. Here I am, talking to David about our divorce and I'm actually smiling. It feel so bizarre, and yet it doesn't – if that makes sense. Though I'm not sure anything makes sense any more.

Perhaps I'm smiling because I'm grateful David blew it all up, so that I could build something better. Because now, seeing him again, I realize I was looking to him for all the answers as to why it went wrong, and yet he never really had any. All that time I beat myself up, when really it was nothing to do with me at all.

Or perhaps I can smile because, when two people are woven so tightly into the fabric of each other's lives, the creases of comfort and the folds of familiarity will always be there. Even after all the hurt and anger and crushing heartbreak have forced you to unpick the threads. He's no longer a stranger. He's David. My ex-husband. A huge part of my past, who will always play a part in my life. But he's no longer my future.

And I don't love him any more.

'Your house is nice. Colourful.' He adds, his eyes casting around the open-plan kitchen and resting on my bright-red Smeg fridge.

'Thanks.'

'It's very different from the old house.'

'I wanted something different.'

His eyes come back to mine and rest there. There's no need to read between the lines.

'Well, I should go.' Scraping back his chair, he stands up. 'Thanks for the wine and the tea. And for listening. I know I don't deserve it.'

I nod and stand up too.

'Say hi to Will for me.'

'You know he hates me.'

'He doesn't hate you – he's your son, he loves you. He just thinks you're an idiot, that's all.'

'He's not wrong.'

David smiles gratefully then and I follow him to the front door, where we stand awkwardly on the doorstep, exchanging a few pleasantries about driving safely and taking care; while I think of how last time he was leaving I was crying so hard I couldn't breathe. And I have the strongest sense of wanting to reach back into the past to hug that sobbing woman and tell her it's going to get better; that her life isn't over – far from it. That, in many ways, it's only just beginning.

'Bye, David.'

'Bye, Liv.'

And then the door closes and he's gone.

Stanley

Usually he had Auntie Holly to babysit, but she was busy tonight so instead Stanley had Maya. He liked Maya. She was fun. She ordered pizza and let him choose the toppings he liked. He hated mushrooms, but his favourite was pineapple. But only if the cheese wasn't melted on top of the pineapple. Then he couldn't eat it. Once he'd gone to a cafe with his mum, and the waitress had laughed and called him a fussy eater, and his mum had got really mad at her and said, 'He likes what he likes.'

He likes what he likes. Stanley thought that was a good saying. He liked how it rhymed and repeated itself. It was neat. He liked things that were neat. *He likes what he likes.* He said it to Maya tonight when she was ordering the pizza and she laughed and repeated it too.

They ate their pizza on their knees in front of the TV, and Stanley let Harry eat all his crusts. Harry loved crusts. Maya even let him play with her phone. Dad hardly ever let him play with his phone, after he downloaded a game that said it was free. Only it wasn't free, and Dad had to ring someone up and shout a lot. Luckily Maya's phone already had lots of good games on it, so she didn't have to shout at anyone.

Stanley could tell the time now, so when his watch showed eight o'clock, he told her it was time for him to go to bed and he had to count to sixty when he cleaned his teeth. Maya said it was OK to count to thirty tonight, but he showed her his list, where it said sixty, so she said OK and counted with him. Stanley also showed her his telescope and told her about Mummy being a star.

Maya said that was cool, which he thought was confusing. But then she explained that cool didn't always mean cold; sometimes it means really good. She also said that if Mummy was a star, she could also be a rainbow or a snowflake or the bit of sunlight that comes through the gap in his curtains in the morning and shines on his duvet like a light-sabre. Which he thought was *really* cool.

But best of all about tonight was Harry being here. Stanley was afraid of the dark, and sometimes when he went to bed he would get a funny, twisty feeling in his tummy. He told Maya he needed to leave his night-light on, and she said not to be scared as she was going to be downstairs watching TV, and to call if he woke up and needed anything. Better still, she said that Harry could sleep in his room but wasn't allowed on his bed.

As soon as she left, Harry jumped straight on the end of his bed and lay on his feet like a big, heavy, hairy blanket. Stanley knew Harry was there to protect him and he didn't feel scared or twisty in the tummy. He lay in bed and closed his eyes and thought about Mummy being a light-sabre, and how there were exactly eight pieces of pineapple on his pizza. It made him feel happy.

Stanley hoped his dad would put on a suit and go out with Liv again.

Table for Two

The Langley Arms is one of those lovely country hotels filled with chintz and wood panelling, and grandfather clocks that chime softly as you enter, making you feel like you're stepping into another era. The restaurant is intimate, with low lighting and the hum of discreet conversation. It's quite a reach from our local pub, with its salted peanuts and pints of ale.

'Gosh, this is very fancy,' I whisper, leaning across the table as the waiter finishes telling us about the specials and leaves us to consider our menus.

'I thought you'd be used to fancy restaurants, after living in London,' says Ben, fiddling with his collar.

He's had a shave and is wearing a smart jacket and a freshly ironed shirt. When he picked me up in his van, I made some jokey comment about how well he scrubbed up, and Ben said something about how he thought he should make an effort. But what I was really thinking was how handsome he looked. Out of his overalls and with a fresh shave, the transformation is quite startling, and when I went to kiss him on the cheek, I caught the scent of his aftershave and I felt something shift between us. It felt different.

Or is it just me that's different?

'Honestly I think you've got completely the wrong impression about me,' I protest, smoothing my napkin onto my knee. It's made of heavy, starched white linen and is so spotlessly clean I can't help wondering how on earth they get the stains out. 'My life was hardly glamorous. Most of the time you'd find me on the sofa, marking homework.'

Ben laughs then and I feel him relax a bit. I get the feeling he chose this restaurant for me, and he would have been as happy – if not a lot more comfortable – down the local pub. Me too, if I'm honest, but of course I can't tell him that. He's made such an effort.

He turns to the menu. 'What's *pommes purée?*' he asks, lowering his voice.

'I think it's mashed potato.'

'Well, that's not very fancy – even I can make that.' He looks triumphant and I laugh. 'Though mine's probably lumpier,' he admits as an afterthought.

'That's a good thing. My grandma always used to say that's how you know it's home-made.'

'Wise lady, your grandma,' he nods approvingly and I start giggling. I don't know what's got into us. Neither of us is drinking and yet I feel giddy. Aware of the other diners' eyes on us, we both duck behind our menus, trying to straighten our faces.

'Chicken looks good.'

'Ah yes,' I nod, 'but can you make Parmesan Snow?' Reading from the description, I look at Ben over the leather-bound parapet and raise my eyebrows.

Which of course sets us both off again, and it's only when the waiter returns to take our order that we finally manage to stop giggling. Though I do feel a bit guilty about dabbing my eyes on my lovely white napkin, as I get two big smudges of eyeliner all over it.

We both go for the chicken, complete with the Parmesan snow. Ben isn't drinking, so I order sparkling water, even though he tries to persuade me to have some wine.

'Please at least have a glass,' he insists. 'I'm the one driving.'

'It's fine, honestly,' I say, handing the waiter the wine list.

'Or what about a gin and tonic?'

'Are you trying to get me drunk?'

He stops cajoling me and smiles sheepishly as the waiter disappears.

'I just want you to have a nice time.'

'I am having a nice time.'

He studies me, as if making sure I'm telling the truth, then leans back against his chair, satisfied.

'You look nice.'

'Thanks.' I put my hand to my hair, trying to smooth it down. 'I didn't have time to blow-dry my hair properly.'

'I like it like that. Your curls suit you.'

'That's lucky,' I smile. 'I was planning to straighten it, but something came up.'

'Would that something have anything to do with the Porsche I saw parked outside your house?'

I let out a groan. 'You saw David's car.'

'I arrived early to pick you up and couldn't miss it. We don't get too much call for sports cars around here; it's mostly tractors and Land Rovers . . .' His eyes dance mischievously. 'Though I know of a white van that can do nought to sixty in about five minutes, if the wind's in the right direction.'

He pulls a face and, despite myself, I start laughing. I wonder briefly what David would say about me going out for dinner in a white builder's van, which amuses me even more.

'So I take it that was the ex-husband?' he asks and I nod. 'Well, that makes sense.'

'He just turned up. It was completely out of the blue.'

'Break-ups hit men later.'

'But he was the one who had the affair and broke up our marriage.'

'And now you're over it, and he's suddenly realizing what he's lost.' Ben shrugs. 'Trust me, men are idiots.'

'*You* don't seem like an idiot.'

'I'm a reformed idiot. Don't you remember me when I was a teenager?' He grins and reaches for the bread basket.

'Teenagers are allowed to be idiots – their frontal lobes haven't developed yet.'

'I don't think mine fully developed until I had Stanley.'

I watch him buttering a piece of bread. 'God, that looks delicious.'

'It is.' He takes a bite. 'Here, have some.' He holds out the basket, but sees me hesitate. 'What is it with women and bread?'

'Says a man who's never had to try and fit into a pair of skinny jeans.'

'Well, I'd look a bit silly,' he says, and I laugh and take a piece. The bread really is as delicious as it looks, especially with a thick smearing of butter from the little silver round. Well, in for a penny, in for a pound.

'So why did it take you so long? The frontal lobe, I mean?' I ask through a mouthful.

'I suppose part of me didn't want to grow up, but when I became a dad, I had to. Simple as that.' Ben looks at me, his face becoming serious. 'I wanted Stanley to have the kind of dad I never had.'

There's a pause. I think about sweeping it aside, like the crumbs on the table. Like I used to do in the past when the conversation was difficult. But I don't want to do that with Ben – not even when the topics are painful.

'What was your dad like?'

'I wish I knew,' he shakes his head. 'I never met him. I don't think Mum even knew who he was.' He says it matter-of-factly, as if it's of no consequence, but he doesn't fool me.

'Mum had so many useless boyfriends; they liked to knock her about – me too, if they could – so I had to toughen up. That's when I started getting in trouble with the police, drinking, getting into fights . . . I ended up running away from home.'

I listened. Trying to imagine. My childhood had its share of tragedy, but we were always loved and kept safe.

'She passed away just before Stanley was born. We'd made it up by then. She wasn't a bad mum. She just made bad choices.' He shrugs his shoulders. 'But I made a promise to myself that it was never going to be like that when I had Stan.'

'Your relationship with him is amazing.'

'Thanks. He's a great kid. I'm lucky.'

'He's lucky too,' I say, and Ben smiles appreciatively.

The waiter returns with our entrées and our conversation turns to the chicken, which is tiny but mouth-watering, although the Parmesan Snow turns out to be slightly disappointing – it's merely finely shaved Parmesan – which leads us to make up all kinds of silly weather-themed names for ingredients, like Parsley Frost, Tomato Rain and Breadcrumb Drizzle.

'Actually that one's pretty good,' grins Ben, raising his glass of water to toast me.

'I know, right?' Chinking my glass against his, my laughter fades as I catch him studying me. 'What?' I frown. 'Have I got food on me?' I reach for my napkin to brush my mouth.

'No,' he says, shaking his head. 'It's nothing.'

'Ah . . . now I know it's definitely something.'

He smiles then, his eyes crinkling around the edges. 'I was thinking about when we were teenagers. Who would've thought we'd be here now?'

'Not me!'

'Well, don't say it like that.' He looks offended.

'No, I don't mean—' I break off, casting my mind back. Even now I can remember my feelings of inadequacy around him. 'You know, I had such a crush on you,' I confess.

'A crush on me?' He looks incredulous and I nod, embarrassed by my admission.

'But you were so mean to me.'

'Only because I liked you.'

'*You did?*'

It's the last thing I expect him to say and now it's my turn to look astonished. He must have got me mixed up with Josie.

'No, you liked my older sister – you were always flirting with her.'

'Only because I wanted to get your attention, because I was intimidated by you.'

'*Intimidated by me?*'

Seriously, I almost have to check it's water in his wine glass.

'You were so pretty and clever, and you had this air about you – everything I wasn't.' He pulls a face, then peers at me, creasing his forehead. 'You didn't know?'

'No.' I shake my head, still trying to take it all in. 'Of course not. I had no idea.'

Ben's expression is unreadable as he holds my gaze for a few moments.

'It was always you,' he says quietly.

His words unfold themselves and hang in the air between us. And for a few moments we both sit there, realizing how wrong we got it.

'Why didn't you tell me?' I ask finally.

He shrugs and smiles. 'Told you I used to be an idiot.'

Maya

'Damn, my phone's about to die and I've forgotten my charger.'

'No way.'

'Way.'

Stretched out on the sofa, Maya had spent the last hour FaceTiming with Will. Before that she'd been texting friends, scrolling through her socials and updating the rescue shelter's Facebook page.

'I've got less than five per cent.'

'We can do a lot with five per cent,' Will grinned flirtily.

'Ha-ha.' She rolled her eyes.

Maya was trying hard to play it cool, but Will was giving her all the feels. She tried angling the camera so it was more flattering. She'd turned off the overhead lighting, put on some lamps and a lit a candle, to try give it some mood lighting, but her face still looked fat.

'Stop moving the camera – you're breaking up.'

'Sorry, my arm's going to sleep.' She really wished she had cheekbones

'Yeah, me too.' Will let out a wide yawn. 'I didn't get in until three a.m.'

Maya felt a twist of insecurity but tried to hide it. 'Sounds like a good party.'

Will pulled a face. 'It was OK. It would've been a lot better if you were there.'

A look passed between them and she glowed inside.

'I gotta go too. I have to be up early to volunteer at the shelter. It's my last weekend before I leave for uni.'

'For real?'

'Yep.'

'Awesome.'

Breaking into a wide smile, Will shook his head, letting his hair flop into the camera. When Maya had told him about getting her place to study law at Manchester he'd been totally stoked for her, giving her lots of advice about the course, reassuring her that she'd love it. She looked at him now, peering up at her from underneath his fringe. She wondered if he knew how sexy he looked when he did that. Probably, but she didn't care.

'OK, it's down to one per cent.'

'Bye, one per cent.'

'Call you tomorrow.'

Her phone died just as she was saying goodbye. She looked at her watch. Liv and Ben had said they'd be home by midnight at the latest. Yawning, Maya grabbed the remote and flicked through a few channels, but there was nothing interesting on. She was tired. She might take a snooze and, feeling her eyelids growing heavy, she closed her eyes.

Sticky Toffee Pudding

The dessert menu is impressive. Lots of exquisite-sounding cakes and flans, featuring intricate concoctions of puff pastry and exotic-sounding ingredients. And yet, to be honest, despite how wonderful they all sound, nothing takes my fancy.

'There's cheese and biscuits,' proposes Ben. 'I bet they do some nice stinky cheese.'

'Hmm.' I smile politely. Normally I love stinky cheese, but there's nothing normal about tonight. 'Sorbet?' I suggest.

Ben gives me a look but doesn't say anything. He doesn't have to. It's a look that says who, in their right mind, would order sorbet for a pudding? Especially at £7.50 a scoop. Even if it is mango.

We both look back at the menu. It really is very fancy.

'You know what I really feel like,' I blurt out, then quickly stop myself. 'No, forget it.'

'What?'

I hesitate, looking round to make sure no one is listening, then lean closer and lower my voice.

'The sticky toffee pudding they serve at the Crooked Billet.'

'With loads of custard,' Ben adds, his face lighting up.

For a moment we both look at each other, imagining its sweet, gooey deliciousness, then give up with the dessert menu. Because, of course, now the thought's out there, neither of us can think of anything else.

'If we leave now, we should just make last orders . . .'

*

363

Ten minutes later we're in the van and driving back to Nettlewick – Ben at the wheel, me in the passenger seat – feeling like we're on the run, Bonnie and Clyde-style, from the maître d', who tried very hard to convince us to have the *millefeuille* and got very sniffy about it all when we refused. It gave us both the giggles and we're still laughing about it. It's like being drunk, except we're both stone-cold sober and I've never felt more wide awake.

'I make it a rule not to eat a dessert I can't pronounce,' I'm saying now as we wind along the country lanes, full beams on.

'What is bloody *millefeuille* anyway?' says Ben, in a way that no French person has ever said it, which makes me burst out laughing again.

I dig out my phone. 'I'm going to check on Maya . . .'

'You mean Harry,' he grins and, busted, I smile. 'You love that dog, don't you?'

'He's not just a dog – he's my one good thing.'

'Hey!' he cries, pretending to be offended. 'What about me?'

'No, I don't mean it like that,' I shake my head. 'I'm talking about before, when everything fell apart and life felt so hopeless.' As my mind flicks back, I become serious. 'All you need is one good thing to turn life around and make it worth living again. Do you know what I mean?'

For a split second our eyes meet.

'It could be anything really,' I shrug, thinking about the email I wrote to Josie, in which I'd tried to explain it all. 'Just some small, random act of kindness – something seemingly inconsequential. Like a smile from a stranger, or a song on the radio, or a beautiful sunset . . . or the barista giving you a love heart on your coffee.' I smile, thinking how sometimes brightening up someone's day can be life-changing.

'Or it can be something much bigger,' I say, my mind running over all the possibilities. 'Like a phone call from the doctor giving you the all-clear, or an email saying you got the job, or a hug from someone you love . . .' My mind casts itself back and I think about Valentine and Gisele that day on the beach. 'Just one good thing that changes the course of everything . . .'

Ben is listening, but he doesn't say anything.

'For me, that one good thing was Harry. He came into my life when I was so lost. He was the reason I got up in the morning, went out for a walk, met Valentine and Maya and Stanley . . . And I'm so grateful, because when I desperately needed one good thing, he was it.' I break off, suddenly feeling self-conscious. 'Does that make me sound crazy?'

'No, not at all.'

Ben briefly takes his eyes off the road to glance across at me.

'After Janet died, there were lots of dark days. Some days I didn't want to carry on, if it hadn't been for Stanley—' His voice catches in his throat and he swallows hard. 'He's my one good thing.'

I nod and for a moment we both fall silent, watching the open road.

'I have a question, though.'

I turn to look at Ben and he's smiling.

'Can you have more than one good thing?'

'Are you flirting?' I ask with mock-indignation, and he laughs and I feel the mood lighten, as outside the windows the Dales flash past, cloaked in darkness. 'Yeah, and that's what's so brilliant,' I nod, in answer to his question, 'because once you have one good thing, you start to find more and more – it's like a chain reaction.' I pause and think of all the wonderful things that have happened since I first brought Harry home and then, remembering the phone call I was going to make, I glance down at my phone. 'No service.'

'Don't worry, I texted Maya earlier when you were in the loo. She said everything was fine. Anyway, we'll be home soon enough.'

'We'll get one pudding, two spoons,' I suggest.

He looks horrified. 'Crikey, steady on. I don't know about that.'

I laugh and slip my phone back in my pocket. I've got that warm, fuzziness inside that comes from feeling that, whatever's happened in the past, all is now right in the world. I look across at Ben, who has both hands steady on the wheel, remembering when I first accepted that lift home. I glance at his chaos of receipts shoved between the dashboard and the windscreen. He's made a valiant attempt at tidying up – the empty takeout cups and chocolate wrappers have been thrown away at least – but whereas the mess freaked me out the first time he gave me a lift, now I feel a strange affection for it.

I like that Ben doesn't care about stuff like that. That he's too busy caring about his son, and working hard, to give two hoots about what things look like on the outside. Because it's what's on the inside that matters. For so many years I gathered things neatly around me: the nice house and the happy marriage, and the good job with promotions. No chaos here. No messy emotions or drama and disorder stuffed into the dashboard of my life.

Oh, how wrong I was.

Ben slips his hand onto my knee and leaves it resting there. I rest my hand on top, threading my fingers through his. Neither of us says anything. No one needs to. In my mind's eye I have an image of us from above: this little white van speeding through the countryside, a white dot in the darkness. There's a chill tonight and the heaters are blowing, but cocooned together in the warmth, I can't remember the last time I felt this happy.

'What's that?'

Abruptly I catch sight of flashing lights in the wing mirror, followed seconds later by the sound of a siren wailing behind us.

'It looks like the police,' says Ben, checking his rear-view. 'There must have been an accident.'

He takes his hand off my knee and puts both hands on the wheel as he pulls over, allowing them to pass on the narrow lane.

A police car races past, sirens shrieking. I feel a beat of alarm.

'I hope the people are OK,' I murmur, my mood suddenly sober. 'I wonder where it's going?'

'Looks like it's heading to Nettlewick.' Ben's voice is drowned out by more sirens. 'Shit!'

This time it's a fire engine. Two of them.

As they hurtle past, the atmosphere inside the van suddenly darkens. Checking the road's clear, Ben pulls back onto the road. Neither of us says anything, but I notice his knuckles are white on the wheel as we follow them. He speeds up. Anxiety twists in the pit of my stomach.

'I'm sure it's fine. Probably a false alarm from someone.'

But even as I'm saying it, we're pulling into the village and ahead of us I can see the cluster of fire engines and police cars, the flashing lights . . .

'There's a fire! A house is on fire!'

The panic in Ben's voice cuts through me, and my heart starts to race.

'No. It can't be.'

I strain forward, trying to see. Dread and fear clutch at my throat. *Which house? Which house?* I smell the smoke before I see it, billowing into the sky. Feel my worst fears realized as I recognize the house that's ablaze.

'Please God. No!'

PC Neesha Sharma

The call came through to the station as she was about to go off-duty and head home. It was from the operator at the control room of the Fire and Rescue Service. Someone had called 999 to report a house fire. A Mrs Iris Shackleton from the village of Nettlewick. She gave the address of her neighbour's house. At first it didn't register. Nettlewick was ten miles away and a rural community in the northernmost part of the district. They weren't the village's local police station, but it was asking for backup. Apparently it was a pretty bad house fire.

PC Sharma thought about passing it on to a colleague. It had been a long shift and all she could think about was a takeaway and a hot bath. But it was her job. She had a duty. It could be her family one day that needed help. It was only when she was in the patrol car on the way that she remembered Nettlewick was where Maya had said she was babysitting tonight. Straight away she called her daughter, but it went to voicemail. Maya never turned her phone off. That's when Neesha's blood ran cold.

By the time she arrived, the ground floor of the terraced house was alight. Two fire crews were attending the scene, and there was an ambulance waiting and another patrol car. House fires were terrifying. They could be unpredictable and uncontrollable and they happened so fast. PC Sharma had been doing this job for more than twenty years, but house fires still got to her. Especially when there were children involved. Your house is where you feel safe; it's there to protect you and the people you love. No one goes to bed at night thinking they might never get out alive.

But she was lucky. Maya had got out alive and when her daughter saw her, she ran over and collapsed, crying and shaking in Neesha's arms. She was hysterical. The little boy was still trapped inside. She hadn't been able to get to him as the fire had blocked the staircase. She kept saying it over and over again. Talking about the flames and the smoke. Thick black smoke. And how she couldn't breathe. That's when she'd run outside, screaming for someone to call 999.

As her mum, Neesha tried to comfort her daughter. She'd done the right thing. It wasn't her fault. That's when Maya told her that she'd lit a candle and left it burning as she'd fallen asleep. She was sobbing so hard it was difficult to hear her speaking, so PC Neesha Sharma did what she was trained to do: she switched from her role as a mother to that of a police officer. She told Maya calmly but firmly that the highly trained firefighters would rescue the boy; that they had special breathing apparatus and would find a safe escape route.

But then PC Sharma saw him: a desperate figure that she knew at once must be the father. His anguish was visceral and, as a parent, it tore at her. Jumping out of his van, he was trying to get into the house, shouting his son's name over and over again as the firefighters tried to restrain him. He couldn't go in. It was far too dangerous. He wouldn't survive the flames and the smoke.

He was with a woman. She was trying to comfort him, while calling out for Harry. PC Sharma didn't know who that was. The rescue crews only had reports of a young boy trapped inside. That's when Maya told her mother that there was also a dog in the house. That's the reason she was alive.

370

A rescue dog, from the shelter that she worked at, had woken her up by barking and alerting her to the fire. If he hadn't been there, well, it didn't bear thinking about . . .

PC Sharma looked at the couple, clutching each other now as the firefighters put ladders up against the house, trying to reach the attic bedroom at the back. She felt her breath hold tight inside her chest, as two of them broke a window and disappeared inside. Waited for what felt like the longest time, until one emerged with a small boy in his arms. Watched as the ambulance crew rushed forward with a stretcher. Witnessed the father collapsing to his knees in relief.

She felt the euphoria, followed seconds later by anguish, as the second firefighter reappeared through the window carrying the limp body of a dog.

Harry the Hero

In all the commotion, it's only after the fire is under control and the paramedics have checked everyone over that a police-woman comes over to talk to me. She introduces herself as PC Sharma, and I later learn that she's Maya's mum. We've exchanged texts and spoken on the phone, but it's the first time we've met. No one could ever have imagined it would be in these circumstances.

'I don't know how to thank you. Your dog saved my daughter's life.' She speaks to me as a mother, not as a police officer.

'Don't thank me, thank Harry.'

Hugging him as he lies wrapped in a blanket in the back of a patrol car, I find my face streaked with smoke and tears. According to the firefighters' reports, Harry didn't just save Maya's life, he saved Stanley's too. He refused to leave him, and it was his whimpering that led them to Stanley, and they were both found curled up together under the bed. Stanley has been rushed to hospital; they're confident he's going to make a full recovery. Meanwhile the firefighters gave Harry oxygen, in a desperate attempt to resuscitate him.

PC Sharma bends down and strokes his soft head.

'He's a hero,' she says and a look passes between us I bury my nose in Harry's fur, which smells of smoke and fire and bravery.

'Harry the hero,' I murmur, wondering how it's possible

that you can love something so much and feeling a tidal wave of relief as, still wobbly from the smoke inhalation, he manages to wag his tail.

STAGE 7

The Best is Yet to Come

Hey you,

Sorry I haven't written for a while. The last few weeks have been crazy. So much has happened since my last email about the fire. It's only now I've finally had the chance to sit down and write.

After Stanley was discharged from hospital he went to live at his aunt's with Ben. They're going to stay there until their house is fixed up. Luckily the fire damage looks a lot worse than it actually is. It's mostly smoke damage, but it's going to need a lot of clearing up and the furniture replacing. Thankfully the insurance has agreed to pay out.

Still, like Ben said, none of that stuff's important – it can all be replaced. What's important is that everyone got out safely and Stanley's made a full recovery. He's even started at his new school. I think Ben was worried Stanley might be too traumatized to take up his place. Stanley doesn't like change. It scares him. But when the reporter from the local paper interviewed him, Stanley said that Harry's bravery had given him courage and made him brave too.

The article made the front page, and there was a photo of Stanley with Harry. The headline was 'HARRY THE HERO'. Can you believe it? Thrown away like a piece of trash, Harry is now a national treasure. But then I always knew he was special. When I think how close I came to nearly losing him in the fire . . . well, it doesn't bear thinking about. I couldn't imagine my life without him now. Maya says I rescued Harry, so now he's rescued us back.

Afterwards the story was picked up by the national press, and the past couple of weeks have been a bit bonkers. It's like the world can't get enough of Harry. Maya set up a Facebook and Instagram page for him and he's got thousands of followers. She even started a hashtag #bemoreharry. Apparently it trended on Twitter. I say 'apparently' because I leave all the social-media stuff up to Maya. She says it's incredible publicity for the rescue charity and donations have been flooding in, plus sponsorship for free dog food and an influx of potential adopters, so they're delighted. I'm really pleased about that.

I wish you could meet Maya; she reminds me a lot of you at her age. She's so ballsy and opinionated: ☺ She's going to university at the end of September. I'm glad she's got that to focus on. She's been really upset since the fire and she's been seeing a counsellor. She's racked with guilt about what happened, but I keep telling her it was an accident; that it was no one's fault, and what's important is that she managed to raise the alarm and everyone got out safely.

But she says Ben blames her, and that he hasn't answered any of her texts. I don't know if that's true. I haven't had a chance to talk to him properly. There was so much going on that night – the terror and then the relief – and we were just so grateful everyone was alive. That's the only thing that mattered.

Since then I've only see Ben once. It was when the reporters came to do the interview, and he was being both proud and protective of his son. I think having come so close to losing him, Ben wanted to wrap him in cotton wool, but he knew it would be the worst thing for him. 'Stan needs to be able to enjoy every opportunity. He's not the one that's scared. I am,' were his very words.

I wanted to talk to him about it – about the fire, about what happened before – but there were too many people around. It feels weird. Like something changed that night. We'd got so close to something, but now we're further apart than ever. I don't know what to do. Maybe I shouldn't do anything.

Sorry, I don't know why I'm telling you all this. I suppose I could really do with my big sister's advice right now.

Anyway I've saved the best to last. You'll never guess what else happened. Yesterday I got an email from a TV producer in Hollywood and we've been invited onto some big talk show! Me and Harry. Isn't that the craziest thing you've ever heard? Turns out his story's gone viral around the world and everyone wants to meet him. They said we can do it via a live link, so Harry doesn't have to fly. I think it's going to be next week, so maybe you'll see it. Though I don't know if you watch TV where you are.

Where are you, Josie?

I know you told me you needed to be alone and not to contact you, but it's been two years now, and I have no idea where you are or how you are. Sometimes I worry whether you're even alive. I try not to think like that because I believe you are. I believe you're safe and well somewhere. I have no idea if you're even reading these emails, but I'm never going to stop sending them. I'm never going to stop hoping that one day you're going to get back in touch.

OK, I know this email is very long, so I'll stop writing now.

I love you.

x

A Celebration of Life

'I don't think I've ever seen you without your flat cap. You look very smart.'

'Gisele always liked me in this suit. Said I looked like Cary Grant.'

'Cary Grant was gorgeous.'

'I used to say to her, "I look nothing like bloody Cary Grant, you daft bugger—"'

'Do you want a tissue?'

'Nay, I'll be right.'

'I've got tissues.'

'Look at me. Now who's being a daft bugger?'

'Here you go.'

'Thanks, love.'

'OK, Cary Grant, are you ready?'

'As ready as I'll ever be.'

Gisele passed away a few days after the fire. I was still reeling from recent events when I received the phone call. Valentine was with her, holding her hand. He said it was very peaceful. It wasn't unexpected – she'd recently developed pneumonia and had been moved to the local hospital – but we still wept together on plastic chairs, when I went to pick Valentine up and found him sitting in the side ward with a carrier bag of her things.

The funeral was arranged for two weeks later and I helped him organize it. There's a lot of practical stuff to sort out when someone dies. It brought back memories of Dad's death; Josie couldn't stop crying, so it had been down to me to make all the decisions. And there are so many decisions. Before you can even begin to grieve and deal with your emotions, you're making tea for funeral directors who sit at your kitchen table, handing you brochures of coffins and asking if you want to fork out a grand for wicker or double that for oak. In which case, have you thought about what kind of handles you want? And will that be burial or cremation? And have you spoken to the local vicar to ask when he's free to do the service?

Two weeks on Tuesday, as it turned out. Valentine wanted everything kept simple. Gisele wouldn't have wanted a fuss. Just a few of her favourite hymns and some nice flowers to decorate the village church. She loved flowers. Pinks and purples were her favourite, so I contacted the local florists. I also made a simple notice and put it in the post-office window, announcing when the service would be. There was only one thing Valentine was adamant about. 'Don't call it a funeral. It's a celebration of her life.'

He didn't expect many people to come – putting the notice in the window was really a ticking of a box: what people do when someone dies. He and Gisele had always been one of those couples that you never see without the other. Nowadays they'd probably call it being co-dependent, but the simple fact was they didn't need anyone else; they were happiest in each other's company. Valentine said that on their day-trips in the camper van, one of them would start singing and the other would automatically join in the melody, singing the descant or adding a riff. They harmonized with each other, not just in song, but in life too.

*

It's one of those unseasonably warm days in September when summer has second thoughts and decides it's not quite ready to give centre stage to autumn. Blue skies and sunshine greet the three of us as we walk along the small path from Valentine's bungalow and descend the hill into the village for Gisele's celebration.

Harry is coming with us too. Having seen him on the national news, the vicar made no objection to him attending the service, instead making some comment about welcoming all creatures great and small. As the cobbled lane leads us towards the entrance to the church, Valentine asks to hold Harry's lead. He needs to do something with his hands, which have been flapping around like a trapped bird all morning. I don't think I've ever seen him so nervous. I loop my arm through his supportively.

'Are you all right?'

He's quiet for a moment, his expression unreadable. 'I was just thinking. I don't have any family left. It's only me now.' He says it so plainly it almost breaks my heart.

'You've got me and Harry,' I say firmly. 'We're your family.'

He manages a smile, but his red-rimmed eyes betray him. I hold him tighter. Normally so stout, Valentine suddenly seems so fragile.

'Afterwards we can go to the pub, just us three, and raise a glass to Gisele,' I continue as we gather pace.

He looks grateful. 'That'll be grand.'

I haven't said anything, but I'm hoping for at least a small turn-out. Evelyn has promised to be there, and Ben replied to my text to say he's coming too. It sounds silly, but I noticed there wasn't a kiss at the end of his text. Sadly, Gisele's sister, Agnès, who lives in Paris, isn't well enough to make the journey, but apparently her son is going to try and make it. And I've had confirmation from some old friends in Leeds, and from a couple of nurses at the care home. Even if only a small handful of people come to pay their respects, it will mean a lot to Valentine. He pretends he doesn't care, but I know he does.

The vicar is waiting for us as we turn the corner. He smiles kindly and steps forward to greet us. I've never been particularly religious, but today I feel a burst of gratitude for his reassuring presence.

'A beautiful day to celebrate the life of your wife Gisele,' he's saying now, shaking Valentine's hand.

'Yes. Thank you.'

'Luckily you've been blessed by the weather, so we've found some extra chairs and put them on the grass.'

'Excuse me?' Valentine looks confused.

'For those standing outside. I'm afraid inside we're at full capacity.'

'Sorry, Vicar, but I don't know what you're on about.'

The vicar frowns and, stepping aside, turns and opens his arms in welcome. 'The whole village is here to pay their respects.'

And that's when we see them. Crowds of people, gathered around the porticoed entrance to the church – so many they're lining the flagstoned path and spilling out into the lane. For a few moments neither of us reacts. We stand and stare, taking it all in. My eyes flick over the faces, so many of them familiar. There's the landlord from the Crooked Billet, with his family and his bar staff. The ladies who run the local cafe, smartly dressed and without their striped aprons. Sheila the postmistress and Gary the postman.

Oh, look, and there's Evelyn and the Three Degrees, and several others that I recognize from the different pub-quiz teams. And Maya. She's here too. Looking red-eyed and emotional, she's standing apart from Ben, who nods respect-fully towards Valentine, but avoids my gaze. I've texted him a few times to check on how he and Stanley are doing, but while he always replies, it's obvious that his feelings towards me have changed since that evening at the hotel.

My throat tightens, but I look away: at volunteers from the village hall, whom Valentine has been showing how to paint and decorate. The farmer and his wife. Local hikers that I've seen sitting outside the pub. Dog-walkers, whose faces are less familiar than those of their dogs, which are wagging their tales furiously at the sight of Harry. He responds just as excitedly, pulling at his lead, and I quickly take it from Valentine, who turns to me, his expression one of bewilderment.

'They're all here for Gisele?' His voice wavers, and I squeeze his arm and smile.

'They're all here for Gisele.'

And yet while that may be true, it's more than that. They're here for Valentine. To support him. To show him he's not alone. That he's part of this community, ever since Harry forced Valentine to stop watching life from his window and become part of it again. And as he begins to walk falteringly down the path that leads into the small twelfth-century church, where he's come to say a final goodbye to his wife of sixty years, he's buttressed by the strength of the entire village.

I walk alongside him, my arm still linked through his. Losing someone you love is brutal. No well-meaning words or platitudes can ever change that, and yet the villagers' presence is like a pair of arms hugging Valentine in an embrace. Smiles of affection and solidarity, nods of sympathy and respect, a reassuring hand on his shoulder, a look of understanding. A shared grief. And it doesn't matter that

Valentine might not know every single person here. What matters is that they showed up. They showed up because sometimes it's only by lifting each other up we are able to bear life's heavy load.

Inside we're greeted by the scent and the bloom of flowers. Deep-purple delphiniums and lisianthius, bright-pink cosmos and lilac-edged hydrangeas fill jam jars on the church windowsills, while at the end of the pews the local florists have tied balloons shaped like love hearts. They make Valentine smile, and as the vicar begins his service and we sing hymns, I hear the echo of the crowds singing outside and feel a sense of being a part of something bigger.

It's uplifting and joyous, despite the sad circumstances, and when I walk up to the lectern to say a few words on behalf of Valentine, who'd baulked at the thought of speaking in public, I fold up the poem by Kahlil Gibran that I've rehearsed, with its beautiful words and its profound sentiments. Because, really, is that the best I can do? It might be famous and philosophical, but it's not remotely illustrative of the two people I've got to know, and while my own words will never be as eloquent, they'll come from the heart.

So instead I tell the packed congregation how Valentine first laid eyes on Gisele as a teenager when he asked her to dance. I tell them about their trip to Paris on a scooter, and how they danced in smoky jazz clubs until they had blisters on their feet. I tell them about Gisele's *tarte tatin* and winning second prize at the Dales Show for her dahlias. And I tell them about Valentine winning first prize when she agreed to marry him.

I speak about their daughter Helen, and how much she was loved. About the day we drove to Whitby and they both ate ice-creams and danced together on the beach, to the sounds of the waves and Bill Haley and His Comets. How we weren't here to say goodbye, because people live on in our thoughts and memories, but instead to say 'See You Later, Alligator.' And I tell them how the coffin is wicker and cost a small fortune and, frankly, nobody cares what type of handles it has, because all that's important is that we're surrounded by love.

Afterwards we all go to the pub and stand outside in the dappled sunshine. So many of us: a whole village coming together to heal a broken heart. And we all raise a glass.

'To Gisele!'

And to Valentine.

Turning the Page

By the beginning of October the village hall finally has a brand-new roof and windows, thanks to the hard work of Ben and his builders, who have worked around the clock to get it watertight before the weather turns. Autumn is now upon us. On my daily walks with Harry I've become aware of the morning chill, which causes me to reach for a jumper before leaving the house, and of the changing leaves on the trees.

Standing up high on the Dales this morning, I looked down across the sweeping valley and, whereas for months all I've seen is green, now there's a kaleidoscope of colours transforming the landscape. Russet-coloured bracken that looks ablaze in the sunshine, hedgerows of bright-red berries, golden woodland. On a bright day like today it's breathtaking, but these days are becoming few and far between as the new season brings with it wet weather and the threat of high winds.

And worse.

'You know, two years ago we had a storm that caused the river to flood and brought down my chimney pots,' Evelyn is telling me now as she sits at my kitchen table, nursing a mug of camomile tea and enjoying her captive audience.

I listen dutifully, thinking of how she must miss her school assemblies.

'One minute they were there and the next they were in the road. Gladys at number three was unloading her shopping from her boot. Missed her by a whisker!' Throwing her arms wide, Evelyn spills her tea down the front of her houndstooth gilet and tuts sharply.

'Wow! Sounds intense.' I pass her a piece of kitchen roll.

'It was,' she nods, putting down her mug and dabbing herself. 'You should have heard the crash. Like a ton of bricks!'

'Which I suppose it was,' I say and she looks up with a flash of amusement.

'Ah, very good. Very good,' Evelyn nods, waggling a finger.

'So anyway, about the calendar of events.' I bring her back to the reason for our meeting today. 'In terms of daily clubs and weekly classes, a lot of people in the village have made suggestions as to what they want from the hall.'

'Zumba,' says Evelyn definitively. 'I trust that's on the list.'

'You'll be pleased to know that's scheduled for Monday,' I say, referring to my ringbinder of papers.

'With Ronaldo?'

'With Ronaldo.'

Evelyn positively beams.

'We've also got a whole host of children's clubs and activities, drama classes, creative writing, yoga, a book group, film nights, guest speakers . . .' Referring back to my files, I run down the list.

Coordinating it all had proved a challenge, even for someone like me who likes to organize and has bookshelves arranged by the colour of the books' spines. The needs of the community are diverse, and everyone was excited about the hall reopening.

'There's something for everyone,' I finish. 'Plus I've also being doing a lot of research into what we can offer, in terms of special monthly and annual events, and there's so much we can do – like having concerts or a music festival, for example.'

Opening up my laptop, I turn the screen towards her and begin enthusiastically showing her the PowerPoint presentation I've put together. Naomi had given me Danny's number, and I picked his brain about booking bands and playing different venues and festivals.

'The possibilities are endless. It's such a great space and we could even hire the field behind. I spoke to the farmer and he's agreeable . . . Honestly, the sky's really the limit—'

I break off with excitement. Which makes me laugh as I think how Naomi recently pointed out that I've never actually *been* to a music festival. And no, getting ten-quid tickets to the Proms at the Royal Albert Hall didn't count.

'Alas, that doesn't apply to our budget,' says Evelyn.

I glance up from my screen to see her looking at me pragmatically.

'I'm sorry, I know that's rather pouring cold water on things, but I'm afraid we need to be sensible.'

Disappointment stabs. I know she's only being realistic, but still.

'But what about the opening? We need to do something to mark the occasion.'

'Well, yes, obviously,' she nods and I can see she's thinking. 'I know!' Evelyn claps her hands with satisfaction. 'How about a raffle?'

'*A raffle?*'

'Yes, a raffle. They were always very popular when I was a head teacher.'

I like Evelyn. I really do. But I'm getting the feeling we're not on the same page.

'I was thinking rather more than gift vouchers and a food hamper.'

'Such as?' she asks.

Rather sniffily, I can't help thinking. Maybe it's a

head-teacher thing: the 'my way or the highway'. In staff meetings with Mr Godfrey, our head teacher, his answer to any suggestion deviating from his plan was always, 'No, but . . .'

Only this time I'm determined not to back down.

'Well, I've had some ideas, and I thought, what about a dance?'

'A dance?'

'Yes, like they used to do in the fifties. They were so popular – everyone used to go to them. Valentine has told me so many stories about much fun they were and I think that's what everyone needs, don't they? Some fun. I mean, who doesn't love dancing?'

As I say it, I think briefly of my ex-husband David, which only serves to spur me on even more.

'I thought we could hire a band, and I've been doing some research and found a wonderful six-piece that can do both swing and rock-and-roll . . . We could even have a little competition to see which couple are the best dancers – it could be like *Strictly*.'

'Now let's not get carried away,' Evelyn cautions.

'But why can't we get carried away?' I argue, feeling frustrated.

'Because our finances are stretched as they are,' she replies.

'We could sell tickets,' I suggest.

'But wasn't the whole point that the village hall would be free for everyone to use, whatever their budget?

That is a good point and momentarily it takes the wind out of my sails.

'Absolutely. You're right, of course,' I nod. 'I realize you're only being sensible, Evelyn.'

She shifts now in her seat and I see her shoulders square in righteousness.

'And it's good to be sensible,' I continue, 'only I'm sick of being sensible.' No sooner has the wind dropped than it picks up again. 'Sensible gets you to the station on time, so you don't ever miss a train. It gets you ironed shirts and comfortable shoes, and savings for a rainy day. It gets you mornings without hangovers, and waistbands that never need unbuttoning, and days spent at the beach sitting in the shade. But what it doesn't get you, Evelyn, is a life.'

And now I'm not talking just about a dance – I'm talking about myself.

'Because life is also about spontaneity and fun, and making mistakes and doing the wrong thing. It's about blisters and sunburn, and that extra slice of pizza. It's about the absolute riot of an evening that you had drinking that bottle of wine – hell, make it two bottles and throw in a couple of chasers—'

I break off now, slightly out of breath and not sure exactly where I'm going with this, and look across at Evelyn, who's staring at me, taken aback by my outburst.

'Look, I understand your frustrations, Olivia,' she says, as diplomatically as ever, then adds, 'Trust me, I don't quite have a stick up my arse, you know.' Which isn't quite so diplomatic and makes me smile. 'And I love to dance too. *Strictly* was one of my and Charlie's favourite shows. It still is. Who can ever forget Harry Judd's Viennese waltz?'

For a moment we both fall silent as we remember.

'But we simply don't have the funds.'

'What about asking the council if they could allocate more funding?' But, even as I'm suggesting it, I know the answer.

'With the current cuts, we're lucky to get any funding at all.' Evelyn sighs and leans back in her chair. 'I think we should count our blessings, don't you?'

'Yes. I suppose so.'

'You know, you actually remind me a lot of myself when I was younger,' she says, standing up and gathering her things, and I'm not sure if I should take that as a compliment. 'One can always want more, but one must also know when to be satisfied. You should be proud of how much we've achieved.'

I nod. I am. It's just . . .

She smiles swiftly and gives me a wave. 'No need to get up. I'll show myself out.'

After Evelyn leaves, I sit at my laptop for a few moments longer, trying to think of another solution. Except there isn't one. Evelyn's right. Closing my laptop, I glance across at Harry, who's been asleep in his basket, but is now looking at me expectantly. My eyes flick to the clock on the wall above my bookshelf: six o'clock; time for his dinner. I could set an alarm by him. My gaze drops and it's then that I notice it. Tucked into the row of books on my shelf: the first edition that David bought me as a gift for last year's Valentine's Day.

Scraping back my chair, I go over and slide it from my bookshelf, carefully turning the pages. I'd wanted this book forever. It's one of my all-time favourites and the prose is so wonderful, and yet I haven't looked at it since the day I received it. Too many painful memories.

Clambering out of his basket, Harry yawns and stretches, wagging his tail. Scratching his furry head, I put down the book and reach for his bowl to mix up his food. Since the fire, he gets expensive sardines to go with his kibble. The ones in olive oil.

'There you go.'

Then I pick up my phone from the table and google the number of an antique bookshop I'd noticed next to the castle when I'd visited at Easter. This book will have cost a fortune.

David never skimped on gifts, remember? Then I smile, thinking about what fun I'm going to have, turning those painful memories into good ones.

'Hello, is that Harrison's Rare and Collectable Books? Hi, yes, I wondered if you could help me. I have a first edition I'd like to sell . . .'

Valentine

'A dance at the village hall?'

Valentine stopped digging a hole in the plant pot and turned to stare at her.

'Yes. I've already booked the band. They're a sort of tribute band and do all the Bill Haley hits and some swing too. Anything and everything, really.' Her words came tumbling out excitedly. 'They're called "Shake, Rattle and Roll".'

Kneeling next to him on his patio, Olivia gave a sort of jazz-hands wave in her thick yellow gardening gloves.

'Isn't that a brilliant name?' She grinned. 'Everyone can dress up, and there's going to be a bar selling beer and cocktails. It should be really fun. You know, it's because of you that I got the idea? You inspired me with your stories about you and Gisele.'

'Well, I'll be damned.'

Putting down his trowel, Valentine shook his head and stared at the flagstones. When he looked up, her smile had faded and she looked troubled.

'Is that a good or a bad thing?'

'It's a marvellous thing,' he reassured her, but she obviously didn't believe him as she clutched her forehead with a giant glove and let out a groan.

'Oh God, I'm sorry. I haven't gone and been totally insensitive, have I?'

'Don't be daft,' he tutted, frowning. 'It's . . . well, I don't have anyone to take to a dance, do I?'

It just came out, but as soon as he'd said it, Valentine wished he hadn't. She'd been so excited about telling him all about it, and now he'd gone and spoiled it.

'Well, I'm free, though I know that's not much of a consolation.' She gave him a small smile, almost an apology. 'Plus I'm pretty rubbish. I fell over last time you tried to teach me to jive.'

As he looked at Olivia, Valentine could almost hear Gisele's voice, telling him off for feeling sorry for himself. 'Well, don't just sit there, do something about it,' she would say to him, and he would always grumble and grouch, annoyed that he wasn't allowed to wallow in his own misery and indulge in the unfairness of it all, while grudgingly appreciating her tough love. It made him both sad and happy to think of her. He missed her – by 'eck, did he miss her – but the sad truth was he'd spent the last few years missing her. So many times he'd felt like a widower. Only now, it was official.

'Best start practising then, hadn't we?' he replied and watched Olivia's face brighten. More happy than sad, he decided.

They'd spent the morning at the big garden centre on the edge of town, buying compost and spring bulbs. It was a spur-of-the-moment decision. Waking up, Valentine had put on his dressing gown, pulled back his curtains and looked onto his small front patio, just like he did every day. Only today he'd abruptly made the decision. Right, that was it. The pots and containers had been sitting empty for long enough. There was no excuse for it any more. Gisele's funeral was three weeks ago and, as much as he missed her, he knew he needed to start looking forward to the future. Not to mention that she'd have his guts for garters, if she saw the state of her beloved patio.

When Olivia had walked past with Harry, he'd mentioned

it to her and she'd kindly offered to take him in the Land Rover. Well, he could hardly carry heavy bags of compost on the bus, and the mechanic had finally called last week to say the camper van was *kaput*.

'You're probably better off selling it as a scrap.'

'Scrap!' Valentine had been both horrified and insulted. 'Bugger that! I'm not selling my van for scrap. There's nowt wrong with it.'

'Nothing except the alternator's gone, it needs a clutch and the floor is almost rusted through,' replied the mechanic, running through a long list.

'Well, can't you fix it? I don't care what it costs. It's got sentimental value. You can't put a price on that.'

At which the mechanic had really put his tail between his legs and apologized and said yes, of course he could fix it; and several hours later he'd called back with an estimate. To which Valentine had said there was being sentimental and there was being crackers, and how much could he get for scrap?

Two hundred quid in cash, it turned out, which was the money he was going to use to transform his patio. Though he knew nothing about gardening. All those years watching Gisele and he hadn't a clue. It had been the same with the washing machine. Still, he'd picked that up – though not until he'd shrunk all his jumpers and his shirts turned pink (well, how was he supposed to know you separated the colours?) – and now he was a dab hand at all the different programmes.

That said, buying new jumpers had been costly, so he'd rather not repeat his mistakes. Olivia was helpful, though she said she was still learning, and went on about Monty Don's Jewel Garden a lot. Luckily there was a very nice assistant who explained about all the different spring bulbs and how to plant them, and Valentine ended up buying a huge selection. Daffs, crocuses, grape hyacinths, alliums and so many different colours of tulips. Some even had stripes and frilly edges.

'You know, I could have lent you the money to fix up the camper van,' Olivia was saying now as she reached for more compost.

Harry was lying up against the bags of multi-use potting compost, basking in the weak October sunshine that was shining through the low branches of the trees. He lifted his head grumpily as she removed his back-support.

'I've still got some money left over from paying for the band, and I sold some of my old clothes on eBay recently. A lot of it was vintage designer stuff that I bought in London, but my lifestyle's changed now. I'll never wear them again. Or fit into them,' she added with a roll of her eyes.

'That's very kind of you, but no need.' Valentine shook his head. 'That part of my life's over.'

'Oh, don't say that.' She looked dismayed.

'It's all right, love. It's how it should be. We had some wonderful times in that van and I'll never forget them, but life moves on and you've got to move with it.' He gestured to the packets of bulbs. 'Look to the future, eh?'

A look passed between them.

'That doesn't apply only to me, you know,' he added.

'I know.' Olivia shrugged, averting her eyes and opening a packet of small narcissus bulbs. She shook them into the palm of her hand. They were like little silver pearls.

'So how come you're going to the dance with an old bugger like me then?' he continued. 'Why don't you have a nice fella to take you?'

'I've got a nice fella,' she teased, winking at him.

397

'You know what I mean. What happened to your builder, Ben? He seemed to have taken a shine to you when I was last round your house.'

She looked self-conscious then. 'He's been busy, what with repairing the damage from the fire, and work – we both have . . . anyway, he's just a friend.' Grabbing the gardening fork, she began raking the soil industriously. It was obvious that she didn't want to talk about it. 'Right then, that's the last one planted. How about a cup of tea?'

Along with everyone in the village, Valentine had been shocked by the fire. Thankfully, everyone got out safely and there was no harm done – nothing the insurance couldn't fix anyhow. At least that's what he thought. He watched Olivia stand up, brushing the soil from her knees, and her distracted expression before she caught him looking and forced a bright smile. He wasn't so sure now.

'Only if I make it,' he nodded, raising himself stiffly to his feet and wondering if he should try those yoga classes at the village hall that Olivia had been telling him about. After all, he needed to get fit for all that dancing he was going to be doing. 'None of that teabag stuff.'

The central heating in the bungalow felt toasty and warm after being outside and, removing his layers, he went into the kitchen to start brewing the tea. Olivia joined him, reaching for the tray on top of the cabinets and getting out cups and saucers. She was taller than him, so she didn't need the little stepladder, and she knew where everything was now. As she reached for the cutlery drawer, he felt a reassuring companionship that comes from someone else knowing where you keep your teaspoons.

She was just putting them on the saucers when there was a chirping noise. It sounded like a cricket.

'What's that?'

'Oh, it's my phone. It's to say I've got a new email.'

'Well, I never.' Valentine watched as she pulled it out of her pocket and tapped the screen.

'You know, we should get you a smartphone, Valentine – you'd love it.'

'I've got a mobile phone.'

'Which you never turn on. Plus it's about a hundred years old.'

Choosing not to hear her, he reached for a canister of loose-leaf tea. All these newfangled gadgets. He couldn't understand the obsession. They only lasted two minutes before you had to buy a brand-new one. 'Upgrade' – that's what the sales assistant had called it, when he'd popped into the phone shop in town to see about a new battery, only to be told they didn't make them for that model any more. 'Daylight robbery' more like. Now tea: that had been around for thousands of years and the practice was still the same as it always was.

'Ooh, look, it's from the genealogy website – you've got your results.'

'I'd forgotten all about that.' His finger curled around the Orange Pekoe, but at the list minute he changed his mind. Today called for Lapsang Souchong with its smoky pinewood flavour, which always reminded him of autumn.

'*Great news! The moment you've been waiting for is here. Click the link to see the results and your matches.*' Olivia read aloud from her phone while the kettle boiled and then flicked off.

'Matches – what kind of matches?'

'Oh, they always find distant cousins.' She tapped the screen of her phone. 'But you never know, it might really help you with your family tree.'

'Well, that's the thing. I've been wondering what's the point, what with Gisele and Helen both being gone now.'

Olivia raised her eyes to him then, her face sympathetic.

'Does there have to be a point to everything?' she asked, shrugging her shoulders. 'Can't you do something simply because you enjoy it? Like dancing. Or birdwatching. Or trainspotting.'

'Nay, it's not that bad – let's not go that far,' Valentine grumbled, and she laughed as he poured the water into the teapot and added two scoops of tea.

'Anyway, I think genealogy is far from pointless. I love finding out about our ancestors. How we're all intercon-nected. It's fascinating.'

'So tell me, am I related to royalty then?'

Lifting the tray, he carried it into the living room. Harry had made himself comfortable on the blanket that he'd put on the sofa, and was asleep in the patch of sunlight streaming in the window. Olivia pretended not to notice.

'Hang on, I'm logging in . . . I just need to remember your username.'

'Username? What's that for?'

'It's an alternative to using your real name, for security purposes.'

'Bloody hell, they don't half make it complicated.'

Sitting down at the table, he poured the tea while she peered at her screen.

'It says your ethnicity is forty per cent British, thirty-five per cent Scottish, twenty per cent Irish—'

'Well, that'll be on my mother's side.'

'And there's even five per cent Iberian Peninsula.'

'Where's that, then?'

'Spain and Portugal.'

'Well, the Spanish Armada did capsize off Ireland,' he nodded, passing her the milk.

'Ooh, and you've got some matches.'

'What did I tell you? I'm landed gentry. Duke Valentine of North Yorkshire,' he chuckled and sipped his tea, only Olivia didn't laugh.

'Well, that can't be right.' Her forehead creased into a sharp frown. 'There must be some mistake.'

'Why, what's up?'

'It says you've got a ninety-nine per cent match.'

Now it was Valentine's turn to frown. 'What does that mean?'

'Hang on, there's a thumbnail photo . . .' She peered at her screen. 'No, but that's impossible.' She turned the phone to him, so that he could see, but he shook his head.

'It's all blurry – I need my glasses.'

There was a pause and he noticed Olivia looking at him funnily.

'It says parent/child . . .'

'What?'

'It says you've got another child.'

Silence. It was as if someone suddenly sucked the air out of the room. Valentine felt his cup slip from his fingers, the china splintering as it crashed onto the table, the tea spilling onto the carpet.

'Oh God!'

'It's OK, don't worry, I'll get a cloth.' Olivia jumped up.

'What I have done? I've made such a mess.' He tried to scoop up the pieces of broken china, but a shard pierced his skin.

'Oh no, you're bleeding.' Quickly grabbing a napkin, she reached for his hands.

'I'm sorry.'

'Don't worry. It's nothing.'

'No, you don't understand.'

She looked up at Valentine then, holding his hands tightly in hers, stopping him from falling, as shame washed over him. 'I had an affair.'

WhatsApp with Naomi

Can you and Danny swing?

Is this a sex
question?

No! I've organized a dance at the
village hall for the grand opening.
Do you want to come?

Yes.

I've hired a band
and there'll be a bar.

I've already said yes.

Great! Btw you won't have
to sleep in a tent this time.

I loved sleeping in a tent!

Not in December.

Brrr. Good point.
What's the band called?

Shake, Rattle and Roll.

That sounds like your sex
life when you're fifty.

Ha!

I'm serious.
You sure it's not a sex thing?

Forgiveness

With the opening night of the village hall drawing ever closer, the next few weeks are taken up with preparations to make sure everything is ready in time. November passes in a bit of a blur. Bonfire night comes and goes. I stay home with Harry because of the fireworks, although I'm glad of the excuse; after the fire at Ben's house, I worried it would bring back too many painful memories.

The days are much shorter now, but I wake to beautiful misty mornings. Trees shed their leaves while the rest of us pull on layers of gloves and scarves and jumpers. I rake the leaves into a big pile in the garden and harvest the last of my vegetables. The slugs ate the beans, but I have so many carrots and beets that I find myself googling how to make chutney. Me, making chutney! Who would have thought it?

As the nights draw in, I'm thankful for my new log-burner and spend my evenings cosied up in front of it with Harry who, despite the no-dogs-on-the-sofa rule, has now taken up residence next to me on the sofa. Though technically he's not *on* the sofa, as I cover it with a blanket. And yes, I know I'm fooling myself.

But mostly my life is spent at my kitchen table drawing up endless lists, which seem to grow ever longer. As quickly as I cross one thing off, another is added. In a way I'm pleased I'm so busy as it stops me thinking about Ben. He gradually stopped replying to my texts, so in the end I stopped sending them.

In between organizing caterers, printing posters and finalizing the calendar of events, at the beginning of December I make a quick trip into town to try to find a dress for the dance. The high street is decorated for Christmas and there's a steady stream of shoppers. I duck away from the crowds and into the quieter back streets and narrow Victorian alleyways, where there's a string of vintage and charity shops, selling clothes and jewellery.

It's there I run into Ajay. We smile and say our hellos. He read about the fire in the newspaper and asks how I am. Fine, I say, asking how he is. He's good, finally having decided to take the plunge and do what he loves: I'm looking at a personal trainer now. We laugh about something that I can't remember. I tell him I'm looking for a dress for the dance and invite him to come. He replies that he's looking for a present for his girlfriend and I invite her too. Is that weird? I don't know. It doesn't feel weird.

We say our goodbyes and he gives me a hug. I hug him back and we go our separate ways – our lives like train tracks, crossing briefly and crossing over again. Which makes me think about Valentine. Is that he how he felt about his affair? Just a brief encounter, someone with whom his life fleetingly crossed over, before crossing back again. Never knowing that it had produced a child.

With December come the plunging temperatures and wet weather that the forecasters have been promising. It rains for days, and I skip my morning walks as it's too cold and wet for Harry's arthritis. One morning, watching the rivulets run down the panes of my bedroom window, I notice a familiar flash of pink-and-white polka dots bobbing through the graveyard. It's Valentine with his umbrella. I wonder how he's feeling. It was all such a shock that day. I'd sent off the DNA test with such casual curiosity, as a fun way of helping with his hobby, but now his life had been rocked with an emotional fallout that neither of us could have imagined.

Since then we haven't seen much of each other. He's been busy too, in charge of an army of volunteers helping to finish painting and decorating the village hall. But in truth I think we've both been avoiding the consequences of our actions. He unknowingly fathered a child, and I unintentionally found that child. And, like a genie that's been let out of the bottle, a secret has been discovered and Valentine needs to decide what to do about it.

'You had an affair?'

I think back to our conversation that day several weeks ago in Valentine's living room. I remember my disbelief. How he'd gone pale, almost grey, as he tried to explain.

'It was after Helen was born. Gisele wasn't herself. They've got a name for it now, but they didn't in those days. She'd just sit on her bed and cry.' He started speaking, his voice low. 'She wasn't interested in the baby, or me, or anything. I didn't know what to do. I was out working all hours to try and pay the rent. At first I was sympathetic, but after a while I lost patience . . .'

He swallowed hard, the guilt in his eyes palpable.

'I got frustrated. I told Gisele to pull herself together – that she had a daughter to look after.'

'You were probably tired.' I tried to make excuses, but he wouldn't let me.

'There's no excuse for what I did.' He shook his head, his voice almost breaking. 'If that wasn't bad enough, when she did finally bond with Helen, instead of being happy I felt rejected. It was like I didn't exist and I got jealous. Jealous of my own daughter: what kind man does that make me?'

Pain flashed across Valentine's face and my instinct was to comfort him, but I couldn't find the right words.

'And there was this woman I was doing some decorating for. She lived on the other side of town. She paid me attention. Flattered me, I suppose. And I was weak and stupid and . . .' His voice trailed off and he couldn't bear to look at me. 'It only lasted a couple of weeks, if that. One evening I walked into the house and Gisele was in the chair rocking Helen, fast asleep, and they looked perfect. *They were perfect*. And I suddenly realized I risked losing everything I'd ever wanted.'

He hung his head with shame then, while I absorbed his story, trying to make sense of the emotions being triggered in me.

'I swore I'd never take them for granted again – never do anything like that again – and I swear to God I kept my word. I never saw the woman again.'

Valentine was asking me to believe him and I did believe him. And I believed that he was sorry. And yet I couldn't help thinking how he'd cheated on Gisele, just as David had cheated on me, and that his confession felt almost like a personal betrayal.

'But then when Helen died all those years later, I felt like it was my fault. Like I was being punished. I'm not a religious man, but it felt as if God was making me pay for what I'd done – for being unfaithful, for being jealous of my little girl.'

'But that's nonsense.'

'Is it, though?' His face was racked with pain and, despite my own hurt, I felt a sudden need to protect him.

'No God worth believing in is going to sit in judgement,'

I told Valentine firmly and, even as I said it, I knew that I couldn't, either.

'But I did something very wrong. I betrayed Gisele. I was jealous of my own daughter.'

'Helen had an asthma attack,' I said firmly. 'She didn't have her inhaler. It was nothing to do with you. It was an accident. It's not your fault.'

'But if I hadn't cheated on my wife . . .'

'What? Helen wouldn't have suffered from asthma? She wouldn't have forgotten her inhaler?' I looked at him then across the table, my face stern. 'You know that's not true, don't you? You loved your daughter, and she loved you. You mustn't blame yourself. It was a tragic, tragic accident. You have to believe me.' I heard my voice rising and felt a sense of urgency.

'Why?'

'Because if you're responsible for what happened to Helen, then I'm responsible for what happened to my sister, Josie,' I blurted out.

He stared at me, his attention caught.

There's a beat and then, 'What happened to your sister?'

I hesitated and swallowed hard. 'That's just it – I don't know. She's been missing for two years. She could be dead, for all I know.'

It was the first time I'd said those words out loud, so terrified had I been that by articulating my worst fear, I'd make it come true. Yet at the same I felt suddenly unburdened, freed of their crushing weight.

'Missing? You never said.' Valentine's face creased with concern. 'But why is that your fault?

It was a question I'd asked myself a million times.

'Because I was supposed to look after her,' I said simply. 'Before my mum died, I always remember her telling me to be a good girl. "Look after your sister for me, she's not as strong as you are—"' I break off, casting my mind back. 'My sister's older than me, but she's always been more fragile. Though you'd never think it.'

I stared down at my hands, twisting them in my lap.

'She was always so creative and witty; all the boys wanted to be with her, and all the girls wanted to be her. But she'd get so homesick on school trips that Dad would have to bring her home. We used to share a bedroom when we stayed at my grandparents, and she used to cry in the night . . . I'd crawl under the covers and spoon her until she fell asleep.'

Reminded of her soft warmth, I drifted back for a few moments. 'I don't know why I'm telling you all this – it's not important.'

But Valentine shook his head. 'Yes, it is,' he urged. 'It is important. Memories are important. It's what we're all made up of.' He blinked hard and I knew he was thinking of Gisele and Helen. 'I want you to tell me about her.'

There was so much to say. Where did I start?

'Josie's like a bright light. She's either on or off.' I conjured up my big sister, starting with the broadest strokes. 'She'll get ideas and be so excited; she was so much fun when we were growing up . . .' I smiled, remembering. 'But then she'd exhaust herself and get in these dark moods where I couldn't reach her.'

I paused, the memories painful.

'When we were young we didn't understand mental illness, nobody spoke about it then; it would be years till she was finally diagnosed with bipolar.'

I raised my eyes to meet Valentine's. He was looking at me, his face filled with concern.

'She got a scholarship to art college to do photography,

but she fell into the wrong crowd, drinking, doing drugs . . . For a while it was like we lost her, but then she got on the right medication and won a prestigious award and moved to New York.' I smiled, remembering her excitement. 'Dad and I were so proud – it's what she'd dreamed of, yet we were worried . . . but America seemed to suit her. Everything here always felt too small for Josie, like wearing clothes that don't fit. She seemed to find it constricting, too claustrophobic. But there it's like she bloomed; she made friends, had boyfriends, she seemed happy—'

I broke off, feeling the familiar pangs of guilt. Was she really happy or had that just been me, newly married and projecting my own thoughts?

'But after Dad died, everything seemed to unravel. Josie stopped taking her medication and started drinking again. She asked to borrow money. I was always helping her with her rent and David and I used to argue about it. He said she was old enough to look after herself, that she had to sort herself out, that we couldn't keep bailing her out . . . Thing is, I'd never admit it, but I knew he was right. I was just enabling her.'

I'd gone over this in my mind so many times, replaying the chain of events.

'So the last time Josie asked for a loan, I said no. I offered to fly out there instead, to go and see her doctors, help her get the right treatment, but she said she didn't want my pity. We got into a big row and she slammed the phone down. I think she was drunk or high, or both. A week later I got word from her landlord that she'd moved out of her apartment without paying the rent. No one knew where. She wouldn't answer emails, texts . . . After a while her phone was disconnected . . .'

I had a sudden memory of the panic.

411

'I tried contacting her friends, her ex-boyfriend, but no one's heard from her. I even filed a missing persons, but the police aren't interested; she's a grown woman, and as far as they're concerned, she can take care of herself.'

I shook my head, feeling the tears prickling my eyelashes.

'The thing is, I don't think she can. You know, I still write to her, even though she never replies. I send emails about what I'm doing and where I am. It makes feel close to her; it makes me feel like I haven't given up—' I broke off, realizing how stupid I must sound.

Valentine hadn't said anything the whole time I'd been talking. He just listened. But now he reached his bandaged hand across the table and placed it on mine.

'Sometimes it's easier to be lost than it is to be found.'

I raised my eyes to see he was looking at me, with that steady, solid gaze of his.

'That's how I felt when you waved at me that day in the window. After Gisele went into care, I didn't want to see anyone or do anything. I wanted to disappear. But then you came along with Harry and you pushed your way in, with your persistence and bloody cheerfulness.'

He smiled then, which made me smile, and raised his eyebrows.

'Have you ever wanted to disappear?'

'Yes,' I nodded, remembering how I felt after my marriage broke down and I left London. 'Yes, I have.'

'Well then, don't worry. She'll be in touch when she's ready. It's like that bird feeder I made you.'

'You mean the one that no birds have found yet?' I said ruefully, but his gaze didn't waver.

'Be patient. They'll come.'

*

Downstairs in the kitchen the kettle flicks off and I pour boiling water into the small stainless-steel flask. As the teabags steep, I reach for my coat hanging over the back of the chair and the packet of mince pies I bought when I was in town. I know I should try to make my own, but I also know I can never make shortcrust pastry to rival M&S's. Popping a couple in my deep pockets, I add a splash of milk to the flask, making sure to fish out the teabags. I've learned my lesson.

Afterwards Valentine told me it was only years later that he learned Gisele had known of his affair, but had chosen not to say anything. When he asked her why she had stayed and not left him – why she had chosen to forgive and trust him again – she'd simply replied that she loved him and knew he loved her, and that love was always worth the risk. Which made me think how often the hardest person to forgive is yourself.

It was then that I told him why my marriage ended. Valentine had never asked me, but it felt dishonest to keep it from him, when we'd been so honest with each other. At the mention of David's affair, he looked upset and asked me if I was disappointed in him, and I said of course not and told him what Josie once told me: that the same story is different for everyone. You just have to live the one that's right for you.

I find Valentine sitting on Helen's bench, to which he's added a dedication to Gisele. I take a seat beside him as Harry beats his legs with his tail, overjoyed to see his friend again. I think how simple life is for Harry, and how complicated we humans make our own lives.

'It's cold – I thought you might want some tea.' Producing the flask, I unscrew the lid and pour him a cup. 'Don't worry,

I took out the teabag,' I add, passing it to him, along with a mince pie that I fish out of my pocket.

'Thanks, love.' He smiles at the gesture and moves his umbrella so that we can both shelter underneath it. Pouring the hot, steaming liquid into an extra cup, I settle myself next to him, looking out across the graveyard, watching the dusk falling quickly.

'Will he know about me yet?'

He doesn't need to explain that he's talking about the child he's discovered he fathered. Both of us have thought of nothing else.

'He could, yes.' I admit, feeling the weight of responsibility. My breath exhales and I go over my thought process from the last few days. 'But the likelihood is he probably hasn't logged into his account for ages. DNA tests were popular Christmas presents a few years ago – my ex and I got them, though it didn't throw up any surprises . . . My ex-husband was very disappointed he wasn't royalty, either.'

I try to make a joke, but we both know how serious it is and Valentine nods, absorbing the information.

'I imagine a lot of people have forgotten about them. Plus, even if he does remember, he won't be able to identify you.'

'But I saw his photograph.'

'Yes, but I didn't upload one of you or use your real name—'

'I'm not ashamed of him, he's my son.' He cuts me off and turns to me, his jaw set determinedly.

'No, I know.'

'And I don't want to try to forget the past. If Gisele's disease taught me anything, it's that.' Shaking his head, he gestures towards the small garden of remembrance where Gisele's ashes are scattered, his voice quietly filled with resolve. 'That's why I came here today. I owed it to her to tell her first . . . I want to contact him.'

414

I listen, but don't say anything.

'But I don't want to cause any trouble. He might not want to know me. Not after all these years. So I was thinking . . .'

He doesn't finish the sentence. For a moment it hangs there as he raises his eyes to mine.

'Will you?'

Like with so many momentous choices in life, it's made without fanfare. And as Valentine's words disappear into the darkness, we remain there, sitting on the bench, savouring hot tea and sweet pastry. Lost in our thoughts of what's to come, being lulled by the soft pattering of the rain on a pink polka-dot umbrella.

The Grand Opening

'This place looks amazing! I wouldn't recognize it!'

With her arms flung wide, Naomi is racing through every room in the house, showering me with compliments and exclaiming at every detail. 'I love that old French chandelier in the kitchen. Are those gorgeous paintings the ones we found in the shed? Oh, wow, I can't believe it's the same garden!' Her enthusiasm is exactly the reaction you want from a friend, whether it's in response to a new hairstyle, or a dress, or a house renovation. Though in my case, it's all three.

'Danny, come look at Liv's roll-top bath,' she cries, bounding into the guest bedroom where her fiancé lies, dozing on the bed before we get ready to go out. 'She found it in a field. It used to be a water trough for the cows! You're gonna love it.'

'Babe, do you have to emote so loudly?' I hear him groan, before minutes later dutifully appearing at the doorway of the bedroom to inspect it.

It's the dance tonight, to mark the opening of the village hall, and they've travelled up from London to stay for the weekend. Ellie has come too and Ben was right about converting the attic. She couldn't have been more excited to discover her bed under the eaves, which I've strung with fairy lights, and is now firmly ensconced up there with Harry. The last time I looked, she was playing hairdressers and Harry was sitting there obediently, having his fur brushed and plaited.

'You know, maybe we should get married here,' Danny is

saying now. It's his first visit to the Yorkshire Dales, and earlier he caused quite a stir as he walked around the village dressed in his leather jacket, bandana and sunglasses. *Sunglasses in December*. I think Sheila at the post office thought he was Bono. 'Hire a field, get some yurts, put on a music festival.'

'Now who's emoting?' laughs Naomi. 'Not sure I can imagine my parents in a yurt.'

'They must be pleased about the engagement,' I say.

'That I'm finally going to be respectable?' Naomi rolls her eyes and sighs. 'Still, I suppose if it makes them happy, and their church-group happy.'

'Are we going to be respectable?' says Danny, slipping his hand around her waist and making her smile.

Which is lovely to see, as Naomi has always had such a tough time with her parents, though I can imagine Danny might not be quite the son-in-law they're imagining.

'No, you're right, this place is amazing,' he's saying now in admiration, looking over at me. 'Total respect, Liv.' With his free hand he gives me a fist-bump.

'Thanks.' I laugh with embarrassment as I fist-bump him back.

'And I'm not just talking about the house and garden, when I say I don't recognize it,' adds Naomi. 'Remember when I told you that life was going to get bigger and better?'

My mind flicks back to that moment, standing outside my old house in London, feeling like life was over. It seems so long ago, and yet I can still conjure it up in a heartbeat.

'See, I'm always right,' she says pointedly at Danny.

'Yes, she is,' I nod and he groans good-naturedly, which makes us all laugh.

But what no one tells you is that the darkest moments make you look for the light. And I looked for it and found it.

*

We get ready for the dance in a haze of hair spray and high spirits, and as we step out into the night there's a veritable feeling of festivity. The air has that crisp coldness that makes your breath appear like cobwebs, and the village has been decorated for Christmas. A large trimmed tree shimmers in the cobbled square and warm white fairy lights are strung across the lane leading to the top of the village.

The sounds of the band warming up are wafting into the darkness, and up ahead the village hall is lit up. Earlier an army of volunteers draped a banner across the front with the words 'Grand Opening' painted by the local primary school, while others erected ladders against the old oak tree that grows in front of the hall and hung garlands of carnival lights in the branches. The effect is magical.

'It looks like the Faraway Tree,' whispers Ellie, her voice heavy with excitement as we pick our way across the cobbles. I'm usually always wearing wellies, but now I tiptoe carefully, trying not get the kitten heels of my slingback stilettos stuck.

'You're right, it does,' says Naomi. 'I wonder where it's going to take us?'

'Back to the 1950s,' quips Danny as he smooths a hand over his quiff, which is set rock-hard with sugar and water.

Danny has gone full Teddy boy, in a dark suit with drain-pipe trousers. Naomi is resplendent in a canary-yellow tea dress, cinched at her tiny waist, with a full skirt and netted petticoats. They look like two exotic birds, cooing and chattering in the darkness, as they hold Ellie's hands and swing her between them.

Meanwhile I've taken my inspiration from an old photograph that I found of my mum, the one where I think she looks like Audrey Hepburn, and have worn my hair up in a French pleat, with red lips, black eyeliner and pearl-button earrings. I'm wearing an original fifties swing coat and a black satin dress that I found in one of the vintage shops in town. The owner informed me it was called a 'wiggle dress', as that's how the pencil skirt makes you walk. I mentioned that it wasn't the walking I was worried about so much; it was the dancing, but she assured me that's what the split up the back was for.

Plus the dress looked and felt fabulous, and after a lifetime spent putting practicality first, I took a leaf out of Harry's guide to life and put fun first. One thing's for sure: it won't be long before I find out what it's like to dance in it, as the first person I see when we walk inside is Valentine.

'You're early!'

'Well, I didn't want to keep my date waiting.' He beams, taking my coat and handing it to the one of volunteer cloak-room assistants. 'And don't you look grand!'

'So do you. Love the suit. Very sharp. Is it vintage?'

'Aye, like its owner,' he laughs and holds out his elbow for me to take.

I smile gratefully. He knows how nervous I am about tonight and, slipping my arm through his, we walk inside.

We're early, but there are quite a few people here already, mingling around on the edges of the dance floor, which are lined with chairs, just like they used to be in traditional dance halls. A small pop-up bar is serving beers and Babycham and Cherry Bs, a cherry-flavoured drink that comes in little bottles and was all the rage in the 1950s. That's according to quite a few of the elderly villagers who, on discovering news of the dance, were more than happy to help with the research. Margaret, who lives in one of new retirement flats, has even donated several bottles of Advocaat and is on hand to make Snowballs.

'The place looks wonderful.'

'Isn't it amazing!'

'What a transformation!'

As we make our way across the dance floor I catch snippets of conversation and people's eyes, and am greeted with nods and smiles and waves of hello as they come over to offer their congratulations on tonight and the opening of the village hall. Though really we all end up congratulating each other, as it's been such a team effort.

'Evelyn, you look marvellous!'

Spotting her by the bar, I go to kiss her on the cheek and get a mouthful of her feather boa. She seems to have missed the memo and appears to be dressed for the Roaring Twenties.

'So much better than a raffle,' she beams, sipping a Babycham.

Music is being piped through the speakers as we wait for the band to go onstage. It's set with a drum kit, a double bass and the hall's original stand-up piano, which has been retuned and wheeled in against the silver curtain that is serving as a backdrop. Apparently we had it in storage from when they last put on a production of *The Wizard of Oz* and it's been cleaned and retuned. All part of Evelyn's recycling and sustainability programme, of course.

As the hall begins to fill up, it buzzes with the sound of laughter and merriment and I get a warm glow of satisfaction at seeing it all finally come together – and the local community too. I never would have believed it when I moved here, less than a year ago, but this tiny village, which once seemed so full of strangers, is now filled with all my friends.

And I feel something else: a sense of belonging. I've moved around such a lot in life and, while I was happy when I lived in London, now I know what people mean when they talk about feeling like they've come home.

That's not to say I'm not as nervous as hell. There's so much riding on tonight. I don't want anything to go wrong.

As Valentine goes to get me a Cherry B to calm my butter-flies, I watch the tiny lights swirling around the room and gaze up at the glitter ball above my head. Well, it wouldn't be a dance without a glitter ball, would it?

'The band's coming on,' says Valentine, as he returns with our drinks, and I look over to see them walking onto the stage. Dressed in matching red jackets with Brylcreemed hair, they take up their positions. I gulp back my Cherry B, feeling the fizz of alcohol and anticipation.

'Do you think we've done enough practise?'

During the past week we met up to run through the steps. Valentine had put together a routine and we rehearsed it a few times. Still, I can't remember the last time I was this jittery.

'We'll soon find out.'

As the first chords strike up, he grabs me by my hand.

'Right, we're on.'

Quickstep. Slow dance. Jive. Swing.

Oh, wow, I'm having so much fun. The band is amazing. Brilliant, in fact. They blast out tunes, and any nerves or fears vanish into thin air as Valentine expertly under-arm-twirls, swivels and dips me. Plus the lady in the shop was right: who knew you could move so freely in a pencil skirt? The dance floor quickly fills up. I soon realize that my generation, and younger, don't know how to dance.

White-haired locals that I've seen wheeling shopping trol-leys and strolling along the river with walking poles are bouncing, kicking and swinging their partners around with the kind of energy and fancy footwork that could rival anything I've seen on *Strictly*. And I'm talking about the professional dancers, not the contestants.

High on adrenaline and filled with exhilaration, we dance to one hit after another and, believe it or not, I don't trip over once. *1-2-3-and-4-5-and-6*. As the band blasts out one boppy melody after the other, we lift our knees and rock our hips, and all the while I'm trying desperately to stay in time. *Rock step. Chassé to the left. Chassé to the right.* Pretty soon I'm exhausted – unlike Valentine, who's been practising for weeks with a chair in the garage. Apparently old habits die hard.

Breathlessly I make my apologies: I'm going to have to sit a few out. Though I needn't have worried. No sooner do I find my seat than he's swooped upon by the legion of widows who live in the village; older, spirited ladies who are perfectly happy being single and independent, with no one but themselves to cook and clean for, but who just for one evening would really like a man to dance with.

With his fancy footwork and underarm twirls, Valentine is in high demand and I watch him doing the Lindy Hop, thinking about how different he is now from when I first met him, and not only in terms of his fitness. I know how much he misses Gisele – it should have been her that he was dancing with tonight – but it gives me a swell of happiness to see how much he's valued by everyone. People have been asking if he'll teach some decorating classes and I think it's a great idea, though Valentine said in that case he'll need a new jotter pad. Which I didn't quite understand, but anyway he looked really pleased.

'Maya, hi – you made it!'

I spot her pink hair first, as it emerges through the crowd.

'Yeah, uni broke up. Wouldn't miss it for the world.'

It's swept up in a high ponytail and she's wearing a full skirt and trainers. She looks like a pink-haired Sandy from *Grease*.

'Well, if it wasn't for you starting the crowdfunder.'

'Oh, it was nothing.' She bats it away. 'My parents said they'd come by later, when Mum's finished her shift.'

'Great! Though you might end up having to dance with your dad,' I warn.

'I am never dancing with my dad!' Maya laughs and pulls a horrified expression.

'Well, there's not that many men here – the women seem to be outnumbering them.'

'I've brought my own dance partner.'

'You have?'

I turn then and shriek as I spot Will resembling a blond Danny Zuko.

'What are you doing here? Why didn't you tell me!'

'I wanted it to be a surprise.'

I jump up and Will gives me a hug and I decide that it's official; I now love surprises, and nothing beats a really good one.

'Where are you staying? My place is full, but I've got the sofa.'

'Thanks, but I'm sorted,' he says, slipping his arm around Maya's waist as she giggles, and I think how ridiculously cute they are together.

We go to the bar and get drinks, and it's there that Will apologizes for giving his dad my address. I tell him not to worry; that actually it was good that he did, as it gave me the opportunity to get a lot off my chest, and that I hope the two of them have made up. He tells me they're going away together at Christmas to do some father-and-son bonding. Skiing? No, the Maldives. Apparently David had booked to go there with his now ex-fiancée on honeymoon, and he can't get his money back.

'We're in the honeymoon suite,' says Will and laughs. Which makes me laugh. Because you have to, don't you? And actually the thought of David and Will with petals sprinkled in the shape of love hearts on their bed is really very funny.

Talking of exes, one person who I know isn't going to show up is Ajay. Not that I'm sure I can officially call him an ex, but still. He texted earlier to thank me for the invite, but said that he had a very jealous girlfriend and feared there could be Murder on the Dance Floor. To which I replied ha-ha, very funny. To which he replied that only I would get that joke, which was exactly the reason he couldn't come.

Life's funny, isn't it? Who you click with, and who you don't. Who you see as just as a friend, and who you see as something more. They call it chemistry, but it's so much more than that – that magical connection you feel when it clicks for both of you at exactly the same time. It's a phenomenon. Some people never feel it. Others get lucky once; some people several times over.

Whether it lasts is another thing. It didn't stand the test of time for me and David, but now that I've stopped grieving over my marriage, I don't see it as a failure any more. Just because something doesn't last forever doesn't make it less valuable. A relationship shouldn't be measured by time and how it ends, in order to be seen as a success. It was great and brilliant and wonderful for a while, until it wasn't. And maybe that's how life's supposed to be.

And maybe some relationships don't even start. Maybe they're only a spark and, if you don't catch it quickly enough, it goes out. Maybe that's what happened to me and Ben.

Where is he?

As the evening wears on, I find myself distracted, watching the entrance, waiting for Ben to arrive. We haven't spoken for weeks now and I stopped texting when he stopped replying. I know he's been avoiding me. But tonight brought with it a hope for reconciliation – a chance to talk and clear the air. To at least try and be friends. But as it gets later and later, doubts begin to form, until suddenly a thought strikes me: *what if he's not coming?* And I'm hit with such a crushing sense of disappointment that I realize, for the first time, just how much I want him to.

I've almost given up when I finally catch sight of him. I'm dancing with Valentine when I see Ben through the crowds. I know instantly it's him before he's even turned round. I recognize the broad square of his shoulders in his jacket, and the quiet ease of the way he holds himself, like he doesn't have to prove anything. And I feel such a sense of relief that I lose my step. Valentine catches me, twirling me around, and I laugh and we continue dancing. But I can't concentrate. All I can think about is: *Ben's here.* About how much I want to talk to him, even though I haven't a clue what to say.

It's when the music slows down that I realize I've run out of time anyway. It's too late. It's the end of the evening. Time for the last dance. At which point Valentine apologizes and disappears to the loo, leaving me sitting on the sidelines, feeling like a bit of a wallflower. I look for Ben, but I can't see him any more. He must have gone home already. That tiny bit of hope I've been holding on to crumples inside me, and I rub the heels of my stockinged feet and watch Naomi and Danny slow-dancing; Ellie is fast asleep in his arms and squeezed between them. Maya and Will, arms wrapped around each other, are trying to be all romantic while not looking in the direction of her parents, who are swaying cheek-to-cheek nearby.

My eyes flick across the dance floor at all the different couples: Evelyn towering above the vicar, his head on her shoulder, her feather boa wrapped around his neck; the farmer who for the first time I've seen without muddy wellies, with his wife; Sheila the postmistress, tiny and oh-so-happy to be dancing with her soldier son who's come home for

Christmas; the ladies who own the walkers' cafe, still wearing their striped aprons, as they've been serving up pie and mash. All the familiar faces. Except one.

'Can I have this last dance?'

And then I look up and he's there.

The Last Dance

Ben holds out his hand. I raise my eyes to his. He looks nervous.

That makes two of us.

'Yes,' I nod.

Standing up, I slip my hand into his and he leads me to the dance floor. It feels absurdly formal. Both of us are all dressed up. Like we're in another era and there are different rules. He slips his arm around my waist.

'You look nice.'

'You too.'

'How's Stanley?'

'He's great. With his Aunt Holly. It would be too loud for him in here.'

Our bodies are suddenly pressed together, yet we've barely talked for weeks.

'What about Harry? Quite the celebrity.'

'He's at home. Too loud for him, too. Hopefully the celebrity is not chewing up the house.'

Ben laughs politely as we begin moving slowly around more than just the dance floor – we'll be talking about the weather next. I feel a sudden sense of urgency, in case I lose my nerve.

'Look, there's something I have to tell you.'

'I need to say something.'

We both speak at once and break off, both of us smiling.

'You go first,' I say quickly, aware of wanting to catch whatever it is before it slips away. I know if I go first, everything will change.

'I'm sorry, I'm not good with words.' His eyes meet mine and his face is full of apology. 'But I owe you an explanation.'

'For what?'

'For why I've been avoiding you. For not saying goodbye at the funeral and for ignoring your texts. For being a jerk to Maya.'

He's taken off his jacket and I can feel the broadness of his shoulder through the white cotton of his shirt.

'It wasn't Maya's fault. She's just a kid. It was an accident.'

'I know, and I've apologized to her tonight. I was a teen-ager once and we all remember what a total idiot I was.'

Ben's eyes search mine for recognition, recalling that night in the restaurant, as if wanting to make sure I haven't forgotten.

I haven't forgotten, I want to tell him. Not even a second of it.

As he holds me close, our bodies gently sway together. It's a slow, romantic ballad and I can feel the pressure of his fingertips on my back, guiding me. It makes me feel safe. It's a lovely thing, feeling safe.

'I wish I hadn't suggested we go out, then none of it would ever have happened.'

'Don't say that.' Ben looks upset.

'It's true.'

'No, it's not.'

His head jerks back and I catch flashes of pain and frus-tration in his face. 'What's true is I had the best evening, and I don't regret that for a second. What's true is I got scared. I thought I'd lost Stan, like I lost Janet.'

I've never seen Ben like this, and I can tell it's really important for him that I believe him.

'Like I'm scared of losing you.' There's a beat as his eyes search out mine. 'I'm scared of loving someone, in case I lose them again.'

The whole time I've been listening, waiting, and now I feel my breath held tight inside me, because if I exhale I might blow those words away. Do you know what it feels like to have someone say something to you that you never dared hope they would say? To hear it put into words – that very thing you've been thinking too.

'I thought you said you weren't good with words,' I say finally.

He smiles then. That lovely, slow smile of his that crinkles up the corners of his eyes, and I feel all warm and fuzzy with love and too many Cherry Bs.

'I've missed you.'

'I've missed you too.'

'Though maybe not the mouldy teabags,' I add and we both laugh, and just like all that, all the stuff keeping us apart seems to disappear, and it's just two people. On a dance floor. In a village hall. Somewhere in the middle of the Yorkshire Dales. And as the music plays and the tiny magical refractions of light from the glitter ball swirl around us, I loop my arms around Ben's neck and rest my head against his chest, breathing in his scent as he holds me closer. I could stay like this forever.

'Sorry, I forgot to ask . . . What was it you wanted to tell me?'

His voice murmurs in my ear and we pull apart slightly. And it's then, across the other side of the room, I catch sight of Valentine. He's standing on the edge of the dance floor, looking over at us. I see his expression and know instinctively that it's time. Because life isn't always about perfect timing.

'Ben.' I stop dancing.

'Yes?'

'Can we go somewhere quieter. It's about your dad.'

Dearest Sis,

I've never been much good at knowing where to start. You were always the organized one, not me. Start at the beginning – isn't that what Granddad always used to say? Only I don't really know where it all started and, when I try, I get tangled up in knots.

So instead of trying to find the beginning, I'm going to start right now. Here. On the balcony of an old hacienda, overlooking a courtyard filled with the most beautiful crimson bougainvillea, in a little town in north-western Mexico. I like to sit here and have my morning coffee and eggs. They do the best eggs here, Liv. I like to eat them with fresh flour tortillas and green salsa, and watch the geckos sunning themselves on the old adobe walls.

I read all your emails. I just never knew how to reply. There was so much to say, and it all felt so hard. I'm sorry. I let you down. I should've got in touch, only the longer I left it, the harder it got. I wasn't mad at you. I was never mad at you; I was mad at myself. For not getting it together, for screwing things up. After Dad died, I fell apart and I hurt a lot of people. I hurt you. And it felt easier for everyone if I disappeared.

Ever get that feeling?

I didn't have any kind of plan. You know me. I just wanted to get away, switch off, check out of my life. So I threw some stuff and my cameras in a backpack and started travelling. When I ran out of money I'd hitch a ride, do some odd jobs, wait on a few tables. There was always something I could do. I ended up in South America for a while, travelling around, taking photos. I never really intended not to come back, but every day it got easier to stay away.

I was hiking in Patagonia with a group of people when I met a couple who owned a hotel. They saw my camera and asked to see my photos, and whether they could buy some of them to hang in their rooms. Turns out they own a large chain of exclusive boutique hotels – and several thousand hotel rooms all over the world. So that's what I do now. I take photographs for them, mostly of nature and wildlife, and of everyone's favourite: sunsets.

One of their hotels is this lovely old hacienda in Mexico. I'm staying here for Christmas and the holidays. I like it here. I'm back on my meds and I feel so much better. I've been doing a lot of therapy. But mostly the best therapy for me is being out in nature: just me and my camera, doing what I love best.

I never stopped thinking of you, though. Wherever I went, you came with me. It's been like that my whole life. That's why I was able to hide in the dungeon of a castle, or float out to sea in an old dinghy, or move to New York. Because I knew you were always there, keeping me safe. I was never the brave one. It was always you.

Oh, how I've missed you, Liv. I miss seeing your face. Hearing your voice. And then I was walking through the hotel lobby last week and suddenly I heard your voice and there you were: on the TV. My little sis and her dog called Harry. Imagine what Granddad and Grandma would say! Our Liv on the telly!

I knew then that I had to write. I hope you can forgive me. I wanted to call, but my nerve failed me. I'm on WhatsApp if you want to call me – my number's at the bottom of this email. Or you can come to Mexico, if you

432

feel like a holiday? There's plenty of room and the weather is lovely this time of year. And they make the best Margaritas, though I don't drink any more, but you can have one for me too.

We've got a lot to catch up on.

I love you, little sis.

Josie

Stanley

Today at school they had art and Miss Hattersley, his teacher, asked the class to draw a picture of one good thing that made them happy. She said they could use paints or crayons, or cut things out of magazines and make a collage. She said it was the last week before they broke up for Christmas, so to let their imaginations 'run wild'.

So he drew his trampoline, and Harry and Dad and Auntie Holly and the fireman who rescued him, and the bright-red fire engine that he got to sit in when he went to say thank you. Because he was in a fire and he got to climb out of a window with a fireman. Which he told Maya was *really cool*, when she came home from university and visited him. And they saved Harry, who showed him how to be brave so that he didn't get that funny feeling in his tummy any more – that made him *very* happy.

Stanley liked drawing, but he wasn't very good at drawing people. He was better at animals. He drew Liv too, but he made her head all wonky. She brought them a chocolate cake when they moved back into their old house, and Dad looked really happy to see her. Stanley used a red felt-tip for Liv's mouth, because when she arrived she was wearing red lipstick, but it must have rubbed off somehow, as she wasn't wearing lipstick when she left and he didn't see her eat any cake.

Stanley liked living at Auntie Holly's, but he loved his new bedroom. He had lots of new things now. A new duvet. A new train set. A new pair of binoculars. A new school. New friends. Even a new granddad. And they all made him happy. That was the problem: there were so many happy things in his picture that he couldn't fit them all in. The piece of paper wasn't big enough. It got him a bit stressed.

Overwhelmed. That's the word Miss Hattersley used. But she said that was OK, and sometimes in life we get overwhelmed trying to express ourselves and everything we feel. She said that in art lots of artists used something called symbolism and they painted feelings, not things. So she gave him a fresh piece of white paper and said that instead of painting everything, to choose just one thing that symbolized happiness.

So Stanley drew a pizza. Because pizza makes everyone happy.

Valentine

He drew back the curtains. It was still early, but he could tell it promised to be a lovely day. There was snow on the hilltops and the sun was shining. Pulling on his dressing gown, he went into the kitchen, filled the kettle and turned on the radio. Every morning he had a routine. Picking up a pen, he reached for the jotter pad he kept on the side to make daily lists. As he turned the page to start a new one, he smiled to himself.

monday 18th December
1. Pick up grandson from school
2. wish Liv safe travels

The Rest of Your Life

'I thought you were only going for two weeks.'

'I am!'

'How can you need this much stuff for two weeks in Mexico?' Carrying my suitcase down the stairs, Ben grimaces. 'This weighs a ton!'

'I wasn't sure what to take.'

'So you thought you'd take everything?' He grins and I smile sheepishly.

'Here, let me help.' Following behind him, I try and reach for the handle, and for the first time I notice his left hand. He's taken off his wedding ring. He catches my eye and a look passes between us. No words. No fuss. Just an understanding.

'I've got this,' he says.

I think it was a Greek philosopher who said that change is the only constant in life. I never used to like change. It unsettled me. Scared me even. I had so much change as a child that I grew up to fear it – something to be resisted. And for a while there I did a pretty good job of keeping in my comfort zone, until one day my marriage ended and life fell apart and suddenly I had no choice. It was do or die.

And I wasn't going to die. Not yet, anyway. And as scary and shitty and hard as it was at times, I've slowly come to realize that my sister was right when she told me that life is what happens at the edge of your comfort zone. To embrace change is to embrace life. It can open you up to all kinds of wonderful things. And if I ever needed any confirmation, then I only have to look at the events of this past week to prove it.

Since the dance there's been so much change. After Ben's initial shock at finding out that Valentine was his real father, they've been doing a lot of talking. There's a lot to talk about. A whole lifetime to catch up on. But what's important is that Valentine's fears were unfounded. Ben didn't reject him – far from it. There's been no talk of blame or guilt or fault; just acceptance and recognition of how lucky they both are to have found each other, after all these years. Perhaps, in some strange way, that's the gift grief gives you. Because having known what it's like to suffer loss, these two men could only see how much they had to gain.

As for my sister's email, it was waiting for me in my in-box the morning after the dance, and I read it and wept with relief and joy and called her immediately. And woke her up, as it was the middle of the night and I'd been in such a rush to speak to her that I hadn't worked out the time difference. But it didn't matter. Nothing mattered. And we picked up, right where we left off – like we were having a conversation ten minutes ago. We talked for hours, and when finally I got off the phone, I went online and promptly booked my plane ticket.

'OK, well, I'd better say my goodbyes.'

I walk into the kitchen, expecting to find Stanley, but instead I see the French windows have been left open and he's outside in the garden with Valentine. Wrapped up in scarves and gloves, Stanley has his binoculars, while Valentine is pointing at something. I walk over to them.

'Were you both born in a barn,' I chide, but Valentine turns to me quickly, his finger over his mouth.

'Ssshh.'

I frown, then look up to see where he's pointing. It's my bird feeder. High up in the sycamore tree. There's a bird.

'It's a robin,' he whispers, his face brightening. 'Can you see his red chest – look?'

I peer more closely, squinting into the weak late-afternoon sunshine.

'Do you want my binoculars?'

I look down to see Stanley holding them out to me.

'Thanks, Stan.' I nod and take them from him. Everything's blurry at first and I have to turn the apertures until they come into focus. And then I see it, close up: its tiny beak and glistening eyes, its feathers, the red of its chest. It's pecking hungrily at the bird feeder, checking this way and that, as if to make sure no one has seen it yet.

'See. I told you they'd come. You just have to be patient. Birds get scared of new things. Takes them a while to pluck up the courage. The first one is the hardest, but now the rest will follow.'

I can hear Valentine and I dip the binoculars and look at him. He's smiling at me.

'Took a while, but it's worth waiting for, isn't it?'

And then we both smile at each other, and I know he's not just talking about the birds.

'Liv.'

'Yes?' I look down at Stanley, who's peering at me.

'Is that your real name?'

'Well, it's Olivia really, but you can shorten it to Liv.'

'Like the word "live" that means to be alive?'

'No, mine's spelled differently. There's no e.'

'But it sounds the same.'

'Yes.' I nod and take a deep lungful of wintry air. 'It feels the same too.'

I can see Stan frowning, looking a bit confused, as I hand him back his binoculars and shake his hand goodbye and hug Valentine, who for the first time doesn't just let me hug him, but squeezes me right back.

'Where's Ben?'

'He's putting my suitcase in the car. Have you seen Harry?'

As if on cue, there's a loud barking and Harry comes barrelling out of the kitchen as he spots the squirrel. I don't know whether it's the turmeric paste that Valentine suggested or all the wild swimming that's acted like hydrotherapy, but his arthritis does seem to be a lot better.

'Is he still after that bloody squirrel?' says Valentine. 'He'll never catch it.'

'I know.' I smile, thinking about life. 'I don't think he really wants to. The fun would be over then, wouldn't it?'

I find Ben outside with the engine running, trying to warm up the Land Rover. His van is full of building materials, so we're taking mine.

'Got your passport?'

'Yep,' I nod, glancing at my suitcase in the back. I pause, noticing the sun sinking behind the trees across the graveyard, and feel Harry brush against my legs. 'Can we just walk up the lane to the fields and watch the sunset? We've got time.'

Ben looks at his watch. For someone who's never seemed that bothered by time-keeping, he's taking his job of driving me to the airport to catch my flight to Mexico City very seriously. Satisfied, he nods.

'You know I'm never one to miss a sunset,' he grins.

Cutting the engine, he climbs out of the Land Rover as I unhook Harry's lead from inside the door and clip it to his collar. Then Ben reaches for my hand and together we weave our way through the village lit with twinkling Christmas lights, past the shops and the beery warmth of the pub, its windows decorated with tinsel, to the top of the lane, where it meets the open fields and you can see right across the stone rooftops and spires of wood-smoke to the Dales. It's almost the winter solstice and we're fast losing the light and, with it, the temperature, and Ben pulls me closer. We climb higher. The conversation between us is circling and swooping like starlings at dusk, both of us avoiding any of the big stuff.

'So we all go through the same stages, but the journey's different for everyone,' I finish, my breath coming out in little white clouds. I've been telling him about the theory of the seven stages, but by the confused look on Ben's face, I'm not doing a very good job. 'Sorry, I'm not explaining this very well, am I?' I apologize.

He frowns. 'So, wait a minute. What happens after stage seven?'

I shrug. 'You get to start the rest of your life.'

There was a time when I couldn't imagine a future. I didn't believe I had one. So I stopped looking and concentrated on just putting one foot in front of the other. When I first got Harry he was pretty much the only reason I got out of bed in the morning.

But so much has changed since that morning when I slipped on his lead and we both took our first tentative steps into our new lives. I've found friendship where I never expected to find it and a sense of belonging that feels like coming home. And I've learned so much. About faith and trust and patience and resilience; about living in the moment and having fun; and the simple wonder of a new day and the promise of another walk.

And how it took an old, scruffy dog with the bravest,

441

biggest heart to help heal my broken one, by showing me I wasn't alone.

As we reach the top of the hill, we come to a pause and rest against the drystone wall. The whole of the valley sweeps below us and, as we look across the Dales, Ben kisses me. His nose is cold, but his lips are warm, and it's sweet and slow and just right. And I think how all it took was one good thing to change my life, and now it's filled with so many.

'So what does the rest of your life look like?'

He looks at me, his eyes searching mine.

'This.' I smile. 'It looks like this.'

An Epilogue of Sorts

I used to hear people talking to their dogs in pubs, or on walks in the park, and think they were a bit barmy. But then Harry came into my life and I was let into the secret: animals are just so great to talk to. Especially dogs. Not only because they're brilliant listeners and don't answer back, but because they make the best confidants.

I can tell Harry anything and he's never going to judge or criticize me. I don't have to worry that he's going to think me silly or pathetic. Whatever I say, I know he'll still love me, because a dog's love is unconditional. Moreover, I've never been able to open up to anyone in the way I do to Harry. It's like a form of therapy. On our daily walks, at home on the sofa, or in the middle of the night when I used to be unable to sleep, I'll find myself having conversations with him.

And I'm not the only one.

I often hear Valentine talking to Harry on the sofa, when I'm in the kitchen making tea and he thinks I can't hear. And the other day Stanley told me he tells Harry all his secrets, as he knows they're safe with him. He also pointed out that 'Dog' is 'God' spelled backwards, and how cool was that? Stanley also said that talking to Harry helps him articulate his feelings. Well, he didn't say the word 'articulate' – that was his teacher. She also asked if I'd ever thought about training Harry as a therapy dog, which is something Gisele's old care home suggested, as he was such a huge hit with their residents that time.

To be honest, Harry is no spring chicken; I don't know if it would be too much for him or even if he'd pass all the necessary assessments; still, it's something to think about. Stanley says Harry is a hero and would definitely pass. As proof, he insisted that we draw up a list of all the wonderful things he's taught us. Big and small. So, for example, these are the things we've learned from Harry:

1. *Live in the moment*
2. *Be brave*
3. *Don't hold a grudge or sulk*
4. *Play every day*
5. *There are few things in life better than a sunny patch on the sofa, going for a walk in nature or curling up in front of a real fire*
6. *Drink lots of water!*
7. *Be loyal and dependable*
8. *Giving up is only the sure way to fail (he hasn't caught that squirrel, but he's still trying)*
9. *Love unconditionally*
10. *Looks aren't important, and neither is age (Harry never looks in a mirror and has no idea how old he is)*
11. *Actions speak louder than words*
12. *Be enthusiastic*
13. *Don't judge anyone by their sex, race, age, IQ or how straight their shoe laces are (Stanley was very firm about the shoe laces). We're all just human*
14. *Have faith*
15. *Be patient (no one is more patient than Harry, when it comes to begging for scraps)*
16. *Go for it!*

17. *Joy can be found in the unlikeliest of places – like an old, stinky tennis ball, a muddy puddle or a walk in the rain*
18. *Be open to adventure*
19. *Walk more*
20. *You can never have too much sleep*
21. *Greet everyone you meet as a friend (because to Harry there are no strangers, just friends you haven't met yet)*

And, like Stanley said, if it's on the list it must be true.

Acknowledgements

I want to say a huge thank you to my wonderful editor Trisha Jackson, for all your hard work, boundless enthusiasm and for making me feel so valued and supported as an author.

It takes a village to publish a book, so thank you also to the brilliant team at Pan Macmillan: Sara Lloyd, Lucy Hale, Stuart Dwyer, Hannah Corbett, Eleanor Bailey, Jon Mitchell, Sophie Brewer, Anna Shora, Maired Loftus, Jayne Osborne, and to designer Mel Four for such a brilliant cover.

Also, huge thanks go to proofreader Fraser Crichton and copy-editor Mandy Greenfield, Sian Chilvers and Holly Sheldrake in the production department and text designer Lindsay Nash. A special thank you to Charlotte Wright for all your hard work and patience. I really am the luckiest author in the world to work with such talented people and am so grateful for everyone's contribution towards getting this book out into the world.

My agent Stephanie Cabot has been in my corner from the very beginning and is both a fantastic agent and a very dear friend. I am so grateful for your wise counsel and a huge thank you for everything you do.

Writing can be a lonely job and I want to thank all my friends, near and far, for keeping me company, cheering me on and making me laugh with all your funny texts, voice messages, videos, dog walks and drinks in the pub.

To my readers all over the world, thank you from the

bottom of my heart. It's because of you I get to do the job I always dreamed of.

As always, I want to thank my mum, Anita, for a lifetime of love and support. I also want to say a special thank you for all your invaluable advice about doing the jive, Fifties fashion and being one of my very first readers. To my sister, Kelly, thank you for being the best big sister anyone could hope to have and for being a complete inspiration. I am so proud of you for all your tireless work with ADF and for transforming the lives of so many street dogs in Mexico.

And to my beloved AC, for all the Manhattans, notes of encouragement, beautiful flowers and daily menu of delicious meals while I was on deadline. Thank you for so many good things!

Much of this novel was written during the three national COVID lockdowns, and I have never been more grateful for the beauty of nature, which gave me so much comfort and joy. During this time, I was lucky to spend time in the Yorkshire Dales, a part of the world that is very close to my heart; in many ways this novel is a love letter to the Dales and to my dad, who would tell anyone that would listen that he lived in paradise. Nettlewick is a fictional village, but the dramatic landscape, beauty of the seasons and warmth of the people is very real.

Finally, I was inspired to write this book after adopting Elton, our dog, from Bosnia and witnessing first-hand the difference a dog can make, not only to my own life, but to the lives of other people. So I would like to give a huge thank you to just a few of the wonderful animal rescue charities for all the amazing work they do:

Wild at Heart Foundation 📷 @wild_at_heart_foundation
Animals Care Mostar 📷 @animals_we_care_mostar

Alamos Dog Foundation 📷 @alamosdogfoundation
And last but not least to Elton, for being the best canine companion an author could have; this one's for you.

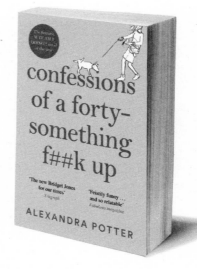